"Kate Noble brings the delicate elements of Regency England brilliantly alive with her prose."

—*USA Today*

"An extraordinary and unique romance worth savoring."
—*Smart Bitches, Trashy Books* on *Let It Be Me*

"The story's prologue literally gave me goose bumps—goose bumps that never went away throughout the whole book. This is the kind of deep, touching read that romance fans search for. I have a new favorite author!"

—*RT Book Reviews* editor Morgan Doremus on
Seal of Excellence pick *Let It Be Me*

"Despite being a delight and thoroughly winning, the book is 300 pages of confirmation to what I'd suspected and now know: The Regency belongs to Kate Noble, and it's in very, very good hands."

—*All About Romance* on *If I Fall*

"If Austen were alive and writing novels today, the result might be something exactly like *Follow My Lead*, a wickedly witty and superbly satisfying romance."

—*Chicago Tribune*

"Believable and captivating . . . an outstanding and memorable tale."

—*Publishers Weekly* starred review on *Follow My Lead*

"Clever and graceful . . . simply sublime."
—*Booklist* on *Compromised*

KATE NOBLE

THE GAME AND THE GOVERNESS

POCKET BOOKS

New York • London • Toronto • Sydney • New Delhi

Pocket Books
A Division of Simon & Schuster, Inc.
1230 Avenue of the Americas
New York, NY 10020

This book is a work of fiction. Any references to historical events, real people, or real places are used fictitiously. Other names, characters, places, and events are products of the author's imagination, and any resemblance to actual events or places or persons, living or dead, is entirely coincidental.

First Pocket Books paperback edition August 2014

POCKET and colophon are registered trademarks of Simon & Schuster, Inc.

For information about special discounts for bulk purchases, please contact Simon & Schuster Special Sales at 1-866-506-1949 or business@simonandschuster.com.

The Simon & Schuster Speakers Bureau can bring authors to your live event. For more information or to book an event, contact the Simon & Schuster Speakers Bureau at 1-866-248-3049 or visit our website at www.simonspeakers.com.

Interior design by Meryll Rae Preposi

Manufactured in the United States of America

10 9 8 7 6 5 4 3 2

ISBN 978-1-4767-4938-9
ISBN 978-1-4767-4941-9 (ebook)

To those who find happiness in the little things.
And to Harrison. For creating those little things.

ACKNOWLEDGMENTS

This book only exists because of the support of many fantastic people. Annelise Robey at the Jane Rotrosen Agency is the best advocate I could ever have asked for. Abby Zidle and my new Pocket family have been incredibly welcoming.

Thank you to my fantastic writing group, the Shamers, in whose membership I am eternally grateful, and who have kept the snickering at my attempts to title my books to a minimum. Also, the community of fellow authors fostered by the Romance Writers of America has been such a huge gift to anyone attempting a career in this crazy genre.

And as always, endless thanks to my family—Harrison, Mom, Dad, Liz, Jake, Andy, Josh, Evie, Haley, Daniel, Harry, and Suzanne. I learn new things from you every day.

 **PROLOGUE**

The light on the floor slanted gray, another horrible dawn. But that was nothing new.

Every day of the last two months had been horrible.

However, today's dawn was the last that Phoebe Baker would spend here, in her little room at the little, elegant school that had been her home for the past five years.

She was already awake. Already sitting on the bed, the gray wool cloak about her shoulders, covering up some of the unrelieved black of her gown. Which gown, Phoebe couldn't tell. Was it the one that used to have the stripes? Or the little flowered cambric? It didn't matter.

All the pretty pinks and yellows of her wardrobe were now this awful, inky black. The only one she had refused to dye was her soft blue ball gown. Her father had given it to her in one of his fits of generosity. Meant to be worn at her debut next year in London.

She would never go to London now. Never dance with young, handsome men. Never be a part of that world.

Who was she going to be?

How was she going to be?

And whom would she share it with, now that her father was gone?

In some respects, Phoebe had been lucky. Her father had paid her tuition at Mrs. Beveridge's School through the end of term, so she had been able to stay until now. And their house had been enough to cover his debts, so she was not responsible for any further monies lost.

Lost by his foolishness. Lost by his trusting nature.

Lost, she thought as she crumpled the brief note she had found among her father's belongings on that last visit, because some men did not have the decency to clean up their own messes. They left them for others to deal with.

But even though she was able to stay at Mrs. Beveridge's, everything had changed. People looked at her differently. Girls she had thought were friends began to shun her, refuse to associate with her, told by their parents and their teachers that she was no longer "one of them." Like she was poison.

Also, her lessons had shifted course. Where she had once been one of the girls their painting master always held up as an example of good work, suddenly Miss Earhart asked her to step out and assist the younger girls with their reading lessons. Then, during the dancing hour, Miss Earhart had come in and requested that she help correct Latin slates.

But requested was the wrong word. "Demanded" was more like it. There were no apologetic smiles from Miss Earhart, no kindness within her. She simply commandeered Phoebe as she saw fit.

Funny. Phoebe had used to like Miss Earhart. Back when she had first arrived at the gawky age of twelve. She had been firm, but good to her.

But not anymore, apparently.

It didn't take her long to realize that skinny, pinched Miss Earhart had been elected by the rest of the instructors to take care of the "problem" of Phoebe. To keep her away, out of sight. The hateful looks she got from the other teachers mirrored those of their students, and even the eponymous Mrs. Beveridge herself sniffed the air as if something had gone sour whenever Phoebe was near.

It made her hate Miss Earhart all the more.

But not nearly as much as she hated *him*.

Phoebe looked down at the note in her hand. The words she had pored over the past few weeks were among her few remaining possessions. She had sold most of her personal belongings at the school— hairpins, shoe buckles, frilly bonnets, her books. All gone to greedy girls for the coins she would need to feed herself, as soon as the houseboys came to throw her out on the street.

He had done this. The Earl of Ashby. He had let this happen to her father, warning him too late, taking no precautions to protect those less fortunate than himself.

If she had told anyone of her hatred of a man she'd never met, she would have been informed it was ludicrous, irrational. But then again, she had no one to confide in.

Besides, there was no one else left to shoulder the blame.

Suddenly, she was overcome with the desire to make

him feel as terrible as he was. Overcome with the need to spit in his face, and make him recognize that other people existed in the world. That actions—or lack thereof—had consequences.

She stood abruptly, marching over to the little desk under the window. It was stocked with paper and fresh ink, as all the rooms were at the school. The supplies might have been placed there for the rich, spoiled girl who would occupy the room next, but at this moment, they still belonged to Phoebe. She lit a candle—the weak light of dawn not enough for what she must do. She sat. Placed pen to page.

Sir—
This will be a short letter. I have little time to write and not much to say. Other than . . .

Phoebe was just signing her name at the bottom when the knock came. It was short, direct. It did not frighten, but it offered no sympathy. Nor did the woman who let herself inside.

"Miss Baker," Miss Earhart said calmly, "it is time to go."

Phoebe sprinkled the sand on the page, folded it neatly, and wrote the direction—as best she could guess—on the front.

"Phoebe," Miss Earhart repeated. "Did you hear me?"

"Yes, Miss Earhart," Phoebe replied obediently. "As you said, it is time to go."

Phoebe took the candle in hand, let its wax drip onto the paper, making a seal. Finally, she rose from her desk and turned to face the cursed woman.

Miss Earhart stood in the center of the room, her stillness presenting an outward sense of calm that made Phoebe want to rage and scream. But there was nothing to rage and scream about anymore.

Behind the teacher stood two houseboys. Gruff and mute, ready to force her out if she put up any resistance.

"Where are they taking me?" Phoebe asked, nodding to the two menservants.

"They will drive you as far as the Brighton Road in the cart. There is an inn at the cross-section," Miss Earhart answered evenly.

Ah yes, the inn. Where parents stayed while visiting their daughters. Phoebe would not be able to afford a single night there with the coins in her pocket, such did the innkeepers gouge their patrons.

"And where do I go after that?"

"Wherever you like," Miss Earhart answered.

And that was the difficulty. Phoebe had nowhere to go. Her father's relatives were thousands of miles away in America. She had never met them. She would have to write, tell them of his death. And her mother's family would sooner spit on her than take her in.

She must have looked pitiful, because for the first time in the past two acrimonious months, Miss Earhart showed her some pity.

"If you find you do not know where to go, I have a suggestion." Miss Earhart reached into the folds of her school-issued plain gray gown. "This is the direction of a family near Portsmouth. They are in dire need of a governess for their three little girls, and asked me for a recommendation. I told them about you."

Phoebe's head whipped up. "A . . . a governess?"

"You are good with the younger students. I have written you a fine reference, and I forced Mrs. Beveridge to do the same. They are expecting you. If you want the position, that is."

"I . . . I don't understand." Phoebe looked down at the note in Miss Earhart's hand. "What do you mean you *forced* Mrs. Beveridge . . . ?"

Miss Earhart just snorted. "If it was up to her, you would have been thrown out two months ago. You're lucky to have stayed here this long—I taught you what I could in that little time."

Phoebe felt the ground spinning. Then suddenly, everything locked into place. She had been pulled out of her beloved painting lessons, out of dance class, not as punishment, not to be kept away from her former friends. Instead, it had been to learn something far more valuable.

How to teach.

And Phoebe instantly knew how far she had fallen in the world. She was not a pampered, loved daughter destined for a shining future. No. She was destined to be a governess.

Her eyes fell to the letter in her hand. Her knuckles went white she gripped it so tightly.

Her life, altered irrevocably. Because of one man's carelessness.

"I know this is not easy," Miss Earhart said, taking a quiet step forward. "You are one of the few young ladies to graduate from this school with the knowledge that life is rarely easy. Or fair."

A hysterical sob escaped Phoebe's lips. She stifled it ruthlessly.

"Your security . . . your *future* is up to you now. No one else will look after you. You must be strong. It is the only way through this."

"Through this," Phoebe repeated dully. "Does that mean there is a way out of this darkness?"

"Of a kind," Miss Earhart said, hesitant. "It will get easier. With time. And one day you will realize that this new self you have become is not so bad. You may even find some happiness in it."

"Happiness?" she replied. "In being alone? In being a governess?"

"Yes." Miss Earhart gave a ghost of a smile. "If happiness is in one's nature—as it is in yours."

Phoebe could only scoff.

"Once upon a time, you were one of my happiest students. You took pleasure in little things and found joy where you could." Miss Earhart laid a tentative hand on Phoebe's shoulder. "You can let this break you, leaving you bitter and hateful. Or you can try to find some good in the world, and let that comfort you. Life will be hard either way, but I hope you find your happiness again."

Phoebe looked at the hand on her shoulder, at the woman before her, who had somehow lost some of her pinched disapproval in the last few minutes. Now she wore her concern plain as day.

Then Phoebe's eyes drifted to the letter in her hand. Addressed to an earl. The man who was the reason she was faced with a different letter now. A different future.

"Thank you, Miss Earhart," she said, taking the letter with the address near Portsmouth. "But I cannot think there is any good left in the world."

She turned to one of the houseboys behind Miss

Earhart and handed him the earl's letter, with one of her few pennies for his trouble. "Please see that this makes its way into the morning post."

Then she picked up her small valise and marched past Miss Earhart.

She would go to this family in Portsmouth. It was the only option she had. But Phoebe knew that from now on, she would be alone. As Miss Earhart had said, her security and future were up to her now. No one else was looking after her.

After all, who gave a damn about the governess?

TO LORD EDWARD GRANVILLE,
  EARL OF ASHBY
GROSVENOR SQUARE
LONDON

1817

Sir –
This will be a short letter. I have little time to write
and not much to say. Other than "damn you." Damn
you for what you have done—directly or indirectly,
you have caused the greatest possible pain, and it
is you who should bear the blame for it.

My father, God rest his soul, has left this world.
Although he quit this world miserably, and I fear God
will not let his soul rest.

I read the letter you wrote to my father. What I
found most telling in it was that, in your warning to
stay away from Mr. Sharp, you gave information
that implied he had rooked you too. That he had

stolen from you, in the guise of investments gone bad, and diverting funds from your estates. But none of that made the papers. It was discreetly hushed up. Mr. Sharp was never taken away and made to pay for that crime. Doing so would have made you a laughingstock. Instead, he was let loose into the country, where he could use your name and association to take advantage of those of us who are not as connected as those in town. Who are not as clever.

You protected your precious reputation, and let my father pay the price for it.

I doubt you and I will ever have the chance to meet. My circumstances are changing swiftly now, and I must make my own way in the world. I want nothing from you. I simply wish for you to feel the horror of your carelessness. And I want you to know one simple truth:

If I ever have the opportunity to cause you pain, know it will happen. I will take the chance as God given and my right as my father's daughter. But it will not be malicious.

It will be justice.

Miss P. Baker
Mrs. Beveridge's School
Surrey

1

It begins with a wager. . . .

*I*t has been said that one should not hire one's friends.

No doubt, those who have said this have a deep wisdom about life, a spark of intelligence that recognizes inherent truths—or perhaps, simply the experience that proves the veracity of such a statement.

The Earl of Ashby had none of these qualities.

"Determined I was. And luckily, I came of age at the very right moment: I join the army, much to my great-uncle's dismay—but two days later, Napoleon abdicates and is sent to Elba!"

What the Earl of Ashby did have was luck. In abundance. He was lucky at cards. He was lucky with the fairer sex. He was even lucky in his title.

"Of course, at the time, I did not think of it as lucky, although my great-uncle certainly did, I being the only heir to Ashby he could find in the British Empire. At the time I would have believed that the old man had marched to the Continent and locked Boney up himself to thwart me."

It was nothing but luck that had the old Earl of Ashby's son and grandson dying in a tragic accident involving an overly friendly badger, making the nearest living male relative young Edward Granville—or Ned, as he had always been called—the heir to one of the oldest earldoms in the country. It was just such luck that had the old earl swoop in and take little Ned away from the piddling town of Hollyhock and his mother's genteel poverty at the age of twelve, and raise him in the tradition of the aristocracy.

"But then that French smudge manages to weasel his way off the island, and this time, true luck! I actually get to go to war! But the real luck was getting placed in the same regiment as Dr. Gray here. And— Oh, Turner, stop standing back in the shadows, this story is about you too!"

It was luck, and only luck, that found Ned Granville in the right place at the right time to save his friend and commanding officer, Captain John Turner, as well as seventeen others of their regiment on the last battlefield.

"So there we are in the hazy mist of battle on a field in Belgium, of all places—and thank God too, because I was beginning to think war was going to entirely be marching in straight lines and taking Turner's and Gray's money at cards—and suddenly, our flank falls behind a rise and takes a hail of fire from a bunch of Frenchies on top of it.

"So we're pinned down, waiting for the runner with

extra ammunition to arrive, when Turner spots the poor runner shot dead on the field a hundred feet away. And Turner, he jumps up before the rest of us can cover him, and runs out into the field. He grabs the ammunition and is halfway back before a bullet rips through the meat of his leg. There he is, lying on the field, and holding our ammunition. But all I see is my friend bleeding out—so of course, I'm the idiot who runs into the fray after him."

His actions that day would earn him commendations from the Crown for his bravery. They would also earn Ned Granville his nickname.

"It was just luck that none of their bullets hit me. And once I got Turner back behind the line, and the ammunition to our flank so we could hold our position, we beat the enemy back from whence they came. The next morning, Rhys—Dr. Gray here—had patched Turner up enough to have him walking, and he came over, clapped me on the shoulder, and named me Lucky Ned. Been stuck with it—and him!—ever since."

It was from that point on that "Lucky Ned"—and everyone else around him—had to simply accept that luck ruled his life.

And since such luck ruled his life, it could be said that Lucky Ned was, indeed, happy-go-lucky. Why bother with worries, when you had luck? Why heed those warnings about hiring your friends? Bah—so bothersome! It would be far more convenient to have a friend in a position of trust than to worry all the time that the servants would cheat you.

Yes, it might breed resentment.

Yes, that resentment might fester.

But not toward Ned. No, he was too good, too lucky for that.

Thus, Ned Granville, the Earl of Ashby, hired his best friend, John Turner, formerly a Captain of His Majesty's Army, to the exalted post of his secretary.

And he was about to regret it.

They were at a club whose name is not mentioned within earshot of wives and daughters, in their private card room. Well, the earl's private room. And the earl was engaging in that favorite of his activities: telling the tale of his heroism at Waterloo to a room full of jovial cronies.

But as the night wore on, said cronies moved off to their own vices, and soon only three men remained at the card table: Mr. John Turner, silent and stiff-backed; Dr. Rhys Gray, contemplative and considerate; and the Earl of Ashby, "Lucky Ned," living up to his name.

"*Vingt-et-un!*" Lucky Ned cried, a gleeful smile breaking over his features, turning over an ace.

The two other men at the table groaned as they tossed their useless cards across the baize. But then again, the men should be used to such results by now. After all, they had been losing to Ned at cards for years.

"That's it," Rhys said, pushing himself back from the table. "I will not play anymore. It's foolish to go against someone with that much luck."

"It's not as if I can help it." Ned shrugged. "I was simply dealt a better hand."

"It would be one thing if you shared your luck," Rhys replied, good-naturedly. "But you have always been the sole man left at the table, even when we were playing for scraps of dried beef in camp."

"I take exception to that," Ned replied indignantly. "I do so share my luck. If I recall correctly, Turner here pocketed a number of those beef scraps."

"And little else since," John Turner said enigmatically.

Annoyed, the Earl of Ashby gritted his teeth slightly. But perhaps that was simply in response to his latest hand of cards, which the good doctor was dealing out.

"Besides"—Ned instead turned to Rhys—"you were so busy tending to the wounded that you likely saw little of those games. Even tonight you refuse to play for barely more than dried beef."

"As a man of science, I see little point in games of chance. I have long observed their progress and the only consistent conclusion I come to is that I lose money," Rhys replied with good humor.

"Little point?" Ned cried on a laugh. "The point is that it's *exciting*. You go through life with your observations and your little laboratory in Greenwich and never play for deep stakes. What's the point of that?" He looked over to the stern-mouthed Turner across from him. "What say you, Turner?"

John Turner looked up from his hand. He seemed to consider the statement for a moment, then . . .

"Yes. Sometimes life is made better by a high-stakes gamble. But you have to choose your moment."

"There, Turner agrees with me. A rarity these days, I assure you," Ned replied, settling back into his hand. "Honestly, you are such a stick in the mud of late, Turner, I even thought you might stay home tonight poring over your precious papers—the one night Rhys is in London!"

"If you had chosen to go to any other club, I would have had to," Turner replied, his voice a soft rebuke. "You know the realities as well as I. And I am afraid being a stick in the mud goes with the territory of being a secretary, instead of—"

The silence that fell on the room was broken only by the flipping over of cards, until Rhys, his eyes on his hand, asked in his distracted way, "Instead of what, Turner?"

A dark look passed between the earl and his employee.

"Instead of a man of my own," Turner finished.

The earl visibly rolled his eyes.

"Whatever do you mean?" Rhys inquired. As a doctor, he was permanently curious, yet amazingly oblivious to the tension that was mounting in the dark and smoky room.

"He means his mill," the earl answered for him, taking a loose and familiar tone that might seem odd from a man of the earl's standing, but that was simply how it was with Ashby. With these two men, the wall had come down long ago.

Or so he had assumed.

"He's been whining about it for three weeks now. And if you, Turner, had been a mill owner and not my secretary, you would not have been admitted even here . . . so . . ."

"What about the mill?" Rhys asked, looking to Turner.

"My family's mill has suffered another setback," Turner sighed, but held his posture straight.

"But I thought you had rebuilt after the fire?" Rhys questioned, his blond brow coming down in a scowl.

"I had, but that was just the building, not the equipment. I sank every penny into purchasing new works from America, but last month the ship was lost at sea."

"Oh, Turner, I am so sorry," Rhys began. "Surely you can borrow . . ."

But Turner shook his head. "The banks do not see a mill that has not functioned in five years as a worthwhile investment."

It went unasked about the other possible source of lending; the source that was present in that very room. But a quick look between Turner and the good doctor told Rhys that that avenue was a dead end as well.

"Turner maintains that if he had the ability to save his family mill, he would be far less of a stick in the mud, and more pleasant to be around. But I have to counter that it simply wouldn't be true," Ned intoned as he flipped over an ace.

"You don't think that working to make my family business a success again, making my own name, would make me more of a pleasure to be around?" Turner asked, his dark eyes narrowing.

"Of course not!" Ned said with an easy smile. "If only for the simple fact that you would be working all the time! That makes no man pleasant."

"I work all the time now," Turner replied. "Trust me, running your five estates does not leave me many afternoons free."

"Yes, everything is always *so* important," Ned said dramatically. "All those fields that need dredging require constant updates and letters and all that other nonsense."

Turner's mouth formed a hard line. "Far be it from

me to bore you with business matters. After all, I was not a man of learning when I took the position. I spent the first three years untangling the old finances and teaching myself the job."

At the mention of "old finances," Ned visibly tensed.

"Well . . ." Ned tried, judiciously dropping that line of argument. "At least here you are in London. There is more to do and see here, more to stimulate the mind on one block in London than there can be in all of Lincolnshire."

"More for you, perhaps."

"What does that mean?"

"What it means is that the world is different for an earl than it is for his secretary."

"Fellows," Rhys tried, finally reacting to the rising voices of his friends. "Perhaps we should just play cards? I would be willing to wager a whole farthing on this hand."

But they ignored him.

"Don't be so boring, Turner. Nothing worse than being boring," Ned said sternly. Then, with relish, "What you need more than anything else is a woman underneath you. Take your stick out of the mud and put it to better use for a few hours. That'll change your outlook."

"You might be surprised to learn that most women don't throw themselves at a secretary with the same frequency they do at an earl."

"Then *buy* one." Ned showed his (very good) cards to the table, exasperated. "There are more than a few in this house who would be willing to oblige. Mme Delacroix keeps her girls clean. Hell, I'll even pay."

"Thank you, no." Turner smiled ruefully. He tossed his cards into the center of the table as Ned raked up his chips. Lucky Ned had won again. "I prefer my companionship earned, not purchased."

"Which is *never* going to happen as long as you keep that dour face!" Ned took the cards on the table, gathered them up, and began to shuffle. "And by the by, I resent the implication that I am nothing more than my title."

"Now, Ashby, he didn't say that," Rhys began, but Turner strangely kept silent.

"Yes he did. He said that life is different for an earl than it is for a secretary. And while that is true, it implies that any good thing, any bit of luck I may have had in my life, is incumbent upon the fact that I inherited an earldom. And any lack of happiness Turner suffers from is incumbent upon his recent bad luck. Whereas the reverse is true. He is serious and unsmiling, *thus* he has bad luck. With his mill, with women, with life. I am in general of a good nature and I have good luck. It has very little to do with my title. It has to do with who I am. Lucky Ned." A beat passed. "And if I have been too generous with you, *Mr.* Turner, allow me to correct that mistake."

The hand that Ned slammed down on the table echoed throughout the room. Eerily quiet, shamed by the highest-ranking man there, the walls echoed with the rebuke. The earl was, after all, an earl. And Turner was dancing far too close to the line.

"I apologize if my words gave the impression that you owe your happier philosophy to your title and not to your nature," Turner said quietly.

"Good." Ned harrumphed, turning his attention back to the deal. A knave and a six for himself. An ace for Turner, and a card facedown, which . . .

Turner gave his own set of cards his attention then, and flipped over the king of hearts, earning him a natural. But instead of crying "*Vingt-et-un!*" like his employer, he simply said quietly, "But the title certainly helps."

"Oh, for God's sake!" Ned cried, throwing his cards across the baize.

All eyes in the room fell on the earl.

"Turner. I am not an idiot. I know that there are people in the world who only value me because of my title, and who try to get close to me because of it. That is why I value your friendship—both of you. And why I value the work you do for me, Turner. It's all too important to have someone I can trust in your role. But I thoroughly reject the notion that *all* of my life is shaped by the title. I didn't always have it, you know. Do you think Lady Brimley would have anything to do with me if I was nothing more than a stuffed-shirt jackanape?"

At the mention of the earl's latest entanglement— a married society woman more bored even than Ned, and most willing to find a way to occupy them both— Turner and Rhys cocked up similar eyebrows.

"So you are saying your prowess with women is not dependent on your title either?" Turner ventured calmly.

"Of course it's not!" Ned replied. "In my not insignificant experience—"

At this point, the good doctor must have taken a drink in an ill manner, because he suddenly gave in to a violent cough.

"As I was saying . . ." Ned continued, once Rhys apologized for the interruption. "In my not insignificant experience, when it comes to *women*, who you are is far more important that what you have."

He took in the blank stares of his friends.

"Go ahead, call me romantic." Ned could not hide the sardonic tone in his voice. "But if a woman found me dull, boring, or, God forbid, *dour* like you, I would not last five minutes with them, be I a prince or a . . . a pauper!"

"Well, there is certainly something about your humble charm that must woo them," Rhys tried kindly, his smile forcing an equal one out of Ned.

But Turner was quiet. Considering.

"I promise you, Turner, it is your bad attitude that hinders you—be it with women or bankers. It is my good attitude that brings me good luck. Not the other way around."

"So you are saying you could do it?" Turner asked, his stillness and calm eerie.

"Do what?"

"Get a woman to fall for you, without a title. If instead you were, say, a man of my station."

Ned leaned back smugly, lacing his hands over his flat stomach. "I could do it even if I was *you*. It would be as easy as winning your money at cards. And it would take less time too."

It happened quickly, but it was unmistakable. Turner flashed a smile. His first smile all evening.

"How long do you think it would take?" he asked, his eyes sparks in the dark room.

Ned leaned back in his chair, rubbing his chin in

thought. "Usually the ladies start mooning after me within a few days. But since I would be without my title, it could take a week, I suppose, on the outside."

Turner remained perfectly still as he spoke. "I'll give you two."

Rhys's and Ned's heads came up in unison, their surprised looks just as evenly matched. But Rhys caught the knowing look in Turner's eyes, and made one last effort at diplomacy between his two sparring friends.

"Turner—Ned . . ." Rhys tried again, likely hoping the jovial use of Ned's Christian name would snap him out of it, "I am in London so rarely and only for a night this trip. Can we not just play?"

"Oh, but we are playing," Turner replied. "Can't you see? His lordship is challenging me to a wager."

"He is?"

"I am?" Ned asked. "Er, yes. Yes, I am."

"You have just said that you can get a lady to fall for you within a week, even if you are a man of my station. Hell, even if you *are* me, you said."

"So . . ."

"So, we trade places. *You* become *me*. Woo a lady and win her. And I offer you the benefit of two weeks—which should be more than enough by your estimation."

"But . . . what . . . how—" Ned sputtered, before finally finding his bearings again.

And then . . . he laughed.

But he was alone in that outburst. Not even Rhys joined in.

"That's preposterous," Ned finally said. "Not to mention undoable."

"Why not?"

"Well, other than the fact that I *am* the earl, and everyone knows it."

"Everyone in London knows it. No one in Leicestershire does."

"Leicestershire?" Rhys piped up. "What on earth does Leicestershire have to do with this?"

"We go there tomorrow. To see about Ashby's mother's old house in Hollyhock."

"*Hollyhock?!*" Ned practically jumped out of his chair. It was safe to say any hand of cards had well been forgotten at this point, as the wager currently on the table was of far greater interest. "Why the hell would I want to go to Hollyhock?"

"Because the town has a business proposal for the property, and the land and building must be evaluated before you decide what to do with it," Turner replied sternly. "I cannot and will not sign for you. That was a rule very strictly laid down by yourself, and with good cause, if you recall."

The trio of heads nodded sagely. The Earl of Ashby did have good reason to be cautious with his larger dealings, and to have someone he trusted in the role of his secretary. And the sale of his mother's house in Hollyhock did qualify as a "larger dealing."

"By why on earth should I go to Hollyhock now? At the height of the season? For heaven's sake, Lady Brimley's ball is next week, I would be persona non grata to her . . . charms, if I should miss it."

"I scheduled the trip for now *because* of Lady Brimley's party," Turner offered. Then, pointedly, "At which she has engaged Mrs. Wellburton to sing."

At the mention of the earl's previous paramour—

an actress with a better figure than voice, but an absolutely astonishing imagination—Ned visibly shifted in his seat.

"Yes, well . . . perhaps you are right. Perhaps now is the best time to be out of London. If you catch my meaning."

"We catch your meaning, Ashby," Rhys replied. "As easily as you are going to catch syphilis."

Ned let that statement pass without comment. "Well, what's the proposal about?" Ned asked, before waving the question away. "No, I remember now. Something to do with a hot spring. But, God, *Hollyhock*. Just the name conjures up images of unruly brambled walks and an overabundance of cows. I cannot imagine a more boring way to spend a fortnight. I haven't even been there since I was twelve."

"So there is no reason to expect that anyone would recognize you," Turner replied.

"Well, of course they will recognize me," Ned countered. "I'm me."

"The physical difference between a boy of twelve and a man full grown is roughly the same as for the boy of twelve and the newborn," Rhys interjected, earning him no small look of rebuke from Ned.

"Even if that is so, I look like me, and you look like you," Ned tried, flabbergasted.

"And who is to say we do not look like each other?" Turner shrugged. "We are of a height, and both have brown hair and brown eyes. That is all the people of Hollyhock will remember of a boy long since grown into adulthood. And besides"—Turner leaned in with a smile—"I doubt you would find the trip to Hollyhock boring if I'm you and you are me."

"There is the small issue of your speech," Ned said suddenly. "Your accent is slightly more . . . northern than mine." Which was true; when Ned had been taken from Leicestershire and raised by his great-uncle, any hint of poverty in his accent was smoothed out. Turner, having been born in the rural county of Lincolnshire and raised in trade, had an accent that reflected his lower-class upbringing.

But it appeared he had learned a thing or two in the interim. When he next opened his mouth, Turner spoke with the melodic, cultured tones of a London gentleman.

"I doubt it will be a problem," Turner said—his accent a perfect mimic of Ned's!—with a smile. "But if someone manages to discern our ruse by my speech, I will forfeit, and you will win."

"Gentlemen," Rhys broke in. "This is a remarkably bad idea. I cannot imagine what you could possibly hope to learn from the experiment."

"I shall enlighten you," Turner replied. "If the earl is correct, he will have taught me a valuable lesson about life. If he can, simply through his *natural* good humor, win the heart of a young lady, then there is obviously no reason for me to take the hardness of life so seriously. But if he is wrong . . ."

"I am not wrong," Ned piped up instantly, his eyes going hard, staring at Turner. "But nor am I going to take part in this farce. Why, you want to switch places!"

Rhys exhaled in relief. But Turner still held Ned's gaze. Stared. A dare.

A wager.

"But . . . it could be interesting," Ned mused.

"Oh, no," Rhys said into his hands.

"If we could actually pull it off? Why, it could be a lark! A story to tell for years!"

"You do enjoy telling a good story," Turner said with a placid smile.

"And I get to teach you a lesson at the same time. All the better." Then Ned grinned wolfishly. "What are your terms?"

Turner, even if his heart was pounding exceptionally fast, managed to contain any outside appearance of it. "If you are not so fortunate as to win the heart of a female . . ." He took a breath. "Five thousand pounds."

Rhys began coughing again.

"You want me to give you five thousand pounds?" Ned said on a laugh. "Audacious of you."

"You are the one that said life is nothing without the occasional high stakes."

"And you are the one who said one must choose his game carefully. Which it seems you have. Still, such a sum—"

"Is not outside of your abilities." His smile grew cold. "I should know."

"And what if I am right?" Ned leaned forward in his chair, letting his cool voice grow menacing. "What if I win?"

Turner pricked up his eyebrow. "What do you want?"

Ned pretended to think about it for a moment. "The only thing you have. The only thing you care about." Ned watched as Turner's resolve faltered, ever so slightly. "I'll take that family mill off your hands. Free you to a life of better living and less worry." He mused, rubbing the two-days' beard on his chin again. "As it's not functioning, I suppose it's worth a bit less than five thousand, but I'm willing to call that even."

Turner remained still. So still. A stillness he'd learned in battle, perhaps. Then he thrust his hand across the table.

"I accept."

"No! No, this is madness," Rhys declared as he stood. "I will not be a party to it."

"I am afraid you have to be," Turner drawled. "You are not only our witness, but you will have to serve as our judge."

"Judge?" Rhys cried, retaking his seat as he hung his head in his hands.

"Yes—you can be the only person impartial enough to do it." He turned to Ned. "Is that agreeable to you, *my lord*?"

"Yes. That will suit me," he answered back sharply, stung by Turner's tone.

"So we are agreed, then? It is a wager?" Turner asked, his hand still in the air, waiting to be shook.

"It is." Ned took the hand and pumped it once, firmly. "Good luck," he wished his old friend. "Out of the two of us, you are the one that will need it."

2

The rules are laid out.

I've decided this is not only going to be easy—it's going to be fun."

Ned and Turner had been riding for the better part of the morning, side by side. Silent. They had left the day before from London with Rhys, making their way to Smithfield and the Great North Road before the sun had breached the sky. They had taken the wearying part of the trip on the first day, riding hard all the way to Peterborough on horseback, a carriage with luggage and Ned's valet, Danson, following behind.

But for this second leg of the journey, it was just the two of them.

After the deal had been struck, the wager made, it still had not been easy to convince Rhys to play his part in it.

"First of all, this is a horrific idea and you both will come to regret it," Rhys had argued, crossing his arms petulantly. "Secondly, I do not have the time to come all the way to Leicestershire with the two of you—I have *work* to do. I'm only passing through London on my way to Peterborough—a chemist resides there who has some amazing experiments that we may adapt in our own laboratory—"

"Peterborough!" Turner interrupted. "Perfect. It's only a few hours from Hollyhock. You can go work with your chemist, and then come to us after a fortnight."

"Yes," Ned agreed. "A much better plan, especially if we get to avoid listening to your predictions of doom the entire time. Merely come in at the end, and act as judge."

Rhys had swung his gaze between the two of them, judging, analyzing.

But it had been Turner's seriousness that had forced Rhys's hand.

"Are you willing to risk destroying a friendship," Rhys asked Turner, "that has survived the better part of a decade?"

"What are you talking about?" Ned threw his head back in laughter. "It's meant to be a lark! A bit of fun!"

"No one wagers their entire lives on a lark, Ashby," Rhys intoned darkly. All Ned could do was throw up his hands at his friend's pragmatic approach to the game.

"Do you see another way?" Turner asked quietly, his eyes intent on Rhys.

Something unspoken passed between the two men, something that made Ned feel left out of the joke. Although neither was laughing.

Then Rhys threw up his hands. "Fine, I will be your judge."

Thus it was that Rhys set about penning a letter to

the chemist in Peterborough, which through a number of very fast riders, gave the man a few hours' notice of the auspicious arrival of the Earl of Ashby and his party.

That night, they had readied themselves to switch lives. It turned out the most important thing was limiting the number of people who knew the truth. It was decided that Danson, Ned's valet, was the only servant who could come with them. In fact, if they traveled with any fewer, Danson had been quick to point out, it would be unlikely that *either* of them would be recognized as the Earl of Ashby.

"Fellows, you'll be staying with Dr. Gray here." Ned had addressed his carriage driver and his liveried groom—whom it would pain Abandon, his stallion, to be without. "Danson will hire a carriage in Peterborough to take him to Hollyhock tomorrow. It's not that we don't trust you, but . . . we don't trust you."

Oddly, both the driver and the groom seemed at peace with this decision.

It had been the last night that Ned would be himself for two solid weeks. For when he woke in the morning, he and Turner traded clothes, traded horses, and traded lives.

They had a leisurely breakfast, delaying the inevitable, then waved good-bye to Rhys and their chemist host—a kind, learned man whose hearing had been compromised by his gleeful enjoyment in making things explode in his laboratory.

And now, the sun was high in the sky, they were only a few miles from their destination, and they had not spoken one word to each other since mounting their horses.

Until now.

"I said, I think it will be fun," Ned repeated. "Being you."

"What will be so fun about it?" Turner replied, his tone neutral.

"Simply that I won't have to worry about anything. Not about my clothes, or about paying proper attention to my hostess, all those little annoyances that make up an earldom."

Turner made a noncommittal noise.

"Thus," Ned continued, "I will get to spend all my time wooing any young woman I please."

Turner pulled up on his reins, slowing his—actually Ned's—beautiful black stallion. The horse whinnied in displeasure. Apparently, Turner had not learned the nuances of riding a Thoroughbred like Abandon, who responded to the lightest touch. Unlike the mare Turner usually rode, which was as stubborn as a mule.

"Perhaps we need to establish some rules," Turner murmured. "About the wager."

"Oh?" Ned said. "What kind of rules?"

"Basic things. Such as, if either of us reveals our true selves, that man loses."

"That makes complete sense." Ned nodded. "However, since this is a wager where I bear the brunt of the work," he said reasonably, "I think it should be established that you are expressly forbidden from interfering."

"How could I possibly interfere?" Turner replied, trying his best to keep Abandon from dancing as he came to a stop.

"You could spread lies to any lady who shows interest in me, you could—oh, here, let me." Ned reached over and took Abandon's reins, loosening Turner's grip. "Don't choke up so high on the reins. He will think there is something to fear."

Turner moved his hands farther down the reins, letting them go a bit more slack. Abandon calmed down immediately.

"Thank you," Turner grumbled. He took a moment to resettle himself on Abandon's back. "I agree to your rule. This is a gentlemen's wager, and I will act as a gentleman throughout."

"In fact, I don't think you should be permitted to say anything bad about me," Ned decided. "Not even a minor slight. You can only sing my praises."

"Since you will be wearing my name, if I slight you, I will be slighting myself," Turner reasoned, but at a look from Ned, he held up his hand. "All right. I shall only sing your praises. But—I have a condition as well."

"Of course."

"The object of your affection has to be a lady of good breeding. Someone gently raised. No chambermaids, no cooks."

Ned's brow came down. *How did he guess . . . ?* But Turner just smirked.

"The premise of this wager is that you, as me, could make a lady fall in love with you. Thus, it would have to be someone I would court. And while I may be your secretary, I am still a man of property—"

"For a few more weeks at least."

Turner shot him a glare. "—and was an officer in the army." Although he had not purchased his commission. So many officers had died during the wars and left vacancies, available to anyone wanting to take them. Turner had gotten a non-purchase vacancy as a lieutenant, and was promoted to captain on merit in the field.

"And these qualifications make you as snobbish as the highest lord," Ned replied dryly. Having to limit himself to only ladies would be slightly more difficult, but . . . "Fine, I agree to your stipulation. Besides, I have found that, regardless of social standing, the fairer sex does not differ much when it comes to matters of the heart. If you confess your love, chances are they will confess it back."

"Oh, and that's another stipulation," Turner added, nudging Abandon forward, making their way up the road again. "You cannot declare your feelings. Her declaration must be spontaneous."

"What?" Ned cried, kicking his stubborn steed into moving, catching up to Turner. "That is ridiculous!"

And it thoroughly destroyed Ned's plan. He would meet a girl (although chambermaids and cooks were now out of the question, it seemed), woo her for a se'nnight, then he would declare his love. Then he would have a whole week for her to declare it back, to wear her down. And if, on the off chance he received a firm "no," he would use that extra week to secure his interest with someone else.

"Why is that ridiculous?" Turner countered. "You mean to prove that your good humor wins the day— not your ardent declarations."

"I don't think you understand how this works. No young lady—not of good breeding, anyway, which is *your* stipulation—will make a declaration of love without first hearing one from her object." Ned shook his head. "It simply isn't done."

Turner seemed to consider it for a moment. "Well, then, perhaps we revise what constitutes a declaration of love."

Ned smiled. Finally, a rule that would work in *his* favor.

"All right. What constitutes a declaration?"

"Well, obviously, if you can get the girl to express her feelings, either written or publicly, then that will carry the day."

"But if she doesn't? If she is too well bred for that?"

"Then . . ." He thought for a moment. "If you can collect three things from a lady, it will serve as proof enough."

"And what are these three things?" Ned asked suspiciously.

He ticked them off on his fingers. "A dance, in public."

"Easy enough." Ned conceded.

"Second, a token of affection. A glove, a pressed flower, or some such nonsense. Freely given, not taken without her knowledge."

"Turner, if these are your qualifications, I will not only have one lady in love with me within a fortnight, I will have them all," Ned scoffed.

"And third: an . . . intimate knowledge of the lady."

Ned pulled up short. "An *intimate* knowledge?"

"Yes—the location of a mole on a concealed part of her body, a personal secret from her youth— something to that effect. All women have these little things." Turner grinned like a cat of prey again—his tiger smile. "How you find out the information is up to you."

"Now hold on," Ned said sternly. "You are requiring that I *seduce* someone. That could have longer-reaching consequences than a fortnight."

Turner shrugged. "Only if you cannot get her to declare her love openly. There is still that option. Besides, seduction is not a requirement—only a possible method of obtaining what you require."

A possible method? Hell, it was the only method Ned could think of. Suddenly, he felt as if he had no grounding anymore. He swayed in his seat, grasping hard to keep upright.

"Have you grown uneasy?"

"Not at all," Ned shot back immediately. "I simply prefer to avoid doing things that cannot be undone. But if that's what it takes . . ."

But his bravado masked a strange sensation in his gut. Could it be a . . . a qualm? A hint of guilt?

"If you feel unequal to the task . . . you could always forfeit," Turner said, his voice gruff.

"Before the game's even begun?" Ned's head shot up. "No, of course not."

So this was Turner's tactic, was it? Make more and more ridiculous qualifications in the hopes he would call the whole thing off. Well, he didn't take into account Ned's luck.

His eyes fell to the signet ring he wore on his right hand. The Earl of Ashby's crest. And he could hear his great-uncle's voice echoing in his head, as if he were still twelve years old: *You're lucky to be here, don't you realize? If you were out there, people would want something from you. And without my protection, you might be foolish enough to give it to them.*

His eyes narrowed. Yes, Turner, his old friend, wanted something from him. He wanted to be right, and he wanted Ned to be wrong.

Well, as long as he was the Earl of Ashby, he would not be taken advantage of. He would not be cowed by something as mundane as guilt. He would prove Turner the fool, show him the truth of his good nature, his luck . . .

And he was right. This was going to be fun.

"What has you grinning so?" Turner asked suspiciously.

Ned looked up, surprised to find himself smirking. "Oh, nothing," he said, unable to quell his newfound righteous conviction. "Here, take this—to finalize the transformation." He held out his signet ring. Turner took it, shoving it onto his finger, none too gently.

"Fingers too fat for it?" Ned teased.

"I would argue that your hands are too slim and feminine," Turner threw back, a wry smirk breaking over his features.

It was a small moment of manly jesting, of camaraderie. It had been a long time since he and Turner had thrown easy, happy barbs at each other. Not since . . .

But then Turner straightened and put his heels into Abandon—lightly, Ned noticed—spurring him into a trot down a side path off the main road.

"You're going the wrong way," Ned said, once he caught up to Turner. "Hollyhock is two miles farther down the road."

"We are not staying in Hollyhock. We are staying at Puffington Arms, the home of Sir Nathan and Lady Widcoate."

Ned's eyebrow went up. "Why on earth would we stay there?"

Turner sighed. "Because when I informed the town of our trip, they would not hear of an earl—especially an earl who hails from Hollyhock—staying at an inn. Since your mother's old cottage is uninhabitable, the Widcoates were applied to. I am told theirs is the largest house in the area."

"Which does not mean it is in any way large." Ned narrowed his eyes, searching his memory. "I remember the Widcoates. Barely. Sir Nathan had just married when I left, his wife and her younger sister coming to settle in."

Lady Widcoate had been a meddling woman. Always pretending solicitude, but really being smug and superior to his mother. And he was about to spend two tiresome weeks with her.

But still, there was the chance of a silver lining. "Perhaps they have a daughter or two," Ned mused. "Just of age to be wooed."

Turner's eyes grew hard. "I doubt the Widcoates will do little more than act as introduction to the neighborhood."

"Oh, I think I will do very well acting as my own introduction." Ned smiled, his eyes having fallen on something that sparked his interest.

The road they had turned onto was lined by a long, low wooden fence, protecting a wide field with the odd cow from their path. And there, along the fence, was a woman—a plain wool scarf wrapped around her practical gray dress. Still, such bulk could not hide her thinness. Her flaxen hair was pulled back tight, and in front of her ran two children, a boy and a girl, using sticks as swords.

There was no mistaking this kind of woman. She was, by her very air, her very posture, every inch a governess.

Not exactly a lady. But she was female, and therefore good practice.

"Well, Turner. Or should I say, *my lord*," Ned challenged. "Time to take up our roles."

Ned cantered up to the fence where the children had come to a stop, having seen the approaching horses.

"Hello," Ned called out, jovially. He lifted his hand to his hat in acknowledgment of the lady. "Madam. What a lovely day."

But then something strange happened. Usually, when anyone saw him, even strangers, they smiled back, with happy replies. But the lady was silent. And these children . . .

"That's the most beautiful horse I've ever seen!" One, the girl, all flushed of face and bouncing curls, ducked under the fence and ran up to Turner, admiring his mount. "Can I touch him?"

"She really wants to ride him," the boy said seriously, joining the other at Turner's side.

"Children!" the governess admonished. "Get away from the horse, please. We do not yet know his disposition."

"His disposition is well behaved," Turner offered, without a trace of his usual northern accent.

"Perhaps I was speaking of the rider," she said tartly, causing Ned to smile and Turner's brow to come down in confusion. "However," she continued, "I cannot know if your mount is well behaved with small children. Rose, Henry . . . move back. Now."

"You should obey your governess," Ned added, giving a wink to the woman in question.

But oddly, she did not blush. She did not even crack a smile. Instead, she turned her squinting, unblinking gaze to Turner. As if expecting . . .

Oh, yes! Introductions!

"Ah, my name is Mr. John Turner," Ned offered. It felt odd on his tongue. "And this is—"

"Lord Granville, Earl of Ashby," Turner offered with a slight bow—the best he could manage on horseback. "We are on our way to Puffington Arms. Are we headed in the right direction?"

Then something happened. Ned only caught it because he was watching her so closely, hoping for something, anything that would denote the smallest interest.

But instead of such hopeful signs, she ignored him. Instead, when Turner spoke to the girl, she stiffened.

It was slight, almost imperceptible. But Ned saw it, clear as day. Odd. The pale, squinty governess was alarmed by Turner . . . and completely dismissive of Ned.

If Turner noticed, he said nothing. And she squelched whatever emotion had flitted across her face, and answered calmly.

"You are on the correct path. Puffington Arms is about a mile down the road, around the bend. You should see it shortly."

"We live there!" the little girl called out, excited.

"Do you now?" Ned exclaimed. But again, he was promptly, unbelievably ignored.

"I'm Rose. That's Henry. My lord, if you come home with us, can we ride your horse?"

"Oh—can I draw the horse?" the other, Henry, begged. But the hard-nosed governess kept a tight hold on the two of them.

"You should go, my lord," she said, addressing Turner, but keeping her gaze resolutely low. "Everyone is waiting for you."

And just like that, they were dismissed. The *governess* had dismissed them. There was nothing else to do but tip their hats and ride on.

"That was quite an introduction." Turner flashed a grin. "She could not have ignored you more completely. Feel a little bit like your luck might be running out?"

"She did not seem terribly impressed by you either," Ned countered. Something about how she shifted so quickly from smart to stiff bothered him.

"At least she looked at me. She didn't even spare you a glance." He shrugged. "She is a governess. She has likely never encountered someone with such an elevated title before."

"Hang it," Ned said, shaking off any deep thoughts that might intrude. "Who cares about the opinion of one common, miserable governess? We will find scores more young ladies, far more happy to be pleased."

As they rounded the bend and Puffington Arms came into view, Turner flashed that tiger's smile again.

"Do you know, I think you are right, *Mr. Turner*. I think this is going to be fun."

3

New players enter the game.

*I*s he here? He's here, isn't he? That's him, rounding the bend? Why are there two of them?"

Leticia kept her tongue firmly in her cheek and her eyes coolly on the two gentlemen on horseback who had appeared in the distance.

"Calm yourself, Fanny," Leticia singsonged, never moving from her particular vantage at the window. It was the perfect spot—she was afforded the best view of the lane, but was seated at a long comfortable bench. Why, with a book in hand, one would think that she had spent the morning reading.

Not that Leticia would ever be caught dead spending the morning reading.

But while Leticia cultivated an air of serenity, Fanny's pacing behind her was doing a cracking job on her nerves.

"Do we have everything ready?" Leticia could practically hear Fanny wringing her hands. "You there!" She called out to the poor girl who happened to be clearing the tea tray at that moment. "Oh, Nanny—whatever are you doing here? Where are your charges?"

Nanny, a stout girl with a good temperament for children, bobbed a curtsy. "My lady—the children are having their walk before tea with Miss Baker. And the other girls are busy readying the rooms for the earl, so I told Cook I would help."

"Oh. Well . . ." Fanny seemed momentarily flummoxed, as she often was when things did not go exactly to plan. "Take that tray away! The earl can't think that we eat muffins and cakes all day! And tell the other girls they are beyond lazy."

Fanny then came over and nervously twitched the drapery over Leticia's head, causing a bit of dust to come flying free.

"Dust! Heavens! He'll think us slovenly. Nanny, put that tea tray down and come clean this immediately."

Poor Nanny, Leticia couldn't help but think, shortly followed by *Poor me!* as Fanny forced Nanny into actively beating out the curtain. Directly over Leticia's head.

"Fanny—*ahCHOO!*—that is enough!" Leticia said in her sternest voice. Then, kinder to the girl, "Clear the tea tray, then have one of the regular girls sent up to clean this room—it won't be in use until just before dinner anyway. Just make certain it sparkles before then."

Nanny bobbed her head, a grateful blush spreading across her cheek, as she quickly gathered the tea tray and ducked out of the room.

"And since when do you contradict *my* orders to *my* servants?" Fanny said in a huff.

"Ever since—*achoo!*" Really, Fanny's curtain-twitching was having long-lasting ramifications. Leticia's nose would be as red as an apple by the time the earl made it up the lane. "Ever since you began acting like a ninny. Which was around dinnertime last night."

Fanny shot Leticia a look reserved specifically for elder sisters to give their younger sisters.

"Well, it's true. You began fretting as soon as the first course was served," Leticia replied with a slight smile, even though her eyes stayed on the approaching men. From this distance, she could not distinguish the better man from the other—but she could distinguish the better horse from the other. The large, gorgeous stallion—that one must bear the earl. Of course it did, she could make him out better now—the fine gray of his coat, the way he bore himself upon what was apparently a problematic mount.

"How was I supposed to stay calm with the first course in shambles and a household of guests to oversee?" Fanny pouted defiantly.

"The first course was not in shambles—it merely arrived fifteen seconds later than you expected." Leticia sighed, turning to her sister for the first time since Fanny had entered the room. "And do not fret about the houseguests. They are a very merry group of girls."

"Flibbertigibbets, the lot of them," Fanny huffed, unaware of the irony of her naming anyone else as such. "I have no idea why you insisted I invite them all—and Mrs. Rye! That woman sets my teeth on edge. Why, I thought the point of this was—"

"I know very well what the point of this is," Leticia interrupted, smoothing her skirts as she rose. "Now, the earl will be at the door any moment. Do you think it perhaps a good idea to gather—"

"Lady Widcoate! Countess Churzy!" The shrill voice broke into their conversation as the door to the drawing room opened with a loud crash. Both sisters turned toward the noise—Leticia, with her outward calm, and Fanny, startled to the point of letting a small "Eek!" escape. Miss Henrietta Benson, flushed and breathless, had burst through the door. Now that she had the attention of the two ladies in the room, she seemed for a moment at a loss for what to say.

"Yes, Miss Benson?" Leticia prompted. The girl remembered her purpose and jolted directly into a rapid speech of great import.

"Have you seen down the drive? Clara and Minnie and I were on the side of the house playing bowls in the yard by the large oak tree near the pond and when Minnie lost her ball in the water she had to step into the muck to get it but it afforded her a better view of the lane and we saw two gentlemen approaching on horseback! Mrs. Rye is certain it's the earl, even though he was not expected until this evening, and Minnie went upstairs to change her dress—should we all assemble to greet them, do you think?"

To her credit, Leticia thought, Fanny did nothing more than blink twice before answering the girl.

"Of course, Miss Benson! How very astute of you—why, the countess and I were just saying the same thing.

If you girls would like to assemble in front of the house, we shall meet you there shortly."

Leticia smiled serenely at her sister once Henrietta had bounded her way out the door. But Fanny's brow remained raised to the ceiling.

"They are all very respectable girls," she placated. "And I was indebted to their families for being such good friends in Bath. How could I not invite them up to Puffington Arms for a country respite?"

"I do not pretend to know your sophisticated ways, Letty," Fanny replied, using the nickname she knew would raise Leticia's hackles. "But I do know that those girls—and their chaperone—are only here to win the hand of an earl."

"I know, Fanny."

"But *you* are here to win the hand of the earl."

Leticia just shrugged. "Well, that, and to see my sister and darling niece and nephew."

"Oh heavens!" Fanny started fluttering again. "The children! That dratted governess took them for their walk, and now when the earl meets them they'll be covered in dirt, I'm absolutely certain! I shall have to send someone out to fetch them."

"Never mind that," Leticia replied. "They'll meet properly when the children are brought round before dinner. Having the earl meet them now would simply be a distraction." And any distraction from herself simply would not do.

"Yes . . . yes, that is best. Keep them out of sight when they are covered in dirt, at least," Fanny twitted.

Then her sister made for the door, but Leticia called her back.

"Fanny—just remember: introduce me by my title."

Fanny double-blinked once again. "Why? For heaven's sake, what if he knew Churzy? Then he would know everything."

"He didn't know Churzy, because Churzy didn't know anyone, thank heavens," Leticia snapped. Then, resuming calm, "It's all part of the plan, dearest."

"A plan that had better work," Fanny groused, before she trotted out the door.

Leticia kept the little smile firmly in place until the door closed behind her sister. Then she finally allowed herself the luxury of letting it fall away, for the barest of moments. Whenever Fanny began her nervous affectations, Leticia found it best to remain outwardly serene—however, inside her stomach was flipping over on itself, and she wished fervently she could give in to the apparently hereditary urge to flutter.

No. To appear nervous would undo everything. It would weaken her.

Leticia pulled herself up by an invisible string connected to the top of her spine, rolling her shoulders straight. Then she went over to the polished looking-glass that hung above the buffet, and took stock. Her hair benefited from her being back in the country—the sunshine gave it warmth, turning it from its regular dark brown to a rich mahogany. Her skin still maintained its pale, creamy complexion, her dark eyes their luminosity. And if there was a hint of crow's-feet at the corner of her eyes when she smiled too widely . . . well, there was an easy enough solution. She would simply not smile with abandon. There would likely be little call for it anyway.

All in all, for a widow crossing the border from nine-and-twenty into thirty (she would *never* admit that border had been crossed last year and she was edging her way past one-and-thirty), Leticia could be satisfied that her appearance conveyed neither the grief of widowhood nor the ravages of age.

She was still beautiful. She was still somewhat young. And she was still cunning.

For while Leticia was not above using her good looks to her advantage, she *lived* by her wits.

It was her wits that had convinced her father, their only surviving parent, to allow her at fourteen to come and live with Fanny when she married her Sir Nathan. Thus Leticia received the genteel benefits of growing up in a landed house in the country—and not above their father's lumber mill in Manchester.

It was also Leticia's wits that wheedled a season out of her father and brother-in-law when she turned eighteen. And it was her wits that leveraged her one season into marriage to Count Churzy, an Austrian with a crumbling castle, an unfortunate predilection for horse races, and a family history of heart seizures.

Now, as long as Fanny managed to play her part and all of Leticia's carefully laid pieces fell into place, it was her wits that would have her capturing the attentions of the Earl of Ashby.

Whether he wanted to be captured or not.

With one last look at herself in the mirror, Leticia pulled her face into a gentle smile (careful to avoid the crow's-feet) and let her eyes soften. She was feminine, alluring, and just a touch mysterious.

This was going to go absolutely swimmingly.

~~~

THE FIRST THING NED noticed as he and Turner approached the Widcoates' residence was just how small the house was.

When he had been a boy, Puffington Arms was the largest house in the county—certainly much bigger than his mother's cottage in Hollyhock. They were invited there only on rare special occasions. A place that required him to dress up in his best church clothes that scratched at his neck. But now the house seemed so squat and . . . *ornate*.

In one of the few of his mother's letters he was allowed, he vaguely remembered that she mentioned the young Lady Widcoate had discovered a passion for decoration, and the foolish Sir Nathan was willing to oblige her.

"Passion" might have been an understatement. As was "decoration." There were columns he didn't remember being there before. Balustrades and cornices on every available surface. There were turrets, for God's sake!

And where had all the statuary come from?

The house of his memory had been imposing because of its importance in the neighborhood. Now it was ridiculous in its cries for attention, showing little taste and absolutely no restraint.

It was to be expected. Since his life was so large now, the pretense of Puffington Arms could not help but be easily spotted and suffer by comparison. He doubted much in Hollyhock would measure up.

The second thing Ned noticed was the number of women gathering at the front of the house.

A *lot* of women.

And absolutely no men.

No footmen, no butlers. No Sir Nathan. Instead, they faced down an array of housemaids and kitchen help, and of course, ladies. Some young ladies. And a motherly type—the chaperone, if he ventured to guess. There were ribbons flying and ruffles being ruffled as the ladies shifted and preened and maneuvered their way into an assembly of some kind. A presentation.

Oh, hell. They were all here for him.

Contrary to what Turner thought, Ned was not so blunt-headed as to think that women everywhere traipsed after him on the promise of his natural charm and cheer. He knew very well that being an earl made him a prize to young debutantes and their mothers alike. He knew the difference between being looked at as a good dinner companion and being salivated over as a possible husband. But while Turner avoided anything that did not result in him making an extra penny to put toward his falling-down mill, Ned saw no reason to be short or rude with those who were after him for his title or fortune. Indeed, he doubted he could manage Turner's level of rudeness if he tried. He would rather be a happy dinner partner to whomever he sat next to, regardless of their motives.

And he would be again.

But no, wait—he thought with dawning glee—these ladies weren't preening for *him*, they were here for the Earl of Ashby. Whose signet ring at present rested on the finger of poor, unsuspecting, dull, sour-faced John Turner.

Weren't they in for a surprise?

And once Turner's bad humor had turned everyone but the most fervent fortune hunters off his scent, there would be all these ladies for him to charm into winning this ridiculous bet.

Ned almost smiled. Almost let his face split into a wide grin and chuckled. But then Turner, who rode a half step ahead of him, glanced behind him.

"Well, here's the first real test."

"What do you mean? The governess wasn't test enough for you?"

"The governess has never met you before. The Widcoates have."

Ned's eyebrow went up. Of course! He had met the Widcoates many times in his youth, and surely the past sixteen years had not wrought so much of a change upon him that he was unknowable. And if it turned out he was *not* unknowable . . .

"The terms are that if anyone recognizes me, then you forfeit and I win, correct?"

"No—the terms are that if anyone recognizes you *without your interference,* then I forfeit." Turner gave him a sidelong look. "No trickery with the cards. Keep both hands on the table."

"I don't need trickery, John," Ned retorted. "Remember—I have luck."

Turner jerked his head back to stare directly ahead again, at all those waiting girls. "And I sincerely hope it does not desert you."

A few steps later, they were within hailing distance.

And Lady Widcoate, it seemed, was not one to miss her cue.

"Lord Ashby! Lord Ashby! How marvelous to see you again!" The lady was rounder than Ned remembered but the pinched pink cheeks were the same, as were the tight curls at her temples and the tuffet of a cap on her head—at least a decade out of style, she would be laughed out of Almack's. She waved heartily and stepped forward as Turner dismounted from Abandon. Ned followed suit. A groom—*Ha! So there was a man here!*—moved quickly to take Abandon's reins. The stallion whinnied and danced. Although Turner paid no attention to it, annoyingly.

"Lady Widcoate?" Turner said jovially—*Turner, jovial?*—as he made a quick bow to Lady Widcoate's low curtsy. "Is that you? I swear you haven't changed a lick. It's like stepping back in time."

Lady Widcoate's cheeks grew pinker with pleasure.

"My lord, what flattery! Meanwhile, you have changed a great deal."

"Oh?" Ned piped up behind Turner. "Do you think so?"

As much as Ned wanted to see Turner fail—or rather, as much as he wanted to prove to Turner that he would win—Ned couldn't help thinking that it would be so much easier if he was recognized, and this whole farce could end quickly.

Granted, the fun would be over before it could even begin, but it would be foolish not to try.

Every head in the drive turned to look at Ned. He smiled broadly, but not a single person smiled back at him. Turner's gaze was rightly hard and suspicious, but judging by Lady Widcoate's expression, Ned had just committed a veritable crime of some kind.

"Lady Widcoate," Turner's voice a warning, "this is my man, Mr. Turner."

"Yes," Lady Widcoate returned with clipped politeness, as Ned bent into a flourishing bow.

"I find I could not do without him—here on business, after all." Turner smiled—and Ned was sure he detected notes of obsequiousness in Turner's speech.

That devil. He was sucking up to the Widcoates! Hoping they would not call him out on his complete lack of resemblance to the Ashby line.

Obviously.

"Of course." Lady Widcoate put the adoring smile back on her face. "But hopefully your visit to your old home will not be *all* business, my lord."

"How could it be with such a"—Turner swept a wide hand to the crowd of women around them— "*merry* assembly as this?"

"Yes, quite merry!" Ned tried again to interject himself into the conversation. He tried to move forward, but found he still had a hold on the mare's reins, and she was more stubborn than Turner ever had been.

Another dismissive glance from the assembled crowd kept him as firmly rooted in his place as the mare was.

"Lord Ashby, may I introduce some, ah—*friends* visiting from Bath? This is Mrs. Rye, and her daughter, Miss Clara Rye. This is Miss Henrietta Benson, lately of Bath, and—"

"I'm here, I'm here, I'm here!" A young lady with the shoulders of an ox flew up, knocking into the bright red Miss Henrietta and the small and wide-eyed Miss Clara.

"—and Miss Minnie Rye," Lady Widcoate finished.

"My niece," the too-smiling Mrs. Rye interjected.

"Where were you?" Miss Henrietta whispered.

"I was so worried, you almost missed him!" Miss Clara's little body shook as if freezing.

"I had to change my gown, didn't I? I can't meet a bloody—erm, a *blooming* earl in a muddy dress, can I?" Minnie said, with a quick glance from her mother keeping her language in line.

"Oh, no." Henrietta whispered—her face flushing all the darker, taking in Minnie's new dress. "You chose the wrong dress."

"What?" Minnie whipped her head around, pins raining out of her messy curls.

"You wore pink. I'm wearing pink." Clara's voice was a shaky whisper. "We agreed, either we all wear different colors or the same, but now only you and I are wearing the same and Henrietta is left out! You'll have to change."

"I can't change—all the others are day dresses and muddy besides."

"Well, you're the one who wanted to play bowls by the pond." Henrietta puffed dramatically. "Oh, this is an absolute disaster!"

"And you're the one with the bad aim and I'm the only one not afraid of a little water to keep playing our game," Minnie shot back.

"It was *your* ball, not mine—and I'm not the one who only brought three dresses!"

"Girls!" Mrs. Rye wailed through a tight smile. "Please!"

"Bloody silly if you ask me," Minnie sniffed. "Planning our wardrobe."

"Minnie!" Mrs. Rye shrieked. "Language!"

As the girls veered dangerously toward melee territory, Ned kept his eyes on Turner. If it were he, he would have stepped in by now; would have paid compliments to every girl on their gowns, pink or otherwise. He would have defused the situation, and kept all the females fluttering happily. But Turner just looked as if he were a green private, about to take his first step on the battlefield.

Ned was about to step in. He was about to save Turner and ingratiate himself to the young ladies—after all, they were all going to spend the coming fortnight falling in love with him—when a veritable goddess arrived on the scene.

"Darlings!" The husky voice floated over them, immediately calming the scene. "You are making it very difficult for the gentleman to admire your dresses if you keep admonishing them." The sea of ruffles parted, and a paragon of grace and style emerged in their midst.

A paragon of grace and style whom Ned found strangely familiar.

"Lord Ashby, may I present to you Countess Churzy?" Lady Widcoate said graciously.

"Oh la!" the Countess laughed, a precise peal meant to entice. And from the look on Turner's face, entice it did. "Surely, sister, we need not be so terribly formal? After all, the last time we saw each other, he was young

Ned Granville and I simply Leticia. Or Letty, as you too often called me."

Of course! Ned's memory zipped back to the arrival of the new Lady Widcoate into the neighborhood. Her sister Leticia, then a gawkish thirteen or fourteen (meanwhile, he was a gawkish eleven or so), had come with her. He would be gone to live with his great-uncle in six months' time, but if he remembered anything about the indelible Miss Leticia, it was her sneezing at flowers, her ability to always win at whist, and her insistence on *never* being called Letty.

Which of course he had done. As often as possible.

But now—now no one could mistake her for a Letty. She'd grown too fine. Too knowing, if that smile had anything to say about it.

And far too focused on John Turner for Ned's liking.

"Letty," Turner breathed. "Of course. But I don't think I should call you Letty anymore."

"True, it never was my favorite nickname." Her eyes sparkled as she came forward and took his arm before Turner even realized he'd offered it. "But I don't suppose I mind it from old friends."

"Indeed." Turner smiled at her, his gaze never moving from her face as she guided him through the crowd of girls toward the house. "And you can call me . . ." His voice trailed off for a moment. Of course, Turner answering to Lord Ashby was one thing. Answering to "Ned" was quite another.

But, to his credit, Turner recovered with a tiny bit of finesse. "Well, I suppose you can call me whatever horrible name from childhood you like."

She laughed at that, a light fall of music that had more honesty to it than her practiced peal from before. "You must be famished. Nothing like a spot of tea on the terrace after a long ride?"

"Nothing like it." He grinned back.

As they reached the steps, eyes only for each other, Lady Widcoate called after them. "Oh, Lord Ashby! We shall have your rooms—"

But Turner simply waved a hand, as if his hostess was a bothersome gnat. "My man will handle everything, Lady Widcoate."

And with that, under the eyes of Lady Widcoate, four female guests, and a half dozen maids, John Turner and Leticia, apparently now Countess Churzy, disappeared into the house.

"You see, Clara! Now, that's how you snare an earl!" Mrs. Rye began immediately, causing her shaking daughter to practically vibrate with . . . some emotion only young ladies are capable of feeling, Ned supposed. "All that bloody foolery about your dresses!"

"She started it!" Minnie pointed to Clara.

"You're the one who went into the mud, Minnie," Henrietta piped up, unhelpfully.

The group continued bickering as they moved into the house, forcing Ned to call after them.

"Excuse me, Lady Widcoate? Lady Widcoate?" Ned tried as maidservants shuffled around him, moving back to their various tasks with more alacrity than he had supposed servants capable of. But his entreaties went unheard in the shuffle, as Lady Widcoate disappeared into the house.

"Excuse me," he then tried of a young maid who

wielded an extremely unwieldy-looking broom, brushing the mud and dirt off the front steps. "I have never—that is . . . where are they going?"

The maid looked at him as if he had grown two heads. "They're all following after the earl, ain't they?"

"Well, yes, but Tur—, er, I should not leave the earl alone. After all, I'm his—"

"Best speak to the housekeeper, make your arrangements for your employer's rooms quick then, if he needs you by his side."

"Arrangements?" Ned asked. And he must have looked as bewildered as he felt because the girl gave him a bewildered look back.

"What your master prefers. Rooms facing east, a hot brick at night, all that bit. If he only eats beets. What your schedule will be for the next few days so you can fix it with what Lady Widcoate will want to do with 'im."

"That's the *valet's* job." Ned wrinkled his nose. Everything except the arrangement of schedule entirely fell under his valet Danson's purview. Didn't it?

"Yes . . ." the girl said, nonplussed as she struggled with the large broom.

"The valet is on his way—he is coming with the carriage and trunks. We rode ahead." He gave a hard look to the footman. "I am the earl's secretary. And I will thank you to remember it."

The girl's eyes went wide, and she ducked into a curtsy. "My apologies, Mr. Turner. The earl said you was his man, I think we all assumed . . ."

"Yes, well—don't assume." Ned frowned. "Do I look like a valet? Really?"

The maid gave him an assessing glance. "No, I suppose you don't." Ned felt his frame relax, until . . . "I'd expect an earl's valet to be better kitted out. Anything else I can help you with, sir?"

"No," Ned answered tersely.

The maid simply nodded. "Of course. Sir."

"Thank you," Ned said with a nod. And let his good nature return to him. After all, he had a number of ladies to impress with his affability, thus he should keep it intact and not let the servants' misidentification irk him. There was a group of women in there, ripe for his picking. All he had to do was follow after them.

Of course it only took two steps before he was thwarted.

"You might want to see to your horse before you try to enter the house," the maid called after him as she dragged the broom around the back of the manor. "Sir."

Holy hell, he was still holding the reins of Turner's mare. No groom had come forward to claim him, as they had for the "earl."

He looked left and right and found himself alone outside the house. Alone, of course, except for the mare. "Damn it," he cursed.

"The stables are around that way," came a direct voice from behind him on the path.

Ned turned to see the governess and the two children from the field. Her pale face remained pinched, the corners of her mouth hard set, and the youths at her side had apparently worn themselves out playing in the field, given their subdued nature.

"Go around and you'll see them—they are made up to look like a false Greek temple." She directed, pointing with an elegant gesture. "Come along Rose, Henry. We must wash up before your father returns from town."

Ned gave a slight nod as the governess passed, taking the children inside. But she kept her gaze straight ahead.

Ned would have pondered it, had he nothing else in the whole of the world to care about. But, as Turner's annoyed mare made a nip at his shoulder, Ned realized he had much more pressing issues than the governess's sternness toward him.

He had a mare to drop off at the stables, and then . . .

He had a charm offensive to plan.

4

The first hand is played.

The thing about a charm offensive is, it works best if played on an even field. Any offensive, really. The fields of Waterloo had a slight incline, and some have said it won Wellington the war. Or at least, Ned thought that was the case. In reality, Waterloo was a fairly hazy memory to him, and when he toured the fields a few years after—because touring battlefields you fought on was incredibly impressive to the ladies with him in the carriage—the landscape had been so altered as to be unrecognizable, even by Wellington himself.

But for a charm offensive in particular, an even field of battle is crucial. And Ned knew one thing for certain: the Widcoate house was not even. Not in the slightest.

He was getting *looks*. Or rather, he wasn't getting looks. The looks that did come his way were glances, overviews. Not fully assessing looks. And when a glance held longer than a moment, it was—well, it was *mean*.

Take, for instance, when he walked into the house. After, of course, he'd dropped Turner's mare off at the folly of Grecian ruin stables and checked on Abandon, making certain that he at least was being treated with the diligence reserved for a horse of his caliber. Indeed, he was, happily munching oats in his corner stall like the prince he knew himself to be.

To his credit, the lone groom came over, immediately taking the reins from Ned. "Sorry 'bout that," the man said, with a thick Scottish accent. "The stallion looked a little jumpy, so I walked 'im first."

Ned nodded, accepting the excuse. After all, Abandon likely had the finest breeding of the entire household, human or animal, and therefore was the most high-strung.

Once he had seen Turner's mare situated (and made damn well sure that the mare received a bucket of oats equal in size to Abandon's . . . even though Abandon was a larger animal and therefore should probably be given the greater share of oats, but still, it was the principle of the thing), he had repaired to the house, hoping to catch up with the group.

He strode into the house via the front door, wherein he received his first *look* from someone. It was the young maid, and the *look* was one of disapproval. Ned was determined to ignore it, but then he caught the maid looking down at the mud he'd tracked in from the stables.

Ned decided to ignore that too.

He found the party on the terrace, all sitting back and enjoying a respite of crisp lemonade and a good airing. Turner had a seat of importance, with Lady Widcoate at his left and Countess Churzy at his right. The rest of the female coterie fell in some assembly around them, except for Minnie, who seemed eager to display her physical prowess and browbeat her nervous cousin— what was her name? Clara?—into playing bowls again.

When he cleared his throat and made his presence known . . . well, Ned got his second *look*. And his third, fourth, and fifth.

Finally, Turner managed to pull his attention away from the ladies of Puffington Arms long enough to turn around and see Ned.

That was his next *look*. And the last one Ned was going to take.

"My lord." His voice was tight, trying to not let those words stumble against his tongue. "Might I have a word?"

"Is it important?" Lady Widcoate sniffed. "The earl has just arrived."

"Yes, I know. I just arrived too." Ned couldn't help the snideness in his voice.

The entire terrace went still. And the *look* Ned got from Lady Widcoate far exceeded any that he had previously received.

"Oh, Fanny, let Ashby go," Countess Churzy said with a laugh, smoothing everything over. "Men must have their secrets, and you can ply him with lemonade later."

Turner stood and made a slight stiff bow to the ladies, then came to join Ned.

Ned led him around the side of the house, hopefully putting enough distance between them and prying ears. Then he walked another twenty steps.

"I think we've gone far enough away from prying ears," Turner drawled.

"Multiply your steps by the number of women in the house," Ned replied, "triple it, then maybe you'll be out of earshot."

"Still—what could have possibly happened in the last twenty minutes that necessitates this kind of subterfuge?"

"I cannot possibly imagine—maybe you choosing phrasing that makes the whole of Lady Widcoate's house think I'm your valet?"

Turner blinked twice. Then he cracked a smile out of the corner of his mouth. "Me? Why, I would never do such a thing."

"And yet you did."

"But it would be in opposition to the rules laid down. I cannot denigrate you."

"And yet you did."

"Just like if you tried to force someone into recognizing you, the game would be forfeit." Turner's smile fell away. "And yet you did."

Ned's brow came down. "I did no such thing."

"I beg your pardon, but the very first thing out of your mouth when Lady Widcoate commented on how I—the earl—had changed was, 'Oh, do you really think so?'"

"That was not—"

"I can write to Rhys, have him weigh in as judge?" Turner replied, innocently. "If you cannot handle the wager, call the whole thing off. Just give me five thousand pounds. It is still early enough to explain our little trick, and likely be forgiven."

"You must think very little of me if you imagine I'll give up after twenty minutes." Ned smiled as blandly as possible and knew it would get under Turner's skin. "I have no intention of forfeiting. Adjustments are . . . to be expected. And as soon as you make it clear to the young ladies present that I am not your valet, and will be attending dinner and bowls and all the lovely pastimes they have dreamed up for you, everything will be fine."

An even playing field, Ned thought. That was all he was asking for.

Turner looked into the distance for a moment. He took a breath, as if to gather his will, and then exhaled and submitted to the will of his superior. As always. "I suppose that is a reasonable request. And I shall try to phrase it in such a way that does not make you sound conceited and entitled."

"Good." Ned let the calm come over his shoulders again. Then, to himself, "Maybe that will stop the looks."

Turner mumbled something under his breath, and for a moment, Ned was certain that he heard "It won't."

But before he could ask Turner about it, a rumbling around the front of the house drew their attention. A few quick steps revealed that the carriage bearing the valet Danson and their luggage had made the turn on the road for Puffington Arms, and was quickly bearing in their direction.

"Oh, thank God," Ned breathed. "Danson is here. And our clothes. Now we can be properly settled. And I can take a bath. I must smell something atrocious."

"No more than normal," Turner said wryly, and

Ned resisted the urge to chuff his friend on the arm, like they had back in their army days.

"You're no better. I have a hard time believing the ladies could stand you."

"Twenty minutes in, and I've already discovered that ladies will stand quite a bit in the presence of an earl. Even an illustrious lady like the countess."

"I would be careful with Countess Churzy," Ned ventured.

"Why?" Turner asked. "She seems happy to give me her attentions."

"Yes, well, I would rather not have some Austrian count finding out about those attentions and hunting *me* down because of them."

"Actually," Turner perked up, "Countess Churzy is a widow. No count will come hunting for your honor. Or mine."

"Still . . . don't do anything that I cannot undo, if you please," Ned replied. "I doubt this one is seeking only a warm bed."

"Widows are already undone," Turner countered. "Hence their appeal."

Ned had to acknowledge that he had a point.

It seemed there was little else to discuss.

"Well, then, I suppose I will see you at supper."

"I suppose so."

After a moment Ned ventured, "Are you going to go in?"

"After you," Turner replied. But neither man moved. Until Ned realized . . .

"I'm not going to scrape and bow to you, Turner— not when we're alone."

"But are we really alone?" Turner asked, tilting his head back toward the house.

Ned glanced over. There, safely out of earshot but not eyeshot, were three female heads, popping out from around the corner. Minnie, Clara, and Henrietta.

Gritting his teeth, Ned gave Turner the slightest of bows. Turner returned an even slighter one. Then Ned turned on his heel and walked in one direction; Turner walked in the other.

But before he made the corner, Turner called back after him, "Good luck, my friend."

"Thank you. But I shan't need it."

No, Ned decided as he walked back toward the house, seeking Danson, a bath, and a change of clothes, he did not need luck.

Because, whether he realized it or not, Turner had just shown his hand.

⁓

NED PRACTICALLY SKIPPED up the stairs after the maid—the same one who had pointed out his less-than-valet-level clothes—who carried his (well, actually Turner's) trunk up the stairs. She was struggling a bit with it, but Ned figured that was because she kept looking over her shoulder to shoot Ned displeased looks. As if she expected him to help her.

Meanwhile, Ned had determined to be gleeful, because it had taken only twenty minutes and the arrival of the carriage for him to realize Turner's strategy in this game.

And it was all so simple. Turner was expecting Ned to bow out.

Not because he wasn't charming enough to woo a woman. Not because he wasn't lucky—but because he thought Ned was too squeamish at the idea of having to bow to him and wear unfashionable clothes.

Turner thought Ned had gone dandy. He thought he was too soft to live at a level of comfort less than an earl was used to. Well, Turner didn't know everything about Ned.

Turner knew that Ned had lived among men on the battlefield, but he likely thought that an aberration. He didn't realize that, growing up, Ned's life had not been one of privilege. That he had worked in his mother's vegetable garden from the age of three, and had carried water back and forth from the town well since he was able to walk, for their cooking, their washing, their gardens. He had built fires in a smoky little room. He *had* lived at a level less comfortable than an earl, and he had . . . well, he hadn't liked it. But he had done it. And he could do it again.

They walked to the end of the hall of the second floor, passing by several doors on their way, some opened, offering a peek into the bedrooms of Puffington Arms. They were certainly not as grand as Ned was used to, with overly ornate furniture matching the rest of the house, but they would do, he thought. When they reached the door at the end of the hall, Ned smiled to the little maid, who was dwarfed by the size and weight of the trunk.

"Could you get the door?" she asked, from beneath the trunk. Then added hastily, "Mr. Turner?"

"Oh!" Ned started. "Of course." He opened the door and discovered . . . another set of stairs. This one far more rickety looking and hidden away than that last.

"Er . . . what's this?" he asked the young maid. "Where are we going?"

"To your room, Mr. Turner."

"Well . . . surely my room is on the main floor. With the other guests?"

"Ah . . . I believe every room has been taken. By the house party."

With that, the maid lifted the trunk in her arms again and headed up the stairs—which, true to their appearance, were immensely rickety.

"Of course. Makes perfect sense," Ned said as he followed.

After all, adjustments were to be expected. And if he was to beat Turner's strategy, from now on, nothing could ruffle him. Not being placed away from the rest of the party, not being mistaken for a valet. Nothing would make him lose his good humor.

Not even when he saw his room. Its cramped space and bare floorboards. Its low slanted ceiling and small bed. Its small basin for water, currently empty.

No. This would not undo him.

"Brilliant! Marvelous!" he said, keeping the smile pasted on his face. He let the maid put the overly heavy trunk down, maneuvering out of her way, since the space was so tight.

"Thank you," he remembered to say, trying to wedge his way past again, but in so doing banged his head on a low ceiling beam.

"Are you all right, Mr. Turner?" the girl asked— annoyingly adept at avoiding the low ceiling beam her-self. Although, to be fair, she was shorter.

"Brilliant. Marvelous." He rubbed the spot that

would grow to a goose egg in no time at all. "Have Danson sent up. And a bath, if you please."

"Danson, Mr. Turner?"

"He's my—he's my earl's valet. We have to . . . go over some things."

"I'll let him know to come see you." She nodded. Then, with a relieved roll of her shoulders, left.

Ned surveyed the small room, the small cloudy window, which afforded a glance down onto the pond off to the side of the house. There was no fire, but it was far enough into summer that it would not make much difference. There was no possibility that this room would be used in winter—and that led him to the satisfactory belief that this accommodation really was because of the overcrowding of the actually-not-very-big-at-all house.

Idly, he opened up Turner's trunk. Rifled through his clothes, all of which were free of wear and holes, but none of which were remotely fashionable.

"Brilliant. Marvelous." He smiled wryly.

The bulk of the trunk seemed to be made up of sheaves and sheaves of paper, and a pile of ledgers. Ned rolled his eyes. Of course Turner would bring all this madness with him. Likely for this moment, when Ned would open this trunk and see *all the work* Turner did. How very droll.

Well, he would simply ignore it. He wasn't here to puzzle over ledgers. He was here to woo a lady—any lady—and a bath was the first step toward that.

Where the hell was his bathwater? And Danson?

Ned waited another half hour before he went in search of them.

He had just hit the bottom of the creaky third-floor stairs when he ran into the governess again.

Quite literally.

"Oof!" was all he heard as the thin female form landed against him like a bundle of fragile sticks.

He grabbed her arm, steadying them both. A pair of gray-blue eyes, set in a pale tight face, whipped up to meet his.

"Oh, I beg your pardon," he said, peering into the young woman's face. She looked back at him so clearly, directly, that it unnerved him.

And then he remembered that his hand was on her shoulder. He removed it as if it burned. She seemed to relax, but kept her eyes on his face.

Trying to restore some distance and decorum, he said, "I am looking for the earl's valet."

The governess took a considering moment before answering.

"I believe I saw him moving the earl's things into his room," the governess replied quietly.

"Thank you . . . Miss . . ."

"Baker," she replied, keeping her gaze on him, unblinking. Direct. Judging. Given that she would not meet his eye before, it was beyond disconcerting.

"Thank you, Miss Baker. I am Mr. Turner."

"I remember."

"Right. Well . . ." Perhaps Turner had been right. Some women were simply immune to basic civility. Even so, Ned could not help but try for a spot of conversation. "Where are your charges?"

"They are having their baths, Mr. Turner."

"Ah! So there are baths to be had in this place," he

joked. Miss Baker did not smile, simply raised a surprisingly expressive eyebrow.

"It has been a while since I was out of Leicestershire—has bathing become unfashionable elsewhere?" she asked wryly.

"Er . . . no. It's still considered rather a good thing," he said awkwardly, as a bemused smile tipped up the corners of her mouth. Meanwhile, she never lost her governess's demeanor. "I must hunt the earl's valet down at once."

"Then I bid you happy hunting, Mr. Turner."

Ned paused as she turned to mount the steps. Had the dour governess just told a joke? He shook his head. This place just got stranger and stranger.

"Brilliant," he said under his breath. "Marvelous."

5

In for a penny, in for a pound.

anson!" Ned cried upon entering the rooms Turner had taken. Which were, Ned could not help but notice, far more spacious than what he had been given. But that was incidental, not worthy of comment. That was something that Ned was determined to smile at and say, "Brilliant! Marvelous!"

Danson, his mournful valet, looked up from where he was polishing Ned's favorite pair of boots.

"Why are you polishing my boots?" Ned asked. "I certainly can't wear them. And Turner's feet would not fit in them."

"Just because you have decided to subject yourself to this strange social experiment does not require my standards for your clothing to fall—whether or not you are in a position to wear them." Danson's dry response was typical of his valet. Its consistency was almost comforting. "Dare I hope you have forgone this terrible idea and come to your senses?"

"Not yet, Danson. I am glad you take such care with my clothes. Now, if we could address my person, I would greatly appreciate it."

"Whatever are you referring to, my lord?" Danson replied archly. "Oh, I mean Mr. Turner."

"I mean I sent a maid to fetch you to me."

"I was so informed by a maid, yes."

"So . . ."

"So, my first task was to see *the earl* settled. I could not come and consult with the earl's *secretary* until that was done." Danson finished with the boots and placed them in a spacious wardrobe.

"I am sure the boots that neither of us can wear could wait."

"Indeed. I, on the other hand, do not have your certainty. Sir."

Ned sighed. He knew Danson's reservations about this wager. But he thought his valet had vented his trickle of spleen before they left. Now it seemed that the trickle was more of a steady river.

"Regardless, I am here for your assistance. I rode all the way from Peterborough this morning, and need to bathe before supper tonight."

Danson took a deep sniff. "I agree with your assessment, sir."

"Well . . . ?"

"Well?" Danson replied.

"Well, if you could see to my bath, I would be ever so grateful."

"I believe you told me before we left Peterborough that I was to lower myself to serve Mr. Turner as I would you, and to treat you as I would Mr. Turner," Danson said, trying to hide a smile. "I have never ordered a bath for Mr. Turner."

Brilliant. Marvelous.

"Still. In this instance, if you could take pity on me . . ."

Danson sighed. "Certainly, sir. The bath has been drawn. I will show you to the bathing room."

Danson produced a towel from a drawer and led Ned out into the hall.

It was not surprising that Puffington Arms utilized a bathing room. Among all the decorative changes wrought by Lady Widcoate, this at least was a functional one. The bathing room was tiled, with special access to the kitchens below, where water was being heated and brought up for the bather's pleasure.

However, Ned was not accustomed to *sharing* a bathing room. He was simply used to the convenience of the personal bathing room he had in his London house, right next to his master suite.

But no matter! Sharing a bathing room was no trouble.

Sharing his bathwater, on the other hand, was a bit more disturbing.

"Danson," he asked as the door to the bathing room closed behind them, "what is that?"

"That is your bath, sir."

"But the water is . . ." Cloudy. Dirty. Soapy. "Used."

"Of course it is," Danson replied. "The *earl* had his bath first, as is his due. Followed by Sir Nathan, and then the two little children."

"So I am bathing after four other people?"

"This is good fortune, sir—most of the ladies performed their ablutions this morning, readying themselves for your arrival." Ned's face must have been somewhat telling, because Danson leaned in and whispered, "You cannot expect the house to go through the time and expense of preparing a bath for just you, *Mr. Turner.*"

Ned met Danson's gaze, but his valet very politely took a step back, with a gesture to help Ned disrobe and step into the milky water of the tub.

"Brilliant!" Ned blurted out, mustering his will. "Marvelous!"

⁓

"NOW, YOU TWO," Phoebe Baker commanded in her sternest governess voice as she dodged the thwack of a twisted wet towel, "stop fooling about!"

But Rose and Henry Widcoate, wearing dressing robes, seemed unable to end the Towel Wars, at least not before declaring a clear victor and making the defeated party forfeit their lands and riches.

"Say 'uncle'!" Rose cried.

"Why?" Henry asked, perplexed. He was six to his sister's eight, and therefore not well schooled in the nuances of towel warfare.

"'Uncle' means that you give up!"

"Oh." Henry's eyes went wide with understanding. "But I don't give up. I've hit you six times, you've only hit me four!"

Thwack! "Five now. And the loser has to give over their dessert tonight."

"Then I definitely don't give up!" Henry spun his towel, readying it for a furious strike.

Time for the cavalry to step in.

"If you don't cease hostilities right now, tomorrow will have double the spelling lessons!" Miss Baker said, hands on her hips.

That was, apparently, sanction enough from a stronger empire to force an end to the Towel Wars.

Rose and Henry blinked up at her, as if they had only just realized she was in the room with them. Their hair was still wet from their baths, water dripping into their eyes.

"Oh, yes, hello," she said, giving a short wave. "I've been here this entire time. I have witnessed your crimes and must insist upon a negotiated armistice before dinner."

"Sorry, Miss Baker," they answered in unison.

"What's an armistice?" Rose piped up, bouncing up and down on the balls on her feet. Rose was always the bouncy one. Quick, and with more energy than she knew what to do with. Henry was the quiet, contemplative child, who—as evidenced by the recent conflict—could find trouble very easily when led into it by his sister.

But both were curious—and having curious pupils made up for quite a bit in the governess trade.

"An armistice is a cessation of hostilities." Blank looks were her answer. "A promise of peace."

"Like when the Boney man was shipped off to the island by Wellington?" Henry asked.

"Sort of," Phoebe replied, satisfied with a six-year-old's understanding of a war that had ended only shortly before he was born. One whose legend was quickly outstripping fact, as in all things.

History, of course, was written by the victors.

"Now, you both will be quite sorry if you don't get ready for dinner. Your father has arrived home from Hollyhock, and you are expected in the drawing room before your supper. Nanny has laid out your best suit, Henry. And your lovely pink dress, Rose."

Both froze. Because, as young as they were, and as breezy as Phoebe tried to make her speech, Rose and Henry knew all too well what their best clothes and an audience with their father meant.

"We are going to have a Questioning, aren't we?" Rose asked, suddenly without her bounciness.

Phoebe looked into the imploring eyes of her young charges. She could have lied to them. She could have soothed and petted and cooed the way she wished to.

But that was not what governesses were for.

"Yes," she replied crisply. "I imagine so."

Rose groaned and fell in the most dramatic possible fashion face-first into a stuffed chair, while poor Henry simply brought his thumb to his mouth reflexively.

"Now, now," Phoebe chided, crouching down to Henry's level and gently removing the thumb from between his teeth. "None of that. This is not worthy of the thumb, Henry."

"But we *hate* the Questioning!" Rose moaned, flopping over in the chair.

"Does the prospect of the Questioning make gravity affect you so much you can no longer stand?" she asked with a raised eyebrow. Rose, knowing that tone, managed to pull herself to her feet, however sulkily.

"Why all this nonsense? Your father only wants to make sure you are learning as you ought. And you are. Rose, you did your multiplication tables perfectly yesterday."

Rose seemed to consider that. As if perhaps she had accomplished something worthy of recognition. Although Phoebe knew Lady Widcoate would disagree.

"Can I show Papa my drawing?" Henry asked, holding up a page from his sketchbook. It was a rather lovely picture of a sunflower . . . for a six-year-old. However, if Phoebe knew her employer, it would not be considered masculine enough for the heir of Puffington Arms.

"Hmm . . ." Phoebe hummed, flipping back a page or two. "Why don't we show him the picture of beetles you drew yesterday? And we can write their Latin names underneath?"

Henry considered it, and then nodded in agreement.

"Excellent." Phoebe gave him a swift nod, the highest sign of approval a governess should give to her pupils. Or so Lady Widcoate had told her the first time she had dared to smile at her young charges.

No, smiles and coddling were not permitted from the governess. They were the purview of the mother. Meanwhile, scaring the children witless with probing questions and a distinct lack of patience was the father's.

"But why are we to have a Questioning?" Rose asked, her fears unsoothed by her younger brother's entomological prowess. "We just had one two days ago."

Yes, there had been a Questioning two days ago, when the house party had begun in earnest with the arrival of Countess Churzy's friends from Bath. The loud arrival.

It had been so long since Phoebe had been at school,

she had forgotten the kind of madness a group of young women can trail in their wake. One of them expressed an interest in meeting the children, so before dinner, in front of a room full of strangers, they were trotted out and quizzed on how they were doing with their lessons.

An idea that simply smacked of Lady Widcoate's uncaring brilliance.

Thankfully, Rose and Henry acquitted themselves well enough, considering. Rose had stalled slightly in the beginning of the psalm she'd memorized for the occasion, causing Sir Nathan to begin to turn a mottled purple. But luckily, Countess Churzy happened to say to her sister, "Psalm Twenty-three? Is that the one that starts 'The Lord is my shepherd'? I never remember that one." And Rose was able to take it from there.

Of course, the children had no cause to fear their father. He was all bluff and bluster, his anger and the reason for it forgotten as soon as the event had ended. Sir Nathan was a man of little patience for trying things, but his bite would never actually break skin. Especially not that of his children.

No, it was Phoebe who had cause to worry, should they not do well in front of their audience. For while Sir Nathan had the ire, Lady Widcoate had the memory of it. And she would never direct her anger at her offspring. She would put it on the one she thought responsible.

Sometimes Phoebe actually felt bad for Lady Widcoate. She had two marvelous children. But she could not understand why her energetic daughter enjoyed mathematics and horses, while her son preferred to draw quietly. Surely the reverse should be the case. At least, in that lady's narrow definition of order and normality, it should be. And often, she would glare at Phoebe as if her children's natural inclinations were the governess's fault.

But Phoebe shook that off, put on her calmest Governess Face, and turned to look into the big, frightened eyes of the children. "You remember the very important men that arrived today. We came across them in the field."

"The one with the beautiful horse." Rose nodded, the thought of the stallion perking her up again ever so slightly.

"It's the Earl of Assby," Henry said drolly, and Phoebe found it necessary to stifle a fake cough, lest they see their serious and pinched governess actually crack a smile.

"It's the Earl of Ashby," she corrected, although, secretly, she thought Henry's interpretation was closer to the truth. The Earl of Ashby, the man who had changed her life and damned her to the purgatory of governessing without knowing—or, more likely, without caring—definitely deserved the family crest and title of Ass.

Phoebe felt the bile that had risen in her throat at seeing him this afternoon churn and attempt to fight its way back up again. But no. She had to tamp down those feelings. She had to keep herself still and controlled. A governess who lashes out at an earl does so at her own peril.

"Yes, the man with the horse," she replied, steadying herself with a judicious breath. "I imagine your parents would like for you to meet him."

"But we already met him," Henry's logic had him saying. "On the road."

"Yes," Phoebe reasoned, "but this would be a formal introduction." When Rose and Henry looked at her quizzically, she put her hands on her hips and stood up. "Your parents are quite proud of you, and wish to show to their very important guest that you are two of the brightest, best-behaved children in the county. Now it's time to get dressed, else we shall be late, and that is no way to make an impression."

As the pair shuffled diligently off to their beds, where their clothes and their young but efficient nanny waited for them, Phoebe took the opportunity to brush out her skirts and straighten her spine.

She checked herself in the small looking-glass that hung on the nursery wall. Pinching down the smile that gave away her delight in the ridiculous. Governesses did not delight in anything, other than their students' accomplishments.

Five years of practice being the perfect governess—four years in Portsmouth and the last year with the Widcoates—had made it easier and easier to do every day. She could not present herself downstairs as anything other than what she was. And if she was lucky, the children would acquit themselves well and quickly, and they could be on their way, not to be thought of again for the next two weeks.

If she could make it through the fortnight and entirely avoid the Earl of Ashby, so much the better.

It was of course predictable, then, that Lady Widcoate had placed the earl's secretary on the unadorned third floor, where Phoebe had previously reigned freely. With the family on the second floor, and the small retinue of servants on the ground floor in their quarters, she had been the only person who existed in the strange "in between" space—not family, not serving class. In her sanctuary on the third floor, she could smile and laugh and unbend to her heart's content.

She thought briefly of Mr. Turner with the dusty brown hair whom she had met with such surprise on the staircase. The one who seemed happy, angry, and confused all at once. But then she dismissed him from her mind.

If he worked for the earl, he knew what kind of man he was. And continued to work for him anyway. This did not speak highly of his character.

Oh well, Phoebe thought. It was only two weeks. She would survive it.

She had survived this long, after all.

6

The winner takes the first hand.

After a bath that left him feeling less than clean, Ned moved quickly back down the corridor, careful to avoid anyone in the hall, and dodged his way into his third-floor room. There he rummaged in Turner's trunk for his best coat and trousers.

It had been ages since Ned had to get dressed by himself, especially the intricate work of evening garb. He almost called for Danson twice while trying to fix a wrinkled cravat, but he muddled through—he had, after all, been in the army. No valets in the army. It had been a rule, apparently.

Ned and Turner had arrived at Puffington Arms in the early afternoon, but after settling the horses, finding Turner, giving him the necessary talking-to, and taking the most disgusting bath in the history of bathing, the afternoon was fading to evening, and he suspected that the Widcoates, fashionable as they tried to be, kept country hours. Granted, no one had come to inform him of the time to be ready for tonight's dinner, but he refused to be caught unawares.

He knew Turner's game now. Ned would not let himself be shut out again.

Thus, Ned, dressed in Turner's best suit of clothes and a clean shirt, found himself in the drawing room a full half hour early for dinner, while it was still being dusted by a harried maid.

"Better than being late," he rationalized to the maid. She blinked at him, curtsied quickly, and left even faster.

Leaving Ned alone.

Strange, he thought. He had never really been left alone like this before.

Oh, he had been alone. Usually in his own quarters, while he slept. And even then, if he happened to *want* company, it was never that difficult to come across. But if he had been the earl at this moment, one of those girls or their chaperone, Mrs. Rye, would have come downstairs early "accidentally" to steal a fast five minutes alone with him. Or one or the other of the Widcoates would have rushed to assure he was well looked after and comfortable. At the very least, he would be well informed of the time of supper, and currently be upstairs getting dressed while Danson hovered over him, and Turner (who would be back to his secretarial role) tried to keep him informed of his own life.

But to be alone, with no one checking on him, no one wondering about him, no one clocking his movements . . . it was a rare thing. A strange thing.

The last time he had been alone like this would have

to have been when he was eleven or so, and not account-able to anyone except his mother. Before the old earl had found him, and a walk from the well in Hollyhock to his mother's cottage could take ten minutes or, given the glory of the day's weather and the leisure to idle, might well take thirty. There was a path, he remembered, that veered off the main road and through the woods, to a place where an eleven-year-old boy could lose himself in the wilderness for hours.

Of course, that was before he was somebody. A nobody could idle in the woods for a few minutes while his mother waited impatiently for water back home. An earl had no time for such foolish flights of fancy.

Well, what did one do with such time alone? He let his eyes roam over the bookshelf. Then his fingers, touching dust off the spines. When he pulled a tome off the shelf and pried it open (a proper boring volume titled *The Collected Ichthyology of the Central Counties*), it was easy to tell by the way the spine cracked that it had never been opened.

It was indicative of this place, he supposed. Puffington Arms had a feeling of being inflated and strained at the seams, stuffed with hot air—things he would have never taken note of if he had been the earl, feted and cosseted by the party members and looming duties at every turn. It was like seeing the strings of a puppet show and the paint wash of the thin board sets.

He really shouldn't be left alone like this. It left one time to ruminate on such *boring* things.

Well, it was only going to last two weeks, Ned thought with resolute brightness. And whatever came his way, Ned would simply smile and say, "Brilliant!

Marvelous!" and then go about waiting for Turner to put off the women with his distinctly un-Ashby manners and looks, leaving Ned to collect female admirers in his wake.

He had four women to choose from in this very house. Five, if he included Mrs. Rye. Although the thought of pulling intimate secrets and tokens of love out of that toothy smile and mercenary gaze was less pleasing.

But still, he could find pleasure in the challenge, if not the prize. And he would—yes, he had a much better footing now than he did when they arrived, and with his policy of "Brilliant! Marvelous!" things should go much more smoothly.

Lucky Ned was nothing if not game.

Ned put himself into his normal good mood with thoughts like these, and thus, when the party began to arrive for supper some minutes later, he did not take notice of the slight surprise and unhappiness in Lady Widcoate's voice when she said, "Oh, Mr. Turner. My *apologies* for this afternoon. Sir Nathan expected *you* to stay in town, is all. Nearer the business dealings. Are you sure you would still not be more comfortable there? I promise the earl will be very well taken care of in your absence. Our third floor has unfortunately the only rooms available at the moment and—"

"I promise, Lady Widcoate, I find the third-floor room brilliant. Marvelous."

"Well, then. I will have another place at the table laid for you," she answered brightly, though her smile did not reach her eyes.

But there was no call to be upset over Lady Widcoate's misunderstanding, or when they entered, over the titter of the Misses Rye, who quickly moved on to the other side of the room with Miss Benson, ignoring his wide smile. Nor did he mind much the harrumphing of Sir Nathan upon being introduced.

Sir Nathan, a thick-trunked man with blond hair going white and a ruddy complexion, had been in Hollyhock when their party had arrived, apparently, according to him, making some last-minute arrangements with a Mr. Fennick for "the earl's" arrival and inspection of his late mother's property.

"This earl of yours," Sir Nathan said as an aside, "I have some slight remembrances of the boy, but what is the man like?"

Ned thought briefly about playing a joke on his friend Turner, in retaliation for Turner's letting everyone think he was a valet this afternoon, but thought better of it. He would abide by the rules of the game and not impugn his friend's character (or his own, come to think of it). No, he would play fair.

And, he decided, he would win.

"The earl is a great man," Ned said confidently. "Saved my life on the battlefield on the Continent during the war. We were sent out to secure a flank, and he—"

"Oh, so he must hunt!" Sir Nathan waved his hand, cutting off Ned's story sharply. "Being a crack shot in the war and all."

"Er . . ." Ned began. "No more than the next man, I suppose." In truth, Ned did not love hunting. Nor, to his knowledge, did Turner. Too many unhappily familiar sounds.

"Excellent!" Sir Nathan was saying, blithely unaware

of Ned's discomfort. "We can go shooting. Granted, it's a few weeks shy of pheasant season proper, but it's my land, so who could care?" Sir Nathan slapped him on the back, happy to expound on a favorite topic. "I'll have my Brown Besses cleaned. And I have one of those new Baker rifles, just for fun. And you can come along too, of course."

Ned brightened, trying to be happy to be included, feelings about hunting aside. "Thank you, sir. I would—"

"You can load for us," Sir Nathan said. Ned had to fight to keep his countenance. "It will be jolly good to have a loader again."

"Surely a servant . . ."

Sir Nathan shook his round head. "No menservants to do the job, can't ask a lady's maid." He caught Ned's upturned brow and hastened to assure him, "We are perfectly able to afford menservants! Or, we would be. But the mine in Midville—when it opened up, it took all the local men away with better wages. That's why the bathing retreat is so important, Mr. Turner. Return some sense of order to Hollyhock."

"I see."

"So . . . do you think the earl likely to agree to our scheme?" Sir Nathan leaned close, giving Ned a full dose of his impressively sour breath. "Letting us have the cottage, that is."

Ned narrowed his eyes. In truth, he had thought very little about the cottage or Hollyhock. Not only since his arrival, but in the last half dozen years or so. Whether it remained in existence had mattered very little to him, except . . .

Except when Turner had approached him about selling, he had stalled on the subject before putting it out of his mind again.

"Well, I suppose it would be best that we take a look at the house first. That is the reason Tur—er, I set up this whole trip, after all," Ned reasoned, holding his breath as he said it, forcing himself not to inhale.

Sir Nathan considered him with a slight cock of the head, making him look like nothing so much as a dog, but that could simply be the association with his breath. "I take it the earl relies upon your opinion."

"That he does," Ned said, with some mischievousness. "It is as if the earl's brain is in my own head."

"You know, the town has great plans for that bit of property," Sir Nathan said conspiratorially. "Indeed, a few of us formed a consortium to handle the business. The old lady who owned the house would never give us the time of day, but if we manage to work this out . . . the town and the consortium will do rather well for themselves. And if anyone were to exert their influence over the earl . . . who is to say they cannot profit as well?"

Ned eyed the larger man and tried to seem unruffled. "And I assume that you are a member of this consortium?"

"Yes," Sir Widcoate replied. "As I told you in my letters."

"Interesting," Ned mused, feeling he was teetering at the edge of a rabbit hole of Turner's intentions. "Refresh my memory—what else did you mention in your letters?"

But any answer Sir Nathan was going to give was swallowed by the mercenary grin that lit his face upon seeing the door open and John Turner enter the room, wearing Ned's spotless evening kit and leading Countess Churzy on his arm.

"We met in the hall," the countess said by way of explanation, giving Turner a serene smile before she removed herself from his arm and attached herself to her sister. Turner followed her with his gaze, but made his way over to Sir Nathan before the other ladies could descend on him.

"Sir Nathan!" he cried, with a smile and a short bow. "I doubt you remember me."

"Of course I remember you, my lord!" Sir Nathan replied jovially, but with a hint of hardness behind it. "I've known you and your family since you were a lad."

Turner smiled, letting his eye catch Ned's as Sir Nathan moved to attach himself like a leech to the earl. If Ned didn't know any better, he would say Turner was trying to provoke him.

Who was he kidding? Turner was *absolutely* trying to provoke him. But he wouldn't fall for it. Instead, he gave his widest smile, and after flashing it to Turner, directed it at the ladies.

To her credit, Miss Benson blushed, as did Miss Clara Rye. Miss Minnie simply looked at him strangely, but two out of three wasn't bad, and Ned felt perfectly comfortable moving over to the girls and giving them the full force of his charm.

But before he could bow and utter a word beyond "Good evening," the door to the drawing room creaked open and admitted the last addition to the party.

"Good evening, my lord, my lady," the little governess said coolly, as the children from the fields that

afternoon stood with rigid attention and more stillness than anyone under the age of ten should be able to
achieve. They were kitted up much better too, having
been cleaned and polished—likely cleaner than he was,
as they had the benefit of the bathwater before he did.

"Rose! Henry!" Sir Nathan called out, forcing the
rest of the room's attention to turn to the newcomers.
The governess held herself judiciously back, her eyes
only flicking up once and never meeting his. It was as
if their amused run-in in the hallway never occurred.

She must be quite the governess.

"Don't dawdle, come forward and meet the earl!" Sir
Nathan frowned, causing the two to jump in nervousness. A hand at each of their backs gave the smallest bit
of pressure, and they advanced forward.

"My lord, these are my children," Sir Nathan said
gravely. "Henry, my heir—and Rose."

"Yes, we happened to meet as we were riding in,"
Turner offered graciously.

But Lady Widcoate did not receive it as graciously.

"Did you now?" she said, her smile becoming fixed
and her eyes steely. "Miss Baker, you took it upon yourself to introduce my children to the Earl of Ashby?"

"My lady, I—"

"Actually, it was our fault. Mine and Mr. Turner's,"
Turner offered, with a nod to Ned. "I was relying on
my memory to find our way here, and Turner fussily
thought it better to ask directions and make sure we
arrived at the right house. The children and their governess were taking a . . . constitutional along the road."

"And your memory proved correct?" the Countess
Churzy purred, shifting herself from her sister's side to

Turner's, all without moving her feet an inch. She really was an impressive hunter.

"It did," Turner replied with a smile. "And Mr. Turner's worry was for naught."

The assembled party tittered with laughter. But if Turner thought Ned would let his hackles rise at something so banal as a good-natured ribbing, he was happy to prove him wrong.

"Yes, out of the two of us, I was always a bit more motherly," Ned said with a smile. He was expecting a hearty laugh and denial from Turner at the very least. But perhaps his phrasing wasn't the best, because his joke fell flat, and everyone in the room just stared at him as if he had grown a fourth head.

Except for the governess, who kept her head down. But from his position, he could see the compression of her mouth, and the . . . heat from her eyes. Her deeply squashed sense of anger.

Maybe it was because he was not used to being on the side of the room instead of in its center. Maybe it was because he had just told a flat joke and was forced to observe rather than engage. But regardless of the reason, Ned found himself *looking* at all the adults in the room. And the only one without a smile—scared, ecstatic, bemused, hopeful, false, or real—painted on their face was the governess.

And from where he stood, Turner was the cause.

She was not hiding her displeasure with Turner very well. At least not from Ned. But then again, he was the only one watching. Everyone else had their eyes on Rose and Henry, being presented in front of their father.

They did not hide their nerves very well either.

"Now, children!" the blustery Sir Nathan began in what he likely thought was good humor, but his exclamation was accompanied by a fierce scowl—and therefore no good humor got through.

Goodness, where had all these observations come from?

"What have you learned today?" their father asked, too large and imposing.

"I did a drawing," Henry said bravely and stepped forward to present the page to his father.

"Drawing, Miss Baker?" Lady Widcoate said suspiciously. "Is drawing the best use of my son's time?"

"Henry drew some insects he found interesting, Lady Widcoate," Miss Baker said smoothly. "As a scientific study."

"Yes," Henry agreed. "That is a dung beetle. And that one is a grasshopper. And that is—"

"Oh, bugs! How horrid!" Countess Churzy said with a smile. "Just like a boy to bring beetles into the drawing room."

The room gave an appreciative hum of laughter, and Lady Widcoate sighed.

"I suppose that is sufficient." Then she turned a smile to Rose. "And you, my darling? Have you a drawing for us too?"

"I . . . uh . . . no," Rose began, beginning to tap her toe against the ground in nervousness.

"Well, girl? Come off it—have you learned anything today?" Sir Nathan growled. "Or did you spend all your time traipsing in a field?" He glanced up at Miss Baker, who had smoothed her features back into something like kind compliance.

Rose looked back at Miss Baker, but that only prompted Lady Widcoate to join the fray. "Rose, stop tapping your feet and face your father!"

"Yes, Rose," Countess Churzy spoke up. "If you can find him under that huge bushy mustache."

It would have been a rebuke if not spoken so sweetly, and not received with a smile and bark of laughter from her brother-in-law. That did seem to cut the tension, and Rose was able to answer.

"I know my times tables!"

"Times tables?" her father answered, trying to muster some enthusiasm and failing. "Well, now, that's a bit of a boast."

"Yes," Miss Baker provided, nodding at Rose. "All the single digits."

"Well, then—what is seven times four?"

"Twenty-eight," Rose answered proudly.

"Six times nine?"

"Fifty-four."

"Ten times ten?"

"One hundred!"

Sir Nathan smiled indulgently while Lady Widcoate still bristled.

"Again, Miss Baker, I must question the subjects you choose. Shouldn't little girls be learning sewing and art instead?"

"Come now, Fanny," Countess Churzy interrupted. "I was always horrid at painting, and found it a fairly useless skill. But when Rose is grown and has a house of her own, she will have to manage it—which is much easier with mathematics, I'm told."

Lady Widcoate shot her sister a hot glare but seemed

mollified. Mrs. Rye could be heard saying under her breath, "She would know." A statement Ned found interesting—and informative.

Rose's relief at passing inspection was visible, and she was just about to curtsy, when Turner spoke up.

"What about eleven times eleven?" he asked. "Or twelve times twelve. Or better yet, thirteen times thirteen?"

Rose looked up at him, dumbfounded.

"Now, if you are to truly use mathematics to their greater purpose, you should be able to do all the numbers, not just the easy ones," Turner said, bending down to meet Rose's eye.

All the ladies looked up at Turner with their hearts in their eyes. They saw a man of learning, a man of inspiration, a man with the worldly experience to know the usefulness of mathematics.

Meanwhile, Ned saw Turner being his normal stick-in-the-mud self. And it seemed like it was going to be up to Ned to make everyone else see it as well.

While Rose trembled in terror, trying to think of the answer, Sir Nathan began to peer queerly at her. "Well? What's the answer? Thirteen times thirteen. You can do it. Now, don't make a fool of yourself—and don't make a fool of me!"

It was mere seconds before Lady Widcoate joined the fray, with no small amount of strain, as she tried to urge her daughter on. "Now, Rose, it's not hard. Just think. I'm sure Miss Baker instructed you on this." Her abrupt change on the subject of girls and maths happened in a blink of potential embarrassment. She glared hard at Miss Baker.

"Just answer his lordship's question!" Sir Nathan's face flushed red, making the bristles of his beard stand out like fury. "It's easy!"

"Then what's the answer?" Ned found himself asking the room at large. Every stunned gaze came up to meet his. "Do you know it, Sir Nathan?"

"I . . ."

"Do you know it, *my lord*?" Ned asked, turning his attention to Turner.

Turner blinked at him twice, and then answered, "I don't have to. I have you for the numbers, Mr. Turner. Do you know the answer?"

The corner of his mouth went up. "Do I? Do I?"

"Yes, do you?" Turner asked drolly.

"Well . . . of course I do." Oh God, time to do some quick maths. Never his strong suit—hence the reason he had employed Turner. If twelve times twelve was a gross, he just had to add—

"One hundred sixty-nine!"

The answer came from Rose, still standing at the center of the room.

"Oh!" cried Lady Widcoate. "Well done, Rosie! Well done!" She proceeded to take Rose into her bosom and smother her with kisses in a manner that was neither attractive to the room nor seemingly enjoyable to the child.

But while she did, Ned could not help but see two more of those *looks*. The looks he had thought he'd quashed forever this afternoon. The first being a look from Lady Widcoate, over the shoulder of her embraced child. It was . . . not friendly. As if she saw him as something to be scraped off her shoe.

That was unfamiliar enough. But then he also caught a look from the governess, Miss Baker. Her look was direct, unequivocal. She took in his full gaze with her back straight, considering. Then, ever so slightly, she gave the barest of nods.

And then, a fraction of a second later, she turned away.

*Putting all one's chips on
the first hand is the act of a fool.*

If the before-dinner gathering had an unpleasant tension about it, then dinner itself was, in the over-dramatic Miss Henrietta Benson's words, an unmitigated disaster.

Once the formal inspection of children was over, Miss Baker was about to take her charges out of the room, when Sir Nathan called her back.

"Miss Baker, have them ready to entertain us tomorrow as well," that gentleman said, leaning down so his wife could whisper in his ear again. "And make sure they know the multiplication tables to twenty. Or else."

Ned was about to ask what the "or else" was, but the bone-thin governess seemed unconcerned, simply nodding and giving a quiet "Good night" to the assembled party.

That done, they were free to move into the dining room. And Ned was free to move into the next phase of charming the ladies.

Seeing as the table was so uneven—there were only three men to the six women in the room, after all—Ned thought he would be given the pleasure of escorting at least one of the girls in. But they all ignored him and traipsed after Turner, who, as was custom, took Lady Widcoate in.

And then, when they sat down to the table, something else terribly odd occurred. He was seated across from Mrs. Rye, a perfect place to engage her in conversation, with Miss Henrietta at his left and Miss Minnie at his right. Clara, poor thing, was on the other side of the earl in a place of pride, and shaking like a leaf. She could barely bring the spoon to her lips with any soup left in it.

But that wasn't the odd thing. No, the odd thing was when he leaned forward and asked Mrs. Rye a perfectly benign question.

"So, Mrs. Rye—have you or the girls found any good walks or rides in Hollyhock? I dearly enjoy a good bit of exercise."

"I am not from Hollyhock, so I do not know, Mr. Turner." She smiled at him in that syrupy manner. But before he could recommend to either of the girls that they do some exploring, Mrs. Rye turned away from him and gave her full attention to the man two seats away. "What is that you said, my lord?"

If Ned was a betting man—and he was—he would put Mrs. Rye in the category of widow.

So, three maids and two widows, all here for the Earl of Ashby's pleasure. Marvelous.

But instead of being taken aback by the interjection, Turner smiled at Mrs. Rye and gave her his attention.

"Mrs. Rye, we have been talking of Rose and Henry and their education. You have raised children," he began.

"Yes. Yes, I have." Mrs. Rye's face remained a plastered smile. "But I married so very young. Just sixteen!" she trilled, and then let her voice go husky with invitation. "Why, I can't be that much older than the countess here."

"Indeed," the countess replied. "One reason we got along so well in Bath. I had the remarkable luck to find friends in both you and your daughter. She such a mature young lady and you so . . . youth-seeking."

Mrs. Rye's smile hardened so much Ned thought it would crack.

"I daresay your husband approves of such vitality," the countess continued. "He is one of vitality's chief supporters, especially among females."

Ah. So not widowed. Just unhappily married. And willing to risk her daughter's and niece's chance at an earl to kill a bit of the unhappiness. Ned could almost feel sorry for her.

But more than that, it was something he could work with.

After all, they had never stipulated that the woman he wooed into loving him had to be unmarried. Just that she not be a village girl or a housemaid. That left *endless* opportunities.

And out of all the ladies in the house, Mrs. Rye, at this very moment, seemed the most willing to play the game.

Oh, he could try to cajole one of the younger ladies into enjoying his attentions, but they were all so *young*, and so timid—each in her own way. Miss Clara would likely shake to pieces if he spoke to her directly, while Miss Henrietta would be taking notes. Miss Minnie might be able to be engaged, if he could get her mind off sport for a few moments . . . but there would be an awful lot of effort involved.

Mrs. Rye might need only the barest amount of notice. If it was the right notice, that is.

If given the option, winning the easy way was always preferable to the laborious way.

"Lady Widcoate told me that Puffington Arms has some of the most lovely walks in the county. She has even put in some most romantic follies along the paths. Do you walk, my lord?" Mrs. Rye was asking—and inadvertently taking over the topic of conversation he had tried out not minutes before.

"Yes, my lord," Countess Churzy interjected. "Do you walk? Have you this stunning ability?"

"I do have the ability, Countess," Turner replied, drolly. Then, with all graciousness, "And yes, Mrs. Rye, I enjoy nature walks."

"You didn't when you were a boy," Lady Widcoate piped up. "Or at least that's what your mother said."

"Really?" Turner asked the question Ned couldn't. "How so?"

"She said you dawdled in the woods too much to be walking. That you must have been crawling, you would take so long."

Turner laughed at that—throwing his head back. The rest of the room erupted with him. "That sounds very like me."

Meanwhile, Ned was left to think, *No, that doesn't*

sound like me at all, thank you very much, and *When did Turner learn to enjoy a joke? Was that a joke?* Also, he was left with that queer hollow sensation that always accompanied any thought of his mother. But he squashed it down, back to a place where he could feel jovial and comfortable.

"Well, we should explore some of those walks while we are here," Mrs. Rye tried again.

"I like walking!" Minnie piped up.

"As do I!" Clara ventured, her voice a mere squeak. "Although not nearly as much as Minnie."

"Yes, all us Rye ladies are so fond of exercise and the outdoors." Mrs. Rye smiled, pulling attention back to herself again. "And Henrietta too!"

"No, I don't," Henrietta replied, pouting. "I should much rather be in town than the country. There's so much more to see."

"A girl after my heart, then," Ned said, unthinking. "Nothing so boring as the country."

"Indeed," Lady Widcoate said stiffly. "Well, I am sorry that our country air and walks do not appeal to you, Mr. Turner. We shall not force such hardships upon you."

"Excuse me, I—" Ned began automatically and imperiously, his tone an echo of his title. Luckily for him, Turner cleared his throat and interrupted, saving him from revealing himself—and possibly losing five thousand pounds in the offing.

"You'll have to excuse Mr. Turner—country life only reminds him of our time during the war, marching across fields day in and day out. However," he continued, before the ladies at the table, young and old, could begin their sighs over the idea of military service, "I am happy to partake of any walks or rambles Puffington Arms has to offer. Unfortunately, though, tomorrow will be spent in Hollyhock, looking over the cottage property."

"It will?" Ned ventured, but then remembered himself. "Oh, yes. Of course. It will."

"Quite right!" Sir Nathan added, jovially. "See, Fanny, his lordship is not here to reminisce or to walk through follies. You could have saved yourself the trouble of putting them up."

While Lady Widcoate turned a rather unwholesome shade of red, Sir Nathan continued, "You're here on business, and business shall be done. I'll drive out with you myself. Mr. Fennick will meet us—another member of the consortium—and I'm sure you will be impressed with the proposal. And then maybe a bit of shooting, eh?"

"Yes, what is the proposal?" Ned asked, ignoring the prospect of hunting.

"You should know—we've exchanged enough letters, Mr. Turner," Sir Nathan replied queerly.

"Of course—but for those present who do not know, perhaps you could explain?"

Really, all this ingratiating was becoming most tedious. Next he would find himself having to ask permission to ask a question.

"Well, I should hate to bore the ladies . . ." Sir Nathan demurred, with a glance at his wife. But surprisingly, Miss Henrietta spoke up.

"Oh, but I am curious," she said, her attention suddenly rapt. "What is the proposal for Hollyhock?"

"Well . . ." Sir Nathan began, taking a pleased, pompous tone toward the girl. He lit up seeing someone interested in his interests. "It all began a few years ago, in Midville, which is a town about five miles away. They mine coal there, and while trying to open up a new site, they came across a natural mineral spring."

"A mineral spring?" Henrietta asked, perplexed. "You mean like in Bath?"

"Precisely. And some people in the county struck upon the idea of turning the spring into a bathing resort, much like Bath—but as Midville is a coal-mining town, it was unlikely that anyone fashionable would want to visit there. So the idea was brought up that the spring could be piped to Hollyhock, and we could establish the bathing resort here."

"It would be, I daresay, very good for the town and the county, to have something so attractive to travelers in its midst," Henrietta replied, earning a look of approval from Sir Nathan.

"Right you are!" he cried, and as he and Henrietta began an earnest discussion about what could be built, and what sort of people they hoped to bring in, Ned saw his opportunity with Mrs. Rye.

She had moved her gaze off Turner, and was idly watching as Henrietta peppered Sir Nathan with questions.

Ned leaned into the table, and spoke in a whisper and with a sheepish smile. "At least she's excited about something other than my making a fool of myself."

When in doubt, play the trump card: make fun of one's own self.

And, miraculously, it worked. Mrs. Rye gave him a smile—a real one—and stifled a giggle. Then, amazingly, she whispered back.

"The night is still young—you have plenty of time to make a bigger fool of yourself."

Ned grinned at her.

She wasn't too bad, Mrs. Rye. Oh, she was trying awfully hard to make an impression—and whether it was for her or for the girls in her charge, Ned thought even she didn't know—but she looked well enough, and she was eager.

Mrs. Rye sent him another look under her lashes—one that in the candlelight appeared distinctly amused.

This might turn out to be easy after all, Ned thought with relish.

No time like the present, Ned thought, and slowly eased his foot forward under the table. Seeking, searching . . . and finding the satin skirts of Mrs. Rye.

Then, as the soup bowls were taken away and the next course came out, her attention drifted to the plates of roast pork and mutton that were being presented. Slowly he let his foot dig its way under the laces and petticoats, finally finding the slight plumpness of her ankle above her slipper—a long, slow stroke down the side.

"MR. TURNER!"

Ned straightened up immediately, banging his foot against his chair as he brought it back with force. Mrs. Rye was looking at him in shock and fury, but surprised, too, that she had cried out so loudly.

Everyone else at the table was equally surprised, and they all whipped their heads around and blinked, astonished at the two of them.

Oh, hell. Thus Ned did the only thing he could do. He straightened in his seat, and asked with aching politeness, "Yes, Mrs. Rye? Is something amiss?"

Mrs. Rye took in the blank and blinking faces around her, the shock of her niece and the shaking of her daughter, and did the only thing she could do.

"Indeed, Mr. Turner. But it is resolved now. I thank you."

Everyone else at the table turned back to their meals, the sounds of silverware scraping plates filling the silence while everyone waited for conversations to resume. Once they had, however, Mrs. Rye leaned into the table in much the same conspiratorial fashion as Ned had before, making certain no one else could hear.

"You are remarkable, Mr. Turner," she said harshly. "You managed to make a greater fool of yourself in even less time than I imagined."

❧

"JUST WHO THE hell does this Mr. Turner think he is?" Fanny growled under her breath, seating herself next to Leticia in the window of the drawing room. The younger girls were gathered around the pianoforte, where Clara had begun to play a happy tune. For such a seemingly frail child, she could play the pianoforte with verve, Leticia mused. Henrietta turned the pages for her, while Minnie dealt out cards to Mrs. Rye, happy for games of any sort. Well, *almost* any sort.

"I don't know how the earl puts up with him. Why, the way that man speaks to him!" Fanny continued in a hiss. "The way he spoke to me, and my darling Sir Nathan. I have never heard of such a jumped-up secretary in all my life!"

Leticia made a soothing hum, her eyes continually

on the door, waiting for the men to come in and join the ladies after dinner.

"He not only insulted us, he put us out entirely. Who wants a *secretary* staying under their roof?"

"Now, Fanny," Leticia began. "I don't know why you are being so high and mighty with him. He's not so low as a tenant farmer, and you've had them to dinner. Why, anyone who is a secretary must be a man of at least some education. Think of Mr. Turner not as being in *service* to the earl, but as more of a . . . a clerk. You are only agitated because you did not think to expect him."

"It just unsettles so many of my plans! Besides, we married men of status to get away from such *clerks*," Fanny huffed. "And unless you want to go back there, you had better get the earl—"

"I know, Fanny, hush," Leticia cooed. But the truth was, she did not want to think about the reasons she had to do what she was doing.

"What do you think of the man? The earl, I mean," Fanny asked.

"He's . . . different than I remember," Leticia replied, a frown crossing her brow. "I thought he would have turned out more . . . cheeky. The way he pulled my hair and called me Letty when he was young is proof enough of that. But he's very calm. And serious."

"Serious?" Fanny prompted.

"The way he pauses before he speaks. As if he is very carefully considering his words, his speech. Perhaps his time in the army tempered him." Leticia paused, considering her own words. "I asked him why he pushed Rose to know the answer to more difficult mathematics, and do you know what he said?"

"No . . . but nor do I know why any girl must know multiples of thirteen."

"That's exactly it. He whispered to me that one cannot rest on their laurels. If one wants to succeed, they must be challenged. They must fight."

Which was a philosophy Leticia had herself come to adopt.

"It is unexpected," she said with a dismissive smile. "That is all."

What was more unexpected was the ease with which she had captured his attention. Goodness, he had come to her side immediately, fascinated as she reminisced about old times and flirted slyly. She would have thought a man as sought after as the Earl of Ashby would have been well trained not to fall for the first pretty face that came his way. But he seemed to prefer her company to any other—although, to be fair, he had been here just a few hours. He had showed her preference only by letting her walk him into the house when they arrived, and then by bringing her into the drawing room that evening.

"That Mrs. Rye is a piece of work—trying to pull the earl her way! And to think, she with children full grown, and a husband besides!" Fanny was saying under her breath.

"It was to be expected. Poor dear, her marriage is not a happy one," Leticia replied back in similar volume, knowing the misery that Mrs. Rye had to deal with back in Bath. Giving her—and Clara and Minnie, who also lived in her charge—a respite was half the reason Leticia had invited her out. But only half the reason.

"You certainly took her apart at the dinner table." Fanny was unable to hide the glee in her voice.

"She was trodding on my territory. Clumsily, too." Leticia gave an elegant little shrug. "I'm perfectly willing to be pleasant as long as it does not interfere with my plans. But really, I have to think of myself first."

"Which is why I don't know why you had me invite them," Fanny huffed.

"Don't you?" she asked. "Silly Fanny—it is because they make me look good by comparison."

Fanny blinked rapidly, as if the idea had never occurred to her, when, really, it should have been obvious all along. All the young ladies were good girls of decent enough background, and individually, their characters might have been allowed to blossom and grow and turn them into interesting people. But they lived in one another's pockets—Henrietta having grown up neighbors to the Ryes—and being so young, their closeness tended to exacerbate their worst qualities. Minnie wanting to strong-arm everyone into playing a game. Henrietta wanting to know everything about everything. Clara permanently in some state of nervous indecision. None of them had the mind for seduction.

Top that off with Mrs. Rye, and Leticia, with her grace, beauty, and worldliness, would ultimately rule the day.

Yes, it was still early. And, yes, the earl also seemed careful to give his attention to anyone who asked for it. His deference to Mrs. Rye and each of the girls was evidence of that, she thought grimly.

But so far . . . so far . . . it was going well. She might even have him sewn up inside of a week. And wouldn't that be a relief?

"Well, far be it for me to tell you how to handle

this little escapade," Fanny said stiffly. "But I confess I still would think far better of the earl if he did not require the presence of that *person*. Just what do you think Mr. Turner did to cause such an outburst from Mrs. Rye?"

"I don't know," Leticia mused. Although, given the way Mr. Turner had been slouching at the table before hastily sitting up, she could guess.

"I can only guess something horrid, from such a nasty little man."

It was impossible to judge from Leticia's position what had set Fanny's teeth on edge about the earl's secretary. Maybe he had shown himself up too high when he challenged Sir Nathan to multiply thirteen times thirteen? Maybe she could not get over the mortification of having mistaken him for a valet? Perhaps she was just Fanny and, being the elder by six years, had felt their status as merchant's daughters more keenly. After all, she had been almost full grown when their father's mill suddenly became a success, and they had money enough to attract landed gentlemen in need of a little funding. For Leticia it had been different.

In truth, their father has been relieved to let his growing daughter grow somewhere else. He had never been the most comforting of men, and tending to family did not suit him the way tending to business did. Fanny, a new bride, and infinitely nervous, was happy to have her around to smooth the transition into married life. Thus, Leticia was free to reject their history as just that, history, and to reinvent herself anew.

Fanny had been the first one to step outside of their old lives. She always remembered being a miller's daughter, and as such, was more aware than anyone of class distinction.

In any case, Fanny's ire had come to rest on poor Mr. Turner, and there it would stay.

"You are being an excellent hostess, Fanny," Leticia soothed, squeezing her sister's hand, "throwing a delightfully cozy party for us. I should not worry over much about Mr. Turner. He's a bit of a nuisance, but nothing more."

"Yes," Fanny decided, a gleam in her eye. "He is a bit of a nuisance. But when I'm through with him, he won't even be that."

8

From time to time, one must reevaluate his strategy.

That was the most amazing thing I've ever seen."
Turner laughed, unable to keep his hearty guffaw in
check. Ned did the only thing he could do and shot him
a spiteful look.

"Please try to keep your enthusiasm for my failures
at dinner from causing you to strangle my horse," Ned
said through gritted teeth.

"Careful," Turner chided. "Say that any louder and
Sir Nathan will hear."

It was a beautiful morning in the country, and had
Ned not been living in the shadow of last night's hu-
miliation, he would have likely been enjoying the ride.
Though his ride was less satisfying on Turner's mare
than it would have been on Abandon—who obviously
thought so too, because he kept straining under Turner's control, testing his boundaries, trying to fly free.

Ned could sympathize.

But, while he and Turner were on horseback, Sir Nathan, who had insisted on coming with them to meet with the consortium for the bathing resort, made use of his carriage, trotting along amiably behind them. Indeed, Turner was right. If he and Ned were to speak freely, he had better watch his volume.

"You know I had to fix it with Lady Widcoate so you could still stay at Puffington Arms. Just what did you think you were doing?" Turner asked again, shaking his head.

"Engaging a lady who met your standards in a light flirtation," Ned answered back crisply.

"By running your boot up and down her leg under the table after having spoken two lines to her? And you thought she would be receptive to this?"

"It's worked before, I will have you know."

But Turner scoffed—scoffed!—at him.

"If it has worked before, it is either because that lady welcomed the attentions of an earl, or perhaps that they were too cowed to shout you down the way Mrs. Rye was happy to," he replied.

"Now, that is not the case!" Ned cried, but with a quick glance back at Sir Nathan in the carriage, forced himself to modulate his tone. "I wouldn't . . . that is, I would *never* . . ."

"Not knowingly, no," Turner said, clenching his jaw tight.

They trotted on for a few moments in silence, Ned chewing over what Turner was saying.

"All right," he finally sighed. "So I need to adjust how I approach the ladies. It is to be expected; after all, I am still adjusting to being you."

"And how do you fare?" Turner asked blithely.

"Brilliant. Marvelous."

"Glad to hear it. Although I doubt you will make any headway with any ladies now. You chose extremely poorly last night."

"I chose the one person who paid the slightest attention."

"You chose *Mrs. Rye*. The chaperone of the other girls here. Do you think she is going to let Minnie or Clara or even Henrietta anywhere near you when you have made such unwelcome advances toward herself?" Turner could barely suppress the smile as he added, "I bet you a hundred pounds that you won't even get two sentences with the other girls now."

"You don't have a hundred pounds," Ned countered.

"In two short weeks I'll have fifty times that."

The confidence in Turner's voice set Ned's teeth on edge. He would not be so easily beaten, damn him!

As they turned onto the road to Hollyhock, Ned could see the little town in the distance, its church spire sitting quaintly on a hill, ready to welcome them.

A new, unfamiliar feeling spread throughout his gut. Unease. A whole pit of it.

"Well," Ned said brightly, pushing down that strange and annoying feeling, allowing himself only the lightness he enjoyed. "There is one advantage you unwittingly gained me. You brought me to Hollyhock." At Turner's blank look, he explained. "Didn't you notice there are no male servants at Puffington Arms? Just a vast female populace?"

"It doesn't matter. No chambermaids. No cooks."

"Not at the Widcoates', no. But due to the mine in

Midville, I would wager that Hollyhock is practically devoid of men. My arrival there will not go unnoticed by the ladies. There will be dozens to choose from."

Turner hummed noncommittally, which only annoyed Ned further. So he chose to needle back. "The countess is not accountable to any chaperone. I will simply have to direct all of my charms in her direction."

Ned was rewarded by watching Turner narrow his eyes. "And if Letty were here, she would tell you that there is little less charming than a man who is trying to be charming. Trying so hard to ingratiate himself, as it were, into the proceedings that he calls himself mother, shows up the host with mathematics, and tries to rub ankles with another guest."

"Oh, is it Letty already?" Ned responded in kind. "You offered me your advice, so I'll offer you mine. A countess of means does not go to Bath. She goes to London."

"So?" Turner asked.

"So, ask yourself what her motives are in 'reminiscing' about old times with you. I think you will find they have very little to do with *you*."

"Well, well, well." Turner tried for an observer's voice, but he could not hide the spots of pink that rose on his cheeks. "It seems you are willing to admit that the title has influence—at least, when I am borrowing it."

"Just remember that you *are* borrowing it, my friend. And don't worry, I think sooner rather than later, you will find it has its own faults."

"I'll return it in the same condition it was lent," Turner said, a wry smile twisting his lips. "But for now, resume your role."

He gently drew Abandon to a stop. They had reached the edge of town, the church spire now looming above them on the hillock to the right. To the left was an assembly of a dozen people, smiling at them, and—oh, dear God—holding a banner.

Welcome Home, Earl of Ashby! From The Hollyhock Bathing Consortium.

"It seems we have an audience."

❧

"SO, SO PLEASED to meet you at last!" the reed-thin man with the smallest glasses and bushiest mustache Ned had ever seen said as he bowed low to Turner. "And you too, Mr. Turner." He came forward and, after a shorter bow, aggressively began pumping Ned's hand. "I am Mr. Fennick. I have greatly enjoyed our correspondence about the bathing retreat."

"You have?" Ned asked, his eyes sliding to Turner's. He seemed just as perplexed but merely gave the tiniest of shrugs.

The entirety of Hollyhock had come out to greet them. And it seemed Ned was right—there was little in the way of men here. However, there was also little in the way of romance.

A number of older ladies crowded around, as well as some wives of local farmers and merchants, who saw the opportunity for business for their crops and wares should the town become a destination for travelers. But there was a decided lack of young ladies, their eyes rounded with hope for love.

"Oh, yes," Turner whispered, laughing. "So many eligible ladies to choose from."

The few people who *did* have their eyes rounded with hope were all men. The Hollyhock Bathing Consortium. Sir Nathan loped forward to perform the introductions.

"My lord, this is Mr. Dunlap, manager of the Midville mines, and intrepid discoverer of our hot spring." A hungry-looking man stepped forward, bowing to Turner.

"And you have already met Mr. Fennick, our town solicitor, who has been very eager to make your acquaintance. He even tried to invite himself to dinner last night, didn't you, Fennick?" Sir Nathan laughed, causing Mr. Fennick's mustache to freeze in a rictus smile.

"In fact, my lord, I wrote the business proposal you recei—"

"And Mr. McLeavey," Sir Nathan concluded. "Our very own vicar."

"And host of this little gathering!" Mr. McLeavey beamed his placid smile and shouldered Mr. Fennick out of the way to offer introductions of some of the townspeople as they moved along. "My lord, of course you know Mrs. So and So, you used to play with her son, Jamie—he's running the family farm now, isn't that right, Mrs. So and So? And Mrs. Whatever has kindly provided us with an array of refreshments, if you would like to join us in the rectory . . ."

"Oh, yes!" Mr. Fennick piped up. "There are simply dozens of details to discuss—"

"Perhaps I can give you a history of the mine, my lord, and tell you about how we discovered the hot spring? It was a blustery day, last autumn . . ."

Watching all the smiling faces, the overeager small-town people who seemed to crowd around Turner, swallowing him in their enthusiasm to be near someone of greatness, made Ned smirk wryly.

He had never liked this part. The bit where everyone looked up to you as if you were somehow minted and bronzed. It was one of the reasons he was far more comfortable in London—earls were a bit more commonplace there. They did not throw people into a tizzy by simply existing.

Yes, by the bewildered look on John Turner's face, the disadvantages of being an earl were beginning to become apparent.

"I did not expect such a welcome," Turner was saying, an uneasy smile on his face, as he tried hard to keep Abandon under control. "Although it, er, is very good of you all to come out to greet me."

"We of the Hollyhock Bathing Consortium simply wished for you to know how enthusiastic we are about the prospect of bringing the mineral springs into our little town!" Mr. Fennick began, before Mr. McLeavey could burst in and take over as he had before with the introductions. "As you can see, our enthusiasm abounds!"

". . . Quite. Sir Nathan, Mr. Fennick," Turner said, taking on that tone that he used whenever he wanted Ned back on the subject at hand—usually involving a vast amount of paperwork—"perhaps you could join us on our tour of the—er, my property." Turner turned a pained smile to the rest of the consortium and townsfolk. "Thank you all for the lovely welcome."

And with that, Turner extracted himself from the group with little finesse and absolutely no ceremony.

Mr. Fennick and Sir Nathan scrambled after him, a mumbled chorus of "Yes, of course!" on their lips as they leapt into Sir Nathan's carriage.

Ned turned to the assembled group, their disappointment obvious as they followed Turner's retreating form with their gazes. He gave them the widest grin possible.

"I am sure you can understand the earl is very anxious to see his mother's cottage. It has been quite a long time," Ned placated. Then, turning to the remaining leader of the assembled party, "I believe you mentioned something about refreshments? I am certain that once the earl has completed his tour of his mother's home, he would like nothing better than to see the parsonage, Mr. McLeavey. And to learn something of the hot spring's history, Mr. Dunlap."

The vicar smiled widely in relief. "We shall await you there. And, of course, the earl can visit his mother while he's there."

Ned's smile faltered. "His mother?" he asked, unable to hide the quaver in his voice.

"Her grave. It is in the churchyard," Mr. McLeavey supplied. "He was unable to attend the service, if I recall correctly, having just purchased a commission for the army."

"No. He purchased the commission after." Ned managed to make his voice sound somewhat normal.

"I presided over the service," the vicar continued, ignoring Ned's statement. "A lovely spring day, all those years ago. The old earl even paid for the headstone. Good solid granite."

"Thank you, Mr. McLeavey," Ned managed.

With a quick bow, he excused himself and moved briskly to catch up with Turner, Sir Nathan, and Mr. Fennick.

When he finally did, he slid next to Turner, out of earshot of the other two men. "Tell me, were you raised by alley cats?"

"Not to my knowledge."

"You gave that impression by practically running away from all the townsfolk and the Hollyhock Bathing Consortium."

Turner shot him a look. "I have no known relation to alley cats." But to be fair, he did sound a bit chagrined. "I was a bit overwhelmed, is all."

Ned nodded, and allowed it to pass.

"So, how much should I know about the kind of deals you've struck with the Bathing Consortium?" Ned managed under his breath.

"Deal?" Turner asked, confused.

"Yes. What with all the correspondence between you and Fennick and Sir Nathan," Ned replied. Given what Sir Nathan insinuated the night before, and how Turner would be compensated for making the deal go through, Ned thought Turner had no right to act innocent.

But Turner just shook his head. "There has been no deal struck. If there was we wouldn't be here." At Ned's cocked brow, he just sighed. "If you want to know about the correspondence, you can read it—it's all in my trunk. You will only find their plans for the property and their initial offer. As well as numerous back-and-forths about where you would stay and what kind of food you prefer for breakfast." Turner didn't even spare him a glance. "If that's not too much work for you, that is."

Ned gave a short harrumph, and Turner could only shrug.

They rode on for another few minutes, when . . . "Turn left here," Ned offered, realizing that Turner was about to take them in the wrong direction. He knew this path. He had walked it every Sunday of his youth, home from church. The road into the main part of town, with the short row of shops, the greengrocer, the milliner, the town well. You had to go to Midville to find an apothecary or blacksmith, he recalled, as they passed the tree that had been half the reason he broke his arm at the age of eight. The other half being gravity.

And then, suddenly, the overgrown oaks that lined the walk gave way and . . . there it was.

His mother's cottage. The Granville cottage.

It sat back from the road, in its own world. Small— smaller than most of the other houses in the neighborhood—but it had been perfect for a young widow and her son. They had moved there after the death of his father, when Ned was two, which therefore, blessedly, he did not remember. The little house had been their whole world. And the woods surrounding it that were attached to the property had been a young boy's playground.

Now it floated in front of him, a memory made real.

It still stood, although that was the best he could say for it. The stone of the chimney was almost entirely covered in thick vines, and the shrubbery around the front threatened to overtake the house. And, most alarming, there was a large hole in the thatched roof that exposed most of the sitting room to the elements. Luckily, someone had covered the hole in the roof with a large piece of canvas, but . . .

How could this have happened? Why had Turner allowed the house to fall into such disrepair? His mother would never have . . .

No. No, he had put all this away long, long ago. He refused to care. He was the Earl of Ashby. Not a scampering child growing up half wild in the woods of Leicestershire.

As if answering the question that he could not ask, Turner spoke low to Ned. "There were tenants up until last year. I had hoped to get more this summer, but the roof collapse a few months ago put a stop to that."

"And it wasn't fixed?" Ned asked, more vehemently than he'd intended.

"So much snow this winter made fixing the roof difficult. The canvas kept the weather and animals out, and since there were no tenants, you told me not to bother about it."

"I did?" His eyes flew to Turner's.

"Yes. You did," Turner said. "And then shortly thereafter came the proposal for the property from Mr. Fennick and the town. Adding variables to the decision to repair."

Had he told him not to worry overly about it? It was possible, of course—whenever Turner got some correspondence about one of his holdings, Ned's eyes tended to glaze over in boredom. Perhaps he should have taken better care to pay attention. Perhaps seeing his mother's house in this sorry state was his penance for that.

A pang echoed through his chest. A shudder—as if someone walked over a grave. He violently shook it off. This melancholy reflective state was so unnatural to him. He would conquer it, until it was dust. Lucky Ned did not engage in sentimentality or in this wretched feeling of . . . something. He was happy. He was game.

"Shall we?"

The question came from the carriage, pulling up alongside them. Sir Nathan and Mr. Fennick disembarked, and Turner dismounted without hesitation. But Ned . . .

That pang echoed through his chest again, forcing its way back up. If just looking at the house from the lane did this to him, what was a tour inside going to do?

"Um . . . if you don't mind, my, er, lord, I will stay out here. Watch the horses." This came as something of a surprise to the groom who drove Sir Nathan's carriage—but the man simply shrugged.

"The house is small," Ned continued, "and I am sure Sir Nathan and Mr. Fennick can give you a better estimation of the town's plans without me in the way."

If it was odd for the earl's secretary not to accompany them into his childhood home, no one said anything. Indeed, Turner met eyes with Ned for a moment, considering. And for once, it was Ned who turned away first.

As Mr. Fennick and Sir Nathan led Turner up to the front door of the cottage, Ned let himself exhale. And then he walked Turner's mare around the bend until the oak trees shaded his mother's cottage, and he could sit still and calm, out of its sight.

❧

"YOU DON'T HAVE to care about this business proposal, but since you are taking up my mantle, you should at least pretend," Turner said to him on the way back to Puffington Arms.

They had left the vicarage after being plied with small sandwiches and too-sweet tea for much longer than Ned had anticipated. Sir Nathan, apparently having been familiar with the foodstuffs of Mr. McLeavey's wife and the stories of Mr. Dunlap, begged off, saying he was expected back at home, and that his lordship and Mr. Turner would easily be able to find the way back after luncheon.

They had had to endure the pleasantries of the rest of the eager consortium also for much longer than anticipated, but they managed to escape before it got too far into the afternoon.

Ned had waited until the church spire was in the distance before lobbing his accusation at Turner.

"And, as you are taking up my mantle, it would help if you could at least pretend graciousness with the townspeople." That had been something that had been drilled into him by his great-uncle. With the distance of rank must come unerring politeness.

"I did not expect to be *mobbed*. And can I help it if Mrs. Whatshername's petits fours had actual dust on them?"

No, he supposed Mrs. Whatshername's dusty petits fours could not be helped.

"You didn't mind being mobbed yesterday," Ned pointed out.

"That was . . . different. And I did mind. Until . . ."

But Turner did not allow that thought its full account.

They walked along in silence for a little while, until

they came to the field where they had run into the children and the governess . . . goodness, had it really only been yesterday? It had seemed centuries ago that they'd been in Leicestershire.

"So, tell me about this business proposal for my mother's house," he finally said, breaking the tension in the air.

Turner let out a breath. "It's less for the house and more for the land it sits on. There is an inordinate amount of acreage that goes with the cottage. And it seems like the ideal place for the town to build their bathing retreat. Close enough for visitors to walk in and enjoy the town, but removed enough that it offers seclusion for those coming to seek a respite. It is also directly in the path of the pipeline being built from Midville."

"So, they want to . . . what? Buy the property?"

"It's not one of your entailed estates. Sir Nathan— well, really, Mr. Fennick—formed the consortium to purchase the property, but what they would really like to do is lease the property and build their bathing retreat upon it, pulling you in as a sort of benefactor," Turner said. "It would cost them less. Less risk on their part too."

"But also less reward if successful."

"True," Turner agreed. "But in either case, your mother's cottage would be torn down to make way for a new building."

The queer hollow feeling that he had successfully avoided giving sway to earlier flared up again with a vengeance.

"Torn down?" he asked.

But Turner simply shrugged. "Or you could leave

the house as is, repair the roof, and rent it out to tenants again, forcing the consortium to look elsewhere for their bathing retreat. Those are the options before you."

The options before him. Sell the estate, lease it, or keep it as is.

"Seems simple enough," Ned replied, breezily. "What I don't understand was why you forced me to the country for two weeks to make a decision that could easily be made in two days."

"Lady Brimley's ball was part of the reason, if you recall," Turner said dryly. "But if the decision is so easily made, then make it. And we can go back to London now."

Yes, his options seemed simple enough, Ned thought. But the matter was so far from simple.

But instead, he puffed out his chest and gave Turner his most charming cutthroat grin.

"If we go back to London now, I would be conceding the wager, wouldn't I? And I never throw in my cards, Turner. I play the game to the bitter end."

"Given the slim pickings in Hollyhock and your status at Puffington Arms, the bitter end may be sooner than you think." Turner pulled to a halt. They were in sight of the house now, and much like yesterday, a beruffled and beribboned crowd was gathering to welcome "the earl" back from Hollyhock.

Braggadocio aside, Ned knew he couldn't play the game right now. He couldn't smile and try like hell to get the ladies to forget his performance at dinner last night. That queer, unsettled feeling in his gut wouldn't let him.

"I'll take the horses round to the stables," he offered, earning a surprised look from Turner. Which then transformed into suspicion.

"You want to miss an opportunity to ingratiate yourself with the ladies?" Turner said, basically reading Ned's mind. But then he met Ned's eyes. Whatever he read there made any and all suspicion drop away from his face.

"Well . . . far be it from me to stop an earl from playing my groom," Turner said gruffly, and then dismounted from Abandon.

Ned followed suit and took the reins of both horses. The last thing he saw before disappearing around the side of the house toward the stables was Turner reaching the side of the Countess Churzy and taking her arm before he was swallowed by a chorus of pastel gowns and young female attention.

All the better, he told himself. For the first time in ages, Ned needed to be alone with his thoughts.

9

Sometimes even a middling card can take the trick.

"Careful," Phoebe called out, as Rose and Henry clamored to pull themselves up to see over the gates. It was her general refrain whenever they were in the stables.

Or near the stables, she realized. Or outside. Or inside. Anytime they were awake, the most oft-used word in Phoebe's governess repertoire was *careful*. She had really better begin thinking of some synonyms, she mused, else the children end up with limited vocabularies.

"Caution!" she tried, as Rose bounded her way up the gate and reached a hand over to pet the tail of the butterscotch gelding in its stall. The patient horse was old and slow, only used to pull the cart. However, regardless of the horse's temperament, no one liked having their tail pulled.

"Miss Rose, stroking Sunshine's mane has very little

to do with her tail," Phoebe warned. But as the inattentive young girl's hand still reached toward the horse's rear, she had to reach out and grab it. "Or should we go back inside and begin a lesson in biology and anatomy?"

"I'm just trying to get him to turn around," Rose said mournfully, withdrawing her hand.

"Well, he would turn around, and likely unhappily, too," Phoebe remarked dryly.

"You told us we didn't have to learn inside today, because it's our reward," Henry piped up, his interest in staring into the dark brown eyes of one of Sir Nathan's matched chestnuts in the next stall momentarily interrupted by the threat of going indoors.

"Really?" came a surprised voice at the end of the corridor. "What are you being rewarded for?"

Phoebe whipped her head around. There, in the entrance to the stable, stood a dark-haired man holding two horses by their reins. For the briefest moment she panicked, thinking it was the Earl of Ashby, and she would actually have to *talk* to him. But then he stepped farther into the stable, and the light adjusted around him.

"Oh, Mr. Turner," she said stiffly, choking down any visible sign of relief. Even if he wasn't the earl, he still didn't need to see the governess acting loose with the children.

"Henry, look! It's the pretty one!" Rose's interest in Sunshine's tail disappeared as she ran up to Mr. Turner to gaze raptly at the impressive stallion, so dark a brown he was almost black. The horse danced for a moment in front of the girl, but a steady hand from Mr. Turner settled him.

"They are not being rewarded," Phoebe began quickly. "We are having a lesson on basic physiology."

"We are?" Henry asked.

"What's physiology?" Rose turned her head.

"Physiology is the study of living things. And how they work," Phoebe answered with pointed patience. "And today we are studying the horses. The, uh . . . the foreleg is connected to the . . . well, on a human it would be the shoulder . . ."

"It's the humerus bone," Mr. Turner answered for her.

"Really?" Her eyes shot up to his. Unconsciously, her hand moved to her own upper arm. "But on humans, the humerus is up here."

"Yes, but on horses, it's basically the shoulder."

"But then what is the lower joint?" she asked, fascinated. "Er, on the horse's leg."

"It's like the palm of your hand—the joint's the wrist," he replied. "Animals are stretched out differently than humans."

"Miss Baker, you told us we didn't have to learn any more today," Rose warned. "This stuff sounds a lot like learning."

"Well, perhaps it is something *I* wished to learn," she replied patiently. "Or your brother might like to know it."

Henry did indeed seem to be listening, patient child that he was, but Rose did not have her brother's contemplative nature. She had been promised time to admire the horses, and that was exactly what she wanted.

"But our reward!" Rose said.

"Your reward for what, precisely?" Mr. Turner

asked as he handed to a groom both the horses he had
walked into the stables. Rose's eyes followed the earl's
beautiful stallion as he was taken away to be brushed,
cleaned, fed. Mr. Turner seemed to have the same af-
finity for the horse that Rose did, because he called after
the groom, "Only oats and carrots for Abandon, if you
please!"

He clocked the look the groom gave him—and then
the look Phoebe was giving him. "Er—the earl prefers
a certain diet for his horse."

Phoebe nodded. They were saved from having to
make any further conversation by Rose's jumping up
and down and answering Mr. Turner's now twice-
asked question.

"We get the afternoon off from lessons because of
what a good job I did at the Questioning yesterday!"

"The Questioning?" he replied, his eyes turning to
her.

"Before last night's dinner," Phoebe supplied. "The
children call it a Questioning."

"I can see why," Mr. Turner replied stiffly. "You
deserve your afternoon off. And how did you know the
answer to thirteen times thirteen?"

But Rose just shrugged. "I figured it out."

"Well," Mr. Turner said, blinking, "that's very . . ."

Oh God, what was he going to say? After all, he
hadn't known the answer. Would he be angry at having
been shown up by a child? A girl?

"Very clever," he finished, and this time Phoebe
could not contain her relief.

"Thank you." Rose beamed.

"But if you don't have to learn anything else this

afternoon, then what are you going to tell your parents at the Questioning tonight?"

Two little faces fell in unison, into confused recollection.

"We've already decided what we learned today. Right, children?" Phoebe prodded. "Rose did the multiplication tables to twenty this morning, as requested." Rose nodded brightly, as if—oh, yes!—she *did* learn something today. "And Henry, what did you learn?"

"That the arm bone is funny."

Phoebe could only blink at him. Mr. Turner blinked in concert.

"Where did you learn that?" she asked.

"From you—you said it was humorous," Henry replied. Then, changing topics with the audacious speed of a child, "May Rose and I go watch them brush down the horses?"

She threw a glance to Mr. Turner. Who seemed frozen. His dark eyes sought hers, and with them, a decision.

"All right, but don't get in Kevin's way." The children ran off to the other end of the stables, where the earl's horse and Mr. Turner's were enjoying their dinners. "The groom," she clarified to Mr. Turner.

He nodded his understanding.

"Be careful," she called after the children. "Guarded! Mindful!"

"Punctilious?" Mr. Turner supplied from beside her.

"Punctilious." She nodded. "I will have to make use of that one."

And then . . . silence.

Now that they were left alone by themselves in the

far side of the stables, the awkwardness that had been apparent in Mr. Turner's interactions with the children now spread to her. What did one say to an earl's secretary? Particularly the Earl of Ashby's secretary?

But she was luckily saved from having to start a conversation or to make her excuses and join the children by Mr. Turner jumping into the fray.

"That little girl is quite intelligent. And better at maths than me."

Phoebe relaxed. "She is smarter than she's been told. And her brother, too, in a quieter way."

"How do you know so much about human physiology?" he asked, conversationally. "The humerus bone, and all."

She started. "I was previously a governess for three young girls in Portsmouth who were interested in the sciences. Or rather, they were interested in the more morbid parts of it." She looked askance at him. "How do you know so much about horse physiology?"

The corner of his mouth quirked up. She couldn't help staring at it. For some reason, her heart began to beat just a hair faster upon seeing that oddly charming, lopsided smile.

"I have a friend from the war who is a doctor. I asked him a lot of bored questions while we were waiting to fight. Since I was having no luck learning the Latin names of the bones in the human body, he started teaching me the bones in horses instead." She must not have been able to hide her true feelings for once, because he immediately tried to explain. "I liked horses—it was easier to learn. And has come in handy on occasion. I made a wager once with the Duke . . ." He paused for a moment, and coughed. "Er, that is, a duke's . . . head groom, and I managed to name more horse parts correctly than him. Won myself a few shillings in the bargain."

"It sounds like you are quite the inveterate gambler," she said sternly, her mouth getting tight at the corners again. *That* quality was more indicative of a man who would work for the Earl of Ashby, she thought callously. Not this seemingly polite, if awkward, man with the lopsided smile.

"Never more than I can afford to lose," he replied with a shrug. "And I never lose anyway."

"Be warned, Mr. Turner," she said in her best governess voice. "Everyone loses a gamble eventually. And usually when you can least afford the loss."

She had learned that much from her father.

"Not I," he replied with a smile. But there was something behind it. Something strange and urgent. As if he were willing himself into believing his statement, and therefore, it would be unequivocally true.

This man, who had smiled so broadly upon their first meeting in the field that she thought his teeth in danger of falling out, had lost his overcertainty. That cheerfulness was now fueled by sheer will.

Perhaps she had spent too long contemplating that smile, staring into his face curiously, because soon enough his eyes turned wary. His smile faltered.

"Is there something in my teeth?" he asked, amazingly without stopping his smile.

And *that* made her want to laugh. Almost.

"No," she promised. But she couldn't keep the humor out of her voice. She knew her cheeks were under enormous pressure to give way and smile and, God forbid, dimple.

Governesses, she was told, did not have dimples.

But it was nice. It was so nice to stand here with someone in an awkward sort of companionable silence. Normally, she stood alone . . . too high for the servants and too low for the family. She was outside of everything.

But then again, so was this odd secretary with the stretched, lopsided smile and the fear that something was in his teeth.

Oh, dear. She could feel herself slipping into smiling again.

"Mr. Turner," she began, covering her mouth with a cough to hide her discomfort. "Is it always your practice to encourage young children in underhanded practices?"

"Encourage . . . ?" he asked, that frozen smile slipping off his features in confusion.

"You see them with an afternoon of freedom and do nothing about it?" she asked, unable to hide her dry humor. Yes, it was always best to cover any discomfort with humor.

That she had learned from her father as well.

And she was allowed, wasn't she? After all, he was not a guest per se, he did not seem like a man to go haring off to Lady Widcoate and revealing that the governess had a sense of humor. Or to Lord Ashby.

Bloody hell—she really had to do better at remembering that he was Lord Ashby's man. But it seemed to slip out of her mind so easily. Suddenly, her quick tongue and archness seemed too much of a risk.

This was suddenly a gamble.

"Oh, that!" Mr. Turner replied, in a thankfully similar arch tone. "Yes, well—I find that if one encourages underhanded practices in the young, it usually helps to make them more despicable when they are older."

"And you wish to foster despicableness."

"Of course!" Mr. Turner cried. "The world is in great need of the truly despicable. Think about it. All these decent people, walking around being kind to one another—nothing will ever get done!"

"Yes—sometimes it does take the truly despicable to force society into movement."

"Precisely. And how fortunate Rose and Henry have you as their governess, who is gifted in the underhanded arts."

"Perhaps when they outgrow a governess, they should have you as their tutor," she replied, biting the inside of her cheek to keep from smiling. "You seem to understand their ways quite well."

"Oh, no"—he shook his head—"I am not . . . er, suited to children. In general."

She frowned and let her gaze travel to where Rose and Henry watched, from a safe distance, Abandon being brushed down. Kevin the groom seemed to have warned them away, so they stood in the opposite empty stall. But she could tell Rose was just itching to run forward and touch the horse.

"No? You seemed fine with Rose and Henry just now." But then she remembered how he tensed up when Rose approached him. "If a little stiff."

"Truth be told, I haven't spent any time with children since I was a child myself."

"Honestly?" She turned to him. "They are not that hard. Just shorter people who require naps on occasion. Same as us."

He laughed at that. A short, appreciative chuckle. "Well, you seem to be a bit better at it than others, Miss Baker."

Just then, Rose made her break for it. Kevin the groom was occupied with the back end of the horse; Rose ran forward and made to reach for Abandon's glossy neck.

"Rose!" she called out, her voice shifting from her playful tones into hard governess in an instant. "What did I tell you?"

"You said be careful?" came the mournful voice of a girl trying to get away with something. "And I am?"

But the groom had been alerted by Phoebe's voice just as Rose had, and came forward, shooing the children further back.

"Miss Baker, you know Lady Widcoate says Rose an' Henry were too little to be in here," Kevin said as Phoebe moved quickly forward. "We would both get in trouble . . ."

"Yes, you're right." She whipped her head around and was shocked to find Mr. Turner standing next to her. He had followed her to the front of the stables. "Oh—ah, Mr. Turner, you'll have to forgive us. The new horses, especially Abandon, simply provided too much temptation."

"Indeed," he agreed.

"Usually there are only three horses—Sunshine for the cart and the matched chestnuts for the carriage," she explained. "For Rose, seeing a Thoroughbred stallion in these stables is akin to seeing a unicorn."

"No one rides?" Mr. Turner asked quizzically.

"Sir Nathan used to love riding, apparently, but he had reached an, ah, age—"

"And by age, you mean girth," he smirked.

"—when he was no longer comfortable on a horse," she finished crisply. "Regardless, I think it's time for my young charges to get ready for the evening."

Rose and Henry audibly groaned, but they moved toward Miss Baker, their fate decided.

"Yes," he said with a bow. "I shall see you tonight before dinner, I presume."

"I imagine so," she replied.

Phoebe was about to take the children out of the stables, but suddenly she stopped herself. His mention of seeing them before dinner for the Questioning brought to mind last night's questioning, and what he had done then. The kindness he had done them.

And what the consequences could be now.

"Mr. Turner," she began, biting her lip. "Might I offer a bit of advice?"

He seemed taken aback, but replied, "Certainly."

She took a step toward him and pitched her voice low, hoping Rose and Henry wouldn't hear.

"You should be a bit . . . careful around Lady Widcoate."

"Now you're telling me to be careful?" His lip quirked up in that half smile, but then he saw she was serious. "Whatever for?"

"Last night, when you challenged Sir Nathan and . . . and the earl if they knew the answer to the mathmatics problem . . . Lady Widcoate does not like that kind of arrogance. Especially from . . ."

She let her voice trail off, hoping he would infer her meaning.

"I . . . I did not intend to be arrogant." Mr. Turner's brow came down. "I will apologize."

"No! That will only call attention to it and make her think that you think she was affronted."

"But you're saying she was."

"Yes. And I caution you to be wary. She might find a way to seek . . ." She searched for the word. "Retaliation."

"Why on earth would she do that?" he mused. Then suddenly, his voice becoming hard, "Has she ever done anything like that to you?"

"No," Phoebe was quick to assure. "But I have been in her employ for a year now. I know what she's like."

"And what is she like?"

Phoebe pressed her lips together.

"She is like one of those girls at Mrs. Beveridge's School—where the slightest criticism from another would result in an all-out war. Some girls never grow up past the dramatics of their youth."

He cocked his head to one side, considering. But when he finally spoke, it was not about Lady Widcoate, or her warning.

No, it was about something else altogether.

"Mrs. Beveridge's School. In Surrey?" He shook his head. "Did you teach there?"

"No," she replied warily. "I was a student."

A single eyebrow quirked up, and a sudden jolt of fear shot through Phoebe. Oh, God—had she revealed too much?

"In any case, good day, Mr. Turner," she said, her breath coming out in one great rush. "Come along, children!" Turning on her heel, she marched rapid-fire out of the stables, Rose and Henry trotting on their short legs to keep up.

It was a good fifty yards before she felt safe enough to slow down—for heaven's sake, Rose and Henry were practically running at her side. But it was harder to steady her feelings.

It had been that spark of interest in his voice. That upturned brow. Had this secretary of the Earl of Ashby put her name and Mrs. Beveridge's School together and finally recognized who she was?

All she wanted was to stay hidden. All she wanted was to get these two weeks over with, and not let the bile and hatred that had consumed her for far too long threaten to take over once again.

She had gambled today, being kind to Mr. Turner.

And she had lost.

❧

NED STAYED IN the stables awhile after the curious Miss Baker disappeared, marching off like a general leading her short child-troops into battle. And apparently, he was standing stock-still long enough to elicit some worry from the groom.

"Mr. Turner?" Kevin the groom asked, poking his head out from behind Abandon. "You . . . all right?"

"Yes, of course," he replied, shaking his head.

"I ask because you're standing in horse droppings."

"Oh!" Ned's eyes shot to his feet. Indeed, in the one or two steps he had taken since Miss Baker left, he had stepped into a fresh pile of soft, slightly green horse droppings.

Danson would have a fit.

And then he remembered, he did not have Danson at his disposal.

"Ergh," he made a strangled noise as he stepped out of the pile. "Good Lord, man, can't you keep a better stable?"

The groom just shrugged. "Hazard of the job, being the only groom here."

Ned's eyes narrowed. "And the only man?"

"I am right now," the groom replied. "Why put up with the Widcoates when there's a mine offering good wages ten miles away?"

"And why are you still here, then?" Ned's eyebrow went up. "Sweet on someone? Miss Baker perhaps?"

Kevin cracked a rueful smile. "Naw. I canna go down the mine. My mind don't like being in small places. I get agitated-like."

Ned hummed, understanding. "Plus, Miss Baker's too strict for your liking?" he teased.

Kevin shook his head. "I'd heed Miss Baker's advice if I were you."

"Really?"

"She's the best governess those two could have hoped for. Been with them a year, and they are better for it. Whether or not she is I canna say. And how she manages Lady Widcoate I do not know. Likely out of affection for the tykes," was the reply. "Soft for 'em. She knows they are not supposed to be in the stables, because the lady thinks her children are still wee babes. But that girl is horse mad—so Miss Baker breaks the rules. I don't mind so much—but it'd be better if I had more help here, so I could keep an eye on them, teach them properly about the horses."

She breaks the rules. A small smile began to creep up over his face, as he completely ignored the scent of horse dung wafting from his feet. He was beginning to get an idea. An idea that could turn this entire trip to Hollyhock around.

He had been enjoying himself with Miss Baker, hadn't he? They had spoken for only a few minutes, but it had been easy—he didn't have to try to make her pay attention to him, the way he did with the other women in the house. And for a few moments, he had been relieved of the burden of thinking about his mother's house and its uncertain fate.

And she had attended Mrs. Beveridge's School.

Which was one of the premiere finishing schools in England.

He only knew about Mrs. Beveridge's because Lady Brimley, his latest paramour—and oddly, easily forgotten in the past two days—kept going on and on about it. She was attempting to get her own daughter in and, apparently, admission was highly sought after, and required connection.

In fact, hadn't Lady Brimley mentioned something about Mrs. Beveridge's the night they had first consummated their relationship? Something about how a peer of the realm such as himself could exert his influence even in places he'd never been?

Good Lord—had . . . had Lady Brimley begun their relationship to get a recommendation? To get her daughter into a school?

But this personal, more unpleasant revelation was tempered by the present situation.

And that situation was that, in terms of the wager, Miss Baker was fair game.

To have attended Mrs. Beveridge's, Miss Baker must have been a young woman of some family. Meaning she was not a foundling, a lost child who through patronage worked her way into her present position. Whatever unfortunate circumstance had led to her becoming a governess could not change that fact.

She was completely adequate as someone Turner would pursue and, therefore, adequate as someone for Ned to pursue as Turner.

True, Miss Baker would have never been his first choice. She was as thin as a rail, all angles and closed-off posture. The gray wool gown she wore—indeed, the only gown he had seen her wear—was basically armor. Up to her throat, stiff, thick, protective.

But when she had made a joke on the stairs yesterday—when he had steadied her with his hand on her shoulder—something different slipped through.

She breaks the rules.

Then there was that moment today when she allowed the armor to fall and let her dry humor out to breathe. They had talked—bantered!—with ease.

And she had smiled.

She had tried not to, tried to keep her features pale and unremarkable. Indeed, with her white-blond hair and brows, she was as colorless as a glass of water, but when she smiled . . . something sparked to life. She had cheekbones. She had vibrancy.

She had dimples.

And considering that Hollyhock seemed populated

by old biddies, and Ned had managed to isolate himself from every other female in Puffington Arms, Miss Baker was his best opportunity for winning.

"Mr. Turner?" the groom asked again. He was holding Abandon's reins now, ready to lead him to his stall. "Are you going to be standing statue-like for much longer? Dead smack in the center of the way?"

"No," Ned replied, shaking off his musings. His plottings. "No, I have to go get ready for dinner."

As he strode out of the stables, he caught a trace of the smell wafting up from his shoes. Damn—he had been outside all day too, riding. He had better bathe if he was going to make himself presentable for the evening—where he would see Miss Baker again. And begin his wooing of a governess.

And then he remembered.

The bathwater. Which Rose and Henry Widcoate were likely frolicking in at that very moment.

No matter his aroma, Ned was not doing *that* again.

There was a pond on the far side of Puffington Arms, if he remembered correctly. One that collected bowling balls but otherwise seemed clean.

Certainly cleaner than that bathwater.

A shiver ran over him—the sun was dipping lower in the sky and it was getting markedly chillier into the evening. But, much like Miss Baker, it would have to do.

10

Keep a good eye on the cards in your hand—
they can change with a blink.

Ned went downstairs to the drawing room precisely on time. Not too early, not too late, and smelling of clean, clear pond water. His evening clothes were acceptable. His coat could have used a brushing, but the shirt was fresh.

He smiled politely at Lady Widcoate and Countess Churzy—the former smiled very politely back and the latter seemed to shake her head in pity. Mrs. Rye, as Turner had predicted, was keeping her daughter and niece and Miss Benson well out of Ned's path, shooting him dark looks whenever she happened to catch him looking her way. Which wasn't often. She just happened to be standing by the door.

Mrs. Rye did, however, manage to direct her charges to fawning over Turner, who was nearby, cornered by Sir Nathan. They listened patiently, leaning in (in the case of Miss Clara Rye, leaning on—she might have been pushed forward by Miss Minnie) as Sir Nathan pumped Turner for information about what he thought of Hollyhock now and should he like to go hunting tomorrow? And oh, yes, what did he think of the consortium's proposal?

But before too long, Lady Widcoate began to lead everyone into the dining room. Without Miss Baker or the children making their appearance for the Questioning.

"Uh, excuse me," he asked, earning no small number of looks from the assembly. "But what about the children? Are . . . are they coming down?"

Lady Widcoate's expression grew markedly displeased, an angry line forming between her eyebrows. "If you must know, *Mr.* Turner, the children—"

"Henry has a bit of a cough, poor thing," Countess Churzy finished for her sister. Then she moved lightly toward him, back through the guests, to come and take *his* arm. "Do me the favor of walking me in to dinner, Mr. Turner?" she asked, turning her big hazel eyes to his. "I feel as if we have barely been introduced."

Taken aback, Ned shot Turner a look of triumph. Now, *this* was more like it. Perhaps Turner had done or said something to offend the lovely Leticia in the short time between returning and dinner, and now she was turning her attentions to someone more worthy of them . . .

But no. Her smile did not reach her eyes. As far as she knew, his name did not have an "Earl" in front of it. And she was the kind who required it—even if Turner refused to see it.

"You must forgive the children," Countess Churzy said in a whisper as he led her in to dinner. "Their governess sent word that Henry was not feeling well. My sister was torn between sitting by their bedsides and hosting her guests. Hence her . . . shortness."

"That is most unfortunate," Ned said, turning his most genial smile to Countess Churzy. "I hope they are not ill with regularity."

"From what I understand, it is quite rare," she replied. "But the governess insisted that Rose and Henry could not be presented tonight. For her sake, I certainly hope they are able to be brought out tomorrow."

"Indeed," Ned agreed, perhaps a bit too fervently. "It would be very bad for Miss Baker."

Countess Churzy turned to him, a considering glint in her eye. "I think you and I should be friends, Mr. Turner. I imagine we could be of use to each other. I could tell you all kinds of things about Hollyhock, and the consortium's proposal, and oh, *anyone* else you might be interested in. And you could tell me all sorts of things about . . ."

"About Ashby?" he finished for her.

"You know him better than anyone here."

Ned quirked up an eyebrow at that. "That, Countess, is more true than you know."

ے

DINNER WAS A better affair than the night before, Ned would give them that much. Since the ratio of men to women was so off balance, and the party was so intimate, Ned knew he would be seated next to at least one person who would rather he be anywhere else. Tonight it was Mrs. Rye. But with a single glare she twisted her body away from him, becoming a wall between himself and Miss Minnie on her other side. Luckily, Ned was happy enough to be left alone with a minimum of interaction. After all, he had an alternative—the plain governess with surprising dimples, Miss Baker, was going to succumb to his charms, and Turner would never see it coming.

He could easily use the hours at the dining table to contemplate the governess. How would he go about wooing her? Maybe spend his energies on the children to garner her interest? Of course, he was not terribly comfortable with children. What about during her free time? Did governesses have free time? An afternoon off? Could he wait that long to perchance meet with her?

While he would have been happy to use his time thus, unluckily, Ned was seated at Sir Nathan's left, forcing at least a modicum of conversation.

And as expected, that conversation was entirely about the business of bathing.

"It will be grander than anything Bath has! Bigger than Brighton's Carlton House!"

Sir Nathan had managed to keep his enthusiasm in check for most of the evening, but as the meal went on and the wine flowed, he became more and more expansive, especially about the consortium's plans for the bathing retreat.

"Fennick could explain the whole thing—Mr. McLeavey is the one who sold the town on the idea. Straight from his pulpit." Sir Nathan waved his fork in the air, his ecstasy causing food to go flying.

Now that their plates of mutton were being taken away, dessert was being served. And one could only hope Sir Nathan could make it through the meal without promising the king himself in attendance at the bathing retreat's opening ceremonies.

"And since the inn in Hollyhock will be inadequate for the illustrious guests we attract—dukes and duchesses will come to us!—so I have devised a plan to build a number of quaint cottages on the town side of Puffington Arms, to be let during the bathing season."

"And I get to design them!" Lady Widcoate added from the other end of the table. "Cottages for dukes! Can you imagine? Oh, my lord, I hope you enjoy tonight's dessert—Cook made it especially. Blackberry tarts. I hope you don't mind, but we took the blackberries from the brambles on your mother's property." Her eyes fell on Ned, and she gave him a surprisingly anticipatory look. "And you as well, Mr. Turner. I hope you especially enjoy it."

"My wife's designs for tarts almost outmatch her designs for cottages." Sir Nathan winked at his wife, causing her to giggle before returning her attention to Turner and the countess on her opposites sides.

The evidence of Lady Widcoate's design schemes all around them (the dining room in particular featured a fireplace so large and covered with cherubs, it took up an entire wall in the relatively small space, and seemed to be very difficult for the servers to maneuver around), Ned was vaguely concerned about the ornateness of the impending tart.

But, in the past twenty-four hours or so, he had learned enough to bite his tongue and turn the topic of conversation. Besides, he did not want to invite the wrath of Lady W, who seemed to be at peace with him, warnings to the contrary aside.

"There's a bathing season?" Ned asked Sir Nathan.

"But of course!" he replied. "Brighton, Lyme—they all have seasons."

His tart was placed in front of him. He was pleased to see that it relied on the structural simplicity of blackberries, sugar, and crust. Indeed, it smelled delicious, and faintly of memory.

"Yes, but those are sea-bathing establishments. They are beholden to the weather," he went on, lifting his fork. Seeing Sir Nathan's blank stare, he continued, remembering to be kinder about it, "Forgive me, but wouldn't a bathing retreat built from mineral springs have the baths indoors?"

Sir Nathan turned a bit pink at that, but it could be that he was chewing too hard on his blackberry tart. When he swallowed, he waved his fork in the air dismissively. "People visit Bath more at certain times than others. It's all in the proposal, Mr. Turner." Then his eyes shot up from his plate. "You *have* read the proposal, haven't you?"

Ned hesitated, his first bite of tart only inches from his mouth. "Of course . . ." he began. But then, for the second time that evening, he was rescued by an unexpected person.

"Mr. Turner has read the proposal, and is apparently pointing out some issues with it," Turner said imperiously from the other end of the table.

"What possible issues could he have?" Sir Nathan growled. "It's a huge boon to the area, and to you, if he allows it to be."

Sir Nathan turned his bright, bloodshot eyes on Ned. "And it's to his benefit to allow it to be."

Ned's vision started turning red around the edges. How dare Sir Nathan try to bully him? Why, just last night, he was trying to bribe him!

He would show him who he was dealing with . . .

"Don't worry, Sir Nathan," Turner soothed, reading the red on his host's face more properly than Ned had previously. "Mr. Turner is my right-hand man—I assure you that he is going to review the proposal with all the care he puts into every aspect of his life." Turner sent Ned a smirk, reminding Ned how much "care" he'd put into his performance for the past few days.

"Well, I should think that a good amount of time and care should and will be put into this decision. After all, we arranged to stay for a fortnight, so the earl would not be swayed unduly," Ned said carefully.

"And so you can attend the town's festival," Lady Widcoate added, smugly.

Ned and Turner shared a glance. "The town festival?" Turner asked.

"Don't you remember, my lord?" Lady Widcoate replied with a laugh. "Hollyhock's summer festival is the biggest event in the county!"

"Forgive me, Lady Widcoate," Ned said cautiously, "but if I recall—er, from our correspondence— the festival is not until much later in the summer."

"Yes, well"—Lady Widcoate sniffed—"we moved it forward this year. At the consortium's suggestion."

And likely at their expense too. Of course they moved it forward. Nothing was too much to impress the Earl of Ashby. Now perhaps Turner would have a greater appreciation for why Ned preferred town.

But Lady Widcoate was still talking. ". . . farmers bring out their best livestock and crops, which everyone has been looking forward to. And you are to be the master of ceremonies!"

"I am?" Turner asked, aghast.

"You were voted unanimously. It will be the perfect way for the town to show you their enthusiasm."

"I . . . saw their enthusiasm. There was plenty on display today." Turner's voice came out a bit strangled.

No, forget strangled. Turner looked positively apoplectic. Good God, did the idea of being lauded at the town festival really fill him with that much dread?

Unlike Turner, Ned actually did remember the Hollyhock town festival. Now, of course, he knew it for what it was—a rather ordinary, small-town or village-type celebration of their general smallness. But back when he was a child . . .

It had been something to get excited about. He wasn't given any chores on festival days. He was given a sixpence to spend on cakes or apples or games.

But no . . . Ned shook his head, shook off those memories. No time for such silliness. Besides, now he had the vision of Turner's being forced into ceremonial duties to look forward to. He would have to cut the ribbon, make a speech, and if he recalled correctly . . .

"You get to lead the dance, my lord!" Miss Henrietta piped up, her eyes shining with the deliciousness of this news.

"The dance?"

"The Summer Ball! The Master of the Festival leads out the first dance. And whomever he picks to dance with is the Summer Lady!" Henrietta supplied.

When Minnie shot her a questioning look, she sniffed and explained, "Lady Widcoate told us yesterday. You were too busy trying to get us to play bowls again to listen."

"Well, I'm certain it will be great fun," Ned supplied, shooting Henrietta a smile. She, to her credit, smiled kindly at him, before seeing Mrs. Rye's harsh look and shying away.

"The earl is an excellent dancer." Ned smiled down at Turner. Among many other more refined talents, dancing was one that Turner decidedly lacked.

"Whom do you think you'll choose, my lord?" Miss Benson asked, breathless. "Of course, you don't *have* to choose now . . ."

"I'm sure he'll choose wisely, Miss Benson," Ned added, turning her attention back to him. He puffed up with smug pride. "The earl has never made a bad decision as long as I've known him."

"Indeed," Turner added, his eyes narrowing, "and the best decision I ever made was to hire Mr. Turner."

Apparently, two could play this game.

"It was?" Countess Churzy asked with polite interest. "How very complimentary."

"I could not be happier in my position, my lady," Ned said innocently. "After all, I owe the earl my life."

"Do you?" the countess said with happy intrigue. "Oh, but this is a story we must hear."

"I don't think . . ." Turner tried to demur, but the countess turned her big dark eyes to him and gave him their full force.

"Please? We ladies enjoy a story of derring-do. Don't we?" She pouted gorgeously. Ned was again tempted to forget that she was as smart as she was lovely, and had an agenda. And her expression wasn't even directed at him.

Turner didn't stand a chance with her.

"Oh, please, let us hear it!" came the chorus from the three younger ladies. And even Mrs. Rye notably brooked no opposition.

Oh, well, he thought with relish. His blackberry tart could wait.

"It was on the battlefield in Brussels," Ned began, enjoying himself for the first time all evening. "I—er, that is, the earl—was a very young officer and new to the regiment, and I was then Captain Turner. We were trying to hold a flank and taking fire, and were desperate for our runner to return with necessary ammunition—"

"No, Mr. Turner," Turner interrupted, his face a hard line. "Allow me to tell the story, my friend."

Ned's eyebrow went up, betraying his slight shock at the interruption. But Turner was the earl tonight, so he acquiesced to him.

"Mr. Turner and I were in the same regiment—I arrived only after the majority of the fighting was done, having only just come of age and selfishly run away from my obligations to my great-uncle and joining the army. Indeed, two days after I joined up, Napoleon surrendered."

Ned's brow creased in confusion. Turner *seemed* to be telling the story correctly . . .

"My experience with war was marching in lines and cleaning my Baker rifle, and talking about how if *I* had the chance to be in battle, I would take on ten Frenchmen at once. I imagine I was insufferable, but, to my captain's credit, he never told me so." Turner smirked ruefully, and all the ladies gave a little laugh at his supposed self-deprecation.

"Then, of course, Napoleon escaped Elba, and set us all on a course to that field in Belgium. I jumped with excitement at the idea of finally being in battle, but the truth is, I was scared. As scared as I'd ever been in my life. But I hid it with bravado, and good humor, and playing cards with Turner here and our other friend Dr. Gray, and that took my mind off the drills and maneuvers, and let me think only of the present. Which was a great gift." Turner couldn't help smiling. "I also won all their rations."

Minnie Rye laughed at that, and she leaned forward on her elbow, enraptured by the tale. Ned looked around the table. They all were. Including him.

"The battle began in the morning, and lasted all day. Our regiment—one of hundreds—was out on a far flank, and our orders were to hold that flank, no matter what. But when ammunition became low, holding the flank became . . . more difficult.

"We had a runner—a boy no more than fourteen. I don't know how he managed to lie his way into a uniform, but we needed every man. He was the fastest runner this side of Marathon. Mr. Turner—Captain Turner—sent him running back to get more ammunition, and honestly, he must have thought it was the safer job. A child shouldn't have been facing direct fire. But he must have gotten lost or turned around in the madness, because suddenly, I spotted the boy in the middle of the field. Our ammunition, our saving grace, strapped across his chest."

Ned could feel himself getting sick, and grave. His stomach roiled, smoke filling up his mind, and the image of the boy lying in a heap, his gangly limbs twisted awkwardly, his eye—the one that hadn't been blown away—staring right at him.

"I spotted him first. I must have, I was closest to him. Pointed, but couldn't yell. I didn't have any breath." Turner continued. "I was frozen on the edge of the field, a pile of dirt protecting me from fire. If we didn't get that ammunition, we would have to run out into the field and begin using our bayonets against their bullets. But I couldn't move. Then I felt a hand on my shoulder."

Ned's eyes met Turner's. Everyone else in the room fell away, and they were standing again on that battlefield. Madness on every side.

"It was Captain Turner, and he didn't hesitate like I had. He ran out into the field. He yelled at me to cover him, and it snapped me out of it. I did my best . . . *we* did our best, and Turner reached the boy quickly. He was obviously dead, there was no saving him. But if he could get the ammunition and bring it back, he could save the rest of us.

"He cut the boy's satchel off of him, tugged it free. Then, on his way back to the safety of the line, a ball went through his thigh, felling him to the ground."

Turner took a moment, a sip of wine. You could hear a pin drop in the room. He subconsciously began rubbing his leg . . . but luckily, Ned was the only one who noticed. Everyone else was lost in the story—their starry eyes gone grave and large, their fear palpable.

"Then, somehow, I had the fortitude—or the

stupidity—to run out from behind my position of relative safety and make for Turner. He was limping to his feet, trying to drag his way up. But even though he was fueled by his fear, he was slowed by his wound. I came up to his side and took the satchel off of him. I was shaking so hard, tears in my eyes, I almost forgot to bring back Turner too!

"But he leaned on me, and together we managed to crab-walk our way back. I couldn't see straight, so Turner had to direct me. My eyes, his legs . . . and bullets dogging our feet every step. And somehow, that was the luckiest bit. The dust that rose from those bullets hitting the ground gave us enough cover to get back to the line. Get back to fighting."

Turner shrugged, pasting a smile on his face, eerily similar to one of Ned's happy-go-lucky expressions.

"After the battle was over, Captain Turner put me up for a medal, and christened me Lucky Ned. The rest is in the history books." Turner took another sip of his wine, but this time the room took the opportunity to exhale.

"Well," the countess finally said, breathlessly breaking the silence. "I fear you give the earl too much credit, Mr. Turner. It seems to me that you saved each other."

"Oh, I don't know about that," Ned finally managed, his mouth dry.

"Well, it is the case, if the earl is telling the truth," the countess countered.

"Is he?" Miss Clara asked, in her small but rapt voice.

"Yes, Mr. Turner," his friend said from the other end of the table. "Do you remember it differently? Or was my retelling accurate?"

Every eye in the room looked at him. Ned wanted to scream. He wanted the floor to swallow him up. He wanted to point at Turner and call him a liar, expose him as a fraud, a manipulator. The difficulty was . . . he couldn't.

"Yes. You have it right, I believe."

"Then you are both to be commended," Sir Nathan said gruffly. He teetered to his feet, holding his glass out to be refilled. A servant moved swiftly to top it off.

"To Lord Ashby, and Mr. Turner. And surviving the war."

"Hear, hear!" came the subdued cry around the table, the ladies lifting their glasses to their lips.

But Ned couldn't drink. Couldn't eat. Couldn't do anything, other than give in to that hollow feeling that had plagued him all day.

That sadness.

"If you would excuse me," he said by way of no explanation, rising to his feet and leaving the room with the shortest of bows. Leaving his new glass of wine and his blackberry tart untouched.

11

The rules don't change in a game of chance.
Until they do.

The knock on the door was a surprise.

Ned hadn't known what to do after he left the dining room. He thought about wandering outside, sitting by the pond, and watching the stars come out, but the chances that he would run into the rest of the party upon reentry were too high. He didn't want to see anyone. He didn't want to be around anyone. He *wanted* to be left alone with his thoughts.

So he went up to the third floor, and back to his cramped room without a fire. Alone with his ruminations.

In many ways, he supposed he should thank God for the knock on his door.

"Who is it?"

"Danson, sir," came the forlorn voice of his valet.

Ned opened the door to find that, yes indeed, it was Danson. Bearing, of all things, a blackberry tart.

"I am told you left the dining room abruptly this evening?" Danson said as he stepped into the room. His tone was distinctly disapproving . . . more so than usual.

"I didn't feel . . ." Ned sighed, "like playing along."

Danson's harrumph was familiar and comforting. He put the tart down on the small table next to the papers from Mr. Fennick that outlined the proposal for the bathing retreat and Ned's mother's property. Ned had glanced at it yesterday when he returned to the room after the evening and then had promptly fallen asleep. He'd actively avoided looking at it tonight, fearful that it would make that hollow feeling in his gut grow wider.

"Lady Widcoate was particularly distressed that you left before you even tasted her blackberry tarts, which were made as a specialty of the cook's. She directed that this one be delivered to you, in the hope that your, er, willingness to play along is restored."

Danson turned and stood directly in front of him. His withering gaze took in Ned's appearance, from the tops of his boots to the self-tied neckcloth.

His expression said it all.

"Come, now, Danson, do I really look that bad?" Ned sighed, giving in to the impulse to run his hand through his hair.

"You look as if you have fleas. Sir."

Ned immediately pulled his hand out of his hair, putting it back at his side.

"Brilliant. Marvelous. And here I thought you had had my suit of clothes cleaned!"

Danson didn't bother to deny it. "And apparently, it did little good." But then his expression relented, and he met his master's eye. "It is not so much in your attire—however untailored and unappealing—as it is in your expression."

"My expression?"

"You may have a talent for reading people," Danson allowed. "But you do not realize how easily read you are yourself. In this game, you need to learn not to let your countenance betray the workings of your mind."

Ned didn't know what to say. First the hollow feeling began in town, and then at dinner, listening to Turner give his account of a story that Ned told so often, he could hardly recognize the truth of another man's version. Now Danson was telling him his disappointment was on display for all to see.

"How do you think he does it?" he asked suddenly.

"Sir?"

"Turner. How does he hide his true feelings?"

Danson gave the question some consideration.

"Some men are not made for service. They do not appreciate the precision and glory of tradition." He sniffed derisively. "Some are made to be their own masters, as unruly as they may be. And to place the latter type of man in the role of the former . . . it would take a great deal of fortitude to last, say five years, with one's ambitions intact. Personally, I believe he bites the inside of his cheek."

"Bites the inside of . . . ?"

"If nothing else, it would keep your mind off other things. Perhaps it will help you not seem so flea-ridden." He let his eyes flick over his employer's appearance again. "Although I will take your suit for tomorrow and make certain it gets laundered tonight, if you please, sir."

"Need I remind you that you are under direct orders to do nothing to give our wager away? And if you do, I lose?" Ned crossed his arms over his chest.

"You will have no chance of winning if you are not presentable," Danson replied coolly. "And I will be damned if any wardrobe *I* am in charge of is less than perfect. Sir."

As much as he wanted to protest, to demand that his orders be respected and insist that he could do for himself . . . right now, he was grateful for this small bit of caretaking.

"Brilliant, Danson. Marvelous. Take whatever clothes you see fit." He waved his hand over to the rickety wardrobe, where he had placed Turner's bag.

Danson opened the wardrobe and made a sound akin to a Pekingese being strangled. "You didn't even *hang* anything!" he wailed. Then, with a quick, bracing inhale, Danson gathered a pile of offensive clothing, then straightened and turned, heading for the door to the small room. "Sir, if I may," he said, his hand on the doorknob.

"Why stop now?" Ned said under his breath, but with a bit of a smile.

"I think it would be in everyone's best interest if you were to hurry up and win this wager. Then we can all go home."

Ned nodded, and Danson took that as the dismissal it was. But, as he opened the door and and turned toward the spindly stairs, Ned caught sight of something interesting.

At the other end of the corridor, a door was shutting. The governess's door. He caught a glimpse of warm candlelight falling on the stiff gray wool of skirts. A braid of hair, coming out of a tight coil.

Of course—he and the governess were on the same floor! Here he'd been worried about finding the time for wooing her, sneaking in a moment here and there between her lessons and his duties as the earl's secretary . . . but luck had given him all the nights.

"Yes, Danson," he said under his breath to the long-departed valet. "I think it is high time I started winning this wager."

～

THE KNOCK ON the door was a surprise.

Phoebe had just finally allowed herself the luxury of the rest of the evening to herself. The children had long since retired to bed, but she had stayed in the schoolroom preparing her lessons for tomorrow.

Making an excuse to get out of the Questioning had been risky, and she had to be certain that Henry and Rose were prepared when they faced their parents tomorrow. Not a single answer or fact could be wrong. She had a feeling her employment counted on it.

She had never seen Lady Widcoate this fractious. Not even the countess soothed her entirely. Sir Nathan, too, was trying overly hard to impress their guests at this strangest of house parties, and their nerves were contagious.

Phoebe just couldn't face the earl, or his secretary. Not with what she had given away this afternoon in the stables. She was scared to death that she would see recognition on their faces. They would remember the name from her letter and tie it to the girl who had been left behind in the scandal.

A scandal the earl himself had caused, no matter what anyone else thought.

So, she had been late coming up to her rooms, and late relaxing into herself. If it was either of the Widcoates or Nanny at the door, she would likely not get the opportunity to be herself tonight at all.

"Who is it?" she asked, threading the narrow field between wary and deferential.

"It's Mr. Turner, Miss Baker," came the mellifluous tenor.

Oh, heavens! Why on earth was *he* at her door?

She hesitated, uncertain if she should open the door or send him off without a word.

He sounded more cheerful than he had that afternoon—did that mean that he had found something out? Or perhaps that he had found nothing out and just had a good dinner?

Her stomach grumbled at the thought. She herself had not had dinner at all.

"Er . . . Miss Baker?" Mr. Turner's voice was tentative now. She could almost hear his smile faltering, causing her to have to squash her own. "I know this might be considered inappropriate, but I was . . . I was given this blackberry tart and thought you might enjoy it."

There was a pause.

"Miss Baker?"

Another pause.

"All right, then. Have a good night, Miss Baker."

Her stomach gave a protesting gurgle. What harm could there be in facing him now? After all, there was no way for her to get out of facing him or his employer tomorrow. And she was hungry enough to ignore any qualms that might be roiling in her gut.

"Just a moment!" she called out. Phoebe took the few seconds to hastily straighten her bedcovers and the books and papers on her little desk and to light her second candle, providing more—if not decent—illumination.

She ran a hand over her hair, the braid no longer pinned up in its bun at the nape of her neck, but falling over her shoulder. Oh, well, it would have to do. She did not have the time or the patience for pins.

One last hand running over her skirts, straightening the shawl on her shoulders, and she opened the door.

Just a crack. Just enough to peer out. There she saw Mr. Turner straightening his dark locks with one hand, holding a plate in the other.

Bearing the blackberry tart.

Her stomach gurgled again.

"Mr. Turner." She forced herself to meet his eyes.

"Miss Baker," he replied in kind, with a short bow.

And they stood there. Neither one knowing what to do or say next.

"Er . . . how was your day?" Mr. Turner began, standing in the hall, oddly formal with that plate in his hand.

"Fine," she replied, unable to think of any other reply.

"I heard that young Henry had taken ill," he continued.

"Oh, yes!" she replied, remembering the story she had given Lady Widcoate. "He was feeling better by the time he went to sleep. I have every expectation he will be right as rain in the morning."

"Let us hope so," Mr. Turner replied.

"And how was your day, Mr. Turner?" she tried, hoping at least to keep the scales of awkward conversation balanced. "Or, ah . . . your dinner?"

"Fine, as well." He coughed. "I was not feeling very well myself, so I left before eating dessert."

He indicated the tart in his hand.

"I do hope it is nothing serious."

"No. Likely the same affliction as poor Henry. I will no doubt be fine in the morning."

She eyed the tart, willing her stomach not to betray her audibly.

"I thought you might like it," he continued.

"I should hate to take your whole dessert . . ." Although she was thinking the exact opposite.

"Well, perhaps we can split it," he replied. "Do you have a knife, or . . . ?"

She nodded. "I think I have a penknife. Just a moment."

She turned and took the few short steps to her small writing desk. The piece was a relic from a different Widcoate of Puffington Arms, and had been in the attic since the present Lady Widcoate's interior renovations began. It was sturdy and useful—two aspects Lady Widcoate had apparently despised—and had deep drawers, in which Phoebe now rifled through for her old penknife. When she finally located it, she spun around to move back toward the door—

Only to bang—for the second time in two days—directly into the chest of Mr. Turner.

The broad chest, it must be said. One she had very nearly accidentally stabbed. Granted, the room was small, and he had taken barely more than a step inside it, but still—

"Oh!" she exclaimed. "Mr. Turner! You . . . you should not be—"

But she was rendered silent by the look of wonder on his face.

"These are wonderful," he breathed, his eyes fixed on the walls.

The two candles only gave the dimmest impression of what she had transformed her rooms into but, combined with the moonlight from the small window, it was enough to see the framed pictures she had hung in a precise line on the wall.

There were rivers and waterfalls cutting through mountains. A city at night in another. The one that Mr. Turner was staring at placed the viewer deep in a forest, looking up through the trees, the branches forming a circle, its own frame of a swirling, beautiful night sky. A comforting canopy, a place of imagination and welcome.

Everything blended together. Each picture in the line took the occupants of the ordinary third-floor room and transported them to somewhere new, different, and amazing.

She could be herself here.

But . . . now *he* was here. In her private sanctuary.

She wanted to curl in on herself. It was as if he had tripped his way into this inner sanctum with no thought to how vulnerable it made her—and she was not speaking of her reputation. No . . . it exposed *her*. The inside of this room was like the inside of her mind. And he was an intruder.

But was he an unwelcome one?

"Did you do this?" His eyes still on the picture of the night sky through trees.

"Yes," she replied defensively.

"The Widcoates have a painting master under their roof."

"They don't know. No one does," Phoebe admitted. "No one comes up here."

"Not even servants?"

She tried to think of a judicious way to explain. "Lady Widcoate—can be short with the maids. The staff often changes from one month to the next. To make their lives easier, I carry up firewood and wash water myself. I would wager half of them think I live in the nursery."

"I am amazed you have survived the Widcoates this long," he mumbled, likely not thinking that he could be heard.

"Luckily, my purview is the children's education. Indeed, I can go days, sometimes weeks, without seeing my employers." To his unasked question, she supplied, "The Questionings are more frequent when there are visitors to be impressed."

He nodded in understanding and, drawn like a moth to the proverbial flame, went back to examining the paintings.

And she had little to do but examine him.

He had barged his way in here—although, at the moment, she could not feel that was the right word. Followed where he should not have? As inappropriate as it was to have him in her rooms, he was not *acting* as if he was going to ravage her.

Indeed, the way he crouched in the small space, peering close at the wall, was almost comical.

He was a man of height. He made the painted forest and town and rivers recede into the background, an imposing figure that took up all the space in the little room. For a hundred different reasons, Phoebe knew she should be feeling wary of him.

And yet . . . she didn't.

"You are remarkably talented."

"Thank you," she replied.

"No modesty?" he asked, his head coming up.

"None false," Phoebe remarked dryly.

His mouth quirked up into that half smile—which sent a flutter through her insides to match the flickering candlelight.

Oh, dear. Perhaps she did have cause to be wary.

"I, ah . . . I studied art in my youth, and had a talent for it."

"I would imagine it is a good skill for a governess to have," he remarked, now letting his attention rove over the rest of the room. "What is this one?"

"Oh. That." She blushed. "It's a ship."

"I can tell," he observed. "It is rendered quite fine. But I know of very few lady painters interested in nautical art. Especially those landlocked in Leicestershire."

"Well . . ." she offered, feeling bolder than she should. "It is a special ship."

"The—" He peered at the name on the transom. "*Blooming Daisy*? How so?"

"It is the ship that is going to take me to America. I will not be landlocked forever."

His head and eyebrow came up in swift succession.

"I have some cousins there—on my father's side. In Connecticut. In two years' time, Rose will be sent off to school and Henry will be given over to tutors. And I will have saved up enough money to travel."

She looked at him for some reaction to her revelation that the governess had aspirations for a life beyond her charges. It was not in her nature to simply tell people about her dreams, her goals. After all, they had been dashed before, and she'd felt people's pity and disdain in equal measure. She had closed herself off, long ago. But there was something about Mr. Turner, standing in the middle of her room, of her world, that made her feel like talking.

But he simply nodded and said, "I see." Then, "May I?" He gestured to her desk chair. She waved a hand, allowing him to seat himself.

"Er, your penknife, Miss Baker?" He held out his hand. Oh, right. The tart.

She handed him the knife and took a seat in her other chair, the soft one that she had also rescued from the attic—where she did most of her reading.

"You have a very comfortable room here," he said as he cut into the tart, releasing a delicious tangy aroma of blackberries and summer. "More comfortable, than I daresay, than the rest of the house."

She could not help but smile at that. "Oh, I can forgive Lady Widcoate her enthusiasm for ornate decoration. Why, without it, I would not have any of the furniture in this room."

"How do you mean?" He finished cutting the tart and gestured for her to join him at the small desk. She did, scooting her soft chair forward to be within arm's reach.

"Nothing," she replied. It was one thing to commiserate and share a tart with a man, but she should not speak ill of her employers. "Lady Widcoate is not all bad."

"You are the one who warned me to watch out for her today." He handed the penknife back to her. "There are no forks, so, by all means, you go first."

She moved the plate closer to her and picked up her half of the tart, taking the smallest of bites.

It was *delicious*.

She made a small, throaty sound, a sigh of appreciation. Her eyes closed, and she let the blackberry juices fill the inside of her mouth, savoring.

When she opened her eyes, Mr. Turner was giving her the most curious look, his own mouth hanging open.

And he didn't stop staring.

A self-conscious hand flew to her mouth. "I'm sorry, did I . . . am I a mess?" she asked.

"No!" he cried. "Not at all," he remarked with a smile, one so wide it reminded Phoebe of a few short hours ago, when he had thought he had something stuck in his teeth. "I am pleased to see you enjoying the tart. It really must be exceptional."

She dropped her hand, relieved. "I missed my supper. And I am not often given treats."

"Given treats?" He blinked several times. "They don't feed you?"

"Of course they feed me," she replied hastily. Not as much as the family, of course, but she was fed sufficiently. Over the past five years of being a governess, she had become used to making do with less. Although her previous family in Portsmouth had been much more generous than Lady Widcoate.

Still, when she was young, she used to have weight to her body. Substance. Now she was reedy—like everyone expected a governess to be.

"I simply do not often have sweets," she elaborated. "Only on special occasions."

"Then by all means, have more." He nudged the plate toward her and watched as she took another bite, more full this time, more of the sweetness and the crust and the ripe fullness of the summer blackberries bursting in her mouth.

She could feel her cheeks pinking under his gaze. Which, in the light of two candles, was warm and intense.

It sent another strange thrill down her spine.

Perhaps too intense.

"There is a dictum that states that two people sharing a blackberry tart should be at least able to hold a conversation," she said, after swallowing. Having him in here would be a great deal more comfortable if he was talking. Instead of just . . . staring.

"I suppose that's a fair—if overly specific—rule of tart consumption," he agreed. "So, why don't you tell me about yourself?"

"Me?" she replied, a flight of panic going through her breast. "Why . . . why would you want to know anything about me?"

After all, he already knew more about her than she would wish.

"You told me you went to Mrs. Beveridge's School. What was that like?"

Was he fishing for something? Oh, dear—was he here under orders from the earl?

No—no, she squashed that fear down. No one thought of her. Least of all the Earl of Ashby. While at one time in her life she would have raged against him, and written scathing letters, now she only wanted to remain anonymous, unnoticed. Her anger had been so useless.

But the fact that the earl's existence still irked her, that his presence here could upset her to the point of paranoia . . . that was what was truly upsetting her.

Ned must have seen something in her reaction to his inquiry, in the space she took to answer, because before she could, he waved a hand, dismissing it entirely. "You're right, who wants to talk about school?"

"No," she offered, trying to sound unconcerned. "It was fine." She took another bite.

"Were you . . . forgive me, were you a charity student? You must have been exceptionally clever, if that's the case. Mrs. Beveridge's is a very competitive environment. Er . . . so I hear."

"You are familiar with girls' schools?" she asked him warily.

"Not through any diligence." He smiled at her, but offered no more explanation.

"I was not a charity student. My circumstances changed when my father died, and I left Beveridge's shortly thereafter."

"I am sorry," he said automatically. "For the loss of your father, I mean. Not that you had to leave school. Although I expect that wasn't a good day either."

"No." She took another mouthful of tart. "It wasn't.

But Mrs. Beveridge's was never very keen on charity. Or cleverness, for that matter." No, the school thrived on status.

"What happened to your father?" he asked suddenly. Maybe he *was* fishing for something.

"He drowned," was all she was willing to offer.

"Ah." Silence reigned for a few moments.

He looked away from her then, his voice someplace very far away. "My father died when I was very young. I don't even remember him."

Her heart, practical as it was, could not help but go out to him. After all, at least she had the memories of her father. His lessons. The good times. There was a bright side—macabre as it may seem.

But Mr. Turner was not sad for long. He shook his head, as if to rid himself of droplets of sorrow, letting them fly off and dry up. Then he looked up at her with that full smile that she had at first thought might be overly toothy but was beginning to grow on her.

"But a night with a blackberry tart is not one for pitiful ruminations! Let's talk about something more jolly!"

"All right," she allowed. "What do you have?"

"What do I have?"

"In your boundless reserves of jollity? I find it very useful to call upon something fun or fanciful to make yourself smile when you need to." She hesitated a moment. "It's my own form of rebellion."

He shook his head, still not understanding. Thus, she explained, "I have found that people expect a governess to be stern and miserable. So, secretly, I refuse."

It had been that philosophy that had ultimately saved

her sanity five years ago. And given her the temerity to plan for America. Her old teacher Miss Earhart had been right about that. She would find joy again, if not in the same places as before. She had managed to piece herself back together.

But Mr. Turner was looking at her queerly, so she cleared her throat.

"So—I always remember to enjoy the little things. Like . . . what was the silliest thing that happened to you yesterday?"

He put his chin in his hand, rubbing thoughtfully.

"I took a bath in water so dirty, it might as well have been piss."

She nearly choked on a bite of tart.

"No, it was!" he continued. "I was the last one to use it—after your charges, mind—and I have no doubt that the scampering fleas and ticks that survived their drowning from the other bodies they came off of have now found a new house somewhere on my person." He gave a little shiver. "I want to bathe again just thinking about it."

She shook her head, trying to ward off the bark of laughter that threatened to escape. "I take it you are not used to such practices? You are a well-pampered secretary, then."

He shrugged, and she could tell he blushed a little in the light. "My time in the army was different, but since then I have lived alone. And enjoyed my bathwater to be mine. But I have discovered that the pond is suitable for my bathing needs from here on out."

You could join me.

Her eyes shot to his. The words were not said, she was

sure of it. But somehow, they snaked their way into her brain. As if his tone and his throaty tenor, the candlelight and the delicious tart had made the suggestion for him.

She closed her shawl more tightly about her. Took another bite of tart. And replied.

"There are eels in that pond."

He threw his hands up in the air. "Then I'm doomed to a rather smelly existence. I think I will manage, but what about my poor dinner companions? Or dessert companions, as the case may be. No—I shall simply have to brave the eels—for their sake. And yours."

"We appreciate your sacrifice." She nodded sagely.

"What about you?" he then asked. "What is your little silliness of yesterday?" Then an idea sparked to him, lighting his eyes with mischief. "Or, better yet— what is your little silliness of tomorrow?"

"Of tomorrow?" she asked, her interest piqued.

"Yes—what little silliness will go into your boundless reserve of jollity tomorrow?" he asked. "Perhaps teaching Henry and Rose to ride?"

She rolled her eyes. "If only Lady Widcoate would allow it.

"I don't know," she mused. "Maybe it will be a swordfight over my honor on the lawn between Napoleon Bonaparte and Julius Caesar." She smirked at his upturned brow. "Rose enjoys swordfighting over my honor. Or over Nanny's."

"It could be seeing the children's faces when they are in the stables."

"A tart shared with a relative stranger," she countered.

"A kiss?"

Her head came up.

"A what?"

Before she could protest any further, her head was in his hands, and his lips were upon hers.

It happened so suddenly, Phoebe didn't know what to do. One second, he had been sitting over there, leaning his arm on her little desk and watching her eat, and then he . . . he got closer. Then he got closer again, as they were talking. And then, he just . . . dove.

Being kissed was alarming in almost any situation, she decided. But this was not just any situation.

His lips were warm, the pressure against hers a startling persuasion. His hands held her by her jaw—more gently than she had supposed—his fingers sinking into her hair. He likely had no idea he was loosening her braid. The sensation that thrilled down her spine before came back with a vengeance.

And he kept his eyes closed.

Did people kiss with their eyes closed?

Then, just as suddenly as it had begun, it ended. He pulled away from her, just an inch or two, his hands still molded against her face, caressing her neck, her ears.

"Brilliant," he murmured to himself, the half-cocked smile in place. "Marvelous."

Then he leaned in, closing the gap between them, and . . .

And it was at about that time, Phoebe decided she'd had enough.

Before his mouth could claim hers again, before she could be kissed more with eyes closed, she remembered that she had limbs of her own that worked, and hauled back and slapped him.

"Ow!" he cried. "You boxed my ear!" His hands came off her face and flew to his own.

"It was the closest thing available," she replied hotly, rising so quickly to her feet that she almost knocked her chair over.

"What was that for?"

"What was that *for*?" she nearly screeched. Instead, she managed to keep her voice to a harsh, angry whisper. "What do you *think* it was for? You think you can just barge into my room and ply me with tarts and take advantage?"

"I . . . I wasn't . . ."

"Oh yes you were, and you well know it!" She called upon the righteous indignation of her profession, shaming him with lack of empathy the way one had to with children.

"We were just talking . . ."

"Precisely. We were just talking. As people who are acquaintances might. What gave you such presumption?" She let herself rant in the most scathing tones, and kept her chair between them. "You have no right! No right at all to force yourself upon a female in the employ of this house, Mr. Turner. You should leave. And think about the consequences of such actions. *Now*."

He stood, pulling himself up to his full (and inimitable) height. Phoebe held her stance, her shoulders hard and tense, ready to spring if she had to, her face a steely resolve. Her knuckles going white around the penknife she kept in her hand.

Her eyes, however, were not quite able to meet his.

Then . . . he gave a short bow.

"I apologize," he said, gravity sinking in. "I misunderstood."

She could have let him go then. He turned and walked away. But something inside Phoebe snapped. And she did not want him letting himself off easily.

"No, you did not."

He turned again to face her.

"You did not misunderstand. You took *advantage*."

On that, she did meet his eye. And what he saw there was enough to make his shoulders fall imperceptibly.

But he said nothing. Instead, he let himself out and closed the door behind him.

And Phoebe let out a breath she hadn't known she was holding.

Good God, she was lucky that worked. Her shaking hands came up to her head. She was completely vulnerable up here with him. Her blackberry-covered penknife would have been of no help. He could have attacked her. Who would have come to her rescue? He could have had no gentlemanly instincts, and instead sought to please himself, and punish her for thwarting him.

She'd heard stories, of course. Of "gentlemen" attacking women of reduced circumstances, thinking they could get away with it. Governesses occupied that in-between space, making them invisible to almost everyone, and therefore vulnerable. But Phoebe had been lucky in her employment—the first family, in Portsmouth, had been fatherless, and Sir Nathan had never given her a second glance, let alone cause to fear for her virtue. Still, she should not have been so careless!

She took two steadying breaths and moved swiftly to her door and turned the lock. Then, for good measure, she placed her chair under the handle, securing it in place.

What other option did she have? she thought to herself. If she moved into the nursery for the duration, Nanny would ask questions, and she would be exposed as a trollop.

If she asked that he be moved to a different floor, it would expose her again, and she would take the brunt of it. There was no question.

How dare he! How *dare* he! She had been right to be wary of him, but she had gone against her common sense when her instincts failed her. *He's not so bad*, they told her. *He's not his employer*, they told her. *Maybe it would be nice to talk to someone.*

The promise of company and a blackberry tart had lured her into a false sense of security.

Well, she would not fall for it again. If he tried anything else, she would move rooms, no matter what anyone had to say about it.

That settled that. Although she doubted very much she would sleep at all tonight.

Her eyes fell on the remainder of the tart on the table.

At least she wouldn't have to be tortured by an empty stomach too, she thought, as she lifted up the remaining half and bit into it with a fury.

There always was a bright side, no matter how macabre.

12

Whist is a different game altogether. One has a partner, and must occasionally take up their cards.

Ned woke up the next morning feeling like a heel, a sensation he was unaccustomed to. Although, in the three days since he'd been at Puffington Arms, it was becoming a bit more the norm.

He had gone back down the long third-floor hallway to his room after leaving Miss Baker's. No more than a quarter of an hour had passed in the interim. And yet so much—so little?—had occurred.

He was numb, his heart beating wildly. Odd jerks of anger and shame coursed through him. He had been rejected. Summarily, completely rejected. By the *governess*. Who had no pretensions and no hopes for anything better in life, who was destined for America, of all places, and was pale and thin besides—dimples or no dimples!

He would give it up, he decided. Declare Turner the

victor and then leave this wretched place where he had no hope of winning his wager. Walk right out the door and never look back. Let them do what they like with his mother's house, he was *done*. Utterly, completely, finally, done.

And with that, he went to bed.

Of course, that was when his conscience—terrible, traitorous thing that it was—began to creep in, keeping him from sleep.

He just kept going over and over those last lines she had said to him.

You did not misunderstand. You took advantage.

Had he? He was fairly certain he had misunderstood. Certainly Miss Baker had been sending out signals all evening that she wanted to be kissed. After all, who made noises like that when they ate blackberry tarts?

Someone who hadn't had a dessert in years, his conscience reasoned, and he tried to shut it up by suffocating himself with his own pillow.

Yes, well . . . why would any woman let a man into her rooms?

Although, he had sort of let himself in. To better see the paintings on the walls.

But the way she had looked at him . . .

Had been the way anyone looks at anyone in low candlelight. As if they are trying to see better.

Oh, hell.

The truth was . . . he had not misunderstood. He had been so focused on charming her, and admittedly was beginning to enjoy their strange conversation, that he only let himself see what he wanted to see. Things he was used to seeing. And now, with the benefit of hindsight and a box to the ear, he could see everything much more clearly.

She had been nervous and reserved. Her posture was unbending, closed off, and relaxed only when they began to talk, putting her at greater ease. She had gradually become less standoffish, that was true, but it was only to the degree that one might say a hermit crab was less standoffish than a lobster.

And he *had* taken advantage of the situation.

Then . . . oh, then! She had cut him down with the firmest of rebukes, and made him feel like the heel he was. Made him know to his core that he was no gentleman.

What he had done was something no gentleman ought to do. That no true gentleman would even think of. He had taken advantage of someone in a weaker, more vulnerable position.

And she had bravely, beautifully corrected him.

He should slink back to London. Though not in anger or frustration.

In shame and disgrace.

But before he did, he had to apologize to her—and maybe get back a granule of his self-respect.

Sleep—what he had of it, anyway—was fitful and unpleasant. He kept waking up, his body aware of every movement and creak outside his door, the old boards of the third floor settling with the night and awakening with the sun. Amazingly, sometime in the night, Danson had brought his clothes back from being laundered and had hung them in the small wardrobe.

He wanted to make sure she went downstairs before

him. He suspected she would anyway, since her day began much earlier than his. While he did want to apologize to her—nay, needed to apologize—he thought it best not to do so up here. She would likely feel much more comfortable if there were people nearby. And so would he.

After all, she might hit him again. His ear still rang a bit.

But the sounds outside his door were undistinguishable as footsteps or simply old creaks, so he waited until it seemed impossibly late, then ducked his head out into the hall.

The door at the far end was closed. Whether it was "still" closed or had been closed after she left, there was no way to tell. Either way, Ned had to take the chance. But just in case she *was* there, he silently pivoted out into the hall on his toes, achingly careful as he closed his door behind him, desperate to not make a sound.

He would have to ask Danson for lessons on how to move silently, Ned thought grimly.

When the latch finally took, echoing in the hall, he moved swiftly to the stairs and snuck down them.

He let himself breathe when he hit the second floor. And he let himself slow down to a normal pace when he hit the ground floor.

First things first. He would go to the nursery and schoolroom and see about locating Miss Baker. If she was not in her rooms still (looking at the hour, how could she be?), he would find her there.

A gurgle arose from his stomach.

Then again, perhaps it would be better if he breakfasted first.

After all, he'd missed out on the blackberry tart last night.

He could pop in to the breakfast room, grab some bacon, and *then* search out the schoolroom. Hopefully he would be able to avoid any of his companions from dinner the night before. He was completely unaccustomed to keeping country hours, so he could only assume, since the sun was up, that people were out and about. Yesterday's breakfast was so murky in his memory, he half assumed he had woken on Turner's mare on the way to Hollyhock.

He followed his nose down the hall toward the east side of the house, but as he was discerning which door was the correct one to the breakfast room, he was stopped by the sound of laughter.

Female laughter.

"You'll see, Leticia," came Lady Widcoate's voice. "You can have the earl for the entire day, to do with as you like. He'll not be going into Hollyhock today, I made certain of it."

"But what about Sir Nathan?" Countess Churzy asked. "He will not want to put off anything if it means a decision can be made."

Given the freedom of their speech, they must have been alone.

"My darling Sir Nathan will go into Hollyhock as always and drink—er, I mean plan with Mr. Fennick and the vicar. But I promise you, Ashby will not be among them. Neither will his horrid little secretary."

There was a pause, and it sounded as if someone was slurping tea.

"He absolutely sneered at the idea for the cottages

last night," Lady Widcoate said darkly. "I'm certain of it. Didn't you hear him?"

"Mmm" was the noncommittal reply.

Apparently, it was unsatisfactory for Lady Widcoate, because she continued, "I was horrified by his behavior. Leaving the table in the middle of everything? Not even waiting until the ladies left? Mrs. Rye thinks there is something wrong in his head. One must wonder at the state of the earl's affairs if he leaves that man in charge."

"They are old friends from the battlefield. He trusts Mr. Turner."

"Why, I have no idea. Affection for the lower classes lowers us all."

Again, there was nothing but a noncommittal "Mmm."

Bacon really wasn't worth the trouble of entering this viper's nest. However, Ned found he could not help but stay rooted to the spot and listen.

"I am glad of it if Lord Ashby gets to rusticate today," Countess Churzy tried bravely to change the subject. "He acts so stern and focused—as if a holiday in the country is completely foreign to him."

But Lady Widcoate would not be deterred. "If only I could do away with the other girls as easily as I did away with Mr. Turner, and leave the two of you alone. You would have him sewn up in a few short hours."

Wait—did she say *do away* with Mr. Turner? How had he been done away with?

"I tell you I was positive we were undone when he left the table without taking a bite of it. But then I had the *genius* idea to send it up to his room. Genius, wasn't it?" Lady Widcoate giggled like a girl at school.

"Fanny, I don't know why you do such things."

Countess Churzy sighed, disapproval in her words, if not her voice.

"I do it for you, my dear. But he'll be fine. Just uncomfortable for a little while. With any luck, he'll not only skip today, but dinner tonight too."

An unsettling sense of horror seeped through Ned all the way to his feet.

The tart.

She had sent it up to his room. He had thought it was an attempt to make him feel either guilty or better or both, but really it had been an attempt to poison him with . . . something unpleasant.

And he hadn't taken a single bite of it.

But Miss Baker had.

Suddenly, his feet uprooted from the ground, springing free as if they were three steps ahead of him already.

Damn the bacon—he had to find Miss Baker. Now.

❧

SHE WASN'T IN the schoolroom. He found Henry and Rose under the supervision of a young, stout woman he presumed to be their nanny. Without stopping for an explanation, he bobbed a short bow and ran out as quickly as he had run in.

There was only one place she could be. The reason he hadn't been sure if he'd heard her leave her room was because she had not. He took the steps two, three at a time, up the rickety last flight to the third-floor landing.

And saw Miss Baker standing at the door of her bedroom, hand on the knob, dressed as neat as a pin.

"Miss Baker," he cried, running up to her. When she started at his approach, he remembered why he had to apologize to her in the first place, and slowed, measuring his steps. "You are all right?" he asked, as he reached her side.

"Of course," she said, her voice uncompromising and stiff. "Why wouldn't I be?"

"Because, well . . ." He began to explain. But then he got a good look at her face.

She was pale. Not that that was unusual, she was always pale, but not usually so . . . wan. There was a faint sheen of perspiration on her brow, and her cool blue stare was suddenly quite unfocused.

"Miss Baker?" He asked, "Are you certain you're—"

Then Miss Baker answered his unfinished question definitively. By retching on his shoes.

"Damn," she said hoarsely. "I didn't think I had any left."

And then she fainted.

❧

WOOL SCRATCHED AT her face. A sleeve.

She was in someone's arms. The world spun in dizzying circles as she was lifted from the ground. The ground that she just wanted to sink into, to let gravity hold her in one place and hopefully the spinning would stop.

"No . . ." she said weakly, but she had no ability to physically protest.

"Shh . . ." came that soft tenor. Mr. Turner's voice. Oh, that's right—he had come to her door. Again. Oh, no, he was carrying her? Last night . . . last night he had been rude.

"No," she said again, "you're mean."

"And you weigh no more than a feather," he said,

taking steps with her in his arms. Or at least, that's what she thought he said. The movement made the room spin again.

Then she was no longer in his arms, no longer being scratched by the wool of his coat. Instead, her face was pressed against her cool pillow. Lying down on the bed gave her that gravity she craved, let her feel like the world was settling. She could focus just a little better.

"I cast up accounts. On you," was the only thing she could think of to say.

"You missed most of me—just got the edges of my shoes," he said, pulling a blanket up over her.

"You deserved it."

"Of that there is no doubt," he agreed. "But right now, let's see what we can do to make you comfortable."

His hands went to the buttons at her throat, and her instincts kicked in. She batted at his hands with all the strength she could muster. "How dare you . . ." she said, tears coming to her eyes—amazing, as she was fairly certain she had no fluid left in her body.

"Miss Baker, calm yourself. I am not going to ravage you," he said sternly, pushing her shoulders back into the mattress. Then he undid the top two buttons at the neck of her gown, allowing her to take a deep breath. "Not when you've been poisoned, at least," he added.

"Poisoned?" she asked. Her mind drifting again, she tried desperately to hold on to the thread of the conversation.

He stood, started rooting around the room, looking for something. "Chamber pot?" he asked. She shook her head. There was no way she was letting him see what was in her chamber pot at the moment, hidden in its cabinet. Remnants of a long, unpleasant night. "Water?" was the second question—and she pointed to the pitcher next to her little basin. He looked in and poured out the remaining drops into her small tin cup. She had gone through most of it the night before.

"Here." He sat next to her, pulling her head onto his lap. "Drink this."

She did as she was told, letting the lukewarm liquid trickle down her fiery throat. It was gone all too soon.

"I'll get more," he said. "I overheard Lady Widcoate say it would pass in a day or so. You should be fine, just get some rest."

"No," she cried, trying to sit up. "I have to work. The children . . . the Questioning . . ." she managed, before her strength gave out and she flopped back down on the bed, clinging to it, thankful for its gravity.

If the children missed the Questioning again, she would be out of a job. She had to teach. She had to get up. She had to . . .

"Don't worry," came the gentle tenor from somewhere above her. "I will handle it. I will . . . I will handle everything. You have to get some rest."

"No . . . if I don't . . ." She slid back down against the sheets. "He'll see."

"Who? Sir Nathan?"

"No," she mumbled, her eyes drifting closed. "Ashby."

"You want to impress the earl?" His voice sounded almost amused. Sardonic.

"No," she croaked, letting sweet darkness take over. "He's awful."

She heard him chuckle. "I quite agree."

And then . . . she slept.

13

Sometimes one must wager blindly, and bluff.

The rest of the morning proceeded differently for the various residents of Puffington Arms.

A note was sent from the Earl of Ashby's secretary to Sir Nathan and the earl, detailing that he was not feeling very well and would not be joining them today. While the earl expressed concern at this, intent upon visiting his friend to find out what was the matter, or even perhaps writing to his friend Dr. Gray, asking that he come all the way from Peterborough and attend them, he was assured by Lady Widcoate and the countess that nothing was the matter that a little time and rest would not cure.

"Some people must adjust to the country," Countess Churzy said in her floating tones, before taking the earl's arm and guiding him into escorting her from the breakfast room.

Deciding—with the help of the countess—that

perhaps it was best to let business wait until Mr. Turner was able to join them, the earl acquiesced to his host's suggestion of a shooting party. But since the secretary would not be available to act as loader, and indeed the vast majority of the uneven party was female, the shooting party was modified into an archery outing, and the girls, Miss Minnie Rye in particular, rushed to prepare themselves to display this particular ladylike skill, while Sir Nathan grumbled and called for his carriage to take him to Hollyhock's pub, as Lady Widcoate had predicted.

Later in the afternoon, Miss Minnie was heard to be proud of her victories, but sad over the fact that she was not permitted to shoot a rifle instead of just arrows.

"But I am a much better shot with a rifle!" she was heard saying. "You know, Aunt. You taught me."

But Mrs. Rye shushed her before the earl could hear that she had ever encouraged such vicious pursuits in her niece.

Elsewhere in the house that morning, Danson received a note of his own. He had been thrown into disarray already by the earl's decision to rusticate about the property that day. This required an entirely different suit of clothes, and he was attempting to dress the man—who some maids said was objecting to the practice, most curious!—when he received said missive. It was read with alarm and then, a sigh. This outward sign of exasperation was egregiously out of character. Apparently, the valet had not gotten much in the way of sleep last night, as he had been up late with some errant laundry.

Upon being released by the recalcitrant earl, he

made his way up to the third floor, where he was seen coming and going, bearing a stock of clean towels and water from the kitchens. When questioned, he simply said he was on orders from his employer. As the other servants of Puffington Arms were not, one might say, well trained, they took the valet from an aristocratic background at his imperious word and asked no more questions about it.

And finally, young Henry and Rose Widcoate were surprised to learn that they would be receiving instruction from a substitute tutor today—Mr. Turner.

And the subject? Horses.

Of course, Miss Phoebe Baker knew none of this. No, Miss Baker slept. And when she woke up, it was to be greeted by someone she most certainly did not expect.

"Mr . . . Mr. Danson?" she said as she came to, blinking away sleep.

"Miss Baker," the stiff valet said, bowing slightly at the waist before continuing to arrange things in her room. "I am much relieved to see that you are looking better."

Indeed, she was not the only thing looking better. Her rooms, as tidy as she normally kept them, had undergone a disheveling the night before during her illness, and she was deeply embarrassed that anyone—Mr. Turner especially—had seen them that way. But now the sheets she rested upon were freshly laundered. The window was thrown open wide to allow in a breeze; the fresh, sweet air replacing the sour stench that had taken hold the night before. The only thing out of its neat place was her gown, lying folded over her soft reading chair.

She looked down at herself—she was in only her chemise and petticoats.

"Why is my . . . Why are you . . . What time is it?" She struggled to sit up.

"The answers to your questions are thus: Your gown is off because you were in danger of sweating through it. I removed it in as delicate a manner as possible. Although delicacy is not often required in a material that coarse. I also loosened your corset, but I am unfamiliar with most women's clothes, therefore you might have to reset the laces." He ticked up a second finger. "I am here because the . . . because your Mr. Turner requested that I assist you today. Apparently, your illness, had it become known, would cast a bad light on you both."

Her illness. What was it that Mr. Turner had been saying before she was tucked back into bed? She had been poisoned. And for some reason it was his fault. But he overheard Lady Widcoate saying it would pass . . .

And suddenly, all the pieces fit together. The tart. She had eaten all of it, and it was meant for Mr. Turner— whom Lady Widcoate had decided to hate.

Her eyes flitted to Mr. Danson's, and he nodded sagely.

"My discretion is, of course, absolute. Your Mr. Turner trusts in it, and so, I hope, will you."

And discretion was absolutely necessary. If Lady Widcoate discovered she had been ill, she would know the cause and then ask questions about how the tart came into her possession. Which would, in turn, likely result in her firing for having the immoral turpitude to entertain a man alone.

"And the answer to your third question is that the

time is just past tea, and thus, you should try to eat this."

Danson lifted a tray from her small desk, which bore hot tea and what looked like a simple broth with some bread. Just the sight of the plain bread made her stomach flip over, but perhaps she could try the broth. Her mouth positively watered for some . . . well, for some water.

She struggled to a sitting position. Danson, meanwhile, directed his gaze to somewhere above her head until she realized that the blanket had slipped down, revealing the top of her chemise. Its thick sturdiness did not remove the inappropriateness of his seeing it, so she quickly tucked the blanket up under her chin.

Danson gave her a stiff nod and settled the tray across her lap.

"May I avail myself of this chair?" he asked, lowering himself to the chair, his posture still completely perfect.

Which made her smile. Ever so slightly, but she was in no shape to make the effort to hide her amusement. But if Danson noticed, he was still the consummate professional and said nothing.

The tea was weak. The broth was delicious. And together, they filled Phoebe to the point that she could again think properly. And when she did, she thought . . .

"Oh, my goodness!" she cried, her head coming up from the soup. Her eyes flew to the window. Amber beams shot straight through, parallel to the floor. Sunset. "It's not after tea! It's nearly evening!"

"Yes," Danson replied. "And we consider your waking now to be a fortuitous bit of luck. Although, with your Mr. Turner, luck seems to be in his purview."

"But I must . . . I have the children. They have to be presented to their parents tonight and I . . . I have to teach them *something* today."

She tried to get out of bed, but the tray, the tucked-up blanket, and her own surprising dizziness stopped her before Danson could even rise out of the chair.

"Now, do not strain yourself. For I have not told you the most amazing bit of information." He leaned forward, took her spoon, and made her take another, measured sip of broth. "Your Mr. Turner has taken care of the children's education for the day. As long as you are able to stand and present them, they will be able to answer questions asked."

Of the hundreds of questions running through Phoebe's head at that moment—*He spent the day with Rose and Henry? What did they learn? How am I going to get out of bed?*—the only one that popped out of her mouth was . . .

"Why do you keep calling him that?"

"Calling who what?"

"*My* Mr. Turner."

A fleeting smile painted the valet's lips. "Well, he is most certainly not *mine*."

Phoebe swallowed. "He mentioned that he was uncomfortable with children. I take it his actions today are . . . out of character for him?"

Danson seemed to consider that for a moment. "I can tell you this, ma'am. I have known your Mr. Turner for many years, and I can say very truthfully that I have never seen him do anything quite like this. It really is—as I said—quite amazing."

At that moment, the quite amazing topic of conversation burst into the room, after the briefest of knocks.

"Danson, is she— Oh! Miss Baker," he said as he ducked his head into the small space and peered around the door.

Phoebe, who had been previously unconcerned with her appearance except for Danson's sense of propriety, held that blanket to her chin for dear life. Which must have looked supremely odd with the spoon jammed in her mouth.

But that was nothing compared with how Mr. Turner looked.

His dark hair stuck up on his head in a hundred different directions, and there were patches of mud caked into it. There were patches of mud everywhere else too. His shoes in particular seemed to be caked in the stuff, going up his stockinged feet to his ankles.

But he seemed to have little care for his state and was much more interested in hers.

"You are awake! And eating—oh, that is good news." He wiped a hand across his brow, leaving a streak of mud. "Best news I've had all day. Are you feeling better? You seem to have more color, although you're still quite pale. But then again, you are normally pale. Do you think you feel up to tonight? I don't know what we'll do if you do not, but—"

"*Ahem.*" Danson cleared his throat conspicuously. "If you do not mind, sir, I believe Miss Baker will be much more able to rise and face what comes next if she does not have to answer a string of redundant questions."

Mr. Turner stared openmouthed at the exceptionally nonplussed valet for a moment, before snapping to. "Right. You are sure you are feeling well enough, Miss Baker?"

She opened her lips to answer, but Danson again had the better of her. The better of them both.

"I will make certain Miss Baker is presentable and ready to meet the children in the nursery before they head downstairs." He raked his eyes up and down Mr. Turner in severe, pointed judgment. "And you should make yourself presentable as well, sir."

Mr. Turner looked down at himself then, a spray of dust coming off his head in the jerky movement and falling onto her floor.

Danson gave Mr. Turner a look of such reproach that Phoebe was surprised he did not shrivel up and die on the spot. But Mr. Turner was apparently a more resilient creature than she took him for, or he was more used to Danson, because he simply gave a snort and that lopsided smile.

"Well, perhaps I had better bathe myself. Although Rose and Henry beat me to it—they were quite dirty as well. Oh—you don't have to worry about them, Miss Baker. Nanny has promised to be most discreet about the fact that you were under the weather today. She mentioned that she owed you for her 'afternoon walks'—and I decided to let her keep what that meant to herself."

Phoebe couldn't help a small smile. Nanny was young, and her mind still tended toward romance. She had a beau in Midville, and on a few occasions had relied on Phoebe to occupy her charges with lessons while she took a stroll with him. Of all the servants who had come and gone, this nanny had made it almost six months already, mostly due to the teamwork principle she and Phoebe had managed to establish.

"Well, I should go, then," Mr. Turner said. "The pond gets chillier the lower the sun." He shot her a rueful smirk at that . . . which he was almost certain she reciprocated.

"Ah—and I'm very glad you are feeling better, Miss Baker. You would not believe how glad." Mr. Turner gave one last wipe to his brow, and then ducked out of the room as astonishingly as he had entered it.

Danson turned to her, his unruffled posture effortlessly intact. He said not a word out of place, but his look to her spoke volumes.

You see? it said. *Your Mr. Turner.*

Instead of heeding these annoyingly unspoken facial expressions, Phoebe decided it was her turn to actually speak.

"If you had been my ladies' maid or governess growing up, I would have gotten into either a great deal less trouble, or a great deal more," she said to him, earning an approving nod.

"Of that I have no doubt."

"Well, then," she said, her voice stronger than it had been. She could rest no longer—not with Mr. Turner's harried looks and children she needed to prepare.

She handed the tray of broth and weak tea back to Danson and swung her feet out onto the floor. "I think I had better get out of this bed, and see just how much trouble my Mr. Turner has gotten us all in."

14

*When bluffing, take care
to know what is in your hand.*

That was amazing," Phoebe breathed out as she came to the second-floor landing. "Simply amazing."

"It was?" Rose asked from her left.

She looked down at her, unable to hide her happiness, her relief. "Oh, Rose. I could kiss you."

Rose made a face. Apparently, she had reached the age when the idea of affection became unsavory. But it did not change the sentiment.

The children had been miraculous that evening. They had marched in to the drawing room, and stared down the assembly, and withstood their father's questioning . . . without a blink.

They had been different from the moment she had met with them in the nursery. Rose had been rambunctious as always, and Henry had been relatively quiet, normal too. But they had a determination about them.

As if today they had decided that the Questioning was not something to be dreaded. Instead, it was fun.

"What is it that you learned today, Henry my boy?" their father had bellowed as they approached him. For once, Henry did not fidget or look at his toes. Instead, he gave a familiar half smile.

Oh, dear—what had Mr. Turner been teaching them?

"I learned that there are a number of berries that grow wild in the woods that you should never eat," Henry said proudly. "Like the yew berry, the holly berries, and sometimes even blackberries. I didn't draw pictures, though."

Henry, blessed child that he was, smiled in all innocence at his parents. His father looked quizzical.

His mother looked white as a sheet.

"B-blackberries, poisonous? What on earth have you been teaching, Miss Baker?"

All eyes in the room shot to Phoebe. She felt her knees buckle but remained upright. The day in bed and bowl of broth had made her feel better, but she was still weak. And now, under scrutiny.

"Ah . . . we studied some botany this afternoon," she said, managing to keep the "apparently" at the end of the sentence under her breath.

"But blackberries . . ." Lady Widcoate sputtered.

"I believe it is true that some are not suitable for human consumption, Lady Widcoate," Mr. Turner then interjected, from where he was standing alone in the corner. "I speak from experience."

Lady Widcoate had then gone a very mottled color, and it was obvious that she wanted to say something, but was saved by her more gracious sister, the countess.

"Well, Henry, I think that is a very good thing to know, which berries not to eat." She smiled at him, and Sir Nathan nodded, dismissing his son. "However much it might be better for young gentlemen to simply eat berries from the kitchen, not the woods," she added, earning a smile from the other young ladies assembled and an admiring one from the earl.

"And you, Rose?" Sir Nathan called. "What new and interesting thing did you learn today?"

Rose, for once not bouncing on her toes, glanced only for a moment toward Mr. Turner before she looked her father directly in the eye and said, "I learned that if I want to learn to ride a horse, I should ask my father, not my mother."

The entire room fell silent at that. Phoebe's eyes went wide, as she could feel any color that she might have gained drain from her face all the way down to her feet, rooting them to the floor.

But Rose simply stood there, waiting for the answer.

And then the most amazing thing of all happened. Sir Nathan laughed.

He threw his head back in a guffaw so loud, it shook the crystal on the gaudy chandelier above their heads.

"Miss Baker." The hot-faced Lady Widcoate turned her fierce glare on her. "What have you been teaching them?"

"I'm not . . . That is to say, I am so sorry, I have no idea . . ."

"She's teaching them to experience the world!" Sir Nathan interrupted her objections. "And a good thing too. I had feared that keeping them with a governess would make them too bookish. But now I see you were right, my love."

"I . . . I was?" Lady Widcoate turned an astonished gaze to her husband. "But . . . horses. Surely it is too dangerous, and Rose is too young . . ."

But for once, Sir Nathan was not going to let his wife's fears for their children coddle them. He waved his hand, cutting off all her objections.

"The girl is of an age, my love, and is sitting well on a horse not a ladylike refinement?" And, for the first time in as long as Phoebe had been in Puffington Arms' employ, she saw Lady Widcoate acquiesce to her husband—really, truly give in! Sitting back, she let her husband take control.

"We were about Rose's age when we learned," the countess comforted her sister.

"Well, Rose, I suppose it is time you learned to ride," her father said, leaning back in his seat. "You'll begin your lessons as soon as we find an appropriate teacher."

Rose's face then broke into the most beatific smile, and she rushed forward with her arms spread wide.

"Oh, really, Papa? Hooray! Er . . ." She had stopped herself from bouncing and forced a deep, gracious curtsy. "I mean, thank you, Father."

After that, the children were dismissed, and Phoebe escorted them out of there as quickly as possible. If Lady Widcoate stared daggers after them, she did not see it. Indeed, Lady Widcoate seemed to be taken aback by her husband's countering her own hopes. All Phoebe could do was be grateful that they had overtly pleased one parent and gotten out of there with her employment, and secrets, intact.

"How about me? Could you kiss me?" Henry was asking from her other side, pulling on her skirt. His thumb had not gone into his mouth once all evening, she suddenly realized.

"Yes, I could kiss you too, Henry. But I shan't, to save your sister alarm."

"How about me?" The honeyed tenor came from below.

She did not need to turn to know who it was, but did so anyway.

Mr. Turner was looking up at them, considerably cleaner than the last time she had seen him. Pond water did him a world of good, it seemed.

His dark eyes were joking, that lopsided smile playing about his mouth. Hopefully they were joking, she thought—otherwise his question was more remarkably awkward than anything he had done the previous evening.

"Rose, Henry . . ." She bent down. "You have both done marvelously this evening. Go to Nanny now, she'll have your dinner waiting."

"Just beware of any berry tarts," Mr. Turner admonished, and shot them both a wide grin before they scurried off.

She watched them until they disappeared down the hall, and then turned back to Mr. Turner. Who had once again managed to sneak up on her, and was now standing directly in front of her.

And as he was a step or two below her, they were actually eye to eye.

"How did you manage that?" she asked, tilting her head to one side. "Riding lessons for Rose."

He shrugged and ran his hands through his hair. "It was a guess."

"A guess?"

"Sir Nathan is a man surrounded by women. Henry is too young to take part in his interests yet, so he has no one to share them with. Thus, anytime anyone pays the slightest attention to one of his passions—hunting or the bathing retreat—he is eager to delve into it. Regardless of gender."

"And I told you Sir Nathan liked to ride. Or used to." She nodded with understanding. "But Rose . . . she has never spoken to her father with such . . . directness."

"All I did was tell Rose to pretend she was asking for something she had already received, like an earl or countess would."

Phoebe sighed. "Still, if he had said no . . . it seems like quite the gamble."

But he waved that away, jokingly. "Only if you worry about consequences."

"It seems as if the consequences are that you will have to teach her."

That had been the final amazing thing, the icing on the berry tart. When Sir Nathan declared that a suitable riding instructor must be found, Lord Ashby had recommended, of all people, Mr. Turner.

"For a secretary, he's the best man I know with horses," he had said. "I have no doubt he would be able to occupy the children and instruct Rose on the basics quite well."

A look had passed between Mr. Turner and the earl, a sort of challenge. But then Mr. Turner simply cocked up that eyebrow and happily agreed.

"I'm pleased to be her teacher," Mr. Turner was saying to Phoebe. "But you might have to give me a primer on best practices for dealing with eight-year-olds."

A qualm went through her. While she was grateful for Mr. Turner's assistance today, having him teach Rose to ride would only throw him into her company more. And she was not certain how she felt about that.

Damn it all, before the Questioning, she'd had such a good speech planned too.

She was going to thank him for his help today, although the difficulty was mostly his doing. She would then magnanimously decide that any of his altruistic actions today would serve to cancel out his more base actions of the night before, thus calling them even, and they would part on good terms—he back to the world of land surveys and business deals, and she to her teaching. They would actively avoid crossing paths in the future.

But those eyes . . . those eyes were playful, and pleased. And that lopsided smile was an adorable charm that told her he had every intention of getting away with . . . something.

And all she wanted was to lose herself in both for a little while.

So, instead of saying what she had intended—and letting him off any hook—she said the first words that popped into her head.

"Why did you do it?"

"Because I thought Rose might like to learn to—"

"That's not what I meant."

"Wh-what did you mean, then?" His smile faltered slightly.

"Why did you kiss me last night?"

"Oh." His smile slipped completely now, as red stained his tanned cheeks. "That."

"Yes, that."

"It was stupid," he confessed. If he had been wearing a hat, it would have been in hand at that moment.

"Thank you ever so," she drawled, and watched him blush further at her sarcasm.

"I was overwhelmed by the moment," he tried, and she let her eyebrow go to the roof. "I was! There was candlelight, and a tart, and I was surrounded by beauty."

"And it was freezing, and the tart was poisoned, and no one can see beauty by two candles. Come, Mr. Turner, after the rigors of today, the very least you could do is be honest with me."

He seemed befuddled by the idea of telling the truth, until he simply blurted out, "It was a bet!"

"A bet?" she asked.

"A wager," he clarified, "with the earl."

"I see," she said, her entire body going cold. The earl. The earl was somehow wagering . . . on her?

"No, allow me to explain." He took a deep breath. "The earl has, for some time, described me as a stick-in-the-mud. Boring and businesslike."

"I would never think of you as boring, Mr. Turner. Or businesslike."

"I agree completely."

"Pushy, yes. Overeager. But not boring."

His brow came down. "All right, I deserve that. But the wager was that I could not . . . convince a young lady to kiss me while we were here. And apparently, he was right."

She looked him square in the eye.

"I did not . . . convince you. I took advantage. As you said. It was low and ungentlemanly and I must beg your forgiveness."

She considered him for a moment. A long moment. An apparently unbearable moment, because he began to fidget under her stare, much like her charges.

"All right," she finally said.

"All right?" he replied, unsure.

"All right. That explanation I believe, at least. What are the stakes of the wager?"

He looked confused for a moment. "Er . . . pride, mostly?"

"So, nothing too expensive, then."

He exhaled a short laugh, relieved. And then so did she. She let her dimples show, regardless of who and how she was supposed to be.

She brought her gaze back to his. And found him staring at her, in the most unusual way. As if she had managed, with one simple laugh, to render him dumbstruck.

Which was nonsense, of course. She had never rendered anyone dumbstruck, and certainly not since taking up the mantle of earning her living.

"So . . ."

"So . . ." he countered. His feet not moving, not turning back to leave. He was content to stay there.

As content, it seemed, as she was.

"I . . . fear you will be missed, Mr. Turner," she tried.

"Really? I'm not." He shrugged. "They have all spent the day together, shooting arrows and sipping lemonade, and are much more content reliving newfound jokes with each other than they are with what I spent my day doing."

"What did you spend your day doing?" she asked. "You were covered in dirt."

He shot her a wicked grin. "I tried very hard to remember all the maths and rules for proper grammar that I thought you would be teaching the children . . . then I just took them into the woods to go exploring."

"Exploring?"

"After a stop at the stables, where Rose convinced me of her dire need to pet Abandon's nose, of course. All children need woods to explore. Places to make forts and wage wars and find trouble. There are remnants of an old keep in those woods, did you know?" His eyes lit up with childlike enthusiasm. "I remember when I was young we used to . . ." He paused, pulling out a cloth from his sleeve and coughing into his hand. "That is, near where I grew up there were some ruins too, which I used to declare myself king of on a semiweekly basis."

She was suddenly assaulted by a vision of a young Mr. Turner, scampering over logs and woods and old stones, remarkably dirty, still with that mischievous smile. She had no doubt that he had excelled at finding trouble, and laughing it off.

And at some point that must have changed. He was no longer able to laugh things off. And something in the way he had acted when they first met, trying hard to be pleasing, and failing . . . he seemed to mourn it as if its loss were recent.

She knew what it was to lose like that. And to have to find your ground again.

But instead of contemplating a young Mr. Turner,

and analyzing the current version overmuch, she let her eyes fall to something that, without the awkwardness of the conversation, would not have captured her attention.

"Is that . . . my handkerchief?"

He looked down at the cloth in his hand, an old piece of threadbare linen with a simple identifying *PB* stitched into one corner.

"Yes! You'll have to forgive me . . . I stole it from you this morning to clean off my shoes when you . . . well, you remember that part?"

She blushed furiously, closed her eyes as she nodded. "Yes, I remember that part."

"Anyway"—he cleared his throat—"I washed it. In the pond, but washed it still. I meant to return it to you, but forgot and just stuck it in my pocket."

He held it out to her.

She eyed it ominously. "There is no need. You can feel free to keep it. Or dispose of it."

"Really?" he asked, curiously. "I . . . forgive me, but you cannot have drawers of handkerchiefs to spare."

True, but she also did not have a desire to keep a pond-water-and-vomit handkerchief. "Yes, but that is a scrap of linen from one of Lady Widcoate's old petticoats, repurposed. I will not miss it."

"Oh, well, then." He looked confused, but then with a shrug, shoved the cloth back into his pocket. "Brilliant. Marvelous."

"I should head back," she said suddenly. "I confess, the Questioning took up more of my strength than I thought. I must lie down again."

"Do you need help? I'll escort you upstairs."

His hand was at her back in a moment. It was meant

as kindness, just the smallest pressure, to help hold her up. But it did something strange to her nerves. It made every tired joint and muscle in her body suddenly awake. Through the wool of her gown, she could feel the heat of his palm, the gentle strength of his fingers.

She could feel it as surely as if he had been touching her naked skin.

"That's not necessary," she said, jerking back in surprise. His hand dropped, a shocked look crossing his face. As if he realized the inappropriateness of the touch. As if his skin burned too.

Then her eyes flitted to over his shoulder. He turned, and saw the Earl of Ashby, standing downstairs in the doorway to the drawing room, clearly newly arrived, and not pleased with the scene.

She could feel her body freeze at the sight of the man. And the quizzical look this earned from Mr. Turner.

Indeed, it was time to leave.

"Thank you," she whispered, "for your help today."

"It was my pleasure, Miss Baker." He bowed to her.

She did not let her expression shift from the plain politeness of a governess, but still, a single eyebrow lifted an inch at that.

"All right, perhaps it wasn't 'a pleasure' per se. I had mud in places I don't want to contemplate, but . . . at least I wasn't bored." He smiled as he came up.

She gave a short curtsy.

"Now, that, Mr. Turner, I believe."

❧

"YOU'RE WASTING YOUR time," John Turner said from the base of the stairs. Ned was not pleased, nor surprised, that he had been there. Out of everyone in that drawing room, only Turner would have noticed or cared that he was gone.

"Hello there. My day was very interesting. I nearly got poisoned by a tart last night and spent today in the woods trying to wrangle rambunctious children. How was yours?" Ned began nonchalantly as he descended the stairs, hands in his pockets, as if he hadn't a care in the world.

"Less interesting than yours, I dare say," Turner replied honestly. "You are wasting your time," he repeated. "With the governess."

"Am I? How?"

"She does not meet the standards laid out at the beginning of the wager." Turner's voice was a low rumble, but there was an edge to it.

"I believe the requirements boil down to someone gently reared, am I right?" On Turner's slow nod, Ned shrugged with ill-contained relish. "Miss Baker was gently reared. So much so, in fact, she attended the exclusive Mrs. Beveridge's School. Her circumstances may have changed, but that does not alter her background."

Turner's eyes narrowed. "But that doesn't mean that—"

"Actually, I feel that Miss Baker is very much the type of woman that a secretary would court. Far more likely than, say, a fortune-hunting countess."

Turner did not take that statement with his usual cynical silence. No, instead he closed the distance between them, leaning in to Ned's face with a sneer.

"Don't ever talk that way about Leticia," he growled.

Ned blinked in shock. For Turner to talk to him that

way, either he had fallen too well into the role of the earl, or . . . or the Countess Churzy had really gotten under his skin.

To snap Turner out of it, Ned hardened his gaze and voice. "You forget yourself. Remember who you truly are. And who I truly am. And then take two steps back."

Turner pulled a long breath in, which he apparently needed to bring himself back from acting like an earl with the actual earl. He took the requested steps backward, but kept his eyes on Ned.

"My apologies," he said stiffly. "I am aware of what she is, you know. Her clothes, though stylish, have been turned out from an earlier season. She pointedly does not talk about her marriage or her recent past. And you could not have been so delightful a child that all she wants out of a connection to the earl is enjoyable reminiscences."

"I am glad you are aware. She is a barnacle. Prettiest barnacle I've ever seen, of course," Ned replied, his eyebrow inching up at Turner's mutinous look. Bloody hell, the man was about to forget himself three seconds after remembering. He had the attention span of a fish. "And there is no reason not to bask in her attentions. I simply request that you don't do anything I cannot undo."

Turner shot him a look. "She is the only person here who does not make me feel the weight of her expectations."

"Do any of those expectations include telling fanciful renditions of the Battle of Waterloo?" Ned grunted.

But Turner simply shook his head. "Fanciful? You thought my version fanciful?"

Ned hesitated. If he'd been Henry's age, he would have simply crossed his arms over his chest and started staring at his toes. Made uncomfortable by a simple question. Instead, he did what he always did. Squashed the feeling down and returned to his normal, satisfied self.

"Fanciful or not, it matters little. But I wager those earlish expectations made your day ever so enjoyable."

Turner's mouth twitched in a rueful grimace as he glanced to the side. "Oh, yes, a glorious time. Mr. Fennick and the vicar from Hollyhock came to join us in our leisure today. It was too bad you were feeling unwell. I was treated to a long recitation of Mr. McLeavey's hunting prowess. He apparently shot a buck when he was five years old, and hopes to inherit the family lodge one day. And Mr. Fennick kept edging forward, asking questions about how we found the cottage and . . ." Then, "There is an awful lot of attention paid to an earl."

Ned nodded tentatively, unsure of what Turner was saying.

"And everyone looks to you for . . . things."

Ned cracked a smile. "Things and things on top of things. But when we first arrived, you seemed to enjoy it."

"Yes, well . . ." Turner coughed, his eyes drifting back to the dull cacophony floating from the drawing room beyond the door. "That was three days ago."

Ned let his own attention drift to the stairs, and the echo of a conversation held there, not minutes ago. For the first time in a very, very long time, Ned would much rather go upstairs to his rooms instead of joining the fun at dinner. Would much rather spend time with one person than a dozen.

One particular person, who teased him when he deserved it, and had a braid of blond hair that went to her elbows when let down from her bun.

"And what a difference three days makes. For us both."

Turner must have noticed the way Ned's attention tended, because he snapped out of what could only be called his self-pitying reverie and again focused on Ned. And the competition at hand.

"I still say you are wasting your time with the governess. You won't win that way."

"And why do you think that?" Ned asked, again putting his hands in his pockets.

"Because, much like overburdened and debt-ridden secretaries, women in Miss Baker's position do not have the luxury of indulging in romance." Turner smirked, triumph written all over his face. "She may tolerate your company but she won't encourage your attentions. She cannot afford to."

Ned smiled, enjoying the feeling of having Turner on the defensive. Ever since this wager had been laid down—goodness, only, what, five days ago?—Ned had been the one spinning in circles. Now, for the first time, he was the one who felt like he had the advantage.

"Be that as it may, Miss Baker's position didn't stand in the way of her giving me this."

He pulled his hand out of his pocket and flourished the little piece of linen with the tiny stitched *PB* in the corner, which had cleaned his shoes that morning. "Just now. She told me to keep it. And I believe it qualifies as a token, freely given—or, rather, the first of the required items I must gather." He couldn't help a ferocious smile at a wordless Turner's stunned face. "Since

I'll be teaching Rose to ride, I daresay I will be spending a great deal more time with Miss Baker. Thanks to you. And, with a dance at the end of the week, the second and third requirements won't be far behind." He let his smile drop. "I might be better at being you than you think."

Ned made sure that Turner got an eyeful before he neatly folded the little square and gently placed it back in his pocket. Then, with the swagger of a man without a care in the world, he moved past Turner and toward the drawing room door.

"Shall we head in? I fear they are waiting on us."

But Turner was lost in thought, staring at the spot where Ned had stood, his posture unchanged from the moment of seeing that handkerchief.

"Miss Baker . . . you say she went to Mrs. Beveridge's School?"

"Yes," Ned replied, slightly impatient. Now that he had figuratively rubbed Turner's nose in the handkerchief, his stomach was beginning to growl. He was hungry, damn it.

"And her first name starts with a *P*?"

"I assume so, given her initials."

"Then this is going to be a more difficult campaign than you know." Turner faced him, a knowing grin spreading across his features. "You've chosen the worst possible person to woo."

"Why?"

"You should likely be asking Miss Baker that." The grin grew sharklike, ferocious. "Ask Miss Baker why she despises the Earl of Ashby."

15

*Knowing what is in another person's hand
can be a boon—or destroy one's strategy.*

ou said something the other day."

"Did I?" Miss Baker didn't look at him. She was staring off into the distance, her eyes following Rose and Henry while their eyes followed the horse being led around the field.

It was Abandon and, as it was the earl's horse, the children were allowed only to watch from a safe distance as Kevin the groom led him in circles around the field, giving him a bit of exercise. Again, Turner had decided that the earl and his party would stay at Puffington Arms for a day of relaxation, and therefore Abandon, a very finely tuned Thoroughbred, was again not ridden. Kevin might be overworked, but he knew where his bread was buttered. And therefore the earl's horse got some fresh air, and Rose—having earned points with her father the other night for her forthrightness—got to watch without fear of recrimination from her mother, and under the eye of her new riding master.

"Mr. Turner, are you ever going to let Rose sit on a horse?" she asked.

"Eventually," he replied to the abrupt change of subject. "When my heart can take the fear."

It had been two full days since their meeting on the stairs. Ned had wanted to approach Miss Baker earlier with his questions, but he needed to ease into it. Recent events having been so overwhelming and dramatic, forcing his questions on Miss Baker might make her back away. No—he needed her to see him as nonthreatening. An equal.

And he wanted to make certain she had fully recovered from her bout of blackberry tart first.

This was made easier by the fact that she now had more time in the afternoon to herself, as—after their morning schoolroom lessons—Rose and Henry were left in Ned's care for their riding lessons.

Which were terrifying.

"Now, when you first touch a horse, make sure he can see you," Ned told them at their first lesson. Kevin was lending assistance, holding the reins of Turner's sturdy, gentle mare and nodding at appropriate intervals. "Otherwise you'll startle him. Touch him on the neck or the flank. Don't come up on him from behind . . . and no pulling on the tail, Rose!"

Rose seemed to have no ability to concentrate and just wanted to rush forward and do everything *now*, while Henry hung back, watching wide-eyed. He spent the first lesson just telling them how to properly touch a horse. He spent the second lesson making sure they knew the names and correct use of all a horse's equipment.

Each day, Miss Baker had brought the children out to him in the afternoon, and then returned a couple of hours later to take them inside for their baths. These few moments were all that he allowed himself to see Miss Baker during those days. Except for a time or two he'd stolen a few minutes with Miss Baker, and those moments he found . . . illuminating.

Such as the day after their conversation on the stairs, when they had first made the exchange of children. Rose and Henry took off for the stables, eager to see the horses, leaving Ned and Miss Baker some precious moments alone.

"Do you have any advice for me on my first day?" he'd asked her, trying not to sound nervous.

"Never let them see your fear," she replied dryly.

He smiled at that, and made to lean on the stable door frame, which was so overcome with curlicues and embellishment that it was a miracle Kevin the groom was able to shut the door. As it was, a piece of the plaster broke off in Ned's hand as he put his weight on it.

"Oh, Lord!" he cried, trying to fit the piece back into its spot and watching it fall to the ground each time. "Lady Widcoate is certain to blame this on me."

"To be fair, it is your doing." Miss Baker laughed.

"Well, at least I gave you your moment of absurdity for the day." He stuck the piece of plaster behind a bit of hay, hoping no one would notice. "Or Lady Widcoate did. Honestly, I do not know why Sir Nathan allowed her passion for decoration to travel all the way to the stables."

But Miss Baker had simply turned thoughtful. "I do not find Lady Widcoate as bad as all that."

Ned's brow went up. "This is a woman who tried to poison you."

"No, she tried to poison *you*," Miss Baker corrected. Then, "Do you know why Lady Widcoate became so enthusiastic about decoration?"

He shook his head.

"I was told by the old butler, before his son began earning enough in the Midville mine that he could retire. It was a long time, and a great deal of struggle, for Lady Widcoate to bring her children into the world." She looked off in the distance for a moment. "She'd had no one to talk to, her sister already gone and married. And she turned to decoration to fill her life."

Ned thought about it for a moment. Yes, Lady Widcoate would have been married nearly a decade before Rose was born. For a young wife, it must have been a devastating wait. It would also explain why she was overly protective of them, not wanting them to traipse through the woods or learn to ride or do anything that could hurt them.

"Why did you tell me that?" Ned asked quietly.

Miss Baker gave a slight sad smile. "Because I have found that when someone irks you, it is best to remember that they are human." Then she dropped a small curtsy and turned to go. "And it's also useful to remember with small children."

He had spent all that day thinking about what she had said—a circumstance that Miss Baker had, in an astonishingly short period of time, made a habit with him.

And then there was the evening. She was just down the hall from him on the third floor, after all. It was too tempting to simply walk down to her door, and . . .

No. Given how he had acted last time, how abominably he had treated her, approaching her room, at night, while she was alone was the last thing he should be doing.

And yet he felt sort of compelled to do something . . . what was the word?—*nice* for Miss Baker.

"Who is it?" came the astonished voice from the other side of the door when he knocked.

"It's Mr. Turner," he returned. "I . . . I don't want you to let me in or anything of that nature. I simply wanted to give you this lemon cake."

There was a pause. "A lemon cake?"

"Yes," he responded cheerily. "They served them with dinner. Did you have one already?"

Another pause. "No."

"Excellent. I should like you to have this one. I made Cook set it aside."

"Mr. Turner, do you mean to tell me you are trying to ply me with sweets in my room alone at night—again?" Her voice was crisp, a rebuke.

"Well, when you put it like that . . ." he mumbled. And then he could swear he heard her laughing. And it gave him heart.

"I know you like sweets, given the way you made yourself sick on that blackberry tart—"

"There were extenuating circumstances."

"I also know you don't receive many of them. I should like you to have this one. To say thank you, for your advice with the children today." He shrugged and put the plate down at the door. "Also, I took a bite out of it to make sure it's not laced with ipecac."

"How very thoughtful." He swore he could hear the smile in her voice.

"I am exceedingly thoughtful." When no reply came, he simply turned on his heel and let his footsteps put her at ease. "I bid you good night, Miss Baker."

"Good night, Mr. Turner," was the reply.

He had gone to his room then and slowly shut the door. When he opened it again a few minutes later, he was gratified to see that the plate bearing the lemon cake (with only a small bite out of it) had been taken up from its spot on the floor.

That missing plate on the floor allowed him to hope that maybe he had earned back a sliver of her trust. The smaller moments, the glances of humor beneath her façade, made him think that maybe he was even winning her to him.

He was wooing Miss Baker. But not in any way he was accustomed to wooing a woman. He was not offering her flowers or sparkling baubles, but rather, half-eaten lemon cake and small bits of revealing conversation. He was, he realized with a start, getting to know her.

And it must have been working, because today Miss Baker had escorted the children after their luncheon while Abandon was going through his paces, and now she hung back with him for several minutes, letting the afternoon begin to stretch around them.

"You are scared to death of letting them on the horse, aren't you?" She smiled at him.

"I admit it freely." He chuckled. "I know myself to

be a good horseman, but a teacher? Giving over all of my knowledge to someone with the attention span of a mayfly and praying they retain some of it while on a large animal seems . . . hopeful, at best. I've just been repeating ad nauseam all the safety lessons I can remember."

"And now you know the secret of teaching: repetition, ad nauseam."

She smiled again. But not the enigmatic, archaic smile of the governess. This was the full, dimpled smile of the woman beneath the gray wool.

And for some reason . . . she hated him.

She hated the Earl of Ashby.

"But, as I was saying—you said something a few days ago. Just after you fainted." Ned tried the subject again and watched carefully as Miss Baker blushed ever so faintly. But she did not move her eyes from the children, nor hide her face. That she had fainted had been a fact. She accepted it as such.

He cleared his throat and continued. "You said that you hated the Earl of Ashby."

Her face turned to fire at that. Her body stiffened, her breaths became short and shallow. But still she kept her eyes away from him. Kept them where she could keep herself steady.

"And if I did?" she asked, her voice as placid as a still pond.

"I was simply curious. I have been thinking about it since you said it."

In truth he had not been thinking about it since she said it. He had thought that when she said, "He's awful," she was speaking about how sour Turner was.

No, it was not until Turner made his declaration before they went in to dinner that Ned began to think about what possible grudge Miss Baker could have against the earl—well, against *him*, if he was going to be technical about it.

But was it against him? Perhaps his great-uncle had committed the unknown offense. But no—she had frozen upon first setting eyes upon them, days ago, when they encountered her in the road and asked for directions to Puffington Arms. If the slight was committed by his great-uncle, surely she would not have been thrown by the sight of a young man wearing the earl's mantle.

And . . . was it a slight? Something small could not inspire that much hatred. Thinking back on it, every time she had chanced to be in the same room (or lane) as Turner, she had frozen, shut down, hidden. Why, even the first few times she had been in his own presence, she had the same demeanor. He had been tainted by association.

Of course, the association was technically with himself. Which made the whole thing all that more complicated.

But it didn't have to. There was no reason that Miss Baker should ever know his *true* identity, he rationalized to himself, every time that sick, hollow feeling began creeping up on him again. After all, he need only dance with her and learn some intimacy of her, and then he could leave her be.

And then he would win the wager, and be gone.

But it still did not abate his curiosity about why she might hate him.

Er, the earl, that is.

"I have known the earl for a long time. And I know that you and he have never met before this week," Ned tried, after Miss Baker's long silence.

And she was silent still, staring off after her charges. Until she finally spoke.

"How long?"

"How long have I known him?" Ned asked, and she gave a short, single nod. "Since the war."

"Then you must have known him when one Mr. Sharp was in his employ."

Ned could feel his blood run cold, his feet rooting in the spot, as if icicles had stabbed them in place. *He* remembered Mr. Sharp very well. He tried to place where Turner's memory of the man would begin.

"I do know of him. I never met him. He was the old earl's secretary, and then the current earl's for a little while. Until he left his employ and I took over." Yes, that sounded about right.

"I know of him too." She shot a glance his way then, and her clear, sky-blue eyes were as hard as crystal. "For, you see, after he left the earl's employ, he traveled the country, and eventually came to Dorset, where my father lived."

The color that stained her cheeks had drained, leaving her again the pale, hard governess, the persona that she put up like a wall. Dread swept over him. Whatever had happened, this had been the result.

"Mr. Turner," she said suddenly, "I am going to ask a very strange favor of you and I hope you will oblige me."

"Anything that's in my power," he answered immediately.

"I . . . I don't often speak of my father. And I . . .

whenever I had something hard to get through, my father was always there, listening and holding my hand." She turned her gaze to him now, and he was surprised to find it so controlled. Oh, but just behind her eyes was a sea at storm. "Would you mind if—while I told this story—I held your hand?"

Ned didn't know what to say. It was supremely untoward to hold hands in public with any woman, let alone the governess. But he wanted to hear her story. And it seemed . . . she needed help to tell it.

He moved his hand so it covered hers, resting on the fence. To someone looking closely, it was a breach of conduct, but if anyone merely glanced their way, it would not seem as if they were being scandalous.

"You can tell me anything."

And she did.

"My family—my mother's side—was wealthy. But when my mother married my father, they felt she had limited herself. He was a joyful little man who made her happy, but they could not see past his modest fortune and lack of connection," she began, her eyes shifting back to the children, ever vigilant.

"They're fine," he said gruffly, about Henry and Rose.

"Yes," she agreed with a sigh. After a moment, she continued.

"They were a very happy couple. They enjoyed their life in Dorset. But my father wanted me to have the same advantages my mother had been given. My mother worked toward reconciliation with her family and asked that they send me to school. They were generous enough to do so, and off to Mrs. Beveridge's I went.

"I was nearly sixteen when my mother died. Still in school. My mother's family did not really see the point in continuing my education after that, but my father"—her breath hitched, as if she swallowed a tear—"my father was adamant that I continue. So, my father was grief-stricken over his wife, and desperate to support his daughter—perfectly primed when Mr. Sharp came along."

Ned's voice was a dry rasp. "What did he do?"

Miss Baker simply gave the smallest shrug and answered, "Much what he did to others, I suspect. He presented himself as a man of business. He said he had been in service to the Earl of Ashby for over twenty years, and when the new earl had come in he had tried to advise him, but to no avail. So he was now looking for a place to retire, a small cottage would do, and, oh, while he's at it, if you like, he can triple your investments. After all, he had handled the Earl of Ashby's estate. He knew all the tricks." She looked at him again, but this time her eyes were sad. "For so many, it was a dream come true. As it seemed to my father."

Ned could only nod grimly. Mr. Sharp was a part of his history that he had thought done, completed, put away . . . but, as with many memories recently, those put-away things had been unpacking themselves.

Mr. Sharp had been his great-uncle's secretary for as long as Ned had known of his existence. A man with tufts of white hair coming off the side of his head, he'd been smart, always with a kind word for young Ned when he saw him. For a time, Ned had thought he wished *he* was his great-uncle, rather than the stern, counting man who looked severely down upon him.

But when the severance in his great-uncle's will did not live up to what Mr. Sharp expected, the kindly man with the tufted hair let his true colors show.

He was gone, with a sizable portion of Ned's disposable income, before Ned could even settle into his new role as earl.

"How much did he take?" Ned asked. He wished they were standing at the fence line, like Rose and Henry. He could do with a railing to grab on to. And squeeze until his knuckles turned white.

"Everything my father had—everything my mother had left for me." There was a catch in her voice. Her affect was resigned, but this was not easy for her to relive. Ned felt his fingers grip hers tightly—too tightly. He forced himself to gentle his hold.

"But why—how—does the earl figure into this? Mr. Sharp was not his agent at the time."

"It doesn't matter," she said quietly.

"Yes, it does." Ned was shocked by the vehemence in his voice. It did matter, damn it. He needed to know. He needed to know why this one person disliked him. No one ever disliked him—not Lucky Ned, at least— and yet . . . she did. Without ever having met him, she did. She hated him.

"Miss Baker." His voice was a command. "Why?"

"Because he could have prevented it!" Her voice was suddenly fierce, her head whipping around to face him. "Mr. Sharp was most at fault, but he fled, likely to the Continent, we are told. My father bore the next-heaviest weight, and it was too much for him. He . . . drowned. Shortly after. And when I went through his effects, I found a letter from the earl."

Ned's head whipped up. "I never—that is, I never heard about you. From the earl. Are you certain about the letter?"

"Oh, yes." She nodded. "Apparently, my father had been suspicious of Mr. Sharp in those final days, and wrote a letter to his last employer—coincidentally, your current employer. He was advised that Mr. Sharp was by no means to be trusted, and that he had even taken some of the earl's money and fled. Then he asked that my father not tell anyone that sensitive information, because it would be unbecoming to the earl's legacy, and ruin his social standing.

"So the Earl of Ashby's reputation was more important than making Mr. Sharp's treachery known, or prosecuting him, or keeping him from doing the same thing to anyone else."

She sniffled, taking a stuttering breath.

"I couldn't be angry at anyone else, so I was angry with the Earl of Ashby. I wrote him my own letter, telling him that he was to blame for my current lot in life, and that I would never stop hating him." She took one last calming breath, and the shine of tears that had threatened to fall disappeared from her eyes. She was herself again.

Slowly she extricated her hand from under his. He felt the loss keenly.

"And then I forgot all about him, until he showed up here. With you." She turned her face to him again. "Does that satisfy your curiosity?"

Ned looked out into the field. He saw Abandon, enjoying his freedom, the golden sun of the afternoon cutting through the thick summer trees, turning the scene into a tapestry of light and shadow. Rose and Henry leaning against the fence, watching from the road. A secretary and a governess watching from a distance. It was the essence of pastoral peacefulness.

No one looking on could possibly know that a shift of the most dramatic magnitude had just occurred, right beneath their feet.

Ned could only nod dumbly. "I am sorry. Miss Baker, I am so sorry."

"What could you possibly be sorry for?" she asked him, with that funny, tight smile at the corners of her mouth that made her look like she was swallowing a secret. "It was not your fault, Mr. Turner."

❧

JOHN TURNER LIKED to consider himself a straightforward man. He was raised to it, the son of a mill owner and businessman who taught him he would only ever be as good as his word. His leadership during the war had been born out of that forthrightness, and he had men, women, whole families counting on him back in Lincolnshire because he gave his word. To get the mill up and running again. And he would do what he must to make it so.

But he had never counted on being an earl.

The obfuscation and misdirection of the last week had been . . . trying at best. He was not used to the clothes, to the looks everyone gave him, and even though he'd held a command position on the field of battle, everyone here seemed to expect him not to lead . . . but to decide. He was the one everyone deferred to. He was the one they wanted to hold on to.

It was very much against his nature.

But he had to do it. It was the only way.

He had wagered everything on it.

But now, as he stood at the window of the front drawing room looking out onto the road, which bore a dirty and dusty Ned Granville back from his day at the stables, he could feel his chances for success slipping away.

For next to Ned walked the governess, her charges running ahead of them. They did not touch, they did not even look at each other. But they had fallen into step. Together.

Turner could feel his knuckles turn white. "Bloody hell," he breathed.

He could kick himself. That offhand suggestion to Sir Nathan that Ned be the one to teach Rose to ride! Thinking it would force Ned out of the way of the Ryes and Miss Benson, and of course Leticia. Yet, as he learned mere minutes later, the request had simply put Ned into the path of an apparently eligible young woman.

Perhaps Lucky Ned really was the luckiest person in the world.

But there was no possible way he could be allowed to win this wager.

God, when had he become so hard? So serious? When had he let his friendship with Ned Granville crumble into this battle?

There was a time when Ned had been his best friend. And he missed it.

But he was too desperate now to turn back.

He could remember exactly the moment that had led them to this. No, it was not their card game a week ago. Nor was it when he received news of the ship having been lost at sea, bearing his new machinery. Instead, the moment that had led to the current situation—to the wager, to Ned courting a governess, to his wearing Ned's ill-fitting signet ring and overstarched coat—was the first moment. The day five years ago when he had come to London, and called upon the young man—an earl now!—who had saved his life on the battlefield. And, he had hoped, would save his life again.

He remembered the knocker on the door to the Grosvenor mansion—brass polished to a shine, even on such an intemperate day. He used it, and before the dusting of snow on its bridge could even fall to the ground, an officious-looking servant had opened the door. Before he knew it, he was gravely escorted back past the larger rooms into a private study.

Where he found young Ned Granville, Earl of Ashby, tearing his hair out over a pile of papers.

"Captain!" Ned had cried, and come forward immediately, rushing to greet Turner. Although there was a tinge of desperation to his voice.

"Not Captain anymore, my lord," Turner said, with a bow. "Just Mr. Turner now."

"And if you call me 'my lord' I will assume my greatuncle has risen from his grave." Ned tried to smile, but it was weak. "What brings you to London?"

"I have to meet with some bankers about my mill. There . . . was a fire."

"Oh, Cap—I mean, Mr. Turner. I am so sorry."

"A terrible hazard of the business. But now that the war is over, and my father is gone, I must step up to fill his shoes."

"Yes," Ned had agreed solemnly. His eyes went to the empty chair, hidden behind the overrun desk. "Strange, isn't it? Everyone was always so worried about our living through the war, and yet we come home to empty houses."

Turner could only nod in agreement. He then watched as Ned, lost in his own thoughts, went back to the papers in his hands, his usual cheerful attitude sunken.

"Where are you staying?" Ned tried, with a forced smile. "Oh, never mind that, you shall stay here. Danson will have a room fixed up for you. Perhaps we can scare Dr. Gray out of his laboratory in Greenwich, and go out on the town."

"That is very kind," Turner replied, surprised at the generosity. To be sure, Ned had always been generous—but seeing him as an earl put him in a very different light.

An earl who, right now, seemed to be very, very worried about something.

"My l—er, sir. Ned. What is it? I can tell something is wrong."

Ned looked up from the pages—ledger pages, from the quick glance Turner could obtain. "Thank you, my friend. But unless you can decipher columns of numbers, it would be of no use."

Turner took in Ned's desperate resignation and made a decision. He began to unbutton his coat.

"What are you doing?"

"Preparing to decipher columns of numbers," he said, taking the pages out of Ned's hand. Ned's body practically crumpled with relief. "I may not be a fancy

Londoner, but I do know how a business runs. Now, tell me what these are."

He pulled out a pile of short, squarish pages with embossed printing. Ned glanced at them, his brows coming down in anger.

"They are shares in a company. I think. Mr. Sharp, my great-uncle's secretary—whom I inherited—made the purchase. Apparently, I've been purchasing a small sum of shares every month since I became earl, but I've never heard of the company. Sharp has been nowhere to be found for a week now, and suddenly this pile of paperwork arrives at my door."

"What are they?"

"Bills!" Ned shook his head, pacing the floor as he did so. "And not silly things like the bootmaker or tailor that you can put off." Turner glanced up at that, but let Ned continue. "These are bills for grain. For the farms at Ashby Castle. There's one in here for a dredging that apparently was supposed to have been paid six months ago! The normal running of the Ashby estates has somehow been falling apart while I was still settling into the seat."

Turner looked at the bills, the columns on the ledger pages. He took them all. After a few hours of sorting through the paperwork, he could tell that Ned had been robbed. And quite well.

"He took how much?!" Ned asked.

"Nearly ten thousand pounds. He's been skimming it here and there. Using it to purchase stock in this company—the 'Riversold Building Company'—which provides you with an account of where the money is going, thus balancing the books. But, in reality, I can only assume that Mr. Sharp was the sole owner of Riversold Building."

Ned again put his head in his hands. Then he stood and went over to a small cabinet. "I do believe this calls for some brandy."

Turner glanced at the window. Granted, hours had passed, but it was then still daylight. And then again— "I suppose it does."

"If anyone finds out about this, I'll be a laughingstock in this town." Ned's voice was pitched as high as a matron's. "'Ned Granville, oh, you know him, the country boy whom old Ashby turned into his heir? Should send him back to the village.'"

"The good news is that your income makes it so that you should be able to repay these bills with little hindrance to your lifestyle. Although you will have to live carefully for a little while. And may have to sell a horse or two."

Ned made a small, pitiful sound at that before throwing back his glass of brandy. Then he refilled it and poured one for Turner.

Ned handed Turner his drink and sat down, nodding grimly. "I suppose I can do that. Make that sacrifice."

"Or, better yet, we can set the authorities on your Mr. Sharp, find him, and make him pay back what he took," Turner advised, taking a sip of his (very good) brandy.

But Ned's reaction to that advice was surprisingly harsh.

"No!" He set his snifter down so hard it nearly cracked. "Did you not just hear me? If the authorities get involved, rumors will circulate. And I don't want anyone to know. I just . . . I just want it gone. Then things can be pleasant again."

"But . . ."

"Turner. I just want it done."

"All right," Turner conceded. His first big mistake. His second was now to come. For, after a few moments, he noticed that Ned was regarding him, considering.

"Turner, how long do you think you will be in town?" Ned asked, his voice casual but his eyes calculating.

"I . . . I doubt much longer," Turner replied. "I did not tell you the whole truth. My mill burned, and it will take some cost to repair it. I went to my bank this morning, but the mortgage was already high, and . . . they have decided not to assist in helping me rebuild. I was going to try other banks tomorrow, but I doubt—"

"I will," Ned said suddenly.

"You'll what?"

"I will help you rebuild. In my way."

"What do you mean, 'in your way'?"

"I need a secretary," Ned said, leaning forward on his elbows and letting that sly smile spread across his face. "Someone I can trust. You need an income, immediately."

"Ned—sir. I'm not a secretary. I run a mill!"

"Your mill cannot run without money. And you proved to be a damn better secretary than my last one in a few short hours," Ned argued quickly. "How much will it take to get the banks from calling your loan?"

Turner was so taken aback that he quoted Ned the number.

"That's your salary for the first year—nay, the first six months." Ned clapped his hands together. "Payable in advance. You can keep your mill from imminent death by helping me sort through my own mess. Then, when your mill is back on its feet and ready to run again, you can train your replacement and we part friends."

He thrust out his hand. "What do you say?"

Turner remembered looking from his friend, to the pile of papers on the desk, back to his friend's hand again. His first thought had been outright rejection. In the plainest truth, he had come to this house on the hope that he could convince Ned to invest in his mill. But this was not the situation he had imagined.

He could not abandon his mill in Lincolnshire! It would be impossible. But . . . would it? His mother was still quite strong, and had run the mill by his father's side for years. With the funds he could earn working for the Earl of Ashby, the rebuilding could take place and she would be there to oversee it. He would not worry on that score. And he would be working for the Earl of Ashby—for his friend Ned, who had been at his side for good and bad marching on the fields in Europe. And working for one's friends would certainly be better than working for strangers, wouldn't it?

Turner had grabbed the hand in front of him before his better judgment could stop it.

"I say, let's get started."

Ned grinned at him and pumped his hand. "I'm so pleased you came by, Turner. It's the best of all possible luck!"

❧

THAT HAD BEEN five years ago. Five years of Ned's luck countering his own. Five years of setbacks with the mill, of Ned's demands and dismissive attitudes. And now . . . he was about to lose it all, because of a wager he'd thought he couldn't lose—that Ned's luck would abandon him and Turner would be able to steal it. But, as he watched Ned and the governess stop and speak before entering the house, he knew that simply wasn't the case.

"What has you so pensive?"

The voice floated over him, a dreamy, soothing lilt. He turned and could feel his body relax at the sight of Leticia's pretty frown.

His heart soared at the sight of her. Odd, as his heart was not often given to soaring. But ever since that first moment he had seen Leticia, there were flutters and beats and entirely new rhythms to his pulse.

She was again dressed to impress, and he knew the aim was to impress him. Frankly, he enjoyed every second of it. She wore a saffron-colored Indian shawl, woven intricately with leaves and flowers, wrapped around a light blue gown, which set off the warm tones in her eyes and her dark hair. She was a radiant woman, standing out as such apart from the unformed girls who flitted around Puffington Arms like a marauding troop of magpies. Meanwhile, Leticia, Countess Churzy, was . . . not a peacock, no. Too showy. She was a dove.

His dove.

"Just contemplating what kind of bird you would be," he answered after a moment. He always had to hesitate before he spoke with anyone in the house, but with her especially. Something about her made him forget to breathe, let alone smooth out his natural northern accent.

Her eyes lit up with playfulness. He knew what she was, of course. There was no way her easy charm would be so easy if she did not think him a rich, titled gentleman. But he was like one of those poor souls craving the taste of laudanum—he knew there was no future for them together, but damned if she didn't drug him into believing there was.

"And what was your conclusion?" she asked, clasping her hands in front of her, all innocence. "A bright fat blue jay? An exotic parrot?"

"Neither," he said, clipped, but smiling at her. "Something far more lovely." Then his head turned, caught by motion outside the window. It was Ned and the governess, moving toward the house again.

Leticia must have taken note of his interest, her gaze following his as she moved to stand next to him.

"And what kind of bird do you think the governess is?" she whispered in his ear. "A chickadee? A tufted titmouse?"

"A cuckoo," he answered darkly.

She pulled back a bit at that. "For heaven's sake, why?"

"Because they cause problems for other birds."

He let himself look at her then, her stunned expression. Very quickly, though, she hid it, smoothing it under her beautiful face until such unpleasantness was never there to begin with. But still, he had seen it.

In fact, the surprise was good. It meant she had an opinion—and he could use all the information he could get.

"What do you know of Miss Baker?"

She blinked twice before answering. "Not much. She's been working for my sister for about a year, I believe. I know she had a good education, because

Fanny hopes her connection to Mrs. Beveridge's will serve Rose well, when the time comes. And the children of course adore her." She slid him a look out of the corner of her eye. "But I have not had much to do with her. Why do you ask?"

To answer that, he simply nodded to the window, where they could see Ned taking Miss Baker's elbow as they mounted the steps to the front of the house, and then disappeared from view.

"Oh. Your secretary Mr. Turner seems to have struck up a friendship, I see."

He nodded.

"And you are concerned about him. Such sentiments do you credit."

"It's not only that," Turner replied, his eyes coming away from the window. Now that the party was no longer in sight, there was little reason to keep staring out to the road. Not when he had something so lovely to look at right in front of him.

"Why?" Leticia painted an amused smile on her lips. "Is your Mr. Turner a lothario? Do his charms go over better in London than they did with Mrs. Rye? Are you afraid he will seduce and abandon her?"

There was a silliness in her voice, but also a real concern. And if Turner thought he could get away with planting that seed in her head, he would. Make Ned out to be a lothario—all the other ladies would rally around Miss Baker to "protect" her. But he could not—impugning his competitor was against the rules.

Instead, he did something far more drastic.

He told the truth.

"Not that at all. I am concerned not for her but *about* her."

She cocked her head to one side. "I feel like the parrot you think I am, constantly asking 'why?'"

Turner chose his words with care. "I am afraid she might be related to a Mr. Baker with whom I had dealings in the past."

He hesitated—and decided not to disclose anything about the letter. Actually, two letters, which he happened to remember very well.

It had been a bit less than a year into his service with Ashby. He had been settling into his role, reconstruction on the mill was going swimmingly, and he had thought he would be able to part company with Ned within the next six months. Of course, that hadn't happened, for a myriad of other reasons.

All of the earl's correspondence went through him, except those with flowery script and a personal footman delivering it from the bedroom of some society lady. The first letter came from a Mr. Baker, wanting to double-check Mr. Sharp's references. Turner had written back urging him to avoid Sharp at all costs, using the earl's name and seal, as was his directive from his not-to-be-bothered-with-small-things employer. He had even asked for the direction of Sharp, thinking that he might be able to right a past wrong and have country officials arrest him, keeping London and the Ashby name out of it.

But then, a few months later, he had received the second letter. This one from a girl's school. He didn't connect the names at first, and had thought Ned had a sister or cousin he had forgotten to tell him about. But then he read it . . .

At first he was angry. Angry at Ned for demanding that the business be swept under the rug. Angry at himself for complying. Then he was nervous. The girl wrote so vehemently, so angrily. Could it be that she *would* exact some revenge? Lastly, he was worried for his position. He had been told to make Mr. Sharp go away, quietly. And here was a loose end. He was six months away from having his mill back. Ned had been more and more obdurate of late. More and more the earl. If he fired Turner . . . well, the banks would not be happy.

So, he had put the letter away. Buried it, underneath piles of work that would come after. He'd thought she had simply drifted away. But no—she had been laying in wait. Like a time bomb.

"Baker is a common name," she tried, but he shook his head.

"It's she."

"And you worry that she has reasons for being in his company other than the fact that he is generally handsome?" Leticia mused. She then responded to the look he gave her with the sweetest of smiles. "Not as handsome as some, of course . . . Well, with the caveat that I do not believe Miss Baker could be a callous enough creature to entice your secretary for your possible involvement with her maybe relative, I can only advise one thing."

"And what is that?"

"Separate them."

Now it was his turn to cock his head to the side. "How?"

"And soon enough you will be sounding like an owl." She arched an enticing brow at him. "Mr. Turner is in your employ. Surely there is something that requires his attention in London. Send him away. Simple as that."

Turner shook his head. "I wish I could, but I need him here. For the consortium's business proposal."

"Ah, yes, this business proposal that you have been ignoring for the past three days to spend your time under my sister's oak trees?"

"As long as you happen to be under those oak trees, there is nowhere else to be," he answered simply, for which she rewarded him with a delightful giggle.

"Well"—she shrugged—"if you refuse to send him away, and as you cannot send *her* away, you will simply have to warn your secretary, watch from the sidelines, and hope for the best." She slipped her arm through his. "But come, I was sent to fetch you. Minnie has caught Henrietta up in a game of wickets, and Clara could not decide between them, so you apparently must come judge the last hit to see who is the winner."

Turner let himself be led out of the drawing room and tugged toward the parlor that led to the terrace. There he would be greeted by the Ryes, Miss Benson, Lady Widcoate, Sir Nathan, and, if the last few days were any indication, Mr. Fennick, Mr. McLeavey, and possibly the Midville mine's owner, Mr. Dunlap. They would all look to him for something—praise, adulation, answers, satisfaction. But for once, his mind would not be on the worry of having to deal with them. No, because something Leticia had said worked its way into his ear, echoing there, a grain of an idea forming.

And as you cannot send her *away . . .*

But maybe, just maybe, there was a way he could.

Maybe he could steal a bit of Ned's luck yet.

16

Never bet with money not yet won.

"ut does it have to be spelling *again*?" Rose asked, as only she could: dramatically, clutching her heart and falling over into her eggs.

"Maths and reading in the morning means you get your riding lessons in the afternoon," Phoebe reminded her.

Which was bribe enough to focus her. At least on her eggs.

As usual, Phoebe took breakfast in the nursery with the children and, when she wasn't running around cleaning up or belowstairs, Nanny. Today the frizzy-haired girl was sorting clothes to be sent down to the laundry maids. Tutting at how their riding lessons had, if possible, made them dirtier.

The riding lessons had been phenomenal. Rose especially had something that made her keen and smiling every day. Sir Nathan had even stopped by the stables a time or two, wanting to see how the lessons were progressing. Phoebe no longer had to work hard to get Rose to learn one thing to repeat back to her father—she recited horse-based trivia at lightning speed. And it made her want to learn other things too—as long as they were equally horse-based.

"But couldn't it be *fun* spelling? Not boring letters and things."

"Well, if we don't learn the letters part of spelling, it seems a little difficult." There was a knock at the nursery room door, and she rose to answer it. "Think about that."

She pulled open the door and started when she saw the solemn valet of the Earl of Ashby standing there, as straight-backed as ever.

"Oh! Mr. Danson," she cried, letting a hand go to her chest, her heart suddenly fluttering. *Why would Mr. Danson be there?* "How nice to see you . . . out of my sickroom." She smiled bemusedly.

"Miss Baker." He gave a short nod. And no smile, as per suspected custom. Then, to the children, who were leaning out of their chairs to see who it was, "Sir. Madam."

Phoebe turned around and gave them a sharp, stern look. They immediately ducked their heads into their eggs and porridge.

"Miss Baker, the, er, Earl of Ashby has requested your presence. If you would be so kind, I will escort you."

Phoebe's eyes went wide. "The earl?" Her voice was gone, barely a rasp. "Now?"

"Yes, if you please."

"But . . . why?" Phoebe's heart, already at a flutter from seeing the earl's valet, began to hammer. What could have possibly happened that the earl would want to see *her*?

Then . . . she remembered what she told her Mr. Turner yesterday. Oh, God . . . she had thought he understood . . . that was her secret! Her blackest moment, and he went and told the earl about it? Told him everything?

"I have no idea," Danson replied. "But if I may offer advice: be on your guard. Do not let them play games with you."

Phoebe may have been unsure of what the warning meant, but she gave a short nod anyway. Two deep breaths, to steady herself, and then she turned, to find Nanny watching, a basket of laundry under her arm and a child on either side of her.

"Nanny, once they are done with breakfast, if you could escort them to the schoolroom? I will meet them there."

Then she turned back to Danson, and set her face in those hard lines that allowed no humor to shine through. "Then let us walk into fire."

⚮

WHEN PHOEBE ENTERED the library, it was with her back as straight as a plank, her eyes clear, and her blankest possible expression. Perhaps she was being called forth only to be asked about the riding lessons. Perhaps he had a child in his care, and wished to ask if she would be willing to enter his employ as governess.

And perhaps, on the library ceiling, Lady Widcoate's painted cherubs would start flapping their wings.

But her true surprise upon entering was seeing that the Earl of Ashby was alone in the room.

"Miss Baker," he said with a short bow. She gave a small curtsy in return, but could not help glancing about. If this was Mr. Turner's doing, shouldn't he be here?

"Expecting someone?" the earl asked.

Phoebe, finding she could not yet manage words, simply shook her head.

"Then, please . . ." He indicated two high-backed chairs placed before the unused fireplace. "Have a seat."

Phoebe, though the one most likely to make use of the contents of the library, was in fact very rarely in here. When she tried to use the books for her lessons, Lady Widcoate kicked up quite a fuss about the "lines of the room" being disturbed. It was then that Phoebe figured out that the books were purely decorative. If she were to pull down the books from the higher shelves, she would be met by blank pages. Thus she relied on her own small collection of texts and correspondence for teaching Rose and Henry.

It was this thought—the library being solely for show—that steadied Phoebe as she lowered herself into the overstuffed, high-winged chair. Odd, but it made her feel as if the earl in front of her was mostly for show too.

"Is something funny, Miss Baker?" the earl asked, regarding her with one brow raised. His voice was sharp— sharper than she expected. Curious. As if he was taken aback by the smile she had tried unsuccessfully to hide.

"No," she hastened to assure, shaking her head. "I . . . I wonder why I was called here, that is all."

The earl nodded, taking a steadying breath. When he finally spoke, his voice was normal, as before. "You are straight to the point, Miss Baker. I asked you here this morning before the rest of the family gathers because there is something you have not told them."

Now it was her turn to lift a brow. But she did not speak.

"It has come to my attention that you are not what you seem."

Her second brow joined the first. But again, she kept silent, and watched as the earl shifted somewhat uncomfortably in his seat. She had found when dealing with children that if she kept her attention on the person speaking, and also held her tongue, they would inevitably explain—oftentimes more than they intended to.

She found it also worked with adults.

Though generally not adults as imperious as the Earl of Ashby.

"By that I mean, you have not disclosed the true tragedy of your circumstances."

"The true tragedy of my circumstances?" she prompted. As much as she wanted to end the interview, as much as she wanted to have him go away and never see him again . . . she was granted an opportunity here. She wanted to hear him say it.

"Your father. His death. The loss of your fortune."

"And you know this because . . ."

He clamped his mouth tightly and tried his best to look imperious. But, as governess, Phoebe was too well trained in spotting a guilty conscience. He could not hold her gaze.

"I recognized your name. Your given name begins with a *P*, does it not?"

Phoebe opened her mouth to answer, but suddenly, the door to the library crashed open, revealing a breathless Mr. Turner standing there, looking dumbfounded between the two of them.

"What is going on?" he asked, his eyes landing on his employer.

"Miss Baker and I were having a conversation," the earl answered calmly.

"No, you're not," Mr. Turner shot back.

"Yes, we were." The earl's words were clipped. Hard. "Unless you have something pertinent to add, that is."

"Maybe I will," Mr. Turner replied, crossing his arms over his chest. "What is the topic of conversation?"

"The earl is inquiring after my given name," Phoebe answered, shooting a look to Mr. Turner, effectively shutting him up. However, he remained in the room, his stance as defiant as a child's. "And, yes, it does start with a *P*. My name is Phoebe."

"I thought as much. Phoebe Baker. Whose father died by drowning after some bad investments." The earl leaned back in his chair. "I have become friends again with the Widcoates and I would hate for them to learn of the circumstances of your father's death. After all, it cannot do to have a governess with that kind of black cloud hanging over her name."

"What the hell—" Mr. Turner had taken two steps forward before Phoebe held up a hand to stop his advance, while her eyes never left the earl's.

"Is that all?" she asked, blinking with innocence. "Well, then, let me put your mind at ease." She leaned forward in her chair. "I have never hidden anything from my employers. Sir and Lady Widcoate were informed of everything you have stated. That my father died of drowning, and that bad investments were to blame for my reduction in circumstances. Now, if you'll excuse me, I must teach."

She made to rise, but was stayed by the earl rising out of his seat, placing his hands in the air in a gesture of compliance.

"Miss Baker, you misunderstand."

"I sincerely doubt that," she replied, allowing a little of the venom that she felt to trickle into her voice. She was rewarded by seeing Lord Ashby flinch back for a moment. But then, hands still held out, he continued, "I do not mean to offend. I mean to amend."

That caught her by surprise.

"Amend?" she asked, tentatively.

"How?" came the reply from Mr. Turner—still there, still posed angrily.

The earl sat down and Phoebe noticed the piece of paper and quill positioned on the small table at his elbow. He jotted something on the paper, then he dribbled a little wax on the bottom and pressed the ring on his last finger into it, effectively signing the document, if not sealing it.

"Indirectly, I did play a role in your current circumstances. I would like to correct that." He handed her the piece of paper. "Take that note to my bank in London, and they will transfer five hundred pounds to your name."

"Five hundred pounds?" she asked, astonished. Indeed, there on the page was the number written, and a few other words around it—although her vision swam so much that she couldn't make them out. It took her a moment to realize her hands were shaking.

"What is she to do with five hundred pounds?" Mr. Turner asked, his voice as angry as his stance.

"Whatever she likes. She could build a school. She can quit teaching and use the interest to rent a cottage. Perhaps she would like to travel abroad. But she need not be limited to the choices of a governess any longer."

The earl leaned back in his seat. "I would be happy to hire a carriage to take you to London today, if you like. I am certain that Rose and Henry would be fine in Mr. Turner's care until a suitable replacement could be found."

"Now, hold on—" Mr. Turner began, but the earl interrupted him.

"Well, Mr. Turner? Don't you think the girl deserves something for her troubles?"

Phoebe's eyes flew to Mr. Turner's. He was frog-faced—gaping with lack of an answer.

Luckily, Phoebe *did* have an answer.

She rose slowly, holding the piece of paper in her hands. A piece of paper worth five hundred pounds. More money than she could save working for the Wid-coates for twenty years. She looked the earl dead in the eye.

And tore the piece of paper in half. Then in half again. Then once more, just to make her point.

"Thank you but no," she said in her clipped governess tones, placing the uneven squares of paper in her pocket. "I want nothing from you anymore. Oh, there was a time when I was an angry child with no outlet for my grief. But now I find that the idea of being indebted to you turns my stomach."

She watched the flash of something—anger? rage? frustration?—flicker through his eyes, but he said nothing. Mr. Turner, meanwhile, looked absolutely flummoxed.

As for Phoebe, who had spent years refining her calm, quiet demeanor for public consumption . . . well, in for a penny, in for a pound.

"All you have done today is confirm my original opinion of you. Careless to the point of cruelty."

"How dare—" The warning came with flared nostrils, but Phoebe was not one to be cowed. Not today.

"No, my lord, how dare *you*?" She drew herself up and moved calmly to the door. Before she turned the handle, she looked back at him. "You should be ashamed of yourself. It takes a very small man to threaten someone as unimportant as me."

With that, and with her dignity, she left the room.

❧

NED WATCHED PHOEBE leave the library, a swish of gray skirts and head held high.

He wanted to choke Turner; wanted to rail at him for this trickery and challenge him to the sort of duel men got sent to the Continent for.

But he didn't. Instead, he kept his eyes on the door as it creaked its way back into place.

"Did you enjoy that?" Ned asked harshly.

Turner's voice became raw. Ned didn't turn to look at him, but he imagined his face had for once dropped its hard mask. "Not for a second."

"This is not over between us," he growled, his blood feral.

"I should imagine not," Turner mused, resigned.

Then Ned took off after Phoebe, breaking into a run before he left the library.

"Miss Baker!" he cried, moving swiftly to catch up to her. But hearing her name did not slow her down—indeed, she sped up. Walking as fast as propriety would allow, out of Puffington Arms and down the front lane, as far as she could go.

Ned kept pace behind her until they had passed the bend that hid them from the house, and her steps slowed. Then he finally allowed himself to close the distance.

"Miss Baker—please . . ." he said in between gulps of air (she had been moving very fast, especially for someone in such skirts) and reached out to touch her shoulder. Which, he discovered, was shaking.

"Miss Baker?" She still didn't respond. "Phoebe," he finally said, and turned her to him.

She was crying.

Wet streaks were running straight back from her clear blue eyes, such had been her speed. Her face was red, flushed to the tips of her ears. Her nose . . . well, perhaps it was best not to opine on her nose, Ned thought. Crying had made it swell.

But while her eyes gave her away, her mouth remained a firm line, no sob allowed to escape. No sound even. Until she spoke.

"How could you?" she accused, shoving his hand off her shoulder.

"What are you talking about?" Ned asked, his brows coming together.

"You told him!" she hissed. "You told him what I told you! About my father."

"No, I didn't."

"Then how did he know? Did the Earl of Ashby suddenly remember after a week of staying in the same house that I happened to write him a letter once upon a time?" She placed her hands on her hips, her eyes drying rapidly with her ability to direct her anger at someone.

While Ned would have very much liked to say that, yes, that was very likely what had happened, he knew it would only incite further anger in his direction. And he knew better than to do that. In general.

"It must have been one hell of a letter," he offered half jokingly.

She did not see the amusement. "Is this some sort of game to you? That was the most humiliating time of my life—and a close second was that farce of an interview just moments ago." She shoved her face into her hands. "Oh, God—if the Widcoates find out about this, they will sack me."

"They won't," Ned assured her. "I promise." Tentatively, he reached out and took her hands down from her face, forcing her to look at him. "You have my word."

They stood there for some moments, Ned holding Phoebe's hands as she took the breaths she needed to bring herself back to normal, to put the wall of propriety back up and be able to face the world again.

But Ned had seen behind it now.

"Phoebe," he asked—not the first time he said her name, but the first time he had paused to taste it. "Why didn't you take it?"

Her eyes flew up to meet his. Those clear blue eyes, at that moment filled with a question.

"The money," he clarified. "You could have a different life, if you took it."

She blinked at him. "You don't understand, do you? I was an angry, sad child when my father died and I wrote that letter. I was railing at the only person I could find to hear me. Even though he proved himself to be an unfeeling man simply by his lack of reply, I look back and realize I was utterly foolish. I do not belong in his province. I belong in my own."

"But the money—"

"No amount of money can give me back my father. Nor can it return me to my former life. And I wouldn't want to go back to being that girl. She didn't have a single thought in her head about how the world worked. All she knew was that she would be petted and cosseted her entire life. And there is so *much* more."

There was so much more. How was it that this little governess, hidden away from the world, had a greater appreciation for it than a peer such as himself? It made him feel . . . shallow. Being never troubled, and always bored.

"You reminded yourself he was human. And that bought him forgiveness?"

Phoebe shook her head. "Reminding myself he was human is what saved my sanity, and made it so I let go of my anger at him. But forgiveness is a harder thing."

She wiped her eyes, though they remained dry.

"I knew it would be hard to face the earl—he's become something of a personal demon," she continued. "In fact, when I learned he was coming, my most fervent wish was to hide away, pray that he did not know me, and let this fortnight pass unexceptionally. But that's not what happened." She sighed and looked up, opening herself up to the sky. "And now there is nothing to do but be glad of it."

"I thought you were brilliant in there," Ned suddenly blurted.

"I was?"

"Marvelous. I've never seen anyone talk to . . . an earl that way. And he deserved every word heaped upon him."

Yes, the Earl of Ashby deserved to hear her vitriol—even if she had unknowingly directed it at someone else. Ned would rail at himself later, but right now . . . right now, he found himself caught in the pair of light blue eyes that suddenly met his, and in the pair of hands that he had been holding this whole time.

"Out of everyone I've ever met, in my entire life, you have the most cause to have a grievance with the world." He rubbed his thumb across the back of her hand, the skin soft and exposed. He had never seen the governess out without her gloves before. "Why aren't you angrier?"

"I suppose I can't help it." She shrugged and gave a tentative smile, a rogue dimple peeking out from its hiding place. "After my father died, I could have given into anger. I could have made it so I seethed and was bitter and let it eat me up inside. But I had a teacher who told me that I should not let it break me. That I still had a right to happiness. Instead, I decided to work toward something. America. And I decided to be happy.

"Yes, happiness is a decision. And it is an easy one to

make when everything is going your way, but when it's not? I saved my soul by finding silly things to laugh at every day. Until it became habit. Until all I want to do every day is enjoy it."

He held her eyes then, those clear blue eyes that spoke of summer skies and bald honesty.

"Even with the sadness I have known or the silliness of the Widcoates, I still find something every day that makes me happy."

An easy decision to make when everything is going your way. But when it's not? Those words sank into Ned and he felt them to his bones.

Had he ever decided to be happy? Or had he just let everyone tell him he should be?

"And what is today's happiness?" he asked, suddenly wanting a bit of her joy. "Today's bit from your boundless reserves of jollity."

Her eyebrow went up. "So far, very little has come forward that impressed me. But the day is still quite young. My students have only just finished their breakfast. I'm sure something will come along."

"I'm sure it will. For me as well. And when I finally come across that thing that makes me smile today, I will think of you."

"Why?"

"I suppose I won't be able to help it," he said, with a shrug to mirror hers. His mouth quirked up at the corners. And suddenly, her eyes, which had been so steady on his, glanced down to his mouth.

And stayed there.

He had her hands in his, their warmth and strength spreading through him. Her eyes on his mouth inevitably led to his eyes flicking to her mouth. It was parted slightly, a light gasp revealing that when she wasn't pressing her lips into a hard line, they were actually pink, a few shades darker than her pale skin. The lower lip was fuller than the upper, a slight dent in the center giving her a natural pout. And there was a freckle, just underneath the left side . . .

It wasn't a thought per se which swept down from his brain to all points of his body. It wasn't that formed. But once the notion was there—the feeling . . . no, the *want*—he could not escape it.

"Until then," he rasped, his throat suddenly dry, "perhaps I can give you something impressive the rest of the day can try to live up to."

Her eyes flew up to his. And then . . . one delicate eyebrow lifted.

Giving him permission.

"And what would that be?" she said, before he swooped down to capture her mouth with his.

This was nothing like the last time. There was no surprise, no strangeness, no folly. This was reverence. This was something he wanted. Wanted desperately enough to forget his place, and hers, and just let them be.

This was the first kiss that she'd deserved before.

Gently, he brought his hands up to her face, let his fingers dance across her soft skin. Her hands went to rest lightly at his waist. He took that as the invitation to close the distance between their bodies, taking a half step forward, the edge of her skirts dusting the toes of his boots.

This warmth, this drug, that came from the touch of lips to lips. The scent of skin. The intoxication had been brewing between them for days now. He wanted everything said and unsaid between them.

He let his eyes flutter open for a moment, just a peek, and then he broke into a smile when he saw Phoebe's eyes were open too. But instead of a languid glance, she was staring at him.

"Phoebe," he chuckled, pressing his forehead to hers, "you're supposed to close your eyes, darling."

"Oh! Right," she replied, unable to hide her grin. "I was wondering about that." He then did something he had been wanting to do for days, but didn't know it—he let his thumb graze across the dimple in her cheek.

Yes, it was real. Deliciously, wonderfully real.

"Interesting," he murmured.

"What?" she asked, her voice no more than a breath.

He grinned. "For once, the teacher is the pupil."

And then, watching her eyes fall shut, he kissed her again. But there was no reverence this time. This time he pulled her to him, chest to chest, wrapping his arms around her body and holding her there. The length of him went hard with need, and he fought back every impulse to crush her to him, bury himself in wool skirts until he could feel her yielding body beneath.

Her hands tightened on the coat at his waist, her kiss became stronger, more certain. He knew what she was feeling, what she was fighting toward, and gently urged her mouth open.

This felt so . . . *right*. More right than anything he'd felt in a long time, Ned thought. She fit against him perfectly, and while she was unschooled, she was an exceptionally fast learner. And he knew, knew to his toes, that when he broke the kiss, he would mourn the loss of it, and then celebrate it the rest of the day.

Because it was a moment of happiness.

He tried to hold on to the moment for as long as possible, but before he knew it, Phoebe had pulled away, and inches of intolerable space existed between them again.

His eyes opened lazily and found hers. Her face was flushed, her breath short, but her eyes—oh, her eyes were focused. Direct.

"You're . . . you're not still trying to win your wager, are you?"

Ned froze. "The wager?" His voice came out harsher than he intended.

"Yes," she said cautiously. "The one where you have to kiss someone?"

He should have been relieved. He should have remembered the lie he told her to conceal his other lies, and smiled and joked about it. But instead, he abruptly released her. Took two steps back. Straightened his coat and trousers over his uncomfortable anatomy, and . . .

And stared.

She was so lovely. He hadn't seen it before. Either he had been blind or she had refused to allow him to see it, but her tight bun had been ravaged by his hands. The flush of her cheeks spread down her neck and disappeared at her throat under the high collar of her gown, which heaved in staccato breaths. Her lips were bruised by his kisses, and her mouth parted, wanting more.

And then there were her eyes.

And the question in them.

"Excuse me. I should not have . . . I should go." He

gave a short bow, turned on his heel, and moved quickly back toward Puffington Arms.

He couldn't answer that question. Not out loud. Whether she knew it or not, Phoebe Baker had asked something that threw Ned off his game and made him more worried than he could say.

Because the truth was, he hadn't been thinking about the wager. It hadn't even crossed his mind.

17

A badly played hand will always have consequences.

I knew you were determined to win, Turner," Ned sneered under his breath. "I did not know you were a liar and a deceitful bastard as well."

"'Liar' and 'deceitful' mean the same thing," Turner drawled in his natural accent as he dismounted from Abandon in front of Ned's mother's dilapidated cottage. Now that they had finally lost the rest of the group, they could speak more freely.

After the business of the morning, it had been an easy decision to forgo whatever banal pleasures had been planned for the day of rustication and *finally* get down to the business of business. After all, the entire reason they were in Hollyhock was to decide what to do with the house. And now that it seemed Turner's attempts to thwart Ned in the courting of the governess had failed, best to get it over with as soon as possible.

But when the rest of the party was told of the earl's

plans over breakfast, they did not mourn his loss, as expected. No, they instead decided to accompany him.

"Oh, yes!" Lady Widcoate cried. "It will be lovely. Won't it be lovely, my dear?" She leaned over to her husband, who seemed taken aback not only because the earl and his secretary wanted to go into town, but because his wife was inviting everyone else along too.

"Well, after all, the Hollyhock festival and Summer Ball are mere days away—and as ladies, it is our duty to shop," the countess purred, raising her cup of tea to her lips.

This sparked no small amount of enthusiasm from the other girls.

"Oh! I can get hair ribbons!" Clara cried, before blushing furiously.

"And I need new gloves—my good pair ripped while playing croquet." This from Minnie.

"You were playing croquet in your evening gloves?" her aunt asked, aghast.

By the time Sir Nathan had declared, "A good day for an outing! Fennick will be well pleased to see us all coming down the lane," there was little to be done but go along with the scheme.

Indeed, Mr. Fennick had been well pleased to see the party. Luckily, the outing was unannounced, so the entire town and their banners were happily off doing other tasks, preparing for the festival. Stalls and carts were being readied in front of shops on the main road, bunting was being sewed, games constructed.

Still, Sir Nathan insisted on stopping and informing Mr. Fennick and Mr. McLeavey. But McLeavey was off visiting some poor soul who needed religion, so the party—consisting of the lone carriage bearing the crush of six women and a supremely uncomfortable Sir Nathan, with Ned and Turner on horseback—pulled to a stop in front of Fennick's offices on the main road of Hollyhock.

"My lord! Mr. Turner!" Mr. Fennick cried. "Can it be that you've made a decision at last?"

"Not quite, Mr. Fennick," Turner answered, with a quick look to Ned.

"Not that much has changed since you came by the house yesterday." Sir Nathan guffawed. "And the day before that. And the day before that."

Mr. Fennick shot daggers at his compatriot in the business venture. Then he turned his overeager smile back to Turner, who was caught off-guard and uneasy yet again by the way he was looked to.

"Er . . . But I intend to tour the property and come to one."

"Excellent! I shall just grab Mr. McLeavey and Dunlap and escort you!"

"No!" Turner said abruptly. "I mean, that is—"

"Mr. Fennick," Ned broke in, saving Turner from being rude again, despite his current dislike of his old friend. But he had things to speak to Turner about, and an audience would not do. "I have to congratulate you on your business prospectus. It is very well written and lays out the plans for the town's conversion into a bathing retreat most admirably."

Mr. Fennick blinked in surprise, but then nodded. Ned continued, smiling smoothly. "However, the decision of what to do with his mother's property is an emotional one for the earl, and therefore, we must beg that we be allowed to contemplate the matter on our own."

While he looked disappointed, Mr. Fennick nodded in agreement.

"Right, Fennick!" Sir Nathan immediately changed tack. "Don't want to go bothering the man too much when he's got a decision to make." Then he leaned over from his seat in the carriage and whispered to Ned, next to him on Turner's mare. "Remember, it will be worthwhile for everyone if this deal is made. You included."

And since they were in the middle of town, surrounded by all the shops that the ladies could possibly wish to frequent, it was as good a place as any for the group to separate: the ladies to their shopping; Sir Nathan stepping out of his gig and into an immediate hushed argument with Mr. Fennick, likely about the pros and cons of changing their overtly enthusiastic approach to courting an earl so far; Ned and Turner to ride toward Ned's mother's cottage.

Luckily, any trepidation he felt at seeing the house again was muted by his red-hot rage at Turner.

"I don't care if 'liar' and 'deceitful' have the same meaning—they both apply!" Ned said, dismounting. He kept his voice to a harsh whisper—until they were inside the house, there were too many possibilities for being overheard.

Turner just sighed. "I didn't break any of the rules we laid out. I did not impugn you in any way, or myself. I did not reveal our true identities. My play was fair."

"And underhanded. Where would you get the money anyway?"

"Your bank extends a small floating fund that I can sign out in your name. To be used to pay off less substantial creditors and the like." Turner jiggled the door handle of the old house, tried to get it to turn.

"So you were going to use my money for your bribe?"

"If she had taken it, I would have won our wager, and I would have been able to pay for it out of my winnings. If not, there was no payment to be made, and nothing lost in the offering."

Turner stepped aside from the door. "It's stuck. Didn't open easily last time either. Is there a garden door, or . . . ?"

"Oh, hell, give me a go." Ned then turned the handle, lifted it up, and put his shoulder into the door. His muscles remembered the rhythm of his youth without his even knowing it was happening.

And then . . . they were inside.

The house was so much smaller than he remembered. He had left it when he was twelve, before he had reached his full height and breadth. The drawing room was a complete mess—beams hung loose from the hole in the ceiling. Dark, too, as the tarp covering the hole was made of heavy canvas, double and triple folded to keep out the elements. All the furniture was familiar— his mother's writing desk, the settee that she had read to him on—but it had been moved in topsy-turvy fashion to the corners of the room, and covered in dust cloths to protect it from the elements. But the paper on the walls was the same striped pattern, and the door to the kitchen revealed that the warmth of that small, practical room still remained.

It was everything and nothing that he remembered. It was terribly the same.

He glanced up at the ceiling, the large, gaping hole.

"The report said this tarp was provided by a retired seaman who rents a house on the other side of Hollyhock. It was the only piece of canvas big enough to be found," Ned murmured.

"Apparently, he took the pieces of his ship he could carry with him," Turner replied. Then, "You actually read the report?"

"And the business proposal, and every other piece of paper in your trunk," Ned replied. "When no one wants your company, there is plenty of time to do work in the interim."

Turner grunted in agreement. And perhaps envy. "I would kill for such solitude. But what is your opinion?"

Ned sighed. "It's good for the town, although they would do better to open their own mine and keep up with industry."

"They are trying to preserve their way of life, not actively keep up with industry."

"And a bathing retreat would allow for that?"

"For a while, at any rate. Who knows, it could become popular."

"Which is why you feel that leasing the property is the better move," Ned concluded.

"You are not pressed for funds. You recovered from your losses with Mr. Sharp ages ago. Lease the land and make a profit from it. Become even richer. It's as simple as can be."

Ned slowly wandered from the drawing room to

the far side, through an entryway that led to the sitting room, then to the stairs leading to the bedrooms.

"Except for the fact that this house would be gone."

Ned idled his way through the sitting room. Pulled open a drawer here, took a book off the shelf there. His whole life, bound up in this place, and yet none of it familiar, or his.

"Turner, when we first met, did I seem like a happy person?"

"What?" His friend's head came up.

"Did I seem happy? When I first came into the regiment."

"Ned, you are the luckiest goddamn person I have ever met," Turner sighed. "Of course you were happy."

"Was I?" Ned looked down at his hands. "All I remember is . . . craving distraction. And letting those distractions amuse me, as much as they could."

In camp he had distracted his misery with cards. When he was a new earl and faced with the terrible truth of Mr. Sharp, he had distracted himself from it by hiring his friend.

"What the hell does this have to do with anything?" Turner asked. "What does it have to do with tearing down the house?"

"Nothing," Ned mused, letting his attention drift again over the appointments in the room. When he was a child, this had been where they ate breakfast. A large, polished wood table with three chairs, two of which were only ever used. "Something that Phoebe said to me, that's all."

Happiness is a decision. One Ned had always avoided making. Instead, he pretended.

She was expected to be miserable, and rebelled by secretly holding on to happiness. Meanwhile, Ned was expected to be happy, and . . . he just went along with it.

"Phoebe. Phoebe Baker." Turner shook his head. "Ned, listen to me. She is the last person you should be spending your time with. She is not who you think she is."

Ned shot his friend a calculating look.

"Are you that desperate to separate her from me?"

Turner looked him dead in the eye, as calm and cold as the pond Ned had had to jump in before he returned to the house that morning. "Yes."

"You think I'm going to win, don't you?" Ned crooked up a smile at that.

"Maybe. Or maybe I just think she's dangerous, and that possibly it is a very bad idea to be playing such a tricky game using her as a pawn."

"Dangerous?" Ned practically guffawed. "How could she possibly be dangerous?"

"You didn't read that letter, Ned. I did. And I remember it, for the anger and pain and vitriol she aims at you."

"She was seventeen years old. She was sad, and grieving. People do very rash things while grieving!" Ned yelled, anger turning his vision red. "Hell, I went and joined the army out of grief!"

Turner straightened, blinking in surprise. "Out of grief? You told us you did it to annoy your great-uncle."

"I likely half believed it." Ned went to go look out the window, out onto the overgrown garden, the blackberry bramble that overflowed from the woods into the unkempt lawn. "A week before I quit school and joined our regiment, I received a letter from my great-uncle. Surprising, as my uncle rarely wrote, and I had been expecting a letter from my mother. She wrote monthly, like clockwork." Later he would learn that it was all she had been allowed. "I was informed that my mother had died three weeks past, of a lung complaint."

Turner remained grimly silent. Ned knew there was really nothing to be said.

"My great-uncle said that since exams were looming, he did not wish to inform me until after. Which, incidentally, meant after the funeral and burial." He shrugged. "I hadn't seen my mother in the flesh since I was twelve. Since we were standing in this house together. He could have been simply assuming that I cared more about my schoolwork than I did about her."

"I doubt that," Turner said quietly, earning a small smile of approval from Ned.

"As do I."

No, his great-uncle had not done it out of concern for his heir's studies, and to Ned, it had been the last straw. He knew he wanted to lash out, but more than that, he wanted to go, to be, to do something. Anything else.

He wanted to be distracted.

But instead of drinking, or gambling, or whoring— those distractions were only good in the short term—he turned his attention to something far more drastic, and hurtful to his uncle.

His mother had left him a small sum of money, as well as the house. His luck with cards at school had padded out his allowance from his great-uncle. He took his funds and purchased himself a commission, what he could afford, and before he knew it, he was on his way to the Continent. And it was from there that he dispatched his answering letter to his uncle.

Of course, there was nothing like war to distract a man. The imminent threat of death was a distraction, the long bouts without clean and dry socks were a distraction, and the camaraderie he found with his new friends Turner and Rhys had changed his life.

But had he ever actually mourned his mother's death? Or the life he might have had, had he not been plucked out of obscurity? Ever actually felt it, and let it go, the way Phoebe had with her father? And then made the decision to be happy?

For the first time, Ned could look at his life with open eyes—clear eyes, like Phoebe's—and see that his jovial demeanor had been an act. Trying to convince himself and the world that he did indeed belong. That he was Lucky Ned.

But perhaps he had never been lucky at all.

And it had taken less than a week of living without his title for Ned to realize how much he had been hiding behind it.

"Brilliant," he exhaled. "Marvelous."

"Ned . . . we don't have to lease the land . . ." Turner began, but he was cut off by a wave of Ned's hand.

"The point is," he said, clearing his throat, "Phoebe—er, Miss Baker is in no way a danger to me. She is only a danger to you, as she might cause you to lose your precious wager." His eyes narrowed. "And your mill."

But Turner was not willing to accept that as an answer.

"What is it you said to me about the countess?" he asked. "That she is a barnacle?" He leaned in close to

Ned. "What makes Phoebe Baker any different? What do you think she wants from you? And what is she going to want when she finds out the truth?"

There wasn't a thought that passed through Ned's head then. Not a word or sound could make it past the rush of blood in his ears.

His fists were up before he realized it. Grabbing at Turner's collar, he pressed his fists against the bastard's throat and shoved him against a cupboard, rattling the dishes inside with the force.

"You will keep your goddamn mouth shut, Turner," he growled, his vision red. "She doesn't want anything! She's better than that."

Turner grabbed at Ned's arms, gasping for breath. "Ned—" he croaked.

Only then did Ned realize what he was doing. And let go.

"Christ." Turner gulped for breath, as he steadied himself on his feet again. His eyes met Ned's—they were wide. Stunned. But he had not been stunned by the fists in his shirt, or by Ned's words. No, what stunned him was the feeling behind them.

As Ned looked at his own shaking hands, he realized it stunned the hell out of him too.

They both shuffled themselves upright, not bothering to straighten their coats or cravats.

"Careful, Ned," Turner warned. "Don't do anything you can't undo."

"I'll do what I like, damn you," Ned spat. "Sell the land. The house. At whatever price they can afford."

"Sell it?" Turner asked, surprised. "But that makes no—"

"Get rid of it." Ned shook his head. "I don't ever want to come back here."

❧

IT WAS NOT long after the earl and his secretary went into the little falling-down house that they emerged from it. The earl's secretary came out first, his face a thundercloud, his mind obviously elsewhere. The earl followed shortly thereafter, straightening his cravat and quickly assuming the look and imperious nature of a man who has the world at his fingertips, all he need do is snap.

Both men were so preoccupied with the contents of their short discussion inside the house that they did not notice the person crouched outside, under the sitting-room window, behind some overgrown shrubbery.

They walked away from the house, never glancing back, instead stepping into the afternoon sunshine and to the post where their mounts had been tied up, then riding away.

And they had no idea that, indeed, their conversation—and altercation—had, at least in part, been overheard. Nor what their eavesdropper was prepared to do about it.

18

Breaks are permitted in play, and are often restorative.

*N*early perfect, Rose! Sadly, 'equine' does not have a 'w' in it." Phoebe corrected her slate of vocabulary words with a smile. Since Rose was denied riding lessons today, as the entire house party had gone into Hollyhock, disappointment abounded in the schoolroom. As did inattention. To combat this, Phoebe had turned every single subject into a horse-related lesson.

All mathematic problems involved adding and subtracting horses in the field (multiplication of horses, she did not wish to get into). All vocabulary and spelling lessons were with horse-related words. Henry had even drawn a rather impressive—for a six-year-old—picture of Mr. Turner's mare.

"You do not wish to draw Abandon?" she had asked, a little surprised.

But young, thoughtful Henry had just shrugged. "I like Mr. Turner's horse."

Yes, Phoebe thought to herself, she liked Mr. Turner's horse too. And Mr. Turner, for that matter. But before she let herself get too lost on contemplating that subject, she turned from Henry and began to work with Rose on her spelling, and forced herself to be occupied with her occupation.

"You are quite proficient at all the tack-related words," she mused, looking over Rose's slate, "but it seems the Latin-rooted ones still elude you."

But Rose just cocked her head to one side. A look Phoebe had seen Mr. Turner give on more than one occasion, and felt her heart skip a beat. Goodness, perhaps they were spending too much time in Mr. Turner's company. All of them.

As if giving thought feeling and form, Henry then went over to the window and cried out, "Look! They are back!"

The schoolroom overlooked the pond, on the opposite side of the house from the stables—for which, when it came to teaching one horse-mad girl, Phoebe was grateful. Thus it was surprising that Henry could see anything of the comings and goings of Mr. Turner.

She leaned over and spied out the window herself, and there were the Rye girls and Miss Benson beginning a game of croquet on the lawn by the pond.

Phoebe wanted to kick herself. Of course—the *entire* house party went into town. Not just Mr. Turner. She had known it moments ago and the thought flew out of her head to make more room for a pair of mischievous brown eyes and dusty dark hair.

As she watched the sun play across the still waters

of the pond, she realized the shadows were longer than she expected.

"Goodness! Is that the time?" she gasped. "You two are late for tea. Nanny will be waiting."

Rose and Henry scampered off, not needing to be told twice to go eat scones and jam as opposed to learning how to spell and define swingletree—incidentally, a word Phoebe had to ask Kevin the groom to define for her. A bar used to balance the pull of a harnessed horse. She smiled to herself. One learns something new every day.

Apparently, using horse-related terminology to teach worked better than much else she tried, as the children had, without complaint, gone well past the time they were usually taken for their walk out-of-doors.

She had an hour to herself before Nanny tired of them. Her hand went to her coiled braid—fine hairs were beginning to stick out, and, oh! She should likely change her fichu. Not that she had reason to, mind. But she should not look amiss, under any circumstances. It had absolutely nothing to do with a certain someone who had kissed her for the second time that morning.

And much more successfully.

As she moved from the schoolroom down the hall, headed for the rickety flight of stairs to the third floor, her mind went to the place it had been simply dying to go all day. Back to that morning, to the lane, and to him.

It had been . . . well, in a word, educational. She had been a student herself when she was last allowed the leisure of thinking romantically, so all her experience with the opposite sex came after—and, thanks to her ill-fitting dress and sour expression, it was minimal. But with her Mr. Turner, her guard had been lowering further with each time they spoke. With every touch.

An errant hand to the small of her back. His hand covering hers on a fence post—but their bodies inching so close that she could feel his warmth.

There was something about him that overruled common sense.

She had actually wanted to be kissed. Oh, Lord! She had been thinking about it mere moments before. And then his lips were on hers and everything was different. Her body lit up like the wick of a candle, heat coursing through her from his lips to every outreach of her form. A side of herself heretofore unknown.

Well, it must have been obvious that she had never been kissed quite so . . . thoroughly before. Especially when he told her to close her eyes, she realized with horror. And, oh, the things she said! Talking about her father, and her personal feelings about how she made peace with her situation . . . well, no wonder he ran away. Which is basically what he had done. If she had absolute assurance she would pass no one in the halls, Phoebe would bury her face in her hands and give in to the urge to groan at her own odd state of feeling.

But he had been the one to kiss *her*, and then *he* ran away? As if he'd remembered himself and thought that perhaps this was not the best idea, and was mortified by his choice of kissing partner, and suddenly Phoebe found that she had turned into an empty-headed girl who thought in run-on sentences. It did absolutely no good to ponder this subject, and possibly quite a bit of bad. After all, how was she supposed to face him again having all these thoughts running through her head?

Just as she resolved to not let herself ponder any kissing that might have occurred nor the man it might have occurred with, she reached the top of the third-floor stairs and . . .

There he was.

Mr. Turner. All her thoughts made manifest, his hand raised to knock on the door to her rooms at the far end of the hall.

"Miss Baker," he said, his hand pausing mid-knock. He immediately backed away from the door and, after a moment of hesitation, gave a crisp bow.

"I . . . I didn't realize we were so formal," she replied, quashing the instinct to put her hand to her hair or fold her arms over her body.

He was disheveled from his ride, his cravat loose and askew, wearing only his waistcoat—and once again, he had that utterly determined yet confused look on his face. As if he knew where he wished to be but didn't know how to get there.

"Right," he said, trying to find a place to focus his gaze, other than Phoebe. He finally landed somewhere around her elbow. "I was just knocking on your door to see if you were—"

"I ended up teaching rather later than usual," she interrupted, taking hesitant steps toward him. "I started using horses in every lesson and it seems to have taken hold . . ."

"Oh. That makes sense." He nodded, also moving forward.

They stopped some feet apart, and then just . . . stared.

"You look tired," she said softly, after a moment.

"Yes," he sighed. "It's been a trying day."

"Yes," she agreed simply.

"For you as well. Of course, I am sorry," he began. "I . . ."

"You forgot?" but as she said it, she smiled at him, amused.

"No! How could I possibly forget?" he was quick to interject. "I was in fact coming to your door to apologize."

Her heart dropped into her stomach. "Apologize?" she croaked. All of those errant, terrible thoughts she had pushed away came roaring back—he *had* lost his mind that morning when he kissed her and immediately regretted it.

"I . . . I left abruptly," he was saying, and Phoebe snapped back to the conversation, such as it was. "That was terribly rude of me, and I felt I should apologize for it."

"Oh," she exhaled, unaccountably relieved. As long as he was not apologizing for the kiss itself, she felt much better.

Although, why? Shouldn't he be apologizing for the kiss itself? Isn't that what a gentleman would do? And shouldn't she want him to?

"Er . . . Miss Baker? Phoebe?" he asked. Oh, drat, her mind had drifted again.

"Yes?" she said quickly. "I mean, yes. You did leave quickly."

"I . . . expect you were confused by it."

"Not at all," she replied. "It's rather straightforward to me." When he merely kept staring in reply, she continued, "Following me was unplanned, the kiss was un-

planned, therefore when you got to the end of it, you
didn't have a plan. And so you left. I would have likely
done the same thing."

He blinked twice before replying. "Surprisingly, that
is rather accurate."

"Then I accept your apology, even though your actions were easily understood," she replied crisply, her
smile in place.

"Good," he said, distracted. "Good."

And again, silence reigned between them. But this
time, Phoebe was not so fractious in her own mind that
she could not see what was before her.

She looked at him—really looked. Her smile fell.
His usual energy, his quickness, had abandoned him.
He was worn about the edges, a man beginning to fray.

"You really do look tired." Her voice was half
whisper.

"I am," he sighed, giving up on formality and leaning his shoulder against the wall, heavily.

She took a step forward, closing the gap between
them. Placed her hand on his arm.

"Mr. Turner, I—"

And he placed his hand over hers.

"Phoebe . . ." His voice was a gruff comfort. "I
have—I have many things I want to say to you, but
I am afraid they will all come out awkward."

"I don't mind," she replied, but he shook his head.

"It's not that. I have said quite a bit already today—
things not often said aloud. And I just . . . don't wish to
talk anymore."

"I see," Phoebe breathed. "I'll leave you to rest." But
he held her there, his hand refusing to let go of hers.

"I am going to ask a very strange favor of you and I hope you will oblige me," he said.

"If it's in my power to do so," she replied softly.

"May I . . . would it be all right if we simply stood here, in this hallway, and said nothing?" His eyes were a quiet plea. "After today, I could use a little nothing."

Phoebe considered it for a moment. Considered him. "As could I."

And so they did.

They stood silently in the third-floor hallway, forgotten to the rest of the world, and let the day slip off around them. All those thoughts that had invaded her mind all day were gone, lost in the pool of caramel afternoon sun coming in from a small square window near the stairs. Particles of dust floated around them like stars, twinkling surprise in daylight. His hand remained over hers, warm, his thumb idly stroking the soft skin on the back of her hand. And for the life of her, she could not tear her gaze away from his.

But, unlike every other time she had looked into his eyes, or been unable to avoid it, there was not that mischief that seemed to live there. There were only the basic elements of feeling. Happy. Sad. Want. Need.

She could get lost in those dark eyes. Instead, she found peace there. Maybe he found peace in hers too.

Suddenly, she felt . . . better. Not anxious, not fractious. There were no claims on her time or attention. No children to teach. She simply felt she was where she was supposed to be.

"I want to kiss you again." The words were a whisper. And it was a moment before Phoebe realized she had been the one to say them. Aloud.

The look on his face went from surprise to hope to hunger in a matter of seconds. And then that lopsided, heart-flipping smile spread across his features.

"Anything that's in my power," he murmured, lowering his head.

His hands framed her face. His lips met hers.

What started out as easy, warm, and golden as honey, soon because something more. Hands wrapped around waists, exploring higher and lower. And his mouth . . . oh, God, his mouth . . .

Her mind was not as innocent as her body. A lifetime in the country and a profession in education made her aware of certain facts. She knew why her skin flushed with heat. Why she wanted to burrow into him. But she had never felt such things before. Such fire.

Where before, the kiss had lit up her nerves, making them tingle and dance . . . this kiss melted them.

The knowledge that her bedroom and his were mere feet away flashed through her with a forbidden thrill. She was not supposed to think this way. She was a governess. She had hard-and-fast rules. Goals. But at that moment, all she wanted was to keep burning.

Time passed immeasurably, seconds or hours, and Phoebe found herself unable to care.

Only when a cloud passed over the sun, cutting off the shaft of light that had held them still, did they come back to earth and let go of each other.

The moment was broken.

Only the glow of it remained.

"Thank you," he whispered in her ear.

"It was no hardship," she replied, letting her dimple show.

He smiled in return, and the seconds ticked by again, the two of them lost to the outside world.

Until, of course, the outside world caught up to them.

Muffled footsteps and voices floated up from the bottom of the stairs—servants moving about the second floor, an unusual amount of activity for this time of the afternoon.

"What's going on?" she asked.

"Ah. I have a feeling that there will be something of a celebration over tea today. I actually came upstairs with the intention of changing my shirt," he replied, looking over her shoulder toward the noises. "Sir Nathan invited half the town back with him. I expect you will be spared a Questioning tonight, with all the people about."

"Really? Why?"

He hesitated, measured his words.

"Because the earl has decided to sell his mother's property to the consortium," he finally said.

Her eyebrow went up. "Well, that is news." She regarded him carefully. "But I don't know if you think it is good news."

"I . . ." He coughed and then started again. "It is a little sad, I think. To sell off the home you grew up in."

She nodded, silently.

"I suppose," she ventured tentatively, "you will be eager to get back to London now."

Mr. Turner seemed to consider that. "Yes. And no. Now that . . . a decision has been made about the cottage, I suppose we can leave anytime. Although I wager it will be after the festival, seeing as the earl has been roped into being the master of ceremonies."

That thought made him smile, in his old mischievous manner.

"Will he have to do much?" she asked, cocking her head to one side.

"I doubt it. But one can hope." And then one winged eyebrow went up. "However, there is a dance. The Summer Ball. One that I think you should let me escort you to."

Her head came up instantly. Shock coursed through her. And . . . something else too. A spark of excitement, of possibility.

"The Summer Ball?" She found herself shaking her head. "I do not think—that is, I will have Rose and Henry during the festival—"

"And will the children be attending the dance?" he asked, cajolingly.

"Still, I do not think Lady Widcoate would like it if I were to—"

But he silenced her by holding his finger to her lips.

"If I manage to make it so Nanny is looking after the children, and Lady Widcoate has no objection to your attending the dance, and I remove any other obstacle you might happen to think of . . . would you, Miss Phoebe Baker, care to attend the Summer Ball with me?"

Phoebe's words were caught in her throat. A dance? But she had not danced in years. And then it had been partnered with other girls in her class at Mrs. Beveridge's. But she had loved it. Loved moving in time to music, loved the delightful possibilities that existed only for young ladies in their first ballroom. All that hope, tied together with ribbon.

And she would be attending the dance with him. With Mr. Turner. This confusing man, who had in a matter of days gone from a boor to repentant to someone she felt herself trusting. And it had been so long since she trusted anyone.

She did still have a few of her gowns from her old life. But would they even fit? She had not tried them on in years, and she had changed so much since then.

But apparently, she had not changed nearly as much as she thought, because she found herself nodding slowly.

And saying, "Yes. I will go to the Summer Ball with you."

He grinned wide, and brought her hand to his lips. "Brilliant," he breathed. "Marvelous."

19

Preparations for deep play are as important as the cards themselves.

The next few days were a flurry of activity at Puffington Arms. Every single member of the household had preparations to make, to be ready in time for the festival.

As the local gentry, Sir and Lady Widcoate had the honor of playing host at the Summer Ball, which was held at the assembly rooms in Hollyhock, as the ballroom at Puffington Arms was simply too small to host the entire town. Lady Widcoate would proudly inform anyone who asked, and many who didn't, that she'd suggested the Doric columns on the exterior to the builder when the assembly rooms were first being constructed. Of course, when faced with her sister's logic that the building had been standing since the previous century, Lady Widcoate simply sniffed and said, "Well, I would have done."

As it was, the assembly rooms in Hollyhock needed

a thorough cleaning and decorating, and as the stated hosts of the affair, the Widcoates sent out a bevy of chambermaids to scrub the place from top to bottom. That the caretaker of the assembly rooms cleaned them on a weekly basis did not matter. This was a matter of pride.

As was the decorating. A task to which Lady Widcoate had set every other lady in the house. The Countess, Mrs. Rye, and all three girls were conscripted into her army. They were forced inside (a huge loss to Minnie, who was honing her archery skills) and to the work of sewing bunting, choosing objets d'art that Lady Widcoate decided should cover every available surface in her desire to impress, and deciding on the best of all possible flower arrangements.

Apparently, the argument that broke out over the merits of peonies was to go down in the annals of Puffington Arms history. Rumor had it that the disagreement had been augmented by a letter Mrs. Rye received from Bath.

"And then he said—" Henrietta had been saying as dozens of different flowers were brought before them. But as always, Minnie interrupted her, chafing against the confines of being a lady.

"I can't look at another flower," she whined. "I think they are making my nose run."

Such an idea obviously had come into her head when the countess had declared that the bouquets were making her sneeze, and thus excused herself. Lady Widcoate, never having hidden her preference for her sister's company to that of her guests, had followed suit, thus leaving the Ryes and Miss Benson in charge of all flower decisions.

"If that were the case, you would not be so eager to go outside," Mrs. Rye snapped. Her eyes were on the letter in her hand. When she finished, she looked up to find the eyes of all three of her charges on her.

"Mr. Rye has requested that we return to Bath," Mrs. Rye said by way of explanation, trying to sound breezy, but failing. Instead, her hands shook with anger. "But of course, we cannot return yet. Not when Clara has made such friends with the earl."

Henrietta's eyebrows went up, but she wisely said nothing. Apparently, Mr. Rye's enjoyment of other women and the circumstances of Mrs. Rye's removal to the country had not escaped Henrietta. And, judging by the look she exchanged with Minnie, it had not escaped the older girl either.

Clara, however, seemed oblivious, scoffing at her mother's declaration. "Mother, Lord Ashby wants nothing to do with me."

"Don't be ridiculous, Clara. Of course he does," Mrs. Rye replied hotly.

"Mother, Lord Ashby has twice called me Minnie. *Today.* He's half in love with the countess and he's probably twice my age. He has no interest in me," Clara declared. "Besides, I'm sure Father misses us."

"You father misses being considered respectable," Mrs. Rye scowled. But then, remembering herself, "But that does not mean you should not make a go of it with Lord Ashby."

"Mother, I—"

"You have to *try*, Clara. Not just be a frightened little twig!" The whole room flinched at the words.

But for once, Clara was not silenced.

"I don't want to!" she cried, her bottom lip shaking.

"I don't care! You are going to work at attracting Lord Ashby—and . . . and we are staying here until you do!"

Just then, one of the kitchen girls brought in a large vase of lurid pink peonies from the greenhouse.

"And absolutely no peonies!" she screeched, before knocking the girl over on her way out the door—leaving the floral decisions for the Summer Ball to a group of teenage girls.

Everyone, it seems, was feeling pressured.

The reasoning for Mrs. Rye's dislike of peonies would remain unknown, but the other members of the house went along in their festival preparations without as much dramatic intrigue, and a great deal more labor.

The cook had been permitted to bake and sell some pastries during the festival. Thus she set to work making tray upon tray of thankfully not-poisoned blackberry tarts.

Kevin the groom was put to the task of cleaning and polishing the carriage, so its lacquered finish would gleam bright in everyone's eyes.

Ned was himself frequently in the stables, putting the children through their paces. Rose had set herself a goal of riding into town the day of the festival on the back of Turner's mare. Ned agreed to the scheme, as long as he walked beside the horse. Henry, it seemed, was more than happy to ride in the carriage and let his sister take the lead.

When he was not instructing the children, Ned was busy making arrangements to take Phoebe to her first ball. Nanny was persuaded, with only a moderate bribe—an affection for Phoebe tempering any extravagance—to make certain there were no nursery obstacles. But making sure Lady Widcoate did not have a problem with her children's governess dancing with a secretary required more maneuvering.

He finally hit upon a solution, when he offered to forgo the "commission" Sir Nathan kept promising for turning the Earl of Ashby toward agreeing to the town's proposal, in exchange for Sir Nathan's smoothing the whole thing over with his wife.

Sir Nathan agreed with a hearty clink of his pint of ale.

Sir Nathan, now that the town's future as a bathing retreat was secured, no longer felt such pressure to impress his houseguests. For him, this meant he would go shooting with his fellow consortium members, even though it was not hunting season. Or perhaps he would go into Hollyhock and stop by the pub for a chat, and be home in time for supper. Invariably, it did not much alter how he had been acting before—he simply felt less guilty about it.

Meanwhile, another person who should have been as relaxed as Sir Nathan was instead the reverse. Mr. Fennick—as the representative of the Hollyhock Bathing Consortium—had made the trip to Puffington Arms multiple times with the intention of stabilizing the agreement with the earl, only to be put off multiple times. As a man of the law, he only felt safe once things were put in writing. He asked so many questions, demanded so much time—his eagerness was grating, as was affirmed by the whole party (Sir Nathan remaining markedly silent when it was brought up at dinner), and all declared that the earl was right to avoid him and simply enjoy the time he had left visiting the country.

Mr. Fennick kept a wide smile on his face, making sure to not let anyone see it falter. No one could know of his worry that the deal was too good to be true.

And "too good to be true" was exactly what Miss Phoebe Baker felt about the Summer Ball. Or rather, about her apparent attendance. Somehow, her Mr. Turner had removed every obstacle to it. And in doing so, he also removed the obstacles she had placed in her own mind.

Governesses don't dance. Well, apparently, this one would.

Governesses cannot walk out in public with a man. But at the Summer Ball, she could.

Governesses should not have suitors. Should or not, that was what seemed to be happening. And it made Phoebe feel like her insides were aglow with excitement.

There was, of course, the issue of distraction. And this wonderful, shining ball waiting for her in the distance was a compelling distraction. Phoebe found herself thinking about dancing, while giving lessons. She thought about her old blue silk dress, altering it in the wee hours between dinner and sleep so it would fit her thinner frame.

Over and over again, she thought about that moment in the lane, just before his lips touched hers . . . and the sunlit kiss just outside her bedroom door, when his hand had cupped the side of her face, and it shot fire to her belly.

Governesses are not romantic. And yet . . . every beat of her heart, every wayward thought proved this wrong.

Was this her adventurous heart breaking free from her practical shell? Someone in her position could not afford to be imprudent. She knew that. She had known that for five years, and kept those words at the forefront of her mind. She had her goal, after all. Two more years, and then America. But now, with Mr. Turner . . . it was something new. Something stronger than prudence. Something worth savoring.

It was at that moment that a knock came to the schoolroom door, snapping her out of her reverie.

"Goodness, what's happened?" she said, shaking her head free of the cobwebs.

"You were reading aloud," Rose said. "About different horse breeds? And then you just . . . stopped."

"And someone's at the door!" Henry piped up, running to answer.

"Henry, remember your manners, if you please!" Phoebe tried, but he was already at the door, swinging it open to reveal Nanny.

"Hullo, children. Time for luncheon," she said, flashing a smile at the young master. While Phoebe was in charge of the education, Nanny was in charge of the schedule, and anytime it called for feeding was considered a celebration.

Henry whooped and took off down the hall, Rose close on his heels.

"Do not run. The food is not going away!" Phoebe admonished.

"You'd had them late five minutes," Nanny said, watching the children go off toward the nursery. "And you picked a bad day to do it. Lady Widcoate wants you in the drawing room."

"Me?" Phoebe asked, surprised.

"She actually *came into the nursery* to find you," Nanny warned. "And I bet I know what it's about too. But don't let her bully you, Miss Baker. No reason you can't go dancing with your Mr. Turner, as far as she's concerned."

Phoebe moved with trepidation to the drawing room, but kept her head high. She could not help but worry about what Lady Widcoate might want—seeing as she was not given to involving herself in the affairs of her children—but her mind kept echoing something Nanny had said.

Her Mr. Turner. Nanny was not the first person to say it—Danson had made that observation much earlier. But Danson seemed more privy to Mr. Turner's affairs than Nanny ever was to Phoebe's. Had their association become . . . obvious?

And, more important—was he *her* Mr. Turner?

Such ruminations were quickly put aside as Phoebe knocked on the door to the drawing room, and a feminine but direct "Come in!" gave her entrance.

"Ah, Miss Baker," the Countess Churzy said graciously, her impeccable manners, as always, in place. "Do join us."

A sharp look to her sister had Lady Widcoate joining in. "Yes. Please join us. We have a matter to discuss."

"We do?" Phoebe asked. "Forgive me, is there something amiss with Rose or Henry?"

"No," the countess answered before her sister could. "Not at all. They have been so engaging when they are presented before dinner. You have done well."

"Thank you," Phoebe replied simply. And yet she knew there was more to that sentence.

"The issue is with you," Lady Widcoate interjected.

"Me?"

"You are attracting attention to yourself in a manner that is most unseemly," Lady Widcoate sniffed.

"I am?"

"Well, obviously, if that Mr. Turner is requesting to escort you to the Summer Ball!" Lady Widcoate huffed. "You have not been in good company lately, so I'll have you know that man is nothing of the sort! Teaching Rose to ride—she will fall and break her neck and Henry will follow suit!"

"Now, Fanny . . ." the countess tried, but Lady Widcoate was on a tear and enjoying it.

"And now my husband goes behind my back a second time and forbade me to forbid you from attending the ball with the man!" she snapped, more to herself than anyone else. Her eyes narrowed as she sneered, "Do you think you are the first woman he has tried to lure? Why, on his very first night here, Mrs. Rye says—"

"All right, Fanny, that is enough." Countess Churzy put a hand on her sister's arm, stopping her speech as well as the erratic bobbing of the feather sticking out of her turban. "What my sister means is that she is concerned that you are becoming too close to Mr. Turner. You have known him little more than a week. I know the earl has expressed . . . similar concerns."

"I'm sure he has," Phoebe murmured, her eyes flashing. She expected that the earl's concerns were rather conversely phrased. "How long an association would you consider appropriate, before consenting to an outing, my lady?"

The countess smiled hesitantly. "I suppose enough time to understand their intentions."

"And the Earl of Ashby agrees?"

"I would assume."

"And yet he is escorting you to the Summer Ball, correct? He has only been here a little over a week, after all."

The countess's smile dropped from her face in an instant. "There you are mistaken. I have known his lordship since we were children."

"You watch your tongue, girl!" Lady Widcoate gasped.

"I . . . Forgive me, my lady. Countess. It was a point badly made." Phoebe immediately backed off, and reassumed her role as the meekly employed.

"I understand, Miss Baker." The countess granted amnesty. "And, in fact, *my* point still stands. I know the earl's intentions. Or as much as anyone in my position can," she could not help but purr a little smugly. "Do you know Mr. Turner's?"

"He is a reprobate," Lady Widcoate chimed in. "I never wanted him here. I thought he would have been staying in town. Completely threw any plans I had awry! I tell you, there is something *wrong* with that man."

Phoebe could only blink at Lady Widcoate's misplaced vitriol. Indeed, she could tell it was misplaced from the apologetic look that the countess gave her.

"I am afraid I don't understand. Am I forbidden from attending the dance?"

"No," snapped Lady Widcoate. "Didn't you hear me, girl? I have been forbidden from forbidding it!

My husband has dropped so low as to collude with Mr. Turner—they made some sort of deal. And I would never, ever undermine my dear Nathan when he insists upon something, but he really should just listen to me and everything would be so much—"

"There you have it, Miss Baker," Countess Churzy interrupted, forcing everyone back to the subject. "You are being courted by someone your mistress does not approve of. However, you are neither underage nor under her protection, and she can do nothing to stop you. But Mr. Turner's character has been called into question. And you do represent this household. Do you understand?"

Phoebe nodded slowly, understanding the words, if not their meaning.

"As far as I am aware, your conduct has always been exemplary, Miss Baker. But a woman's reputation is everything. So you are going to have to think very hard about whether or not it is worth it to attend the Summer Ball with your Mr. Turner. After all, he could be playing some sort of game with you. If that's the case, your disgrace would be my sister's disgrace. And we would not wish for that."

Phoebe took a deep, considering breath. "No," she conceded. "We would not wish for that."

❧

"WOULD YOU CARE to tell me what the point of that little exercise was?" Fanny twitted, as she poured herself tea.

"Now, now. You did the girl a kindness," Leticia answered, rising and going to the window, looking out on the lane. "She deserves fair warning about your reservations."

"Fat lot of good it did her." Fanny's brow lifted. "She didn't seem to care at all. You saw her, carrying her head high, proud and defiant as you like."

"Yes," Leticia sighed. "I fear you are right."

"Then again I ask—what was the point of that? Besides unsettling my nerves all over again." Fanny eyed her sister. "Why did you insist upon that interview?"

"Because he asked me to," Leticia murmured.

The earl had asked her to make this last attempt to separate his secretary from the governess. He did not provide the particulars, but she could tell his previous attempts had failed.

If she had concerns about his increasing interest in the governess, they were abated by the way he looked when he asked her for help. By the way his eyes met hers, and the desire he kept banked in its depths.

Desire for her.

She should preen. She should triumph and crow to the heavens that she had done it. She had captured the heart of the man she desperately needed. But she couldn't.

One small thing kept stopping her.

The way *she* felt about *him*.

"Fanny . . . I think I would do anything for that man."

Fanny looked up from her tea, and let out a low whistle. "The plan was to turn his head. Not to have yours turned by him."

"I know," Leticia replied, her eyes still on the window. "But I am very much afraid my head has been turned around so much that I can barely keep my eyes on the horizon."

"After all this time . . ." Fanny mused. "After Churzy . . ."

"I know!" Leticia cried, surprised at her own vehemence. "I should not let this happen."

"Perhaps not," Fanny agreed. "But then again, if there is one man you *could* let this happen with, it would be he."

Leticia thought for a moment. Lord Ashby wanted her. She knew it. And not just in his bed.

Could her silly sister be right? Could it be that falling in love with a man whom she intended to ensnare in marriage was not a catastrophe?

"So you have lost your heart to an earl." Fanny shrugged, returning to her tea. "There are worse things. Just be glad you're not the governess, and risking your entire future on a dance with a secretary."

⁓

THE DRAWING ROOM safely behind her, Phoebe exhaled slowly. How dare Lady Widcoate and the countess try to influence her! She would shake with anger at being so handled, she would rail against it, but that would come when she was on her own. She knew enough of her place to know that she could not outwardly show displeasure—ever, but especially not now.

When she was in her rooms after the day was done, she could seethe by herself—and by that time, she likely wouldn't even care to. By that time, maybe she could laugh at it. But right now she had children to teach.

She sought them out in the nursery, certain they

would still be at their luncheon. But instead, she found Nanny just clearing away the plates, and the children gone.

"Your Mr. Turner came by and took them to the stables, Miss Baker," said Nanny with a wry smile. "Although, if you ask me, he was really looking for you."

She should go down to the schoolroom. Clean up the morning's lessons, correct the children's slates, and prepare for the reading she wanted them to do after tea.

But instead, she found her feet carrying her outside. Found herself idly moving toward the stables. And found her mind caught on the warnings she had just received.

Do you know Mr. Turner's intentions? She . . . she thought she had. True, his intentions may not have been very good at first, but accidentally poisoning her had made him remarkably penitent, and he had been nothing but honest and honorable since. Coming to her aid multiple times—even when she did not know she needed it.

He could be playing some sort of game with you. The game had been played—his wager with the earl regarding his stick-in-the-mud status. She had no idea if he had claimed victory or not with their kiss in the road. But it had the benefit of explaining his early faux pas with Mrs. Rye.

But was a man who agreed to such a wager someone with whom she should be spending time? That was what sent fear rolling through her.

A woman's reputation is everything. It was. Unfair, true, but there was nothing to be done about it. And, as a woman in a situation that was . . . friendless, it was less than ideal. If it happened to be the case that Mr. Turner was not someone to be spending her evenings with, then it was her reputation on the line. Her situation with the Widcoates was on the line as well, it seemed. Was she willing to risk it? She stood so close to her goals—being able to travel, to go to her relatives in America . . . would this one night, this one dance, risk it all?

As she turned the corner, Phoebe was still lost in her own thoughts, her head down, watching as her toes bent over blades of grass in her path.

Then her head came up.

There, in the field abutting the stables, Mr. Turner sat astride the earl's big black horse, Abandon. The midday sunlight caught his hair, giving it a streak of bronze. His coat lay over the fence and his shirt was open at the neck, exposing the bronze hollow of his collarbone. His sleeves were rolled up, revealing tantalizing extra inches of skin and strong forearms.

He was putting the horse through its paces, showing the children, who were safely back by the fence with his coat, what a man and a beast could do together. His thighs gripped the horse's flanks as he took Abandon from a trot to a gallop. His muscular legs clenched when he loosed the horse and let him fly, jumping over a fallen log on the far side of the field.

Rose gasped when she saw the jump. And so did Phoebe. Then they landed perfectly on the far side of the log. The children clapped. Phoebe could only sigh in relief.

They moved together as one, Mr. Turner and the horse. They were beautiful.

He was beautiful.

Suddenly, the roll of fear that had overtaken her belly released its grip, and something new took its place. A warmth, tingling awake, spreading from her chest. Lower, lower, down to the core of her woman's body, and then out in all directions, to the top of her head and the tips of her fingers.

Something went soft inside her, and for the first time in a very, *very* long time, "want" won out over "prudence."

"Hello," he called out as he cantered back up to the fence and brought Abandon to a stop.

"Hello." She smiled back, entranced.

"I want to try!" Rose cried, practically vaulting over the fence.

"Not on your life or my head," her Mr. Turner replied immediately. "You will be doing no more than a trot, and that on the mare."

Rose's bottom lip stuck out, until a moment later, when she realized—"I get to ride today? By myself?"

"Yes, I will not be up behind you. You will be on your own."

Rose practically vibrated with excitement.

"But first you have to help Kevin with the saddle and bridle, understood?" Mr. Turner intoned, and was rewarded with solemn nods of the head from his pupils. "Off you go."

As the children took off at a run for the stables, he turned his wide smile to Phoebe.

"Hello."

"You already said that."

His grin widened further. Strange—she had once thought his smile overly toothy, but now that seemed impossible. Instead, there was something irrepressible about it, like the excitement of a puppy.

"So I did," he replied. "You'll have to forgive my enthusiasm. I have a ball to attend tomorrow, and reason to believe I will get to dance with the most beautiful girl there."

Beautiful. He thought her beautiful? The words went through her like lightning. How long since anyone had claimed her beautiful?

Her stunned silence must have unnerved him, because his smile slipped. "Nanny said you had been called to attend Lady Widcoate over luncheon. Is everything all right?"

Is it worth it to attend the Summer Ball with your Mr. Turner?

Yes, it was, she decided in that moment. It would be entirely worth it.

"Everything is brilliant," she declared. "Marvelous."

20

The final hand is not always the last one played.

The Hollyhock Summer Festival—usually held three weeks later into the summer, when earls were not present—was enough of an event that it drew farmers and tradesmen from all corners of Leicestershire to sell their wares and to connect with friends not often seen the rest of the year. Local gentry was of course an attraction, and with the news that an honest-to-goodness earl would be the honored guest at the festivities—well, even the hasty change in the festival's dates did not deter the populace.

As promised, Rose rode—slowly—into town on her own, on the back of Turner's mare. Luckily it was a very sweet-tempered horse and gave Rose no trouble. Ned made certain to stay beside her, having requisitioned Abandon for the purpose. If Turner had anything to say about it, Ned didn't care. As it was, Turner rode into town with the countess and the Widcoates in the incredibly shiny carriage. Since the house was so full of people, Kevin the groom—and today, carriage driver—had to go back for the Ryes and Miss Benson. Henry was quite happy to ride in the cart with the cook, her tarts, Nanny, and Miss Baker. Everyone else walked the short two miles to Hollyhock.

When Ned and Rose crossed into town, it was to cheers from Sir Nathan, who was as enthusiastic about his daughter's learning to ride as he was usually indifferent to everything else. He helped Rose down from the horse and lifted the girl in the air. Of course, that lasted about three seconds, until Sir Nathan saw someone he needed to speak to and Rose was deposited safely in Phoebe's care. But it was a start.

Lady Widcoate, who'd stuck her head out the carriage window during the entire journey, watching Rose ride, gave Ned a grudging nod. As she stepped away to greet the vicar and other gentry she knew from the far side of Midville, the party began to mill and disperse. Ned moved immediately to join Phoebe and the children, until a hand slapped him on the shoulder.

"Oh, no you don't," Turner said with apparent calm. "I am afraid I am going to need you by my side for the festival."

Ned shot him a look that could flatten a walrus. "Whatever for?"

"I have no doubt I will be assaulted by any number of people wanting me to judge who has the biggest ear of corn, or some such nonsense. You have to help me."

"You'll be fine," Ned assured him, removing Turner's hand from his shoulder. "Cut a ribbon, pick your favorite ear. Even you can manage that."

"And yet I insist." Turner smiled tightly.

Ned rounded on Turner. "You are just trying to keep me from Miss Baker."

"You are absolutely correct," he replied.

"She had an audience with the countess and Lady Widcoate yesterday," Ned speculated. "Nanny told me she thought it was about me."

"You are getting along quite well with the help, aren't you?" Turner drawled. As Ned's eyes narrowed to slits, he sighed. "Yes, I asked the countess to appeal to her common sense. A governess should not be accepting offers of escort from anyone, let alone a secretary who made advances to Mrs. Rye barely a week ago."

"Did you impugn my character, Turner?" Ned asked, his eyes wide in false shock. "That is against the rules. Should I write to Rhys?"

"I was not in that meeting, *Ned*, so I could not impugn anyone." He kept his voice low, but the harshness of his whisper stung. "I believe there is gray area on that score."

"You ganged up on her. You had two ladies of high rank and her employer try to sway her opinion."

"Yes, I did," Turner said simply.

Ned fumed. He thought of Phoebe in that room, her back straight and her head held high, and a strange, soaring sensation grew in his chest at the thought. She could face down anything, it seemed. An earl, a countess, anything.

"I wish I still liked you, Turner," Ned said under his breath.

"I wish I still liked me too," he replied, his voice unable to hide the regret.

Unable or unwilling to ask what that meant, Ned turned away and scanned the crowd. His eyes found hers. She was ushering the children toward a stall whose painted sign declared "Fish for Prizes!" and Henry was already trying his hand with a fishing rod, trying to hook a straw doll on the other side of the stall. Phoebe smiled widely, showing her dimples when she saw Ned looking at her.

"Since it apparently had no effect, I will not call the game on a technicality," Ned decided, trying to let his blood calm with the sight of her smile. However, that did not keep Ned from twisting the knife just a bit. "Besides, I am going to win, so any of your trickery can only be summed up as foolishness."

"You won't win if I can help it."

"I already have the handkerchief. Tonight I'll have the dance. And then . . . who knows?"

"Who knows if you'll be able to find out, considering you will be stuck to my side all day today and all night tonight," Turner declared, before looking over Ned's shoulder and booming out a greeting.

"Mr. Fennick! And Mr. McLeavey and Mr. Dunlap! How pleasant to see you. Again."

"My lord, a pleasure!" The vicar came forward, edging out his two companions with his hand forward and his smile firmly in place.

"Oh, yes, my lord," Dunlap spoke up, his usual hungry look turned blasé by the festivities. "I've been so busy with the mines, a day off to spend time with people of worth is so, so enjoyable."

"Could you gentlemen point us in the right direction?" Turner asked. "I am supposed to be doing something with my master of ceremonies title, but I have no idea what."

"Of . . . of course!" Mr. Fennick squeezed his way in. "So pleased that you are enthusiastic about the honor, sir!" Mr. Fennick did everything he could to restrain himself from pumping Turner's hand, Ned noted wryly. "I'll escort you now. And of course, I would love it if we could talk for just a moment and finalize the sale of your mother's property? It would put such a capper on the day, my lord!"

"Yes, yes." Turner waved. "As Mr. Turner will be spending the day with us, you two can discuss to your heart's content." He smiled at Ned wolfishly. "Come along, Mr. Turner—we have ribbons to cut and ears of corn to pick."

Ned shot a look over his shoulder, hoping to find Phoebe and her smile in the crowd again. But alas, it seemed that Henry had won the straw doll and given it to his sister, and they had moved on.

&

PHOEBE COULD NOT believe the day sped by so quickly. Having Rose and Henry at her side constantly made the festival come alive in the way that only a child's enthusiasm can. Nanny had disappeared in the crowd with her beau—which was the concession Phoebe had made so she could have tonight.

Rose and Henry had each been given a sixpence and could not decide where to spend it first. The caramel apples? (Which, truth be told, could have used those few extra weeks on the tree that moving the festival had stolen from them, but the caramel made up for the sourness.) The tart stall, where Cook's blackberry tarts competed with cherry and gooseberry? Or perhaps they could go look at the livestock, the pigs and the sheep, the goats and the cows that farmers brought to show off—and possibly to sell, if the price was right. Rose started pulling them toward the Punch and Judy puppet show, while Henry wanted again to play the game where you use a fishing rod to snare a prize.

When the earl stood on the dais erected in the center of town, they dutifully went and watched as he was presented with a key to the town. Mr. Turner was next to him the entire time, the oversize iron key being passed off to him by the disdainful earl. He found Phoebe's eyes in the crowd, and gave a shrug and a grin that said, *Look! I've got a key!* like the eager and exasperating man she was getting to know better with every breath.

The vicar and the ladies representing the bathing committee then read a statement *each*. They started short, but got longer and longer, so that by the time the vicar began pontificating, the crowd was twitching with desire to get back to the enjoyable parts of the festival.

Sir Nathan got up last, and thankfully kept it short: "Now that that's over, let's have some food and drink!"

The crowd cheered, Henry and Rose grinned, and a singer who had been brought in from Midville's best pub took the stage and started a rousing rendition of a song with its words modified for children.

They stopped at every stall, each sixpence spent on sugars and sweets that had the children spinning in circles, their minds overloaded with colors and activity. From time to time they passed Mr. Turner, who seemed to have been roped into attending the earl that day. He would tip his hat and, being pulled away by the earl, shrug and roll his eyes as if to say *I would rather be with you.*

But one time, he did not get pulled away immediately, and they managed to exchange a few words.

"Hello," he said.

"Hello." She could not suppress the upturn at the corners of her mouth. "Again."

"Are you having a good time?" he asked, turning his attention to the children.

"I had three tarts!" Henry cried, practically vibrating from the sweets. "And marzipan."

"Yes, I can see that," he replied drolly. "And you, Phoebe? What do you think of Hollyhock's festival?"

She looked around at the festival. The people, the pageantry. The efforts of an entire town, coming together to make something wonderful. "I think it's brilliant. Marvelous," she replied simply, which made him grin.

"Miss Baker, can we watch the bruisers?" Rose asked, as only a bloodthirsty child can.

"Absolutely not. Young ladies do *not* go anywhere near the amateur boxing matches."

"They are not running you ragged, are they?" he asked, nodding to Rose and Henry, who pouted only long enough for something new to catch their attention, this time a man walking a house cat on a leash.

"No," she sighed. "Last year I had only been their governess for about a month before the festival. I was scared to death they would get hurt and I would get sacked. The nerves kept me on edge all day, then I went home and collapsed. Now I know they are basically indestructible. Besides, this time I have wisely requested that we go back to the house when the other ladies do, to rest before the evening."

"Ah," he replied, his eyes lighting up. "Yes, that is indeed a fortunate suggestion."

They stood there, in the middle of the festival, the world loud and laughing around them. But for that moment, when neither of them had a thing to say, lost in each other's eyes, Phoebe could not help but feel as if she and her Mr. Turner were the only two people in the world.

"Mr. Turner!" called the earl, beckoning him.

He nodded at Rose and Henry. "Have a lovely rest of the afternoon, young Master Widcoate, Mistress Widcoate." Then he tilted his head in toward hers and impulsively lifted her hand to his mouth. "And I will see you tonight."

&

THE CHILDREN AND Phoebe were loaded into the cart back to Puffington Arms, along with empty trays once filled with Cook's tarts and a few of the ladies' maids. The sugar was wearing off, Rose and Henry both glassy-eyed and tired on the drive back. The other ladies had squeezed themselves into the carriage. Lord Ashby and Mr. Turner would ride their horses back, and Sir Nathan was happy to be collected at the pub later.

Once they were back at Puffington Arms, the maids were immediately set to work, laying out gowns and gloves and pearls, drawing baths, and serving tea while the ladies of the house leaned back and relaxed into the summer afternoon, happy to be away from the noise and excitement of the crowds.

Phoebe took the children to the nursery, undressed them, and made them lie down for a nap. By the time she had convinced them of the virtues of sleep, Nanny had returned, flushed with joy from a day spent in the company of her young man.

"I'll take over watching them," she said with a wink. "But first, come with me—I've got a surprise."

A little bewildered, Phoebe took Nanny's hand and was led quickly down to the bathing room on the second floor. There Nanny took a bob out of her pocket and handed it to Lady Widcoate's personal lady's maid.

"She's got twenty minutes, at most," the greedy maid said. With that, Nanny pulled Phoebe into the tiled bathing room, where she discovered a bath—a fresh bath of steaming water, waiting for her.

"What is this?"

"Your bath, silly!" Nanny cried proudly. "Everyone will assume someone else got to it first. But you had better hurry up while the ladies are still napping."

Phoebe's mind was torn between wondering where Nanny had gotten a whole shilling and reveling in the brilliance of a bath of her own, when Nanny shoved a towel into Phoebe's arms and commanded that she get herself in the water. "Time is ticking, girl—and don't you go keeping your Mr. Turner waiting like this! Such trickery is for finer ladies."

Then Nanny squeezed Phoebe's arm and shuffled out the door.

Phoebe luxuriated in the bath for as long as she could.

The curls of steam and the release of tension from the long, lithe muscles of her back could not completely block out the fear of being caught . . . but still, it was the most marvelous twenty minutes of her life.

She hastily threw her dress back on and toweled her hair, abandoning the delicious bath just in time. Lady Widcoate's maid had been about to knock and looked relieved to see her dressed. She carried the bundle of her undergarments as she moved to the third-floor staircase at the end of the hall.

By that time, most of the gentlemen had returned; she could hear their low tenors downstairs in this house of women. She was briefly worried that she would run into Mr. Turner in their shared hall again. She did not wish him to see her in her current state of disarray. But he was not there, and she closed the door to her rooms swiftly and latched it, letting her back fall against the door in relief.

Then she caught sight of herself in the reflection from one of the framed pictures on the wall. Goodness, was that really her? She looked so . . . different. So *awake*. Cheeks flushed red with the warmth of the bath and the run up the stairs. Eyes bright with anticipation. Her wet hair hanging down her back, but loose on her head, framing her face, making it seem softer. She reached forward, took the picture off the wall. Strange as it may seem, yes, it was she. Younger looking, lovelier seeming. But it was she.

Putting the picture back, she inspected her body as she had her face. Not having put on her undergarments, the practical gray dress clung to her damp body, transforming it into something sensual, alluring. And though she was still much too thin for fashion, the small curves she did have were apparent now. She ran her hand over the high gentle curves of her breasts, the kick of her hip.

She looked like a woman.

The heavy gray dress felt different against her skin, she realized as she sat on the bed. Or perhaps it was her skin that felt different, as if a million points on her body were waking up to feeling, to sensation.

It was a sensation she had felt only a few times before. When Mr. Turner kissed her in the lane. When they'd spent a few moments on a sun-streaked afternoon just *being* with each other on the other side of those doors.

And when he'd kissed her hand mere hours ago, in front of all of Hollyhock.

This feeling—this *awake* feeling—crawled across her skin and settled low in her belly. With every occurrence it made her want it more. And then beyond it.

Because something told Phoebe that there was more, much more, beyond it.

Suddenly, she heard footsteps in the hall. Mr. Turner was back, his footfalls as distinctive to her as his lopsided smile. Her heart skipped a beat, her body tingling with memories of before and anticipation of what was to come.

A wicked thought crossed her mind. What if she went out into the hall now? What if she let him see her like this? Disheveled. Wanton. She bit her lip. Her hand fisted in her skirts, drawing the material up, exposing calf . . . then thigh. Oh, she could imagine the look on his face. She could see it changing from shock to appreciation to lust.

Lust. Her mind pulled up on the reins of her imagination. Lust. That's what this was, this wanting. Or at least, it was certainly part of it.

At the age of twenty-three, Phoebe was not a child. She was not a green girl fresh out of the schoolroom. However, she had not the sophistication that other young ladies her age enjoyed. Mostly, she had put thoughts of men and romance and lust out of her mind, in her quest to meet her goals. But now . . . now those long-dormant thoughts were waking up.

She *wanted* him. The way bodies clamored for each other. For touch. And it should have scared her. It should have brought her up short and made her rethink stepping outside her door ever, let alone going to a ball. But it didn't. It made her strangely . . . happy.

Happy that little part of herself that thought of men and romance and lust was not gone. That she was fully human, and not someone who could or would have to live without it. And more than anything, it made her happy that this was happening now. With him.

She had to hold her hand over her mouth to keep her laugh from being heard in the hall. She was someone who tried to find the humor in the everyday, who looked for a moment of happiness. And for once, the thing that made her happiest was . . . herself.

The footsteps in the hall paused. Then she heard Mr. Turner's door open and click shut. Her chance to shock him had passed. Ah, well. But, as she grabbed her old wooden comb, she knew she would have another chance. One that she needed to get ready for. When he saw her in her blue gown, her hair pinned up loose and lovely.

And she would not only shock him—she would stop his heart.

21

A winning hand is not in the cards.
It is in how they are played.

I t is truly amazing what some bunting and flowers can do," Ned mused, filling the silence that settled
in between him and Phoebe the moment they entered
the hall.

"Hmm," she replied, her eyes wide, her face going
slightly pale.

"Who'd have thought that mere hours ago, Sir
Nathan had fallen asleep in that corner over there?"

"Hmm?" she asked, tearing her eyes away from
the crowd of the hall and turning to him. "Sir Nathan
was . . . ?"

"Right over there." He nodded toward a corner.
"Rumor has it that's where Kevin the groom found
him, a chicken leg in one hand and a tankard of ale in
the other, taking a nice little snooze, waiting to be fer-
ried home."

She gave a little laugh, and a smile broke out over her

face. And every muscle in Ned's body relaxed. It would be all right, he thought. She had come back to him.

The night—up until they had walked into Hollyhock's assembly hall—had been going perfectly. After Ned got back from town, he took the opportunity of the mad jumble in the house to take a quick jump in the pond. Eels aside, he found it quite bracing. It also had the effect of calming him down, the excitement of the evening already making him want to jump out of his skin.

He had been to other balls. He had seen the inside of Carlton House and Almack's, and the grandest ballrooms in Grosvenor Square. He had danced with ladies dripping in diamonds and drunk brandy that the king of France would have killed for. But for some reason, this country dance shone brighter in his imagination.

Dinner had been a sparse affair, served early, to accommodate everyone in the house who was free to go to the ball. All of the ladies had trays sent up to their rooms so as not to interrupt their preparations. So, at table it was just Ned and, curiously, Minnie Rye, who held much less interest in the dance than her younger cousin and friend did. She was also not as wary of him as the other girls were, and prattled on happily with tales of the horrid process of choosing flowers, and how peonies had been outright rejected. Dinner, it was needless to say, was over quickly.

Once he was dressed and ready (thank goodness for Danson's willingness to bend the rules this once and thus see him outfitted correctly), he waited downstairs with the other gentlemen for the ladies to arrive. The countess led a procession of silk-clad ladies, all frippery and curls and excited energy. The countess, of course, was smooth and sophisticated, and in other circumstances, she would be the woman whose attention he sought. But tonight, he kept his eyes glued to the stairs, waiting for Phoebe.

"Maybe the girl came to her senses," Lady Widcoate sniffed in a false whisper to her sister.

"Let us hope," the countess replied, much more quietly, with a look to Turner, as they made their way toward the door.

Turner shot Ned a look, as if he intended to stay back—but his threats to hold fast to Ned's side were empty. For tonight, at least, he was firmly in the possession of the countess, and when she made to go to the carriage, he had to follow.

And while it made him grind his teeth, Ned knew they were wrong. She would be coming. He just had to wait.

The rest of the party had in fact departed by the time she made her way downstairs, and when she did so, it was in a rush.

"I'm so sorry!" she said as she flew down the stairs. Relief flooded through him. "I fell asleep and I had to borrow hairpins from Nanny, and she told me not to make you wait, and I went and did it anyway and . . . and you are not talking, so now I feel even more foolish."

He blinked at her in astonishment. "I am not saying anything because I am dumbstruck by how lovely you look."

And she did. The periwinkle silk of her gown brought out her clear blue eyes. The dress itself was a few years out of fashion, but she had obviously kept it in pristine condition, a reminder of a previous life. And it fit her beautifully, far more beautifully than that heavy gray wool ever could.

She looked . . . young. Funny, he had never really considered her age before. Given what he had learned about her past, she would be no more than twenty-three now. But this was the first time she looked it—or perhaps, even younger. The tiny puffs of her sleeves would have been childish on less well-formed shoulders, the soft swell of her breasts made him realize just how *female* she truly was.

Her hair was pinned up loosely, allowing some girlish curls to escape at her temples. A plain blue ribbon wound about her crown, and he wondered if it was new; if she had spent some of her precious funds on something as frivolous and yet important as a hair ribbon.

And she was blushing. He took her hand in his and bowed over it, bringing the ungloved skin to his lips.

"And yet there is something missing," he said, feeling the corners of his mouth pinch with humor.

"There is?" she asked. He watched her mind cycle, running over a mental inventory of everything that could possibly be missing.

"Indeed, but it can be quickly remedied." He brought from behind his back a (slightly) haphazard nosegay of summer wildflowers.

Her smile broke wide as she took the flowers from him and, like all women everywhere, buried her nose in them.

And promptly sneezed.

"They are . . . very fragrant," she finally said, once the sneezing subsided. "But lovely. Absolutely lovely."

"Come," he said, relaxing a bit. "We have a dance to attend."

And so, they walked out of the front door, down the steps, and into . . .

"Where do you think you're going?"

She turned. "The dance?" she said with a raised eyebrow. "We shall have to walk quickly, to make up for my tardiness."

He pulled her back up a few steps.

"Indeed, you have made us incomparably late," he remarked drolly, earning him a sideways glance. "But we are not about to walk to Hollyhock. Certainly not in that dress."

Just then, a carriage rolled around the corner of the house, pulling to a stop in front of Ned and Phoebe.

"This is for us?" she asked, her eyes popping out of her head. "Where did it come from?"

"I rented it in Hollyhock," Ned said simply. "I have to confess, I saw Mrs. Rye renting one for tonight. Since all those dresses would be smashed if everyone rode in Sir Nathan's carriage, as evidenced by this morning," he explained. "And I thought, 'That is a marvelous idea.'"

"Well," Phoebe said, "here's to Mrs. Rye!"

"Are you two coming, or what?" Kevin the groom said from the driver's perch, the top hat of his formal driver's uniform sitting high on his head.

"Kevin?" Ned asked, confused. "Aren't you supposed to be driving the Widcoates?"

"I traded with the driver you hired. Sir Nathan will never notice." Kevin winked at them. "I figured I've been your chaperone half the time, I'm not going to miss this now." He looked up at the sky, dipping into purple and black, stars beginning to shine beyond the old oaks. "And we had better get moving, lest you miss the first dance—when the earl chooses the Summer Lady."

With a smile and a shrug, Ned handed Phoebe up into the hired hack.

As they rolled along, Kevin the groom kept an easy pace and let them enjoy the ride, the night, the company. They talked along the way—Ned asking Phoebe about how she'd enjoyed the festival that day, and she telling him all about how Rose had wanted to play every game and win every prize, and Henry wanted to try every single sweet.

"I was like that, as a boy," Ned had said, his memory focusing back to his youth and the festival then. "I would eat tarts and marzipan at the festival until I became comatose."

"You had a summer festival where you grew up?" she asked.

"Er, yes," he replied, catching himself. "It was much like Hollyhock's, actually."

"Tell me about it."

And so he did. The entire day—hell, the past ten days—had been like stepping back into memory. He told her what he remembered. Of the smells of fresh baked goods, of him being eight and watching the Punch and Judy show three times in a row. Of being exhilarated by the excitement of the day . . . and then, of his mother, bright-eyed and happy to be among friends and seeing her son enjoy himself.

"It sounds like a rather charmed youth," she sighed, when he finished. "You were very lucky."

"Yes," he agreed, slowly. He had been lucky. Even then. Even before he was "rescued" from poverty by his great-uncle. He had been lucky, because he'd had his mother, and summer, and Hollyhock.

"Of course, that excludes the time I went into town with my entire body painted in mud, proclaiming I was a savage American Indian, and tried to requisition a pony from the smithy."

She laughed, that high sparkling laugh, and it carried them into the assembly hall.

And that was when the laughter—and conversation—stopped. Her nerves reclaimed her. The idea of being escorted by a man, to an assembly, presented as something other than a governess . . . well, it could not be truly surprising that her bravery fled for a moment.

"Come," he said, offering her his arm. "We do not want to miss the dancing."

They moved through the crowd, already raucous—the townsfolk having already gathered, the vicar talking with the butcher and his wife, the ladies of the Bathing Committee situated in a corner, making their opinions known with nods or furtive whispers, as little old ladies are wont to do. Mr. Fennick was chatting with a tenant farmer, wearing his Sunday best. It was all and everyone, and no one seemed to take notice of the earl's secretary and a governess as they passed by.

They made it to the large hall of the assembly rooms just in time, where a string quartet had been placed and the floor cleared for dancing.

At the top of the hall stood Turner in his earl's

disguise, his face a perfect frown, only his eyes betraying his fear. Next to him were the Widcoates, the countess, Mrs. Rye, and her charges. As the fanciest people here, they seemed to be holding court, both attracting admirers and keeping everyone at arm's length.

Ned's brow came together in a scowl. If he had been up there, he for certain would not be *repelling* people. He would be doing his best to bow and smile to everyone who met his eye.

"What are you thinking?" Phoebe asked. "Your face just became a scrunched-down line."

His eyebrow winged up. "A scrunched-down line? What on earth does that mean?"

"You know . . ." She demonstrated, bringing her brow down and squinting, making him laugh out loud, and attracting a few eyes to them.

Again, Phoebe froze up.

"You mustn't worry so," he whispered to her. "You are at a party, and acting with absolute decorum. There is nothing to make anyone think ill of you."

"I . . . I know," she replied, trying to smile again. "I am not used to being . . . seen."

"Seen? By whom?" he asked, his voice like honey. "Have you not yet realized, Miss Baker, that we are the only two people here?"

And for the barest of moments, time stopped.

Just then, Sir Nathan, at his wife's urging, came forward to address the crowd.

"My wife informs me that it is time for the celebration to commence!" Sir Nathan boomed, and was rewarded with robust cheers. He held up his hands to quiet the crowd. "Now, usually, Fanny and I lead you all out onto the floor, but today, we have a very special guest, who will choose his Summer Lady, with no doubt a discerning eye."

Ned watched as Turner stepped forward and gave a short bow, then began inspecting all the women in the audience.

"Look at them," Ned whispered to Phoebe. "Positively in knots to see who is going to be picked."

He nodded to where Minnie, Clara, and Henrietta stood next to Mrs. Rye. Indeed, they did seem to be preening—albeit at the behest of their chaperone. He nodded at Minnie, leaning over to whisper in Phoebe's ear.

"Oh, yes, he's going to choose me! I can shoot better than any other girl!" he said, mimicking Minnie's bravado. Then, of Henrietta, "He'll choose me. Then I can tell *everyone*."

"Shh . . ." Phoebe tried, but she could not hide the smile pinching at the corners of her mouth. "They are nice girls—don't be cruel." Then, after a moment, "Besides, everyone knows that Lady Widcoate is the one to be chosen. She claims the title as hers every year because, as she says, she is the only woman there who is actually a lady and . . . I doubt Sir Nathan would survive the night if he did not choose her."

Ned stifled a chuckle. "You're right. Lady Widcoate is preening harder than anyone."

Just then, the lady in question fluffed the ostrich feather jutting out of her turban, causing Phoebe and Ned to both smother a laugh. Unfortunately, it was just as Turner happened to be passing by, in his selection process for a Summer Lady. He shot them both a hard look, obviously disappointed that Ned was here, and that Phoebe had made the decision to join him.

For a brief moment, panic shot through Ned when he thought Turner might very well have the audacity to choose Phoebe to dance with. Possessiveness shot through him as he surreptitiously sought her hand and held it tight in his.

Phoebe was *his* Summer Lady, damn it.

Fortunately, Turner let his cold gaze glide over them, and moved directly to . . .

The countess.

Of course, Ned thought, as Turner led the countess out onto the dance floor, a crown of flowers placed upon her elegant coiffure, much to the mottled embarrassment of Lady Widcoate and the disappointment of Mrs. Rye.

"Oh, dear," Phoebe murmured as the quartet struck up a waltz. "I wonder how that will go over." But then she shrugged. "It likely will be smoothed out. He's an earl. And in her pocket."

"Yes," he mused. Deep in her pocket, Ned would say. Turner practically had stars in his eyes.

Poor sod.

When the first turn was made about the room, other couples were invited to join in, led by Sir Nathan and a subdued Lady Widcoate. Ned, Phoebe's hand already in his, took what he wanted and brought her out onto the floor.

"I am going to claim the first two dances with you," Ned whispered in her ear. "I would claim all the rest if it were allowed, but the little old ladies in the corner would not like it."

A blush spread across her cheeks as she put her hand

on his shoulder, and they began to move in time to the music.

"And I would claim you for the rest of the evening," she replied, humor threading under her words, "if only you were not so frightened of old ladies in corners."

He grinned. "You know that if I were the earl, you would have a crown of flowers on your head. I'd choose you as my Summer Lady."

"I'm glad you're not the earl." She sighed, her eyes fixed over his shoulder. "And I'm glad I wasn't chosen. At least to spare my feet the trouble."

Ned let his eyes follow Turner about the room. The man was glancing in their direction frequently, his mind not on his dancing. And it should have been, because Turner was fairly atrocious. The countess was doing him a great favor covering for him, but there was no mistaking his cloddishness.

"God help Letty," he murmured to himself as he took Phoebe through an expert turn.

Her eyes lit up like the dawning sun, her face flushing again with pleasure.

"You are a very accomplished dancer."

"I am a man of many hidden talents, I'll have you know."

"And just how many of those hidden talents will be revealed this evening?" she asked, archly.

Something in him sparked to attention. Was his meek little governess playing at being a saucy minx? His body stirred with awareness.

She blushed again, looking down at her feet in a way that no knowledgeable woman would. And Ned felt his body quiet. Of course she wouldn't make such an insinuation. She was too good, too innocent for that.

Instead, he took her through another turn and replied, "That depends on what the next dance is." He pitched his voice to a comic whisper. "I am an utter phenomenon at the quadrille."

She laughed again, her eyes clear and lovely, lifted to his. And Ned was suddenly overcome with a thought that blocked out all other thoughts in his head, widening like white light and blinding him from anything or anyone else in the room.

No matter what, his life would have led to this moment. If he had stayed in the village and never been made the old earl's heir, they would have met here. He would have owned his mother's cottage, had some sort of profession, and he would have known Phoebe Baker as the governess of the Widcoate children. They would have danced here.

Or, if he had still been the earl, but a better one—one who had caught Mr. Sharp and prevented him from ever meeting her father—they would have met in London, during her season. He and the light-haired girl with dimples and laughing eyes would have danced at Almack's, or in some other elegant ballroom.

Or they could have met this way, and spent this night, dancing in this assembly hall.

Something . . . strange flopped over in his chest. This, he realized, was where he was supposed to be.

But more than that, this was where he *wanted* to be.

⁀৶

THE WHOLE NIGHT had been absolutely magical. There was no other way to describe it.

And, as a teacher, Phoebe was never short on words.

After that first waltz, and the following quadrille, at which Mr. Turner was as much a phenomenon as promised, they moved to the side of the room, where Ned fetched her a glass of summer punch. Then Mr. McLeavey came forward and asked Phoebe to dance.

She was astonished. She had never even considered that she would be asked to dance at this ball. She had expected to shrink into the background when not with her Mr. Turner.

But she hadn't. She didn't.

She was *seen*. And, as odd and uncomfortable as it was at first, there was something marvelous about it. After the vicar, Mr. Dewitt, who ran the milliner's shop, asked her to dance. Then one of the local tenant farmers. She was in no way the best dancer, nor the most popular young lady there—but she was one of them. She was included.

And it was all thanks to him.

When she was dancing, usually Mr. Turner was too—but he was incredibly circumspect, only taking up respectably married ladies, and once even one of the little old ladies from the corner. The only young, marriageable woman he danced with was herself. And when they were not dancing, they were side by side, talking about the dance, the night, their lives. And laughing.

Lord, did Mr. Turner make her laugh. He broke through the wall of sternness she had built over the years, the one that let her keep her sense of humor to herself. He made it all come out. Wide smiles, happy trills, indelicate snorts. She was happier in his presence than she had been in . . . in her entire life, she realized.

And he made her throw caution to the wind, and try for boldness. Although he seemed unable to recognize it when she did. She tried to remember what it was to play coy, to be seductive. But then again, she had never had the opportunity to be coy or seductive in the first place.

But it was important because . . .

She wanted more.

"Will you ask me to dance again?" she had said, in between sets.

"I have already danced with you thrice," he admonished. And indeed, he had stolen her away for a reel, pushing the boundaries of what is proper.

"Well, if not here, then . . . somewhere else," she tried, attempting to be subtle.

"Any time, any place," he said gallantly, bringing her hand to his lips. But that was all.

Perhaps she had been too subtle.

In fact, she was at that moment trying to decide what her next tack should be, while dancing with a young navy man on leave who was visiting his family. Phoebe was trying to think of just what it would take to get Mr. Turner's lips away from her hand and toward her mouth, and debating the various dark corners and walks and maybe even the carriage ride home (although she would never be able to face Kevin the groom again) where such a transference could occur, when the music ended and the pleasant young navy man made to escort her to the edge of the floor.

And he would have done so, too, if the Earl of Ashby had not been standing in his way.

"Miss Baker," he said on a smart bow, as the young

navy man made a judicious exit. "Are you enjoying your evening?"

She was so stunned she could barely squeak. They had not spoken directly since he tried to buy off his guilt in the library days ago. And while she no longer felt hate and anger at the man, she was under no compunction to like him. She would have been perfectly happy never to speak to him again.

"Miss Baker?" he asked again.

"Er, yes, my lord," she said quietly, remembering to drop to a curtsy.

"Excellent. May I have the next dance?"

Her eyes nearly burst out of her head.

"You are not engaged already, are you?"

"No," she finally managed.

"Excellent. I will come collect you in a few minutes." He leaned close to her. "I would have some words with you then too."

And with that, he was gone.

Phoebe could feel her hands shaking. Words with her? What words with her? What could he possibly have to say to her anymore? She moved blindly through the crowd, trying to find her way back. Back to . . .

"What is it?" Mr. Turner asked, appearing like a beacon before her. "What is wrong?"

She let it gush out of her. "The Earl of Ashby asked me to dance."

Any other young lady, shaking as she was, would have been doing so for entirely different reasons. But her Mr. Turner knew exactly why she was so unsettled, and took her hand in his.

He swore softly under his breath. "Did you accept?"

"He didn't exactly allow me to say no."

"Well, then"—he smiled brightly, his entire features changing into his happy, mischievous demeanor— "that's no difficulty at all!"

"It's not?" she asked, unable to hide her surprise.

"Not a bit! Because he can't dance with you if he can't find you."

A light of understanding dawned over her. Her eyebrow went up of its own accord.

"Unless you want to dance with him?"

Slowly, she shook her head no.

"Then would you like to make an escape with me?" The rakish grin spread across his features.

Slowly, she nodded yes.

"Then let us go."

"Where?" she asked.

A spark lit his eyes. "Wherever you like," he growled, his thumb rubbing across the back of her hand, wreaking havoc on her senses.

As they threaded their way through the crowd, making their way to the door, Phoebe couldn't believe her luck, or her brazenness. She was about to stand up the Earl of Ashby. But more than that, she was about to get her Mr. Turner alone, under the cover of stars, with no place they needed to be.

Perhaps she hadn't been so subtle after all.

&

WHEN JOHN TURNER moved through the crowd at the Hollyhock Summer Ball, people parted for him. It was one of the benefits—the few he had found anyway—of being the earl. But when he spotted Phoebe Baker being led to the doors by goddamned Lucky Ned, for once the crowd did not let him follow. No, they were all moving and assembling themselves into lines for the next dance.

And Turner's partner had just escaped.

Out the doors. Gone into the night. Of course, Turner couldn't follow them without causing a scene akin to an uproar. Not when he was the earl. The anonymity of a secretary was but a memory—and something Ned was currently taking advantage of. He stared as their forms retreated, and could only curse himself. This was the last chance he had to make an impression on Miss Baker. To tell her—somehow, without breaking any of the rules— that Ned was not what he seemed, not worthy of her trust. Ned had already gained the first two criteria of the bet. The handkerchief, and tonight, the dance. Would he be willing to go for the third? And was there any way Turner could stop him?

There wasn't, he realized. Short of walking in on one gaining "intimate knowledge" of the other (which would result in an engagement and kerfuffle, and also break the wager's rules), Turner could do nothing. It was in the hands of fate now. And the hands of Miss Baker's judgment, be it good or bad.

"God damn it," he cursed under his breath. "Bloody damn hell." And he decided cursing at that moment was very much allowed. He was, after all, about to lose his mill—or win it. Everything hinged on this night. He had played every card and now all he could do was wait and see if he came out on top.

Either way, it was going to end soon. Their wager, their battle. Their lives in this fiction. And it left Turner feeling like his chest was going to cave in.

And the reason why was across the dance floor, smiling at the young gentleman who was her dance partner, all sophistication and grace and life.

"My lord!" the pleading voice of Mr. Fennick assaulted him. He swung about and faced the tweedy little man, who had Mr. McLeavey and Mr. Dunlap in his wake. "Are you not dancing?" he asked. "Well, perhaps now would be the best time to talk about having your signature affixed to some papers, to make the sale of your mother's house—"

But Mr. Fennick would never get to finish that sentence.

"Hang the goddamned deal, Fennick," Turner growled, causing the annoying fly buzzing about his head to go white with apoplexy. Then he stalked away from him, not giving the consortium another thought, and across the room to where the countess, his Leticia, was about to begin her dance.

"Excuse me," he said gruffly to her partner, and cut between them, taking Leticia by the hand.

"Ashby, what is it?" she asked, her face flush with embarrassment but her eyes full of concern. "Is something wrong?"

Was something wrong? Yes, God damn it, something was wrong. He was about to lose his mill. He was about to give up on his livelihood and his family's name and all he could think about was how he was about to lose *her*.

He just wanted something that was his. Something that couldn't be taken away from him.

And so, in the middle of the Hollyhock assembly hall, amid hundreds of people, he took Letty's face in his hands and kissed her.

As he wrapped his arms around her body, she let him drink of her essence. After her surprise wore off, she melted into him, and the din—gasps of shock and cheers of joy—faded around them. There would be hell to pay for it in the morning, or perhaps even sooner, but Turner couldn't bring himself to care.

This moment, he thought, no one could take away.

22

*Sometimes, even a novice player
has to wager everything.*

They walked. Walked the length of Hollyhock, and no one noticed or cared. Everyone around them—and they were few and far between, as most people were inside the assembly hall—was as much in their own world as the governess and the earl's secretary were.

Blind to anything but each other, they kept walking, further away from the center of town, grasping for a place to be together, until suddenly, Ned looked up and discovered himself standing in front of his mother's cottage.

There was an eerie quiet over the area, as if they were the only two people left, and this the only place.

"I always thought it was a lovely little house," Phoebe said, seeing the direction of his gaze. "It is a pity it will be torn down."

Yes, Ned thought. It was.

"It was halfway down already," he said instead,

"with the hole in the roof. And besides, it will be good for the town. Think of all the funds a new business can bring in."

"Spoken like a secretary." She smiled at him. "All figures and business potential."

"What's wrong with business potential?" he asked, one corner of his mouth turning up.

"Nothing, I suppose. I prefer to think in terms of life potential." Reacting to his look, she continued, "That is exactly the kind of home I hope to make for myself in America. Nothing fancy, or grand. Just enough."

He could see it, he realized. Phoebe in a little house much like this one, standing at a stove or fire, an apron tied about her waist. He could see her reading books in the windowsill, or growing a garden out back, the way his mother had. Or painting. Yes, she would be painting, a little studio given over to her hopes and passions.

He could see her . . . and it made him homesick.

"Come." Her smile turned impish. "Shall we go inside?"

The inside of the house was much as it had been the last time he was here—well kept, excepting the gaping hole in the drawing room ceiling. And small. Smaller than he was used to now, in his life as the earl. And yet, when Phoebe walked in, she seemed to make the place feel wide and open. She inspected the space.

"Oh, yes," she declared, putting her hands on her hips. "This will do nicely."

"You know, I have some sway with the owner of the house," he began cheekily. "He could be persuaded to part with it to you instead of to the town."

It popped out of his mouth as banter. But then he

thought about it. Hell, he could give her this house. And he *should*. She was owed. Turner wasn't wrong to offer her five hundred pounds as recompense for her father's ill judgment. He only offered too little.

Phoebe shot him a smirk. "I do not believe my savings will cover the cost of the property. And heaven forbid I stand in the way of business potential." She sighed longingly, letting her eyes roam over the appointments of the room, the furniture under cloths, the ceiling. "But still, it's nice to dream."

She kept her gaze fixed on the ceiling, looking up at the damage. But she was smiling—that archaic smile that told him she had found something that she enjoyed but was going to keep it to herself.

Well, not tonight, she wasn't.

He came over and stood beside her, then glanced up.

And saw the entire universe.

"The canvas has shifted out of place. Was there wind this morning?" she asked, her eyes never straying from the starry night that poured into the drawing room.

"Not that I recall. Could a gale of wind be strong enough to cause it to stray?"

She shrugged, lowering herself to the floor to sit in the pool of faint starlight. "Perhaps the canvas knew it would be intruding tonight, and took itself off, allowing us a view."

His head swiveled to look at her. She took his hand in hers and gently tugged him down beside her. It was a smooth and calculated move. One that surprised him with its boldness. He wondered whether she realized she was even doing it . . . and then he noticed her hand was shaking.

And he felt every nerve of her body come alive, tingling with understanding.

"Come," she said, her smile suddenly tremulous. "Come look at the stars with me."

He settled in beside her, letting his body brush against her. Looked up through the hole in the ceiling. And kept his hand firmly in hers.

"It reminds me of your painting," he said. "In your room. Looking up at the night sky—the trees surrounding us."

"Except here it is not trees," she remarked dryly. "It is pieces of roof."

"I said it *reminded* me—not that it was an exact copy." But he grinned at her. And she grinned back.

And got caught in his eyes. Held there for long, aching moments.

"Ah . . ." she said, shaking off the reverie, and returning her gaze to the heavens. "Do you see that one? That's Ursa Major. And right next to it is Leo the Lion."

"Always the teacher," he sighed on a smile.

"It is useful to know things. But she's always there— Ursa. She has been in this night sky since before she was given a name. And she has looked down on us the entire time, and seen us in every one of our incarnations."

One eyebrow went up. "Our . . . incarnations?" he asked, hesitantly.

"Us. You and me. As children. As students. As a solider and a teacher. And now, sitting in this house." She leaned close to him, her breath caressing his ear. "I wonder what she's thinking."

A shimmer of relief passed through Ned's already

too-aware body. Her "incarnations" had not included the Earl of Ashby, so he was still safe.

He leaned in, letting his breath tickle the strands of hair that fell from her coiffure at her temples. Entrancing things—so much so, he reached out with his free hand and began to coil the silky curl around his fingers. "I think . . ." he mused, "that Ursa Major is terribly concerned with Ursa Minor, and doesn't really care what we are up to."

His hand gave up the curl and began to caress her cheek, her jaw, the beautiful line of her neck. She leaned in to him, inviting his touch. "However," he continued, "if she were to take notice of us, I think she might guess that we are a young couple who, having made the purchase of their first house, are now debating the virtues of having a window in their roof."

"Ah," she replied, her voice a bare breath. Her eyes came up to meet his. They seemed gray and mysterious in this light. Not the forthright, clear gaze he had known, but something altogether more enticing. "And have you . . . come to a conclusion?" she whispered.

But he couldn't speak. His gaze was trapped by her face. Her eyes, the perfect blush on her cheek, dusky in the starlight. Then her mouth—oh, God, her mouth, parted ever so slightly, waiting breathlessly . . .

"Ah . . ." he said, turning away. *Oh, God, why did I stop myself?* He mentally kicked himself in the head. "I think perhaps there are benefits and drawbacks to a roof window."

He felt her body tense against him—with confusion, with expectation. But he did his best to ignore it, and salvage the rest of any dignity and the evening there was left.

"Yes. The benefits, of course, being light during the day—and a view."

"Mr. Turner," she tried, but he carried on.

"The drawbacks being, well . . . it could rain."

"John . . ." she whispered low—and the name had the effect of splashing cold water all over him. And breaking through his strange, nervous affliction.

"Don't . . . don't call me John," he begged, trying to keep his body from jumping out of its skin.

"Isn't that your name?" she asked, hesitantly. "I thought I heard . . ."

"It is my name," he agreed quickly. Or at least it was Turner's, he thought. "But nobody calls me by it. Not anyone I like, anyway." He gave her that half grin, and watched the corners of her mouth pinch in amusement.

"Then what do people you like call you?" she asked.

Thinking on his feet, he came up with . . . "Edward. It's my, ah, middle name."

"Well, then, Edward," she began, the twinkle in her eye mixed with the nervousness in her voice like a heady new drug he didn't know how to name. "Before we paused briefly to name you properly, were . . . were you about to kiss me again?"

Ned looked at her blankly, caught off guard by the boldness of her question. "Yes," he stated firmly. "I was."

"Good," she replied in a rush of breath. "I have been waiting simply ages."

"You have?" His voice came out strangled. Of course she had. She had been sending him signals all evening, but he was too dunderheaded to see them.

"Yes!" she cried on a laugh, rolling her eyes. "For heaven's sake, Edward. I *need* you to kiss me."

Lust zipped through Ned like a wildfire. *Well*, he thought, taking her head gently in his hands, *wait no more*.

Unable and unwilling to stop himself from taking what he wanted, Ned dove, letting his body enjoy what his incomprehensible brain had been jamming up. The kiss started out as something sweet, something to be savored, but it moved and changed for them, as they themselves did. They sank into the kiss, their bodies pulling toward each other like gravity—irresistible and unending. His fingers sought out her skin, and hers mimicked in turn.

Collars, sleeves, coats—these things all got in the way of what was most wanted. Contact. Their lips never breaking apart, they grasped for each other. What was one measly little layer of clothing, after all? Certainly, it only got in the way. Her hands found their way inside his coat, running up his chest and pushing the hateful and much-too-warm fabric off his shoulders. When he was free of that annoyance, he considered Phoebe might feel the same way, and began urging the tiny puff sleeves of her gown off her own gorgeously formed shoulder.

He let his mouth stray from hers as he feasted on her shoulder, the curve of her throat. She gasped—a sound so charged, he fisted his hand in the silk of the back of her dress. She pulled him into her, wanting to get closer . . . closer . . .

For Phoebe, her mind spun with all the sensations— new and long lost—she learned from the simplest of his touches. She wanted more from him. She wanted *everything*. Her hands precipitating her desires, knowing more than she herself did, she pulled his shirtwaist out of his trousers, craving the touch of his flesh.

"W-wait . . ." he said, his voice a smoky, strained rasp. "Phoebe, we cannot—"

For heaven's sake, why wasn't he kissing her anymore? "Why not?" she asked, dazed.

"Because . . . if we go too far, I fear I will not be able to stop."

"I don't want you to stop."

The words hung in the air, a promise just out of reach. And she could see in his eyes the doubt . . . and the hope.

"Edward—" she began. Oh, how to explain? "I am someone who, it might seem to the casual observer, has had opportunities in my life . . . limited."

He nodded slowly, not fully understanding.

"So," she continued, screwing up her courage, "when a rare opportunity comes along, like this one, I have decided to take it. And live."

She held her breath and waited. And waited.

"Say something?" she finally asked.

"I just . . . Phoebe . . ." His voice was gruff, so he tried again. "I'm just so damned lucky."

And that was all she needed. All they needed, as she pulled his head back down to meet hers.

It seemed that her Mr. Turner did not need to be told twice about her decisions. Because he embraced her with all the fervor, all the promise that had been left hanging in midair—letting it course through them both and melding them together.

His hand went to her skirt. Gathering it in his palm, raising the hem inch by slow, torturous inch, the silk sliding across her skin like butter. The cool air that hit her thigh, above her stocking tie, shocked. But the gentle touch of his warm palm shocked more. He let his fingers slide over her skin, then hooked beneath her knee, deliciously tickling the tender flesh there. Then, smiling against her mouth, he whispered, "Hold on."

"Hold on to wh—eep!" she squeaked, as he deftly pulled, and slid her back, catching her at the same time. Suddenly, she was lying on the floor, with this wonderful, impossible, mischievous man over her, making her body feel so . . . *real*. So womanly. So powerful.

"Wait," he said suddenly.

"Now what?" she practically purred. Her legs were on either side of him, squeezing . . . God, the pressure was so tantalizing, the feel of him there.

"I don't want to see such a beautiful thing ruined."

That made her stop. And her eyebrow go up.

"I'm a thing to be ruined?" she asked, the haze of passion having fled from her voice.

"Not you!" he said hastily. "I meant your dress."

"Oh." She sighed. *Oh*. He wanted her to take off her dress. She stamped down the slight current of fear that ran through her belly.

Seeing her reaction, he leaned down and kissed her mouth. "You"—kiss—"are beautiful"—kiss—"and can never be ruined. Only made more brilliant."

"Marvelous," she sighed, smiling up at him.

They came apart, scrambling to their knees. The dress made its way to the sofa on the far side of the room, draped carefully over the cloth-covered furniture. Mr. Turner's—Edward's—coat was placed beneath them, giving them a cushion for their little paradise in the starlight. Shoes followed, then stockings. A corset. Then his shirt.

She gasped when she saw the solid muscle of his chest, the flat, rippled stomach, both covered with a smattering of dusky curls. All that time on horseback had obviously been in his favor. And she wanted to touch every inch of him, with every inch of her.

And that was exactly what she would do, she decided. For once her fingers not shaking, she took the hem of her plain linen chemise in hand and drew it back over her head. Pins from her hair rained down, tumbling her coiffure about her shoulders. She kept her back straight, her eyes on his.

He drew in a sharp breath, his body going hard with want. He could only be thankful that he still had his trousers on, sparing him from spilling himself at the mere sight of the most erotic, astonishing woman in his life.

"You're beautiful," he whispered. Bending himself down to take her mouth again.

He wanted to take everything. He wanted to feel everything. But more than that, some little altruistic part of him wanted *her* to feel everything, more.

He was her first. Even if he hadn't known about her past, he would know it instinctively. He had to be careful. She deserved someone careful.

So, carefully, he let his hands roam her body, let his weight settle against her on the floor as he explored.

Her pale skin was like moonlight silk beneath him as his mouth kept and held her with him, his hands brushing against her ribs, her full breasts. Down to her hips, his fingers brushing against soft damp curls.

Her breath hitched. And he knew she was feeling something that she did not know how to reach for. And he tested her wetness and warmth with his fingers, causing her to arch toward him.

What was he doing? Phoebe thought. And, *Please don't stop*. Gracious, his fingers were *inside* of her. She was drugged. That was the only explanation. There was too much goodness, too much sweetness to be had, and she was glutting herself on it. On him. Except this time, she did not wake up in agony after eating a blackberry tart. This time she could only beg for more.

A slow stroke, lazy and delicious, had her body keening. Her mind . . . well, her mind had already fled. She only wanted what he had to offer. More pressure, more pleasure, more speed. All of these things she didn't know how to ask for, he gave her.

"That's it, my darling," he whispered against her cheek. "Let yourself go."

As he said it he matched his breath to his rhythm, making her feel a part of something greater, grander. But she didn't know what he wanted, what she was supposed to feel. And just when she thought she could not take it anymore, he moved his tawny head down to her breast and took her pert nipple into his mouth.

She nearly screamed with the pleasure of it, the strangeness. The totality. Every nerve in her body tuned to him, and what he was doing, and she throbbed with it, and then . . . she let go. Fell over the edge and flew down to earth. And when she landed, all she wanted was *him*.

She broke apart around him so beautifully, he thought, his own body nearly betraying him when he saw it. Too wonderful, too powerful, and altogether too perfect.

He wanted his turn. And she clung to him in such a hazy, starry-eyed way.

"There's more?" she asked, her voice husky with passion and curiosity.

He grinned. "Yes. There is so much more."

Ned reached for the band of his trousers. He couldn't believe his luck. He couldn't believe he was here in this night with this beautiful woman. It felt like she had been hidden away, waiting for him to find her. She had made all the boredom and loneliness he had been feeling go away—not just when she was naked underneath him in starlight, but when she stared at him with those clear blue eyes. When she challenged him to remember to be happy. When she trusted him with . . . well, everything.

He couldn't believe this was real.

That's because it's not.

He froze, his hand stilling on his trouser buttons. It *wasn't* real. He wasn't really Mr. Turner. He wasn't really meant to be here right now. And if she knew that, she would never have trusted him. Never have given of herself so boldly and completely. She would, instead, hate him.

She was going to hate him, when she found out. He could never share this with her and walk away. Never let her go to her cousins in America. And she would never, ever give in to the Earl of Ashby.

Not this Earl of Ashby. Not one who traded places

with his secretary on a wager. And who would win it, if he took what he wanted from her.

And he knew—he couldn't do it. Not to her.

"Edward?" came the teasing voice beneath him. Then, more worried, "Edward?"

His brain had known this was wrong from the beginning, he realized. That's why he had stopped himself from kissing her. But his body and his heart formed a blockade against reason.

His heart.

It took all the strength in his body to ease himself off her and away from her, the cool air of the night coming between them like a wall.

"What is it?" Phoebe asked, her worry showing openly now. "Is something wrong?"

"Yes . . . no," he said, raking his hand through his hair in frustration. "There is more," he began after a moment. "But not for tonight."

"I don't understand," she said, crossing her arms over her naked body, her voice sad.

"Phoebe, I . . ." But what could he possibly say to this bewitching creature, looking up at him so confused and so heartbroken. *I'm the Earl of Ashby. I'm a liar. I . . . I love you.*

"I need to take you home."

23

Never fold your hand before the last card is dealt.

When dawn broke the sky, Ned decided he'd had enough. Enough of trying to sleep, enough of waiting. Enough of thinking of the woman who was just down the hall.

He'd done as he said last night; rearranged themselves to look vaguely respectable, then took her back into town and found Kevin the groom. They hadn't been missed. The assembly hall was still lit with warmth and packed with revelers. Kevin hadn't even noticed their absence, having become engaged in a game of dice with some of the other carriage drivers.

"You want to go home?" Kevin had said, surprised. "Now? The night's just getting started!"

"I am afraid Miss Baker doesn't feel well," Ned offered lamely as an excuse. Indeed, Phoebe did look pale and dazed.

She did not utter one word to him on the drive back.

To be fair, neither did he. He wouldn't have known where to start. But neither did she touch him. She sat rigid, her form perfectly governessorial, her eyes forward. She refused to invite those affections that could have made the agony of the ride tolerable.

When they got back to the house, it was quiet and dark—only a few of the maids had not been sent to the Hollyhock assembly hall to clean or serve. A sleepy girl let them in, and then let them be. Ned walked beside Phoebe up the stairs, down the hall, to the third-floor staircase. She did not pause or slow, but marched up those rickety stairs with the same even stride. The same blank expression. When they reached her door at the far end of the hall, he took the only advantage he had left. Ned let his hand slide down her arm, take her hand, and bring it to his lips.

He held it there, longer than was proper, cherishing what of her he could. When he looked up, her eyes were on him for the first time since they had left his mother's cottage. And there were so many questions there.

Questions he could not answer—not then. So he released her hand, and turned away as she shut the door behind her.

The short walk to his own room was not enough to wear off his feelings. But a short dip in the eel-infested pond certainly cooled his body down, which allowed his mind to settle. Settle on all those things that had come forward and stopped him from taking what Phoebe had offered so beautifully. All those things that had made this past fortnight so unaccountably strange and uncomfortable.

And amazing.

He lay in his bed, thinking on all of it. Listening as the rest of the inhabitants came back up the drive, finally home after a full evening of dancing and merriment. Feeling the house settle around them, every nerve in his body attuned to any sound that might emanate from the room at the far end of the hall.

Alas—or perhaps fortunately—there was none.

And when dawn breached the sky, Ned decided it was time to call a stop to it. He crawled out of bed and tiptoed his way to his destination.

He pushed the door open without knocking. Crept across the room, achingly quiet. Then he reached out and drew back the covers.

"What . . ." moaned Turner, who, it seemed, had fallen directly into his bed without even taking off his shoes after the night of dancing.

"It's Ned," he whispered, brooking no opposition. "We need to talk."

⁂

THE MORNING AIR was heavy with dew, clinging to them like wet linen. They walked through the field on the opposite side of the pond, quickly losing themselves in the woods surrounding Puffington Arms.

"This should be far enough," Ned said, when they had reached a safe distance from which no early-morning ears might overhear.

"What the hell do you want?" groused Turner, trying to sound displeased, but to Ned's ear it was nothing but a whine. "I've slept barely two hours."

"Well, I've slept none, so we are in the same boat," Ned quipped.

Turner's bleary eyes grew hard. "Is that it? You dragged me out here to gloat?"

"Gloat?"

"About your lack of sleep and the reason for it. Or should I say the person for it?"

"What are you going on about?"

"Miss Baker!" he spat. "She is the reason you dragged me out here, isn't she?"

"Well . . . yes," Ned admitted, only to watch Turner's face break into a disbelieving grimace.

"I offer my congratulations," he finally said, stiffly. "I hope you enjoy your new equipment-less mill in Lincolnshire. And the mortgage on it." He made to move past Ned, stalking back toward the house. "Now, if you'll excuse me, I need my sleep. I vaguely remember agreeing to go hunting with Sir Nathan this morning, probably with the intention of discussing the terms of my supposed engagement."

"Engagement?" Ned gaped, shocked.

"Apparently, when you kiss a woman in the middle of a crowded dance floor, people assume it is the sign of an engagement."

Ned gave in to the desire to dig his thumb into his temple. "What happened to not doing what couldn't be undone?"

"I don't know, Ned." Turner's sarcasm dripped heavy from his tongue. "Do you have a way of spinning back time and *not* bedding the governess?"

"That's just it—I didn't," Ned ground out.

Turner stilled. "You—"

"Did not," Ned confirmed.

Turner visibly sagged in relief. Then a quirk of a

smile painted his face. "Came to her senses, did she?"

"No." He shook his head. "No, I came to mine."

Turner blinked in shock. And finally Ned asked what he had been wondering for what felt like ages.

"At dinner, about a week ago, you told the story of how . . . of how you got shot in battle and how I got my medal."

Turner nodded silently.

"You told it differently than I do."

"You called me fanciful. But I remember it differently," Turner replied simply.

"The thing is . . . so do I. I remember it much more the way you told it than the way I had been." Ned put his hands behind his back, starting a slow pace in the dirt and leaves of the forest. "But I had been telling it so long in *my* way that I had begun to believe it. I had begun to believe I was that person."

"What person?"

"Lucky Ned."

The name hung in the air between the two men, its creator and its bearer.

"And the thing is," Ned continued, "Lucky Ned didn't have anything to worry about in life. Everything just *happened* to him. I didn't have to do anything for myself. Or anything for anyone else. That's what I had you for."

A rueful smile was the only answer Turner gave.

"But these past two weeks, I have been doing nothing but work for myself or other people. Poring over Hollyhock's business proposition or teaching the children to ride, making my own arrangements for a carriage or—hell, carrying my own water up and down from the kitchens." He threw his arms wide, building up to something, but not entirely certain what. "And I would not trade any of it! Well, perhaps the water carrying, and the bathing after everyone, but that's it. And do you know why?"

"I hope you do." Turner blinked at him.

"I think it's because for the first time since . . . damn, since I became the earl, I wasn't *bored*. I was forced to do for myself and it was—well, if not fun, then certainly worthwhile. And if I hadn't been doing for myself, I would have been stuck up there with you, in the tower—"

"There's a tower?" Turner interrupted, seemingly confused.

"A proverbial tower," Ned replied immediately. "A tower where everything exists only on the surface. A shining place of manners and ambition, and I would have never met *her*."

"Your Miss Baker."

"I would not have met her—but more important, I would not have known her. And I think . . . I think I kept you with me as secretary for so long because we knew each other. Not in the surface way that seems de rigueur for the upper classes. We were friends. And I didn't want that to go away. It's hard for someone in my position to know anyone." That was one truth drilled into him by his great-uncle. "You are always suspicious of motive. But she does not have any." Ned sighed, and ran a hand through his hair. "Do you understand what I'm trying to say?"

Turner nodded slowly. "You're in love with her."

"Yes." He realized it was true. "Yes, I am. She makes

me want to be better, John. She makes me want to do things with what has been given to me, and not just let things happen. She deserves that someone better, but she's not going to take me as I am—when she knows who I really am."

"I see," Turner said solemnly. Then, "Although, just to be clear, you are not in love with *me*. We just happen to be friends."

Ned caught the smirk on his friend's face, and smirked in return. "Very astute of you, jackass."

"So . . . what are you going to do?" Turner asked after a moment, all contentiousness gone. "You cannot be Mr. Turner forever."

Ned started pacing again. "When you proposed this bet, you thought I wouldn't make it a day, did you? That's how you justified this. In my mind, I thought it was a harmless joke to play on silly people. But it's neither. They are not silly and this . . . isn't harmless."

"No. They are not, and it isn't," Turner replied gruffly. "But by the time I figured that out, we were too far into it. I've hated myself for days."

"As have I. I have spent all last night racking my brain, trying to think of a way to make this right. And there is no easy or simple way to do it. Any way it comes out, someone gets hurt, and most often it is Phoebe."

"And Leticia," Turner murmured.

"Yes. So—I have no idea how I am going to fix that. But I can fix something else."

Turner's head came up from his musings. Ned stopped pacing.

"You have long since chafed against the role of secretary. It was never your ambition, but you did it for me. You should have left ages ago, but I kept making it harder for you to do so."

"My own bad luck had something to do with making it harder," Turner noted dryly. "It's not as if you made storms happen and shipments get lost, or any of my other problems."

"I know that. But I could have been a help, not a hindrance." Ned cleared his throat. "So, in my first act of being better, you win."

Turner quirked up a brow. "What?"

"You win the wager, Turner," Ned said clearly. "You win, and you're dismissed from my employ."

Turner opened his mouth to say something, but no sound came out.

Instead, the only answer was the report of a gunshot, echoing from the trees.

24

*Never forget, when stakes are high,
any game can be deadly.*

Help me!" Ned cried as he lumbered through the front door of Puffington Arms, a limp Turner hanging from his side. He crashed into the drawing room, just off the main foyer, throwing Turner as gently as he could (damn, the man was solid) onto the settee.

"Graeahhh!" Turner screamed through gritted teeth as he landed on the couch, the shift causing the bullet wound in his left shoulder to move and twist painfully.

"I'm sorry," Ned said quickly, grabbing some lace throws from the table and pressing them into the wound.

"GRAEAHHH!"

"You have to keep pressure on the wound, you know that," Ned admonished. "Keep your hand here, understand?" He transferred Turner's right hand to his shoulder, making him press, trying to keep as much blood in him as possible. It had already been a long tumble back from the woods, and red liberally streaked not only Turner's clothes but his own.

Ned spun around looking for something, anything that could help him. Luckily, his rumpus upon entering and Turner's screams of pain had attracted some attention from the household, and there were two maids standing in the doorway.

"Wake up your masters," Ned told them. "Bring me clean linens, scissors, some water, and brandy. And get Kevin the groom in here, now!"

While they had stunned expressions, the maids responded to the voice of authority with speed and professionalism. Thus it was only moments before Sir Nathan and Lady Widcoate came plunging through the drawing room door, dressed in their nightgowns and sleep in their eyes.

The sleep went away quickly enough.

"What the devil!" Sir Nathan boomed, rushing over to the prone form on the couch.

"Is that the earl? Oh! Lord Ashby! You have murdered Lord Ashby!" This from Lady Widcoate, who began fluttering the instant she saw the color red. "What have you done, you monstrous brute!"

It took a moment for Ned to realize that her accusatory eyes were on him, and he should likely answer the accusation of murder. "I did nothing," he said, his voice turned stony with authority. "We were walking in the woods, talking, and a shot rang out. And he's not dead."

Lady Widcoate was mollified by either his words or his commanding stature, but in any case, it had the desired effect. She shrunk back, gaping like a fish. "But then, who—?"

That question was cut off by the door flying open and admitting Mrs. Rye and her charges.

"He's bleeding!" Minnie declared with morbid fascination.

"Oh, my goodness!" Henrietta squeaked, trying to see over Mrs. Rye's shoulder.

"I think I need to sit down," Clara added meekly, turning white as her mother's frilly bed cap.

"Girls! Do not look!" Mrs. Rye said sternly. Then, turning an accusatory glare on Ned, she began *her* interrogation. "What did you . . . how did you . . . how *dare* you . . ."

To which Ned let his eyes flash with fury as he replied succinctly, "Madam. I did nothing except bring him here and try to save his life. Now, kindly get out of the doorway."

Mrs. Rye's eyes widened in shock, but she complied—which allowed Kevin the groom to rush in.

"Gor—what happened?" Kevin said, looking at the pale, groaning form on the couch. "The girl said someone was dead, and—"

"He's not dead. Kevin, there's no time," Ned said, grabbing a piece of paper and a quill off the writing desk. He hastily scrawled an address on it. "You have to go to this address in Peterborough. Take Abandon, there is no time to lose. If you fly fast you should be back in a few hours. Ask for Dr. Rhys Gray."

"You're sending to Peterborough for a doctor?" Sir Nathan piped up. "There is an apothecary in Midville, he took my tooth out—"

"The bullet is still in his shoulder. Dr. Gray is not only a surgeon but a physician. He is our friend from the war, he is experienced, and I am not trusting his life to anyone else—especially not a tooth-extracting apothecary," Ned replied firmly. Then he turned his attention to Kevin, who was standing still. "What are you waiting for? Go!"

Kevin started, and quickly ducked his way out of the room, saying, "Pardon me, miss," to the newly arrived—and stock-still with shock—Leticia.

"Ashby?" Her voice became small and broke as she unfroze and came to his side. She kneeled at the sofa's edge and brushed an errant lock of hair out of Turner's eyes. "Darling, what have they done to you?"

"It's . . . all right," Turner said, his eyes locked on hers. "Don't . . . cry." His voice was a struggle, and it tore at Ned's gut to hear it.

"Of . . . of course not," the countess sniffed, and tried to smile. "These are not tears. Just, ah—too many flowers in here. Now—" She wiped her hands over her cheeks. "What can we do? Mr. Turner?"

Ned found those dark, seductive eyes on him, but for once they were straightforward, and keeping fear in check.

"You can help him keep pressure on the wound," Ned said. "That should stop the bleeding. But be careful, I think his—"

"GRAEAHHH!"

"—collarbone was broken by the bullet," he finished lamely, as the countess decreased the pressure she was putting over Turner's hand, which held the now bright red scrap of lace to his shoulder.

"Is that my doily?" Lady Widcoate noticed. Luckily, the doily would be saved from further dampening with the arrival of linens, a pitcher of water, and a decanter of brandy, borne by one of the maids he'd sent.

"Excellent, thank you," Ned said, receiving the tray.

"Really, Mr. Turner, is now a time for drinking?" Mrs. Rye harrumphed.

"And the good brandy too!" Lady Widcoate added.

"I think it's a perfect time for drinking," Sir Nathan mumbled. But to all of them, Ned barely spared a glance.

"It's not for drinking," Ned said through gritted teeth. "Countess, lift your hand—and his, if you can manage it."

She did, whispering sweetly to Turner, encouraging him to lift his hand off the wound. Ned carefully clipped the coat and the shirt away from the wound and exposed the skin.

"What are you doing?" came Danson's voice from the door. "Cutting a coat by Weston?"

"I'm trying to save his life, Danson," Ned said without looking. "Now, come and help me."

The grave valet rushed forward without another word and helped Ned survey the wound.

Blood was still pooling, but it seemed a bit slower than the gush of red that had occurred when he fell in the woods. Danson took one of the linens and damped it in the water, pressing it to the wound, cleaning the area. Turner whimpered in pain but did not move a muscle. Ned attributed this to the presence of the countess, and was thankful for her way with him. Then Ned took up the bottle of brandy.

"Are you ready?" he asked Turner, locking eyes with him. Turner took two deep breaths through his nose, then nodded.

"What are you doing?" Henrietta asked, with more curiosity than relish.

"Something Rhys taught us in the war," Ned replied, and then poured a liberal amount of brandy on the wound.

The sound Turner made was inhuman and echoed through the room. The countess, God save her, held his hand tightly and let him squeeze his pain into her.

When it was over, Turner's body relaxed, slumped. Ned quickly packed fresh linens on the wound. "Keep pressure there," he commanded the countess. "When blood seeps all the way through, add another cloth. Eventually it will stop." He turned to his valet. "Danson, help her."

Ned made to rise, but when he did, Turner caught his arm. Ned met his eye.

"In the . . . in the woods . . ." Turner began, his voice even weaker now from what he had just gone through.

"It's all right—don't tire yourself," the countess murmured in his ear.

"No," Turner coughed. "In . . . woods. Heard . . ."

"Yes?" Ned said, leaning forward.

"It was . . . Baker."

And then Turner slumped, passing out from the pain or loss of blood, or both.

Ned felt the ground shift beneath him. The clock ticked on the mantel, five, six, seven times, before someone finally spoke.

"What did he say?"

"Did he say Miss Baker?"

"Miss Baker? The governess?"

"The governess shot the earl?"

"Everyone stop!" Ned cried, coming to his feet. "I'm certain there is some misunderstanding. Miss Baker was not in the woods this morning. Tur—the earl must have meant something else."

"What else?"

"How do you know she wasn't in the woods?"

"Where is she, then?"

"There is a murderess in this house!"

"She is not a murderess!" Ned cried again. "Not the least reason being that he is not dead. He has simply passed out due to pain. And I refuse to consider any preposterous explanation until he wakes and can explain what he meant."

"That is all very well and good for you," Lady Widcoate sniffed. "But my children are under her care! And cannot be a moment longer!"

"Lady Widcoate, be reasonable," Ned tried on a sigh. "There is no reason for hysterics."

"Oh, really?" Lady Widcoate sneered. "Why not?"

"Well, for one thing, Miss Baker has no reason to shoot him."

"But she does," came the calm, rapidly cooling voice of the countess.

All eyes turned to her.

"He told me that he was worried about her . . . flirtation with you, Mr. Turner. Because she had blamed the earl for her family's past misfortune."

"Revenge!" Henrietta piped up, her eyes as large as saucers, full of the salacious possibilities. "But what about—"

"That's it!" Lady Widcoate cried. "My babies! My darlings! We must rescue them from her evil clutches!"

"My dear, hush." Sir Nathan took his overly dramatic wife in his arms (and now Ned knew where Rose got such flair) and turned a dark gaze on Ned.

"Mr. Turner, it seems Miss Baker would have a motive."

"It's patently ridic—"

"And while we can do nothing for the earl except wait for the doctor, I for one do not intend to let Miss Baker go unquestioned."

Sir Nathan patted his wife on the head and released her, before stomping out of the room. It took only moments for the rest of the party to scurry after him.

Ned looked down at the countess, still kneeling beside Turner's prone form, diligently placing pressure on the wound, under Danson's direction.

"You are wrong about Miss Baker," he ground out to her.

"I sincerely hope so, for both your sakes," the countess replied coolly.

"You'll stay with him?" he asked.

She nodded in return.

Ned did not hesitate. He had to catch up to Sir Nathan. Phoebe had no idea what was coming.

～∾～

"SOMEONE SLEPT LATE," Nanny singsonged as Phoebe rushed into the schoolroom. "Or perhaps didn't sleep at all?"

Phoebe blushed a deep red, but otherwise her features remained utterly controlled. "I apologize for being late, Nanny. Rose, Henry—good morning," she said quickly, turning her attention to her charges. Turning her attention to anything other than Nanny's knowing look.

"We already had breakfast," Nanny said, "and recited the alphabet—"

"Nanny only missed 'L-M-N-O,'" Henry cried. "She did much better today!"

"And I'm running a bit behind myself—needed in the kitchens." Nanny took off her apron and smoothed her hair as she spoke. "Apparently, there's some sort of ruckus, and a few of the girls were called away to help. Cook is going mad trying to ready the kippers and eggs, because everyone got up earlier than she expected for the day after the Summer Ball. Everyone except you, that is." Nanny winked as she passed Phoebe, and headed out the schoolroom door.

In truth, Phoebe had barely slept last night, so fraught was her mind. She kept running over the evening in her head, the wonderful moments at the ball having their shine dulled when compared with her outrageousness at the little cottage, and then Mr. Turner's confusing reaction to them.

And she had thought Mr. Turner seemed confused before! But this time, it infected her. She had gone past boldness into wantonness, and he had made her feel such things . . . and then . . .

He'd stopped. Stopped and changed every feeling of glory she'd had to shame. She had thought he had feelings for her. Feelings enough to leave her with a wonderful memory. But instead, she'd only inherited his confusion.

She'd lain awake most of the night, swinging madly between rejection and rage and courage and cowardice. How would she act when she saw him again? How would he? She'd ached, her body pulsed, at the smallest sound from outside her door. But it was never anything. Finally, in the early, predawn hours, she'd fallen into exhausted sleep, all the energy she'd had coursing through her from the excitement and enormity of the day leaving her spent, and she'd slept. Late.

But she could not stare at the closed schoolroom door and reflect on it any longer. She had Rose and Henry and their lessons for the day to fill her mind.

"Now, children, if you would please fetch your primers . . ."

As Rose and Henry found and took out their primers, there was a knock at the door. Both Rose and Henry cocked their heads, eager to be distracted.

"Turn to the page from yesterday, and start reading," Phoebe admonished as she went to the door.

"Edwa— Mr. Turner," she said, unable to hide her shock. He was red-faced, as if he'd been running. She could not think of anything else to say, her eyes locked on his, until she noticed who was behind him. "And Sir Nathan." She dipped to a curtsy. "How can I help you?"

"Miss Baker," her Mr. Turner began, and she forced herself to keep her expression blank. "There has been—"

"Miss Baker, all you need do is answer one question," Sir Nathan said, elbowing his way past Mr. Turner and into the room, his barrel chest and belly filling up the space so that Phoebe had to take a step back. Rose and Henry immediately stopped pretending to read their primers and watched in awe.

"Certainly," she said, folding her hands in front of her. "Where were you this morning, about an hour ago?"

For the rest of her life, Phoebe would wonder why she lied. Maybe it was because Sir Nathan's presence in the schoolroom was strange and intimidating enough to turn her tongue on itself and make her feel meek and scared. Maybe it was because of the warning she'd received from Lady Widcoate and the countess, telling her that her conduct at the Summer Ball must be above reproach—and she felt that oversleeping would be seen as an admission of some kind of guilty act. Or maybe it was because her Mr. Turner's solemn eyes were on her, and she did not want him to know that she had been so unsettled.

But no matter the reason, lie she did. "I breakfasted with the children at seven, and then we began our lessons."

Mr. Turner sagged in what could only be relief, a strange reaction to Phoebe's eyes. Sir Nathan turned to him, and she had thought the man would nod and go, and it seemed for a moment like he would. But then, quiet, observant Henry decided to speak up.

"But you did not have breakfast with us today," he said. "It was just Nanny."

Mr. Turner's face fell. Sir Nathan's turned bright red, his brow coming down in fury. Phoebe quickly backtracked.

"Yes, that is true. I am sorry, Sir Nathan, for lying. I overslept and did not want you to think me lazy, especially on account of how you so graciously allowed me to attend the ball last night, and I beg your—"

"I found it! I found it!" Lady Widcoate's voice came from beyond her husband, as she knocked Mr. Turner back again to force her way through. "I found proof of your perfidy!"

"Actually, I found it," Henrietta Benson piped up from behind her. Mrs. Rye, Clara, and Minnie followed close behind.

"Rose! Henry!" Mrs. Rye called out. "Come here and, er . . . play with Minnie and Clara!"

But Rose and Henry did not move, their eyes flitting from one grown-up to the other, their faces despairing confusion.

"What perfidy?" Phoebe asked, taken aback. "Edward, what is going on?" She turned her eyes to him, but he could only stare back at her, gravely.

"There was . . . an accident this morning," he began. "The earl—"

"Accident, my foot!" Lady Widcoate cried. "The Earl of Ashby was shot, as well you know, and I have the proof of it."

She held open her hands, and there were little scraps of torn paper.

Paper it took only a moment for Phoebe to recognize.

"It's a note from the earl—that's his seal, right there—and if you piece it together, it offers Miss Baker a great sum of money," Lady Widcoate said triumphantly.

"Actually, *I* pieced it together," Minnie said dryly. "I like puzzles."

"But the fact remains that Miss Baker tore it to pieces! Showing her hatred of the man for the world to see!" Lady Widcoate finished.

"Where did you find that?" Phoebe asked, dazed.

"Your rooms," Lady Widcoate replied. "And by the

bye, had I realized you and Mr. Turner were the only people on the third floor, I would never have allowed you to attend the ball. I can only imagine the illicit goings-on up there! Why, you have made this a house of murder—*and* ill-repute! To think, my babies have been in your presence. Oh, my babies! Rose, Henry, come here and get away from this nasty woman."

As Lady Widcoate rushed to her stunned children, smothering them into her bosom with her brand of affection, Phoebe's mind was reeling. She would have commented on the fact that it was Lady Widcoate who had *placed* them both on the third floor, or that the children looked more frightened by her attentions than anything else, but instead, her mind got stuck on a different part of the accusation.

"Murder?" she asked, faintly. "The Earl of Ashby is . . . dead?"

She could feel her knees going weak. Thankfully, Mr. Turner's voice sailed above the fray.

"No, he isn't dead, merely injured," he said, his eyes shooting daggers at the group. "And when he wakes up, he will tell you that Miss Baker had nothing to do with it."

"I didn't!" Phoebe croaked.

"And yet the earl already said you did." It was Mrs. Rye this time, whose eyes flashed furiously. "I know a liar when I see one."

"Now, hold on," Mr. Turner said, his body coming between Phoebe and the rest of the group. "I will not allow you to impugn Miss Baker this way."

But it was Sir Nathan's voice that boomed over the crowd.

"Mr. Turner is right," he said, the gaggle of women behind him stilling, Lady Widcoate gasping, clutching Henry tight. "It is the earl who will proclaim Miss Baker's fate. But as he cannot do so at present . . . Miss Baker"—he stepped forward and took her arm tightly in his meaty paw—"you had better come with me."

Phoebe's eyes fell on her Mr. Turner's flushed and angry face, but there was nothing he could do, as Sir Nathan dragged her away.

25

*When play turns foul, a gentleman will
be forced to call the cheater out.*

"You are going to let me see her."

Ned squared off with the guard at Phoebe's door,
whose stern expression gave away nothing.

It had been two hours since she had been hauled
away by Sir Nathan. Two hours since she had been
locked away in her own rooms, no other provocation
than a ripped-up letter and a whispered word from
Turner.

When Sir Nathan closed Phoebe up in her rooms,
she was pale but stone-faced, her head held high. She
refused to make any admission of feeling, refused to
give anything away. So, he put the guard in place and
that was that.

Then everyone went back downstairs. Ned didn't wish
to, but he was well aware of the heavy scrutiny that he
was getting from the Widcoates, and he needed to check
on Turner. He wanted to be there when he woke, and

wanted to make sure he had heard him correctly. Or, as he hoped, incorrectly.

Turner was where they had left him, on the sofa in the drawing room, the countess tending to his wound with assistance from a maid. His bleeding had slowed to a crawl, and she had bound some linen around his arm to keep it still lest he aggravate the broken collarbone. He was in and out of consciousness, but never clear enough to be asked questions. Ned had tried anyway, without any luck.

For the umpteenth time since a random rifle shot had rung out from the trees, Ned considered bringing the room and the world to a halt by revealing his true identity. But three things stopped him. First, they had no reason to believe him—after all, he had spent two weeks telling them he was the earl's secretary. There was no proof, and it could backfire so easily. Second, who knows if it would do any good? He would vouch for Miss Baker's character as the earl, but he could not give her an alibi. And, not for the first time, he regretted not having provided her with one. Third, and most selfishly—someone had shot Turner . . . likely thinking he was the earl. Meaning someone out there wanted the Earl of Ashby's blood. He did not want to tell them that they'd missed.

While Ned was trying, to no avail, to get sense out of Turner, Sir Nathan had sent for the county magistrate. However, two things were likely to slow his arrival. First, the magistrate had attended the festival and Summer Ball yesterday, and had stayed until the wee hours. The second was that the only person left in the house who could drive was Cook. She had hitched the old cart herself and taken it out just as soon as breakfast had been served.

There seemed little else to do but eat after that, although the countess refused to leave Turner's side, and Mrs. Rye had no kind of appetite. The children were brought in, as Lady Widcoate was suddenly struck by a bout of motherly love and refused to let them out of her sight—although she complained of such nervous spasms that it was Clara, Minnie, and Henrietta who ended up playing with them, with Nanny looking on. As it was, only Sir Nathan gobbled up the kidney beans and ham.

When Ned finally decided that everyone had been lulled far enough into complacency, he excused himself from the breakfast room, saying he was going to relieve the countess of her watch. If anyone had a brain in their heads they would have followed him, but Sir Nathan, true to his nature, considered the matter settled, Lady Widcoate was far too engrossed in her own flutterings, Mrs. Rye was happy to turn a blind eye to anything she considered unseemly as long as she could, and the girls were entertaining the children. Out of everyone, it was only nosy young Henrietta whose eyes followed him out of the room, but she stayed where she was, on the breakfast room floor, playing a game of sticks with Henry and Minnie.

Thus, Ned crept swiftly up the stairs to the third floor. If he came across anyone, he would say he was only going to his own room. But no one stopped him.

Until he got to the guard, that is.

The guard who, outside of Kevin the groom, was the only other male servant in the house.

"Is that an order, sir?" Danson replied, his face not giving away a flicker of interest.

"You're bloody well right it is."

"Very good, sir," Danson said crisply, stepping neatly aside and producing a key. He unlocked the door as Ned came forward, his skin suddenly itching to get to her. Before Danson opened it, though, he whispered low in Ned's ear, "She's strong. I haven't heard her crying, sir. But if you change that I will come after you with sewing shears."

"Sewing shears?" Ned asked.

"A valet's best friend. Sir. I will be at the end of the hall, should you need me."

It was at that moment Ned realized he would have to give Danson a hefty raise once they extricated themselves from this mess.

Ned eased the door open and found Phoebe sitting on her bed. Her back ineffably straight, her eyes fixed on the small, framed painting that hung on the wall— looking up at the night sky, through a circle of trees. It was, in fact, the only thing of Phoebe's that remained in the room. The other pictures, papers on her desk, the few clothes—all of them were packed up in a valise, sitting next to her on the bed.

"Going somewhere?" Ned asked quietly.

"Yes," was her only answer.

"Somewhere nice?" He tried to be light. "Perhaps I've been there and can recommend accommodations."

"Have you been to prison?" she asked, her voice unable to hold on to amusement, instead becoming bleak.

"You will not go to prison," Ned replied, so savagely that Phoebe couldn't help looking at him.

"Not if the Widcoates have anything to say about it."

"Phoebe, the Widcoates won't have a choice!" Ned came and sat next to her. Unable to stop himself, he grabbed her cold hand in his, held it fast. She did not return his grip, but neither did she remove her hand. "I will protect you. No one as small and mean as the Widcoates will ever be able to touch you again. Besides, the earl will come to, and he will explain to everyone that you had nothing to do with this."

"Even if that is the case, I've been accused of murder by my employers. I doubt I can stay here and be civil any longer." She shook her head. "I can go to America. To my cousins. I have enough money for the voyage. Not as much as I would like, but . . . enough. I'm told Connecticut is pleasant. I just . . . I . . ." Her face began to crumple, as she was unable to hold up the façade of strength any longer. "I don't know why I *lied*."

Big fat tears threatened to fall onto her cheeks. The sight of them broke something in Ned. Something fierce, primal, and protective. He said nothing but pulled Phoebe to him, crushing her against his chest.

"This morning, I . . . I was so tired, I had barely slept, and then I overslept. I should have just told Sir Nathan that, but I made it seem like I had something to h—"—*hic*—"hide."

"Hush, my darling, hush," Ned soothed, unable to hide a smile. "Don't cry. If only because Danson will murder me with sewing shears if he hears you."

That made her shoulders shake with laughter instead of tears. "It was your fault I overslept, you know."

"And you are the reason I slept not at all."

She pulled back and looked at him then, her eyes

drying quickly after their uncharacteristic display of emotion. Those clear blue eyes asked all the questions left over from last night, and several new ones too.

And suddenly, the weight of things unsaid and secrets too long held bore heavy on Ned's chest. He knew he needed to tell her everything. Everything he had taken Turner out to the woods to confess that morning. How he felt about her, what he wanted—and the reason he didn't deserve any of it. His true name. And their foolish, terrible game.

But where to begin? What words would cover the enormity of what he needed to say?

Evidently, he took too long contemplating, because Phoebe let her gaze slip away. Pulling her hand away from his, she composed herself.

"I suppose it doesn't matter now, anyway," she murmured, smoothing her hand over her hair.

She made to rise, to shake out her skirts. The return to decorum—and space. And Ned knew—in the bottom of his very soul—that he could not let her put her walls back up.

"Phoebe." Ned stood with her, taking her hand in his. She let hers lie limply. "You're wrong. It does matter that neither of us got sleep last night."

"Why?" she asked, her entire body lighting like a wire. She tried to pull away from him, but he pulled her back.

"Because . . . of what happened last night between us."

"And what did happen, Edward?" she burst out. "I had an entire night to contemplate, and *I don't know*."

"What could you possibly not understand?" Ned said, his voice getting louder.

"Why did you stop?" she wailed finally, breaking free of his hold. "Why did you pull away from me and make me feel like such a fool?"

"I . . . I never intended you to feel like a fool."

"How could I not?" Her face was a fury of anger and despair, of raw, honest pain. "I bared everything to you, and you walked away. If you didn't want me, you could have simply said so at the beginning and spared me the embarrassment of being . . . wanton and unwanted."

"Not want you?" Ned cried, bewildered. "How could I possibly not want you? Phoebe, I'm in love with you!"

Her breath stopped. "You . . . you're in love with me?"

"Yes," he exclaimed, nearly laughing in relief. He risked a step forward and took her by the shoulders. "I didn't stop because I didn't want you. I stopped because I wanted you so badly. But I didn't want you to hate me. And you would have hated me, Phoebe. I promise. You still might."

"Why would I ever hate you?" she asked, bewildered.

He swallowed, the right words elusive, dancing around and taunting him. "I . . . there are things you do not know about me, Phoebe. I have not been entirely honest with you. About my background. My family."

"I don't care," she said quickly.

"You will, though—"

"No I won't." She shook her head. "Edward, I have been one of those cosseted young women like Minnie or Clara or Henrietta, not a care in the world, and looking down at everyone else. And then I tumbled from that pedestal, and I faced the world's derision for it. Hell, even my own family—my mother's side—saw me as something other than myself. You think I would judge you for not being of a certain social level?"

She stepped closer, raising her eyes, the stubborn faith he saw there nearly unmanning him. "When you talked about your home, the forest or the festival you enjoyed growing up, you would hesitate, and were vague, and I could tell that you were not telling the complete truth."

"You could tell?" Ned rasped.

"I teach children. It trains one to spot the fibs." She smiled at him. "But Edward, I do not care if there was no festival in your little town in Lincolnshire, or if there is no mill. I don't care if you are the child of chimney sweeps. I could never hate you."

"Phoebe, it's not that sim—"

She cut him off with a kiss, threading her hand through his hair, bringing his head down to hers, and melding her body against his. He let his arms come up behind her, envelop her. He fell back against the wall in the small room, taking her with him.

"I could never hate you," she breathed, her mouth coming away from his for the barest of moments. "Because I love you too."

Ned felt something wonderful, truly wonderful, settle into his chest, around his heart. It made him feel like flying. It made him want to hold her tight forever. But more immediately, it made him want to kiss her again.

So he did. Hard and long, with no reservation now, no fears. Because if she loved him . . . surely that was all that mattered.

What did not matter was clothing. In fact, what they wore was little more than an annoying hindrance. He wanted to get closer to her, as close as he could. His fingers roamed over her body, gathering her skirt in his hands, pulling it up and up, until finally he found the skin at the back of her legs underneath all of the fabric. She sighed beneath his touch and it drove him mad. Drove him to lift her, wrap her legs behind his back, and press her against the wall.

"Phoebe." He forced himself to pull his head back. "Are you sure?"

"Sure?" she asked.

"Sure about me."

"Sure that I love you," she replied. "And sure that I want this."

That was all he needed. He moved quickly, diving into her with abandon, losing himself in everything Phoebe.

She could feel him, Phoebe realized, a thrill running through her. She could feel *everything*. The hardness, the pulse. He did not withhold himself from her this time, and a hasty jumble of fingers at the buttons of his pants had him springing free, and the hot length of him pressed against her, wanting entry, wanting more, wanting permission.

"Tell me," he growled. "Tell me you want this."

"I want this," she moaned. "I want you."

They had no time. They only had each other. With all his heart and absolutely no finesse, he took what he wanted.

And she gave it. Took him in, her body balanced between the wall of her small room and her Mr. Turner's strength. He stretched her.

And when the pain lanced through her, she hid it behind a kiss.

Although it didn't fool Ned. He saw it, felt her tense around him, and he wanted to kill himself for it. But it was too late for that. He was already too far gone to stop himself now, let alone commit suicide. It would have to wait, because right now, he wanted all of it. The fast, intense pleasure that was threatening to overtake him. He grabbed hold of her bare bottom, his fingers digging into the flesh there as he moved, watching in awe as she rose and fell, sliding against the wall with the motion of his thrusts.

This is too much. Her mind fought against the feelings that threatened to consume her. That rush of sensation that she had felt only last night, now more familiar but just as frightening. It was this moment, having him like this, that she had wanted, yearned for, and despaired of in her mind all at once. She wanted to stay here, stay with him . . . but the more she fought it, the stronger it got, and suddenly she could not hold herself in any longer.

Ned could tell the moment she began to come, nudged over the edge and beautiful to behold. He let go of his own control then, and gave as much of himself as she had given of her.

All that was left in the space was their breathing, slowing gasps of air, each bringing them closer back to earth. Her eyes met his, wide with wonder, dark as midnight with desire fulfilled.

And then . . . she smiled at him. And he could only smile back. Lopsided and happy.

"You should let me down," she whispered.

"Give it a moment," he said, not wanting to let her go.

"It cannot be comfortable for you, holding me up," she protested.

"I've never felt better in my life," he replied honestly. He would have been happy staying like that for a moment, a minute, a lifetime.

However, Phoebe had to be uncomfortable. She had just lost her virginity in a quick thrust up against a wall. That could not have been the gentlest way to go about it. And there was a perfectly good bed mere feet away.

"I'm sorry," he said suddenly.

"Whatever for?" she asked.

"For not being kinder." He took his weight from her as gently as he could and let her feet slide to the floor. Her shaky knees gave way a little when she put weight on them, so he took the opportunity to keep his hold on her, gather her up in his arms, and deposit her on that perfectly good bed, mere feet away.

"Are you in pain?" he asked, watching her wince as she sat, straightening her dress into a modicum of decorum.

"Not really," she replied. "Not anymore."

He didn't want to let go of her. He wanted to keep contact between them, so he sat on the bed next to her, let his leg touch hers, wrapped his arm around her, and tucked her against him. She leaned into him with a sigh.

"I have made a decision," he announced.

"Have you?" she asked, one eyebrow quirking up.

"Yes. You are *not* going to America. You are staying with me," Ned declared firmly.

A second eyebrow joined the first, accompanied by a wry smile. "Oh, am I?"

"Yes," he reasoned. "We will get through this mess, you'll see. And we will get married, of course."

"Of course," she agreed.

He looked at her askance. "That's it? No arguments? No railing against my declaration as overly . . . declarative?"

"I find it rather silly to argue against something I find that I want," she replied practically. Then her face split into that wide-dimpled smile, and she let her joy show through. "Besides, I think I am ready to retire the name Baker. I should much prefer to be Mrs. Turner."

Ned's expression came down, a sour dread lacing through his happiness and leaving a bitter taste in his mouth. Damn it all, he was the biggest heel of all time. He had taken her against a wall and not told her his name. And he had to. Ideally, before she surrendered the name Baker.

"What is it?" she asked.

"Nothing," he decided to say, once again a coward. "It's just . . . Baker." He rolled her last name over on his tongue. "Why would T— the earl say that? Do you have any idea?"

Phoebe shrugged. "He could have meant anything. Perhaps the baker from Hollyhock?"

"I doubt it." The baker was one Mrs. Dilby, who had been running the pastry shop when he was a lad. She was ninety if she was a day. Barely able to lift a loaf of bread, let alone a rifle.

Realization dawned and smacked Ned in the face like a cold eel from the pond. "Of course!" he cried, coming up from the bed so suddenly, Phoebe fell backward.

It was so *simple*. And it made so much sense. Ned grabbed Phoebe by the hand, pulling her up from the bed.

"Edward! What is it?"

"I've figured it out," he said breathlessly, kissing her hard and joyfully. "Come—let's go prove your innocence."

26

No one can win without incurring losses.

"Sir Nathan, there you are! Oh, and Mr. Fennick too, where did you come from? And you, sir, must be the magistrate—very pleased to meet you."

Phoebe watched, dumbstruck, as her Mr. Turner bounced down the main staircase and into the foyer of Puffington Arms, where Sir Nathan was greeting the newly arrived—and visibly bleary—magistrate.

"Indeed," Sir Nathan said, a bit nonplussed. "This is Mr. Hale, whose estate is east of Midville."

"And much where he would prefer to be." Mr. Hale turned his reddened eyes and veiny nose to peer at her. "Is this the girl?" he asked.

"Yes," Sir Nathan replied, his voice gruff with the surprise of seeing her there.

"Then we'll take her to be held at the jail in Midville," Mr. Hale said, before coughing up a lungful of morning fluid. Clearly, his night at the Summer Ball had been as raucous as theirs.

"Such a sad, sad state of affairs," Mr. Fennick was saying in a quiet undertone to Sir Nathan. Then he turned his attention to her. "As you know, I am more versed in the law of contracts and papers, my dear, but if you should need any advice . . ."

"No call for that!" Mr. Turner said cheerfully. Phoebe's mind reeled at his happiness. How could he be so joyful? She was about to be taken to prison!

"I told you, Mr. Turner," Sir Nathan was saying. "I'm not having a murderer in my house, and especially not near my children."

"Well, then, let her return to the schoolroom, because Miss Baker is no murderer."

Sir Nathan sighed the sigh of the weary. "We all heard what the earl said. He said *Baker*."

"Correct," Mr. Turner replied. "Not Miss Baker. Not Phoebe. He was not identifying his shooter."

"Then what was he identifying?" the curious voice of Henrietta Benson came from the entrance to the breakfast room. There the women stood collectively, except for the countess. Phoebe guessed she was likely attending the earl.

"I am so pleased you asked, Miss Benson," Mr. Turner replied, putting his hands behind his back and rocking back on his heels, happy as a clam. "He was not identifying his shooter. He was identifying the weapon. A Baker *rifle*."

Jaws dropped across the foyer. Sir Nathan, in particular, looked a bit like a fish. "A Baker rifle? How—did he see it?"

"No." Mr. Turner shook his head. "He heard it. Believe me, after time spent on a battlefield surrounded by Baker rifles, you never forget the sound."

Phoebe's hand came to her mouth. *Of course*. Baker rifles had been used during the war, more and more replacing Brown Besses, and had since been populating the countryside.

"Do you own a Baker rifle, Sir Nathan?" Mr. Turner asked casually.

"Of course I do," that man replied. Then, realizing the implications, "But I only use it for hunting! And hundreds of other men in the country have one as well!"

"That . . . that still doesn't mean Miss Baker was not the villain!" Lady Widcoate tried. "We have evidence of her hatred of Lord Ashby! And my husband was with me this morning. He could not have shot the earl. But Miss Baker could have—she could have stolen the rifle from my husband's stores."

"True enough," Mr. Turner replied. "Perhaps you could go fetch the rifle, Sir Nathan?"

"Why?"

"Because you keep your hunting rifles in good working order, do you not?" Mr. Turner queried.

"That I do." Sir Nathan's chest puffed out with pride. "Clean and oil them myself after each use."

Of course he did, Phoebe thought. There was no gamekeeper or manservant here to do it for him.

"So, if the rifle is dirty, that would be definitive proof that it was the one fired this morning, would it not?"

Sir Nathan rubbed his bushy mustache for a moment and then, with a nod, ran off down the hall.

"Mr. . . . Turner, is it?" Magistrate Hale interrupted.

"I am afraid that I have no idea what is going on. I simply wish to collect the girl and go home."

"Your patience, Magistrate, is appreciated," Mr. Turner replied with a grin, then turned back to the assembled women.

"While we are waiting, let us explore the second part of Lady Widcoate's postulation. You say Miss Baker stole the rifle. But what would make you think she knows how to fire it?"

"What?" Lady Widcoate said, putting her hands on her hips. "Now you are being ridiculous."

"Do you know how to fire a rifle, my lady?" he asked. Phoebe could only watch in wonder. Her Mr. Turner had command of the room, being jovial, but not yielding his point. He was a leader of men.

And he was hers.

"Of course not," Lady Widcoate huffed.

"Do you know how to shoot a rifle, Miss Baker?" he asked, causing Phoebe to start. Then she shook her head.

"Of course she would deny it," she heard Lady Widcoate say under her breath. Always feeling the weight of phantom persecution, that one. If Phoebe had not been currently fearing for her very life, she might have broken character and rolled her eyes.

"Do any of you ladies?" he asked blithely.

"I do!" Miss Minnie Rye cried. Her aunt tugged at her arm, silently admonishing her to keep quiet. "What?" Minnie asked. "You do too."

Mrs. Rye blushed deeply. "I only learned because my husband is often . . . traveling for business, and I wished to be able to protect myself and my daughter.

But I couldn't have done it, because I was asleep as well. Besides, I am a terrible shot."

"But I would wager Miss Minnie is quite a good shot."

"Mr. Turner!" cried Mr. Fennick, aghast. "You cannot seriously be accusing a young lady like Miss Rye of shooting the earl?"

"Why not?" Mr. Turner spun on his heel to face the fastidious little lawyer. "It makes as much sense as blaming Miss Baker."

"But there is no reason for Minnie to shoot anyone!" Clara cried, shakily.

"Indeed, she actively tries to avoid it," Henrietta piped up, "ever since she almost shot off my toe with an arrow a few days ago."

"Minnie, Henrietta, be quiet, NOW," Mrs. Rye commanded. "Lady Widcoate, I will not stand to have my girls decried in such a way. The truth is, Mr. Turner, that your lady-love had means to shoot the earl, motive to do so, and, as far as anyone can tell, opportunity. She lied to Sir Nathan about her whereabouts this morning. And now the earl is dying on a sofa. Can you argue any of that?"

"No," Mr. Turner said simply. "Other than the dying part. But the fact remains that Miss Baker didn't shoot the earl because she *could not*. She does not know how to operate a rifle."

"Well, let's put that to the test," Sir Nathan said, coming up the hall. "I have my Baker rifle." He brandished the weapon in his hand. "And, yes, it is clean," he said to Mr. Turner before he could ask. "But it is possible she cleaned it and put it back before we discovered her in the schoolroom, is it not?"

"I sincerely doubt it," Mr. Turner said, his tone brooking no opposition. Although Sir Nathan had some to give.

"You might be right. And the earl might bear your theories out. But unless you want Miss Baker behind bars in Midville . . ."

"Never," Mr. Turner replied savagely.

"Then you will allow us to submit her to a simple test."

He let those words hang in the air. The two men growled at each other, like dogs fighting over a bone, while the magistrate, Mr. Fennick, and the ladies looked on in anticipation.

"I'll do it," she said suddenly. Every eye turned to her, positioned on the stairs. It was almost as if they had forgotten she was there.

"I'll take your . . . your test, Sir Nathan," she clarified, her eyes on Mr. Turner, her stare calming him. "And then, one way or another, I am leaving this house for good."

∗ ❧ ∗

"PLEASE TELL ME you have actually no idea how to use a Baker rifle," Ned said under his breath to Phoebe, as they walked out across the veranda and down to the open space by the pond, which Minnie had been using for archery, bowls, and any other lawn game she could persuade people to play.

"I have never shot a rifle in my life," she replied. "But it can't be that hard, can it?"

The corner of his mouth quirked up. "Go on believing that, and you'll be fine."

They neared the rest of the group. Naturally, *no one* wanted to miss this, the governess-murderess proving her innocence by firing a rifle. All the housemaids and the cook were gathering at the windows. Ned looked for the children, but luckily they were not there. Nanny must have kept them away from the fray.

"Don't be nervous," he whispered to Phoebe. She nodded and gave him a slight, brave smile.

"Mr. Turner, step away from Miss Baker," Lady Widcoate cried. "For all we know, you are telling her how to cheat!"

Ned's eyebrow went up, but he said nothing. With a small squeeze of Phoebe's hand, he released her.

All Ned could do was watch. If this did not work, he did not know how he was going to extricate her from this ridiculous mess. If only Turner had said something else! If only Turner would wake up into coherency. If only Rhys would get here and get him better. Because if Turner took a proverbial turn for the worse, well . . . Ned could lose two people he loved that day.

Sir Nathan handed Phoebe the rifle. She held it by the barrel, at arm's length. Then he handed her the ball and powder.

"What am I supposed to do with this?" she asked.

"Oh, for heaven's sake—she doesn't even know how to load the bloody thing!" Ned could not help but cry out.

"Language, Mr. Turner!" Mrs. Rye called out, pressing hands over Clara's and Minnie's ears. Both girls tried to duck out of the way. "And maybe she is feigning her ignorance, hmm?"

"She is not, Mrs. Rye," Ned countered. "Unlike some, she is incapable of feigning anything."

Mrs. Rye sniffed at the reproach, but she let it go. Really, Mrs. Rye had become terribly prudish since that first night when he thought she might welcome a fling. If he were to guess, he would say that it was that misconception that did it. Perhaps she had been thinking of a fling, and then found herself horrified at the prospect of one.

"Now, if she cannot load the gun, how could she have fired it?" he asked.

"Perhaps she had help?" Lady Widcoate rationalized. "Perhaps the gun was left loaded?"

"Sir Nathan said he always cleans his guns. Why would he clean it and then reload it and then put it back?" Ned drawled.

"Well, what if she used a different gun?" came the wheedling sound of Mr. Fennick's voice. "One that was already loaded. Er, just as a suggestion."

Ned looked over at the little man, considering his words. And then . . . something clicked into place. The last piece of this ludicrous, dangerous puzzle.

"Very true, Mr. Fennick," he said, considering. "Your solicitor's brain has come upon a weak spot in my argument." He watched as Phoebe's eyebrow went up, but said nothing. Ned kept his attention on the calm-faced man in front of him. "Very lucky you happened to be here."

"Well, I had an appointment this morning to go hunting with Sir Nathan and the earl. To firm up plans for the cottage before he left for London, you see."

"Yes, indeed. Have to make certain those plans are firm."

"You have no idea how many people no longer believe that giving one's word constitutes a deal." Mr. Fennick shook his head. "I have had so many difficulties—"

"Well, since you happened to be coming to go hunting, surely you can help Miss Baker load the rifle?" Ned broke in, all innocence. "So we can see if she can fire it. After all, you are right, she could have taken a rifle already loaded from somewhere else."

"Well, I suppose . . ." Mr. Fennick tried, his full eyebrows rising up to his nonexistent hairline.

"Come on, come on, Fennick," Sir Nathan said gruffly, having settled himself into a chair on the veranda, and not looking like he wanted to rise again anytime soon. "Load the thing for the girl, we haven't all day."

With a quick nod, Mr. Fennick crossed to Phoebe and took the rifle out of her hands. With quick, practiced motions, he checked the barrel, loaded and primed the gun. Then, with one last check, he handed the rifle back to Phoebe.

"Now aim," Sir Nathan called out. "Into the pond, if you please—I should rather not have anyone shot."

"My toes escaped mauling once already this week," Henrietta said, causing Clara to snicker and Minnie to turn red with embarrassment.

"Like this?" Phoebe asked, bringing the gun to her side.

"Er, more like this," Mr. Fennick replied, adjusting her position, so the gun was at her shoulder.

When she was in position, Mr. Fennick stepped back, and then . . . Phoebe fired.

"Oof!" she cried as she fell backward. The force of the rifle's kick had sent her flying onto her back, showing no small amount of petticoat when she landed with a thud. She struggled to her feet as rapidly as possible, and quickly restored decorum to her skirts.

"Now I know why ladies don't shoot," she murmured as she rubbed her shoulder.

"Yes, they have quite a force," Mr. Fennick agreed, absentmindedly rubbing his own shoulder in sympathy. "And you, er, missed the pond." They looked and saw a mark in the dirt on the other side of the pond, where her bullet had ended.

"I think you can agree, Sir Nathan, Lady Widcoate," Ned drawled, stepping up to join Phoebe and Mr. Fennick, "that it would be nearly impossible for Miss Baker to have shot the Earl of Ashby."

Lady Widcoate opened her mouth to protest, but she was stayed by a stern look from her husband. "That is . . . a fair assessment," he said grudgingly.

"But . . ." Lady Widcoate tried. But this time Ned cut her off.

"Lady Widcoate, stop. Take a moment. And admit to yourself that you were swept up in the madness and must now let it go." His eyes narrowed. "While you think, perhaps you should take some refreshment? A bite to eat? I understand blackberry tarts are a particular favorite of yours."

Lady Widcoate's cheeks flamed in either horror or embarrassment, but she shut her mouth.

"And can we perhaps all admit the impossibility of Miss Baker's involvement in this event?" Ned called out to the crowd. "A young woman who can neither load a rifle, nor manage to hit an entire pond when standing right in front of it, is hardly likely to be the crack shot who felled the earl from under cover fifty yards away."

He had thought perhaps that there might be a rousing cheer for his efforts, for Phoebe's unshakable bravery. But rather there was some grumbling, some shrugging, and ultimately, a concession of the point.

"Yes, Mr. Turner, it is agreed." Mr. Hale the magistrate spoke for all. Ned wrapped his arms around Phoebe as he felt her knees give way.

"Perhaps I can go back to my bed now?" Mr. Hale yawned.

"In just a moment, Mr. Hale," Ned called out. Then he turned his attention to the man with the gun. "Thank you, Mr. Fennick, for your assistance in proving Miss Baker's innocence."

"Well, you are quite welcome, Mr. Turner," Fennick replied, handing the rifle over to him.

"You say you were coming hunting here today?"

"Yes. Sir Nathan and I—"

"Yes, yes, solidifying business and all that. Must be terribly trying, being the only member of the consortium concerned about the deal."

"That's not wholly true . . ."

"Now, now, as a man of business, I know how it goes," Ned said cheerfully. And he did, too, since he had read through all the paperwork of the business proposal. "The consortium's been laying out a pretty penny to make this work, I assume. Land surveys, having a pipeline built . . . even moving the Summer Festival cost money! You deserve the credit for being the one to make certain all that happens."

"Thank you, Mr. Turner." Mr. Fennick blushed. "It is gratifying to have one's work acknowledged."

"How much does it take to buy into the consortium anyway?"

"How much?"

"You four are equal partners. But equal means different things to different people. After all—Sir Nathan is funded by his wife's fortune. Mr. McLeavey comes from some money, as he'll inherit a hunting lodge upon his mother's death. And Mr. Dunlap owns a profitable mine. But you're just a solicitor. You must have used everything you had."

Mr. Fennick's eyes narrowed, while his grin remained firmly in place. "I don't see the point of enumerating my involvement."

"Don't you, Mr. Fennick?" Ned rubbed his chin. "Where is your rifle?"

Mr. Fennick's obsequious smile faltered. "My rifle?"

"Yes, your rifle. For hunting. You do have your own, correct?" Ned inquired. "After all, you shoot with Sir Nathan often."

Fennick shot a nervous look to Sir Nathan, who had begun to peer at him queerly. "Certainly . . ."

"Then why did you not bring it this morning?"

"I . . ."

"Or perhaps you did." Ned advanced on Fennick. Phoebe fell back and away. "Perhaps you came out early and had your rifle with you. And saw us in the woods."

"I . . . I . . ." Mr. Fennick began to stammer.

"Too good an opportunity to miss, I suppose. After all, so many people no longer honor their word. If the chance at the cottage slipped through the Hollyhock

Bathing Consortium's fingers because the earl changed his mind, it would be terribly problematic."

"You . . . you are spinning ridiculous stories now," Mr. Fennick replied, his nervousness turning to anger.

"Perhaps," Ned conceded. "But if we go into the woods, what are the odds that we are going to find your rifle underneath a pile of leaves somewhere?"

Gasps rose from their audience—which had grown. The gunshot had drawn the housemaids out from behind the windows and onto the veranda.

"Mr. Fennick?" Mr. Hale said, his bleary eyes narrowing, as if he was finally truly waking up.

"Fennick, where is your gun?" Sir Nathan asked.

"I . . . I . . . I cannot believe you are accusing me of such things!" Mr. Fennick cried, puffing out his chest and poking at Ned's chest. "I would never do anything to harm the earl!" The little man's eyes narrowed. "But *you* might."

"Me?" Ned scoffed. "Mr. Fennick, I was the one who brought the earl in."

"Exactly—you were the only one with him," Mr. Fennick returned. His solicitor brain began to pick up speed. "We have only your word for what happened."

"Until he wakes up."

"*If* he wakes up. Who's to say you were not out there early in the morning to end his life yourself!"

"Don't be ridiculous, Fennick," Ned drawled, his ire rising.

"I'm not—it is no secret that the two of you have been at odds since you got here."

"Yes, they have been," Lady Widcoate breathed. Without her sister present she was letting her imagination run wild, and it was making Ned see red. "And most of all over *her*."

She pointed at Phoebe, who turned to the lady herself. "Lady Widcoate, you are not doing your cause any favors."

"How dare you speak to me in such a manner!" Lady Widcoate gasped. "You are as rebellious as your lover. And as dangerous. Why, he could have a hundred reasons to wish the earl harm!"

"Why the hell would I want to hurt the earl? I *am* the earl!" Ned growled.

The minute it was out of his mouth he regretted it. He had been holding on to it for so long, and spent the sleepless night deciding that this would be the day to tell the truth . . . but not like this.

His eyes shot to Phoebe, who was looking at him, her expression curiously blank. Only her eyes, usually so clear, gave her away. They were clouding with confusion.

The rest of the audience—the Ryes, Miss Benson, and especially the Widcoates—simply stood there in openmouthed shock. Until, Lady Widcoate, true to form, began to laugh.

A long trill of laughter, harsh and brittle. "How very droll, Mr. Turner. But you cannot remove the stink of guilt from yourself with further lies."

The rest of the party relaxed, Mrs. Rye snorting a laugh and Sir Nathan adjusting in his chair. Everyone except . . .

"Of course!" Henrietta cried, her face lighting up like a firework. "It all makes sense now!"

"What makes sense?" Clara asked in her small voice.

"What I . . . overheard on Sunday, when we all went into town. I told you I went to the Granville cottage to see what all the fuss was about and I heard voices and I thought one was the earl but it didn't really sound like the earl and then Mr. Turner—or, er, *you*," she said with a nod to Ned, "came storming out, and I've been trying to figure it out ever since! But that's what they did. They traded places!"

Now it was everyone's turn to blink at Henrietta.

"Don't be ridiculous, Henrietta," Mrs. Rye said, her voice steel.

"But—"

"You have long since been too fond of poking your nose where it doesn't belong, and making up stories. I will have to have a talk with your mother upon our return to Bath. Which will be immediately, Lady Widcoate. I am afraid this is all much too dramatic for young ladies."

"Long overdue, if you ask me," Lady Widcoate grumbled. "Although if you wanted to shield them from dramatics, perhaps your departure should have been before we all came outside to witness Miss Baker's shooting ability."

Mrs. Rye turned red as a beet, and opened her mouth to retort, but was stilled by Mr. Hale, whose tired voice rose above the fray.

"This has all become rather confusing," he said. "Perhaps I should come back later."

"Or perhaps you should arrest Mr. Turner now," Mr. Fennick called out, to which Lady Widcoate vehemently nodded. "For attempting to implicate me in crimes, for attempted murder, and for trying to lie his way out of it. Thinking we would go into the woods and find my rifle under a bush, indeed!" he scoffed.

"I said a pile of leaves, Mr. Fennick. Not a bush. Although now I know better where to look," Ned retorted instantly. Mr. Fennick colored, giving himself away. "And I am not lying. I *am* the Earl of Ashby."

"Can you prove it?" Sir Nathan asked. All this time he had been sitting still, rubbing his chin in thought, and listening.

"He doesn't have to." The familiar voice made Ned's shoulders fall with relief, as Dr. Rhys Gray rounded the corner, his medical bag in hand, Kevin the groom close behind. "I can attest to it. I am Dr. Rhys Gray, of Greenwich, and this is Ned Granville, Earl of Ashby." Rhys shot him a look. "And apparently, he has caused just about as much trouble as I predicted."

"Rhys, I'm so glad you're here," Ned said in a rush. "Turner has been—"

"Your groom filled me in on the way," Rhys cut off his explanations. He called out to the assembled crowd, "Can someone take me to my patient, please?" Then, low, to Ned, "Not you. You have a bigger mess to clean up."

Rhys glanced over Ned's shoulder. As his friend followed a maid inside, Ned turned and saw . . .

Phoebe.

Everything happened around them. Lady Widcoate emitted a screech, popping up out of her chair and rushing into the house. Sir Nathan pulled Mr. Hale to his side, whispering and conferring. The Rye girls surrounded Miss Benson as she explained how she had figured it out. Mrs. Rye hung her head, no doubt trying to decide how she was going to explain this madhouse to her girls, and then her face lit up with glee, with the knowledge that she had the most delicious gossip to spread upon their return to Bath. And Mr. Fennick . . . he used the commotion to make a quick escape, thus cementing his guilt. Although it must be questioned whether he thought much further than getting away from the house, because really, once back in Hollyhock, where would he go? As it was, Kevin the groom intercepted him before he rounded the corner, tackling him to the ground, and brought him, crying, over to Magistrate Hale.

And all the while, Phoebe was watching Ned. Staring, her expression becoming hard, her eyes crystalline. Her voice, when she spoke, was as flat and cold as ice.

"Edward," she said, then cocked her head slightly. "Ned."

He nodded slowly.

"They call you Lucky Ned, don't they?"

"Phoebe, this isn't . . . I wanted to tell you before." He took a step toward her, but she quickly held up her hand, stopping him in his tracks.

"Yes," she agreed, her voice clipped. "Before would have been better."

They stood there, in the middle of the lawn, madness breaking all around them. And all Ned could do was hold his breath.

And then, he could only watch as she turned away from him and walked back into the house.

"Phoebe," he called out, running after her, "Phoebe, wait!"

27

Never wager more than you can afford to lose.

etty!" Lady Widcoate's shriek broke through the haze. Turner knew where he was. He knew the hand that held his—and had been doing so for hours. He looked for her face whenever his eyes opened. Her dark, secretive eyes for once gave away everything.

He was not feeling all that well. His shoulder burned like fire, and the rest of him wanted to be absorbed into the sofa. When he came to, all he could see were colors swirling and Leticia's face.

Then he saw Lady Widcoate's bustling form come into the room, on the heels of someone tall. Someone with a calm, soothing voice which was gratefully familiar.

"Rhys . . ." Turner managed.

"Excuse me, please," Rhys said, kneeling down next to Leticia by the sofa.

"Are you the doctor?" Leticia said, the relief evident in her voice.

"Yes. Who has been taking care of him?"

"I have."

"You have done admirably. I'll take it from here. John . . . John, can you hear me?"

"Letty, come away from him!" Lady Widcoate called out.

"Wait, why is he calling him John? Fanny?" Leticia's voice got quieter as she rose, stepping away.

"Rhys," Turner tried again. Rhys was prodding at Turner's chest, putting his horn-shaped listening device to his heart. (He forgot what it was called. He never paid as much attention to Rhys's work as Ned did.) "I . . . wasn't shot . . . there."

"I can see that," Rhys said sarcastically. Then his tone changed to that no-nonsense yet kind tone he used when he wanted his patients to know they would be fine. "This is nothing. I've seen you looking worse. Getting shot should be old hat by now."

Turner chuckled, then winced in pain. Rhys called out behind him, "His heartbeat is quite fast. Have you given him anything?"

"Ah, just water, when he asked for it. And brandy," Leticia answered. "But I still don't understand—"

"I will explain," Lady Widcoate said harshly. "Just come away with me *now*."

Turner wanted to call out, wanted to tell her to come back. But before he could find the words, he could no longer find the color of her dress in the room. She was gone.

"I'm going to take the bullet out of your shoulder,"

Rhys said, opening up his bag of horrors. "And it's really going to hurt. You'll be happy to know, though, that Ned discovered who shot you."

Turner only gave a slow nod. His eyes remained on the door, through which Leticia had vanished.

"I believe this is when I say I told you so. Pursuing your damned wager led you to this point."

Turner didn't move, just kept his eyes on the door.

"From what I saw outside, however, I think perhaps you won."

But the door remained open, and empty. So terribly empty.

"No." He shook his head. "No one wins."

⚏

"PHOEBE!" MR. TURNER—no, no, he was the earl now—called out, as he took the steps to the third floor two at a time. Quickly she grabbed her bag, already packed on the bed. She had no choice but to go past him, but she could do it quickly. She could rush past, not look him in the eye, and be gone.

She just had to do it without her heart breaking in half.

She put her hand on the knob and did exactly as she said. She kept her head high but her eyes low. She pulled the door open and stepped out.

And he was right there.

"Where are you going?" he asked, his eyes falling to her satchel.

"America," she replied calmly.

"Now?"

"I told you, I have the funds to make the crossing. It's

not much but I will manage once I am there and find my cousins."

"Phoebe, please, we need to talk. I can explain everything," he said, trying to take her arm.

She maneuvered out of his way. If he touched her, she might come apart.

"There is no need, my lord," she said instead, holding her ground. He winced at her formality.

"Please don't call me that."

"Then how shall I address you? 'Mr. Turner' will not do. 'Edward?'"

"Ned. Please, Phoebe, I am Ned. And you know me."

"Do I?" she asked coolly. "If that is the case, would you mind answering some questions?"

"Fine!" he said, holding out his hands. "Ask me anything. We will have our own Questioning."

"Did you really grow up in a village in Lincolnshire?"

"No." He shook his head. "I grew up here, in Hollyhock."

"Do you have a family mill?"

"No, I don't."

"Did you really have a wager to see if you could kiss someone while you were here?"

He hesitated. "Not exactly."

She paused, realization dawning. "But there was a wager. And I was part of it. Of course, no wonder the earl—I mean, Mr. Turner—wanted me to leave so badly." She cocked her head to one side. "What was the wager?"

"Phoebe . . ."

"What was the wager?"

He could not meet her eyes. "Turner bet me that I could not get a lady to fall in love with me without benefit of my title."

She could feel the blood drain from her face. She thought she might be sick. "I see."

"No, you don't—"

"You were tired of ladies throwing themselves at your feet, so you decided a poor, plain governess might be a game challenge."

"Phoebe, that's not it at all!" Ned cried, and moved away from the door, toward her. "In fact, I never would have picked you in a hundred years!"

She blinked. "Thank you very much."

"But you were the only person to talk to me. Everyone else was chasing after Turner, mooning over him. And then you became . . . more." His eyes moved to the picture on the wall, her little painting of the night sky peering through a circle of trees. He took it down, let his gaze become lost in the picture.

"Last night . . . suffice to say, last night, I could have won the wager. But I didn't, because I knew that I loved you and you deserved more. From everyone, but especially from me."

She turned her head away, clutching the bag in her hands tightly. It kept them from shaking. Last night had been a dream, a hazy memory of stars so far away that it almost didn't exist anymore.

"And this morning?" she asked, swallowing hard. "You gave up your newfound conscience?"

"No." His eyes came up, sparking like fire. "This morning I simply couldn't fight against what we both wanted anymore."

He took another step toward her, his body moving like a cat, his eyes mesmerizing on hers.

"You wanted me then," he purred. "You want me now."

"No."

"You're in love with me."

She let her eyes flash with anger, with pain. "No."

"Phoebe, you told me you loved me here, in this room, not an hour ago."

"Yes," she said, her voice cracking. "But I know you so much better now."

He leaned into her then, growling. She refused to bend her spine. "You also said it did not matter to you what my past was. You said you didn't care if I was the child of chimney sweeps. Why is this any different?"

"It is different, and you know it," she spat back. "Or else you would have told me the truth much sooner. Certainly, before we . . ." Her eyes drifted to the wall, where they had been wrapped around each other. He caught the line of her gaze and his eyes went black with remembered passion. She snapped her mouth shut, and her eyes away.

"If you had been any other lord, perhaps it would not have made any difference. But you're the *Earl of Ashby*. The person whose carelessness altered my future."

"I'm also the man who loves you. Who would alter your future again. Phoebe, don't you see?" He clasped her hand. "All this little wager has done is allow that to happen."

"No!" She wrenched free of him and finally set him back on his heels enough that she managed to throw open the door and march down the hall. "All this little wager has done is convince me that you are still that careless person—one who does not give a damn about what damage is done or who he hurts as long as things are going his way. *That* is who you are, *Lucky Ned*."

She spat the last words like bile. His face fell; he looked so hurt that it nearly broke her heart. But she had to be strong. She had to walk away.

Her pride was all she had left.

So she hurried down the hall to the rickety stairs. By the time she reached the landing, he was dogging her steps, nearly on her heels. But she kept moving forward.

"Phoebe, please don't do this. Please, let me explain. I will tell you everything."

They reached the main staircase.

"You want to know about me? Fine. I lived in that little cottage until I was twelve, when my great-uncle named me his heir and sent me to school. I never saw my mother alive again, and it haunts me to this day."

The foyer. The front door.

"I never thought I'd come back to this town. I convinced myself I'd hated it here. That it was boring. That men of my standing live in town."

The front walk. Rounding the house toward the stables.

"I went to war because I was a selfish boy, and when I came back I had friends for the first time ever—friends like Turner and Rhys. But I was still selfish then because I stopped treating my friends as friends. And I still am selfish now, because I want you."

"Kevin!" she called out as she reached the stables. The groom popped his head out from the stall where he was brushing down a very tired Abandon. "I need you to drive me into town. Now."

"The cart's rigged up," Kevin said, his gaze swinging from Phoebe to Ned and back again. "We can go right now if you like."

She swallowed and nodded. She didn't trust herself to speak. She didn't trust herself to not cry.

Especially when Ned reached out and gently slid his hand up to her elbow, his touch an aching torture. "Phoebe," her name a prayer. "Please. I'll fix it. You'll see."

"Are you ready, Miss Baker?" Kevin called out.

"Yes," she rasped. "Yes, let's go."

⌁

NED TRUDGED BACK up the drive, lost in thought. He had stood at the stable door until Phoebe and Kevin disappeared around the bend in the lane. It took everything in his power not to force a saddle on poor exhausted Abandon and follow them, but he knew it would be futile. She would not look at him. She would not let him in. Not the Earl of Ashby. Not this version, at least.

"Ned!" The voice came from the front steps of Puffington Arms. Ned looked up to find Rhys walking out into the midday sun. So much had happened since dawn broke, it was hard to believe that it was barely afternoon.

"The bullet is out of Turner's shoulder. With any luck it will heal cleanly," Rhys said, wiping red from his hands on a clean rag. Ned nodded with difficulty. His entire body felt like it had lost its bones. Or something else just as vital.

"Now, would you kindly tell me what the hell has been going on here?" Rhys asked.

He looked down. He was still holding Phoebe's picture in his hand, the night sky edged by trees. She had left it—and him—behind. That's how little both meant to her.

Or it meant too much, a little voice told him, one that dared to hope. *And she could not bear it.*

"I ruined everything," Ned said resolutely. "And I have to repair it."

28

In any game, someone wins, someone loses.
That's the chance you take.

TO: MISS P. BAKER
CARE OF: THE TRIDENT TRANSATLANTIC COMPANY
LONDON

Dear Miss Baker—

Please do not be alarmed by the name at the bottom of this missive. I am not the Mr. Turner you were so familiar with. Rather, I am the real Mr. John Turner, who acted so abominably to you in the guise of the Earl of Ashby. (Although, given those actions, any feeling of alarm on your part is completely justified.)

As ashamed as I am at my actions toward you, I am writing not in regard to our recent association, but rather in regard to our much older one. Your father purchased some shares in a company that, unbeknownst to my friend and employer, bore his seal of approval. After consulting with a solicitor, it has been discovered

*that those shares are still valid, and hold value. If
this letter reaches you before your voyage, would you
consider meeting with me to discuss the matter? I
assure you complete discretion, and the business can
be concluded with all possible speed. However, if that
does not please you, the business can be conducted via
correspondence, although it will take much longer.*

*If you choose the former, I will be in my offices at
the address listed below on Monday, July 1st, between
the hours of noon and five.*

Yours, etc.
Mr. John Turner

Phoebe received the letter exactly seventeen days
after she left Puffington Arms. Seventeen days and six
hours.

Kevin the groom had asked no questions and
quickly bore her through Hollyhock to Midville, where
she caught a mail coach to London. Dear, dear Kevin
had even given her the shilling he had in his pocket—
given to him for driving them the previous night by
her Mr. Tur— by the earl. Kevin had told her to keep
it, but she promised she would post it back to him when
she reached her relatives in America. She asked him to
keep an eye on Rose and Henry. It was another wrench
of her heart to think about leaving them two years earlier than expected, but at least they had Nanny.

At least they had someone.

She had found her way to the docks and the Trident Transatlantic Company, the outfit that owned
the *Blooming Daisy*, and which her cousin said would
give her a good rate. She discovered that the *Blooming*

Daisy was expected to dock in London within the week, and then set back on the ocean in another week. She promptly bought a ticket.

The wait was interminable. She had been moving so fast, so blindly, that now, being forced to a standstill wreaked havoc on her conviction. *Just two weeks*, she told herself. *You only have to wait a simple fortnight, and then you will be free.*

Of course, it was luck in some form or another that delayed the ship in its crossing. And so, when the letter arrived, she was already on pins and needles, and her lodgings and food were eating up her precious savings. And her heart—her traitorous, traitorous heart—had been preying upon her mind.

And so it was, eighteen days and four hours after she left Puffington Arms, that Phoebe made her way to the address listed in Mr. Turner's letter.

An address in Mayfair.

Phoebe let out a long, steadying breath as she mounted the steps to the imposing yet beautiful gray stone mansion, taking up half a block looking out onto the wide expanse of Grosvenor Square. Keeping her head held high, she knocked.

And waited.

"Miss Baker." The familiar voice sent a tingle up her spine. "How pleasant to see you."

"Danson," Phoebe replied, allowing a tiny smile to tug at the corner of her mouth. Even though a small shot of alarm ran through her at seeing the earl's valet, it was the first smile she had managed in eighteen days. And four hours. She had liked Danson. She could only hope his presence did not mean that Mr. Turner's promise of "complete discretion" was a lie. "And how pleasant to see you."

He gave an appreciative nod. "Mr. Turner is expecting you. If you will follow me."

As they began to walk down the long, echoing hallway, she could not help but ask, "I take it you are the earl's valet, not Mr. Turner's."

"Indeed. I was copiously bribed to play my role."

"I should hope so," she said blithely.

"And my regrets are heavy."

"But not as heavy as your purse."

That made the unflappable Danson smirk. "However, I must say, I enjoyed our association, Miss Baker. And what I saw of my master when he was with you. And just so you know"—he leaned forward as they reached a large, engraved oak door—"I do not come down from my lofty heights to open the front door for just anyone."

He turned the doorknob and whispered in her ear. "You will prevail. Of that I have no doubt."

Before Phoebe could ask what he meant, she was in the library, and the door closed behind her.

"Miss Baker."

She came about to find Mr. Turner—the real Mr. Turner—standing behind a large desk that was covered with papers and books. His voice had taken on a sharper, northern accent. His left arm was stiff at his side. He wore clothes she recognized as ill-fitting on someone else.

She dropped to a curtsy, retreating into stiff formality.

"Thank you for coming," he said, crossing over and gently taking her arm. "You were not easy to find.

We scoured the docks until we found the company that owned the *Blooming Daisy*. And when we finally did, I admit, we did not know if you would accept the invitation."

Her body froze. "We?" she asked, her mouth going dry.

Mr. Turner, regardless of her suddenly frozen body, continued to guide her toward a chair. "I mean Danson and I. I promised you discretion—the earl is not here."

"Oh." Something dropped inside her, a trail of feeling falling down her body. But that was silly. She kept her back straight, her expression passive as she took her seat. "Your shoulder is repairing, I see."

He winced a bit as he rolled his left shoulder. "It's slowgoing, but yes, repairing. I have other things to repair as well." His eyes went dark, his mind for a moment fleeing to something else. Then he shook his head and returned to her.

"I won't keep you, Miss Baker, but I am tying up a few last pieces of business for Lord Ashby, and this one was long overdue."

"Last pieces of business?" she asked, trying to steady the thundering beat of her heart.

"Yes. This meeting is, in fact, my last duty as his secretary. I have a mill in Lincolnshire that has long since needed my attention."

"I see," she said slowly. "So that part of the story was true, at least. Although it was your history, not his."

"I think, if you wished to take the time and reflect upon it, you will find that much of what Ned told you was the truth," Mr. Turner replied enigmatically. "The important bits, at least."

Phoebe could make no reply. She was concentrating too intently on not letting the sting in her nose turn to tears on her cheek. Instead, she simply nodded and let her eyes drift to the window, wanting to stare into the distance. But the curtains were drawn.

Mr. Turner coughed and shuffled some papers on the desk, finally finding the ledger he required. "As I said in my letter, it seems the company your father invested in—the Riversold Building Company—is bearing fruit."

That made her eyes shoot back to his. "It is?" she asked, incredulous.

"Hmm. And the earl would like to purchase your shares. In fact, he is going to purchase the shares of everyone he can locate who invested in the company. And he has sent men to the Continent to look for Mr. Sharp."

When she simply blinked at him, Turner coughed again. "As I said, this is long overdue." He took a pen and wrote out a figure on a piece of paper. "This is what we have determined your shares to be worth."

When he handed her the paper, she nearly dropped it. It was a sum of money that seemed impossible. So much more than the five hundred pounds he had offered when they were in this eerily similar position. So much more than she would ever want or need.

"It's not really bearing fruit, is it? The company?" she asked. She didn't need to look up to see his answer. This was not a purchase of property. Nor was it a bribe, like before, to make her go away.

This was atonement.

Her eyes were still on the paper when Mr. Turner leaned into the desk, his voice gruff with kindness.

"I would not blame you for hating him," he began.

Phoebe's eyes shot up to his. "I could never hate him. I've tried, but I could not . . ."

It was only when Mr. Turner reached into his breast pocket and pulled out a handkerchief, offering it to her, that Phoebe realized she was crying.

She wiped at her tears ruthlessly.

"Before the wager, before you . . . none of this"—he waved his hand over the desk—"would have happened. You changed him. And he is trying to put things right."

She took two gulping breaths and forced her eyes to meet his.

"How is he?" she asked shakily.

Mr. Turner considered her for a moment. "If you wish to see him, all you have to do is say the word."

"I . . ." Everything in her begged to see him. She wanted to hold him and slap him and sink into his arms. But that little warning part of her brain, the crack against her heart that he had put there by breaking her trust, swelled angry and red.

Although it was not angry anymore. Now it just hurt.

"I should go. My ship leaves tomorrow. I have many things to do," she said, rising, her voice catching in her throat.

"Of course," Mr. Turner replied, his voice downcast. "One of Lord Ashby's carriages is ready. He will take you to the bank, where we have left instructions for that amount to be transferred to you."

She nodded blindly, not listening. She just had to get out of there. Out of this strange place that did not seem like *her* Mr. Turner—her Edward, her Ned—but oddly smelled like him. Then maybe she would be able to think straight, and breathe again.

"Thank you, Mr. Turner, good-bye," she said, curtsying before moving swiftly to the hall. And then it was all she could do not to break into a run.

༺ ༻

"WHAT THE HELL are you doing?" Turner said as he drew back the curtain to reveal Ned sitting in the window seat.

"That could not possibly have gone worse," Ned replied, bereft.

"Why are you sitting here?" Turner asked, crossing his arms over his chest. "The plan was for you to come out and *talk* to her. The minute she said she didn't hate you, you should have burst out from behind the curtain."

"She didn't want to see me." Ned felt as if his rib cage was breaking in half. Turner had asked her point-blank if she wished to see him. And instead, she had left. Practically run out of the room.

"Am I no longer in your employ?" Turner asked.

Ned slowly nodded.

"Then I will say something that has long needed saying." Turner practically pulled him out of his chair. "You are an idiot."

"Turner—she didn't want me. She left the second she had the money in hand, she wants nothing to do with me. What more proof do you need?"

"What more proof do I need? Ned—that she *came here* is the proof. You are the only reason she did. Her entire manner flattened when I told her you were not here. I was the one who sat across from her, I know. And did you not hear her cry, for God's sake? Her heart is still as tangled up in you as she is in yours," Turner exclaimed. "What did you expect her to do, find you in a ballroom like a high-born debutante? This *was* her coming to you. What more proof do you need?"

Ned took all that in, each word cold water to the face, waking him up.

"I don't know why you didn't run after her when she left Puffington Arms," Turner drawled. "I was a bit unconscious at the time. But I know what it's like to watch the person you want walk away from you. The difference is, I am going to go after mine. I'll chase her to the ends of the earth. Don't let her get away, Ned. If you do, you'll have to change your name to Foolish Ned, because you let the best bit of luck ever to come into your life walk out the door."

Ned looked at his friend, his heart racing.

"What if she says no?"

Turner shrugged. "That's the chance you take."

And in games of chance, Ned had always been lucky.

His face broke out into a grin as he clapped Turner on the shoulder, causing the man to grunt in pain.

"Sorry," he said quickly as he moved to the door, not pausing to watch Turner wave him away. Once in the hall, he broke into a run.

"Danson!" he called out, making for the front door. "Have a carriage—no, have Abandon readied and brought round, I must leave at on—"

And suddenly, she was there. He'd pulled the door open, and standing on the step, her hand raised to knock, was Phoebe. His own clear-eyed, too-thin, plain, beautiful governess. Her eyes meeting his, wide with surprise. Her mouth opened, but no sound coming out.

"Phoebe," he breathed. His eyes searched her face, his own unable to hide the lopsided smile that gave away all the hope that grew inside his chest.

"I . . . I came back because . . ." She fumbled for the words; she tried to school her features into that imperious, governess mask that he knew so well, but her eyes filling with tears gave her away.

"Hello," she finally said, lowering her hand.

"Hello," he replied, taking that same hand in his. "Come in."

"No." She shook her head. "I . . . I came back because of this." With her free hand, she held out the piece of paper that bore the amount Turner had written down. "It's . . . it's not what I want."

Ned felt his heart crash down in his chest, flattening him. Of course, her sense of morality would not let her take money from him. From the hated Earl of Ashby.

"It's what you are owed, Phoebe. No matter how you feel about me, you must take it, it is your future."

"But it's not what I want," she said again, her voice heartbreakingly small.

"Then what do you want?" he asked, unable to stop himself from brushing a curl back behind her ear. "I'll give you anything you want, just tell me. Tell me how to fix this. Tell me . . . tell me how to convince you to stay. I'm sorry I lied. I'm sorry about the wager. But I can't be sorry about everything because I would not have known you otherwise." He held up their clasped hands, his fingers laced between hers. "You make me better, Phoebe. And I make you happy. Admit it. And I'm not letting you go this time. Not to America, not even down the street. I will stand here and hold your hand until you remember our first kiss in the lane, and dancing under the stars. Until you remember that you know me, the true me, and might even have loved me once."

He pressed his forehead to hers, held her gently to him, unwilling to let even a breath of space separate them. "We will stand here like this until time itself blows out, if that's what it takes."

"That's what I want," she sighed, her voice little more than a whisper.

Ned sought her eyes. "What?"

"I don't want to go to America. I want to stay—" she gulped. "I . . . I want you. Until time itself blows out."

Ned could hardly believe his ears. In fact, he couldn't believe it. He simply stood there, trying to work out what she'd just said.

"I couldn't hate you," she continued, lifting her eyes to his. "I love you too much."

His chest, so recently deflated, felt itself swell to near bursting. He leaned down and kissed her—reverent, joyful, the first of millions of kisses to come. When he finally broke free, it was to see tears in her eyes and dimples on her cheeks.

"Well, then . . ." He smiled as he pulled her by their joined hands into his—their—house. "Welcome home."

From that moment on, and for all the years to come, Ned knew without a doubt that he had truly earned his nickname.

He was indeed lucky.

ear Reader,

As a trivia nerd, I thoroughly enjoy the research part
of writing. I get to explore fascinating bits of history and
minutia and try to find a way to weave a story through it.
For The Game and the Governess, history got a little . . .
unsanitary.

You see, in the nineteenth century bathing was a laborious business. Society had finally caught on, at the end
of the eighteenth century, to the idea that being cleaner is
likely healthier, but to transport and heat all the water to
make a bath required a good fire and a lot of strong servants willing to carry it up and down stairs. Therefore, in a
family the size of the Widcoates', bathing was likely done
only once a week. And yes, they shared the water. The head
of the house would bathe first, followed by the lady of the
house, then the children. Any governesses or servant might
have been allowed to use the water after they were done.
Having a whole room separate for bathing was a luxury
and fad I thought Lady Widcoate might have taken a liking to, in her enthusiastic redecoration.

As for the bathing retreat that Hollyhock is desperate to
establish, it existed, in a way. The town of Hollyhock is, of
course, a fiction. However, I based the history of the town
on a very real place in Leicestershire called Ashby-de-la-
Zouch. In 1805, a saline spring was discovered three miles

away in the coal-producing Moira Colliery. When the village of Moira couldn't handle the growing spa, it was decided to pipe the spring to Ashby-de-la-Zouch. There they built the Ivanhoe Baths, named as such because Sir Walter Scott's 1819 novel Ivanhoe had been set in Ashby-de-la-Zouch, and the town traded on that fame. Unfortunately, the baths were demolished in the 1960s.

(And yes, as an homage, I borrowed part of Ashby-de-la-Zouch's name to use as Ned's title.)

The Baker rifle was the first flintlock rifle to be standard issue in the British Army. It was used copiously in the Napoleonic Wars and became very popular at home due to its greater range and accuracy than other rifles, including the more ubiquitous Brown Bess. Being as it was the army's rifle, it certainly would be possible for a former officer like Turner to recognize its sound from yards away.

In fact, when I read about the Baker rifle, I changed my heroine's last name so I could use it in my plot.

The fact that Turner outranked a gentleman of import like Ned during the wars is uncommon but not unheard of. Ned's youth and middling funds made it so he could purchase only a smaller commission, of a lower rank such as ensign or lieutenant. Meanwhile, the long wars fought against Napoleon had made it so officers were dying faster than their commissions could be repurchased. Those ranks had to be filled, so an educated man of the merchant class, like Turner, would have been able to take a non-purchase commission, as well as be promoted in the field when a vacancy (sadly) came up.

And remember, Ned joined the war rather late. Turner had been there for some time when Ned showed up. He'd had time to earn his promotion.

So many more interesting tidbits of history went into this story—from what competitive games young ladies would play, to the differences between a surgeon and a physician—but these details are only worthwhile if the central story rings true. And I hope that Ned and Phoebe rang true for you.

Sincerely,

Kate Noble

Read John's story in the next delightful
historical romance in Kate Noble's
Winner Takes All series.

❧

Coming in 2015 from Pocket Books!